Fox

Published by Brolga Publishing Pty Ltd
ABN 46 063 962 443
PO Box 12544
A'Beckett St
Melbourne, VIC, 8006
Australia

email: markzocchi@brolgapublishing.com.au

National Library of Australia
Cataloguing-in-Publication data
       Author: Robertson, Bill H.
       Title: Fox / Bill Robertson.
       ISBN: 9781925367126 (paperback)
       Subjects: Detective and mystery stories - Australian fiction.
       A823.4

Printed in Australia
Cover design by Chameleon Print Design
Typeset by Tara Wyllie

BE PUBLISHED

Publish Through a Successful Publisher. National Distribution, Macmillan & International Distribution to the United Kingdom, North America. Sales Representation to South East Asia
Email: markzocchi@brolgapublishing.com.au

BILL ROBERTSON

For Bob,
My friend of decades.

Mentor, consummate historian and fearless author.

GLOSSARY OF TERMS

Aboriginal English   The language used by Aboriginal people to identify with each other and to express an Aboriginal world view; how Aboriginal people relate to each other through body movement and language. http://www.whatworks.edu.au/4_2_1.htm

Kartiya   white person

Wadjella   white person

Ngarrangkarni   The Dreaming

Nyigiwa   tomorrow

Wia   no

Yuwii   yes

N

WESTERN AUSTRALIA

TIMOR SEA

o WYNDHAM

Indian Ocean

FITZROY RIVER

TURKEY CREEK

BROOME
LEOPOLD DOWNS
HALLS CREEK

ABORIGINAL o FITZROY CROSSING

DAMPIER I.

NORTHERN TERRITORY

GREAT SANDY DESERT

GIBSON DESERT

LITTLE SANDY DESERT

o WILUNA

SOUTH AUSTRALIA

GREAT VICTORIA DESERT

MOGUMBER MISSION

LAKE DEBORAH E.

o SOUTHERN CROSS

ROTTNEST ISLAND

PERTH
FREEMANTLE

AVALGAN RIVER
STIRLING RANGES

MOUNT BARKER o

PORONGORUPS
ALBANY

PERTH & ENVIRONS:
SISTER KATE'S
ROSSMOYNE TRAINING CENTRE

ORIGINS

Kings will be tyrants from policy
when subjects are rebels from principle.

EDMUND BURKE

(1729 – 1797)

CHAPTER 1

1960

He lay among the sandstone and spinifex, obscured by stunted acacias — watching. Squeals, shrieks and laughter floated upwards as children hurled themselves into the waterhole from the rocks below, each attempting to outdo the other with their bombs and bellywhackers. Focussing on the four-year-old paddling at the bank, his erotic fancies bloomed rapidly. She looked so innocent and plump, a wholesome little morsel. He wanted to rush down and take her but it wasn't safe. Too many kids. And her older brother was a protective little prick — he'd be a bloody handful. Still, they didn't know what they were in for and he could wait. He licked his lips, it wasn't far off.

A dust devil rose lazily in the blistering afternoon air. Sweat trickled into his left eye, flies stuck, gluelike, to his thin whiskered face. Heat from the steely blue cauldron overhead was remorseless, yet the scantily clad *Gija* kids seemed immune to it. Here, in the blistering north east of Western Australia, the cool waters of Turkey Creek were an oasis of fun. Mullett, now tense with anticipation, fondled himself to relieve his maddening desire and groaned with pleasure.

In March, he was back. Mullett and two others, a man and woman. They came in a small truck equipped with a wire cage and bench seats. Empowered by warrants, cloaked in the might of the Anglican Church and authorised by the State of Western Australia, they would seize the kids from Turkey Creek for assimilation into white Australia. Mullett's earlier reconnaissance had confirmed several mixed-race kids scampering about the dusty settlement. The raid wouldn't be large, five boys for stock handling and six girls for domestic work. He was satisfied with that. His pleasure was close now, he could almost feel the four-year-old in his rough hands ...

Still, they had yet to grab the kids. Mullett hated that part. It set him on edge and he resented being out of sorts. All that weeping and wailing. He had no objection to taking the noisy little buggers, they brought him new pleasures, but he detested their howling mothers and the other caterwauling women. Some of the men could be aggressive too. That's where having a copper with them was handy — he could give 'em a righteous tap if they played up!

They sat in the truck about a half mile from the settlement, shaded by an old pandanus. Though not as hot as January, the truck was uncomfortably warm. Rogers, the policeman, was impatient.

'What the hell are we waiting for Mullett? Let's just get in and get 'em,' he grumbled.

'I told ya before Skinny, we have to think about this otherwise the bloody lubras will hide their kids in the caves or cover 'em in charcoal. We've gotta try to get 'em all.' Mullett's pinched face wore a sulky scowl.

John "Skinny" Rogers was a constable from Wyndham. Just over six feet tall, thin as a whip, he had a short fuse and dynamite fists. With his bronzed angular features, his police mates thought rawboned was a kind description.

'Yeah, well I got a new sheila waitin' for me back home Mullett, I just want to get it done. I don't wanna be stuck out here a minute longer than necessary. What about you Brigitte?'

Brigitte Murphy, a former Anglican nun had, at the age of forty-five, passionately fallen for a primary school teacher from Bayswater near Perth. Before marriage, she had worked at the Parkerville Children's Home founded by Katherine Mary Clutterbuck. Sister Kate, as Katherine Mary was affectionately known, had chanced the rough watery passage from Ireland and started the Home in 1903. Previously, Murphy had lived there and cared for its young inmates but she now managed the Anglican Church's response to official Aboriginal integration and protection policy. Over the years, she had become hardened to the complaints of brutality and violence from black kids. Most of them, she thought, didn't appreciate the chance they were being offered. But recently, a "situation" forced her to take stock, a case involving Mullett and a little girl. She had joined Mullett and Rogers on this occasion to see how the collection of Aboriginal children was carried out.

'John, like you, I'd rather be home, back in Perth. But, I'm here to learn. I don't really know how things are done on the ground so I've come to find out.'

Mullett muttered under his breath.

'Did you say something Mullett?' she asked sharply.

'Only that I dunno why you're here. It's not normal and as far as I'm concerned, ya shouldn't bloody be here.' Mullett's surly tone was both cutting and dismissive. The chip on his shoulder was flourishing under her continuing presence. He knew that he had to be careful around her and felt shackled.

'I told you before Mullett, some people in my organisation think we're doing the wrong thing. I don't. As far as I'm concerned, these kids are up for a new life. But, I've been directed to look at the effect on families when the kids are taken. That's why I'm here. So,' she said acidly, 'leave it.' Mullett's skinny frame, constant body odour and thin, reddened features repulsed her as much as his niggling attitude of self-importance. Truly, she felt like whacking him.

Bemused, Rogers listened to the exchange. He had been on these trips with Mullett a few times and thought him a strange coot. He was sleazy and rough with the kids. Not that Rogers cared too much about that. *Shit, they were only coons!*

'Yeah, well, nothing like first-hand experience Brigitte. I reckon you'd best stop with the mothers – they'll be kickin' up a right bloody fuss. Mullett and me will chase the little buggers. And Mullett, if you have any trouble with the bucks, I'll deal with it. Keep out of it. Right?'

'Skinny, why does it have to be like this every time?' Mullett whined. 'I'm in charge! I'm the one with authority from the Commissioner of Native Welfare. I'm the one with the power to take these kids. You're just here to see I'm okay. But, seein' as you're so bloody smart, we'll just go in and grab 'em now. They should all be in for tea anyway.' Pissed off, Adam's apple bobbing in his scrawny throat, Birmingham accent thickened by emotion, Mullett started the truck, threw it into gear, spun the wheels in the sand and fishtailed down the track.

They roared into the camp sliding to a stop in the main clearing. Dust billowed around them. Women, bent over their cooking fires, straightened in fear. Children slid closer to their legs. The men stiffened but stayed under the trees.

Mullett stepped from the truck, pulled a crumpled paper from his hip pocket and began reading, his voice cracked and irritated. The hasty words were meaningless because at law, Aboriginal parents with children of mixed race had no rights or protection. Mullett had all the authority he needed to seize the kids. The Aborigines Act of 1905 gave it to him. Nevertheless, while reading the warrant appealed to his perverse sense of decency, his tone made the women nervous. Then, when he and Rogers marched over to the camp fires and seized four little ones at their mother's sides, all hell erupted!

Women screamed and cried, children ran and the men charged

from the trees. Hurriedly, and none too gently, the white men dragged the shrieking, struggling children to the truck, threw them into the cage and locked the gate. Mullett saw the little girl he'd spied on his January trip squatting unobtrusively beneath a gum at the clearing edge. He made a beeline for her. As he reached her, a woman dashed across and swept the child into her arms. Mullett clutched at the girl, trying to tear her from the woman's grasp. Terrified, the child bawled. The battle was ferocious with the younger woman proving stronger than the older, slightly built Mullett. Suddenly, drawing back his fist, Mullett belted her on the jaw. As she staggered, he kicked her legs from under her and tucked the child beneath his arm. In the same instant, he slipped his hand beneath the little dress, hard against her naked crotch. His eyes dilated and darkened with pleasure — it was just as he had dreamed.

Fuck! He became aware of the nun bitch screeching at him.

'Mullett! Mullett! What are you doing you filthy bastard. Put that child down!'

Reluctantly, he moved his hand to the child's knees. 'She's old enough to go,' he growled defensively, 'I'm puttin' her in the truck.'

Brigitte said no more. Mullett's sordid behaviour had confirmed the need for her presence.

'Mullett!' Rogers roared from the other side of the clearing. 'Round up those bloody kids while I deal with this pack of bastards.' He stood ringed by five or six men, some bearing waddies. Completely fearless, he shuffled forward and rendered the man nearest him unconscious with a massive blow to the head. Whirling, he repeated the assault on a man behind him and then cut loose with a flurry of fists and kicks until the last man ran from the clearing.

Mullett zigzagged around the settlement. Three more children were caught and thrown into the truck, another three ran into the bush. The air was riven by sobbing, screeching, keening mothers and the terrified howling of children.

Looking on, Brigitte felt ill. If this was standard practice, no wonder the kids complained of violence when they reached the Home. She watched, retching, as Mullett viciously thumped two small boys who had valiantly tried to outrun him.

Flushed with success, Rogers returned to the truck.

'Have you got 'em all Mullett?'

'No. Three of the little shits got away. Still, we got eight from eleven, that's not bad. The boss'll be happy with this lot.'

He leaned into the cabin to get a padlock for the cage gate. Looking up, he found two furious unblinking eyes glaring at him through the passenger side window. *It's the brother,* Mullett thought. The boy showed no fear and continued glaring.

'Skinny, grab that bloody kid!'

'No need, he's decided to come with us.'

Unusually, the boy had moved to the corner of the truck. About seven, he was lean and sinewy and his stormy, silvery-grey eyes smouldered angrily from a fine, intelligent face. Mullett stomped to the back of the truck and opened the gate. Unable to contain himself as the boy moved to enter the cage, Mullett unleashed a mighty backhander. With a deft sense of anticipation, the child swayed to his left and Mullett's knuckles hit the iron door with such force that he roared in pain. A sly smile slid over the boy's face. Nimbly, he jumped into the cage and went straight to the tiny girl Mullett had assaulted.

CHAPTER 2

Friday, December 5, 1963, the eve of Lucy Fox's seventh birthday. Or so she claimed. Lucy wasn't absolutely certain when her birthday really was. Three years had passed since that terrifying day at Turkey Creek. Life since had been a gyre of pleasure, pain and despair. Initially, they had gone to the Forrest River Mission near Wyndham. Lucy vividly recalled the bumpy three hour drive. Huddling together for warmth, they had received precious little food – a pannikin of water each and some stale bread.

Miss Brigitte had been kind and Lucy heard her scold Mullett because of the lack of food and rugs. Even though the days were hot, nights in the Kimberly were cold and they had all nearly frozen in the cage as they rumbled along. The policeman had done nothing to help them. Mullett was the one who was creepy and had leered and touched and rubbed. Not just Lucy, all the girls. He was careful in front of Miss Brigitte though. When she was around, the girls were safe. Lucy was also safe with Colin about. Though she had only been tiny then, Lucy remembered Mullett had always been wary of him.

That didn't surprise her, the kids loved Colin. He wasn't the oldest but he was their leader. They respected his hunting and tracking skills, he was afraid of nothing and seemed wise beyond his years. He stood square to Mullett, never backed away, was polite and exuded a force that Mullett was reluctant to tackle. Colin had watched over Lucy and the others too. As she got older, she realised Colin had chosen to be on the truck with her. Lucy loved her big brother and missed him terribly.

After arriving at Forrest River Mission their heads had been shaved and their clothes burned. Lucy and Colin stayed only a couple of months before being transferred to Sister Kate's in Perth, thousands of miles from Turkey Creek. The nuns said they were too white to stay at the mission. At Sister Kate's they quickly realised they would not be seeing their mother or family in a hurry and, as though it might compensate, they had been forced to attend church three times a day: before breakfast, at lunch and after school. They quickly learned it was unwise to cross the nuns — that understanding was instilled with religious fervour and a wet ironing cord.

At Sister Kate's boys and girls slept in separate dormitories. Even that was scary. Lucy and Colin were used to shelters under the stars, their family sleeping around them for warmth and comfort. But here, in this new world, they were separated by corridors, slept in beds high off the floor, petrified of falling out. Most nights, Lucy cried herself to sleep.

Between school times, Lucy and the other girls would spend hours chopping wood, waxing, cleaning or polishing brass. They also cared for the little ones who had to be fed, bathed, toileted and put to bed. And, while they slaved at their chores, the nuns drummed into them: they were *white*, being Aboriginal was degrading, they had no mothers, they were lucky to be getting such a good chance in life.

Colin said they were lying. They did have a mother and she loved them deeply. He told Lucy to never forget Rosie's warm arms and big heart, they *would* see her again. But there were some good times with other kids and food was plentiful, although it did take getting used to. It was nothing like the water fowl, goanna, grubs, yams, fruits, berries and kangaroo they knew.

From time to time, Mullett brought new kids to the home. To her horror, Lucy found that if she was too slow, he would push her into a room, shut the door and stick his hand in her panties and touch her "private" while rubbing himself. If she resisted, he slapped her around the head and once, when she said she would tell the Matron, Mullett had snarled, 'You don't tell anybody Missy otherwise you'll be sent to another state altogether and you'll never see your mother again. Never! And that smart-arse brother of yours, he'll be sent to Mount Barker. So, shut up!' Mullett's behaviour frightened and confused her triggering a deep sense of shame and abandonment.

She had been so scared of Mullett she told neither Matron nor Colin about the things he did. Until a month ago. Mullett had arrived with new babies and surprised her polishing brass in the church. He grabbed her hard and put his hand over her mouth and whispered harshly in her ear, 'Shut the fuck up!' Then he'd put his fingers into her so roughly that she felt a searing pain and began to bleed. He had laughed. The following morning she plucked up courage and told Matron Fisher about Mullett.

'You filthy little slut!' Fisher had screamed at her. 'How dare you speak of Mr. Mullett like that. You're a shameless hussy and no doubt you led him on.' Matron grabbed her hair, dragged her into the toilets and washed her mouth with soapy water. For good measure, she delivered five lashes to Lucy's legs with the wet ironing cord. Then, banished to the dormitory, Lucy was instructed to tell no one of her "filthy, dirty lies". Ashamed, helpless, lonely and humiliated, she lay on her bed sobbing and eventually fell asleep. The following day, Colin was transferred to Moore River without explanation or goodbyes.

Lucy believed she had caused Colin's transfer and was racked with guilt. Treated with deepening contempt and suspicion by the nuns, Lucy needed to do little thereafter to taste the sting of the ironing cord. Her world had become oppressive and sinister.

Now, with Christmas approaching and her birthday tomorrow, Lucy felt sad and isolated. She had not seen Colin for three weeks. He had always made a fuss, giving her little presents: a hair ribbon, a grass wristlet he'd made or one of his small paintings. To the contrary, policy at the Home was to ignore birthdays, although most of the kids wouldn't have known them anyway. Besides, they all had their own problems. Privately, Lucy hoped that somehow Colin would visit.

Colin Fox hated Moore River. Also known as *Mogumber Mission,* he could feel its dark history as soon as he arrived. It was a place full of voices past, of pain, torment and misery. And that misery was everywhere, especially at night when it oozed like pus from the pores of the place and clung like an evil mist. He didn't intend staying.

Moore River was about eighty-five miles north of Perth and Fox didn't know why he was there. A male supervisor from Sister Kate's had come to school one lunch time three weeks ago and said he was to leave. Back at the Home he found his few things already in a bag. He was given a sandwich and put in a truck with some workmen going to Moore River. He had ached at leaving Lucy, especially with no goodbye. He loved his little sister and hoped she would be alright.

Gradually, Fox learned of Moore River's history from Aboriginal workers there. Commenced in 1918, the settlement was intended as a farming venture for Aboriginals to educate their children and provide work for adults. There were to be health facilities too. But the land had proven unsuitable for farming. Over time and through lack of care, the settlement morphed into an orphanage, a place for old people, unmarried mothers and sick children. Black people from all over Western Australia were lumped together. Language groups were mixed, problems festered and simmered while hopeless overcrowding bred despondency. Like an endless stream of flotsam, children constantly arriving added to already high levels of misery. Families were sundered by strict rules of segregation as men, women and children were placed in separate dormitories with little bedding or covering. Overcrowding caused health problems and by the early 1950s, more than 340 people had died there. Despair and isolation were rampant. As no-one could leave without written authority, absconding became commonplace. Aboriginal trackers hunted down and returned the runaways who faced harsh penalties — head shaving, transfer, beatings or solitary confinement.

The elderly workmen told Fox they believed Aborigines, particularly the mixed race kids, were treated in ways that no white people would accept, not even under the welfare system.

'It's as though,' said George Morgan to Fox one day, 'they want to breed us out, like they're scared our kids will have the worst features of both races and none of their good points.'

At ten years of age, and from this brutal history, Fox learned two things: to rely upon his intuition and to keep his own counsel. His resolve to escape strengthened and he began formulating a plan to collect Lucy and return to Turkey Creek.

A week before Lucy's birthday Fox heard that a group of boys was being transferred to Rossmoyne Training Centre near Perth. Rossmoyne was a hostel run by the Pallotine Mission where a high school education or trade was offered to Aboriginal boys and girls. The philosophy was to develop leaders who could successfully live and work in the general community. Rossmoyne, Fox discovered, was close to Sister Kate's. The journey south would be made in Moore River's ancient 1949 Bedford coach, a coach that Fox discovered held a particular advantage.

Like most kids at Moore River, Fox moved around, poked and pried and learned as much about the place as he could. In his first week he stumbled across the old coach locked in a shed and, by the end of that week, had located an unobtrusive entry point to the shed. In the bus he discovered that its rear bench seat was fitted to a box platform running from one side of the cabin to the other. Three lugs at the front of the seat held it in place and four slotted vents punctuated the frame. If he could find a screwdriver, he could undo the lugs and check the space. Late one night, using a stolen screwdriver, he lifted the seat to reveal a cavity about sixteen inches deep by twenty inches wide. His plan was clear. He knew the trip south was intended for the Friday before Lucy's birthday and would commence after lunch. He needed to be present for lunch but under the bench seat straight after.

At three o'clock Friday afternoon the old coach arrived at Rossmoyne. Fox's journey had been cramped, stuffy and incredibly hot. More than once he was tempted to yell to the boys above him to lift the seat, but penalty of discovery didn't bear thinking about. So he stuck it out then waited a good quarter hour after everyone had left the bus before lifting the seat. All clear. Quietly extricating himself, he looked outside over the seat tops. He was in the grounds of the Training Centre and people were wandering about, playing or enjoying the gardens. He would have to sit it out. By six o'clock, with not a soul in sight, he left the bus, slipped into the gardens and made his way out onto Fifth Avenue. His next task was to reach Knutsford Avenue Kewdale — Sister Kate's.

CHAPTER 3

Fox had never been to Rossmoyne but knew from the conversation between the two boys sitting above him they had entered off High Road. High Road would take him towards Sister Kate's. He walked south on Fifth Avenue and could see the highway ahead. He turned into Houtmans Street and started looking for a bike. Eventually, inside a driveway, he found a battered push bike leaning against a fence. Quietly, he walked it out, clambered on and rode up to High Road.

Three miles and a few wrong turns later, he reached Sister Kate's. From the light, he reckoned it must be around seven-thirty or eight o'clock. That meant everyone would be finished eating and the younger kids would be going to bed. Since Lucy would be helping with that task, he knew where to look for her.

He hid the bike in the front hedge and sneaked around the back to a dormitory attached to the main block. This was where the littlies slept. Shielded by bushes, he made his way to a window and peeped inside. Lucy and another girl, whose back was to the window, were fussing over a baby about three feet away. He tapped lightly on the glass. When Lucy looked towards the noise Colin raised a finger to his lips and pointed to the door. He bobbed down as the other girl began to turn.

It was twenty minutes before Lucy appeared to walk slowly into the garden. Her heart was pounding. She had not believed her eyes when that familiar face appeared at the window — Colin! Perhaps there was something in prayer after all. From the darkest corner of the garden she heard the muted call of a red-collared lorikeet, a bird from their swimming hole. After checking the garden, she slipped into the shadows.

'G'day. How ya doin?' Colin stood up from behind a fat old grevillea, a huge grin splitting his face.

Fearing discovery, Lucy flung herself at him silently and hugged him.

'Colin, ya back,' she whispered, 'I'm happy you're 'ere. Will ya get into trouble?'

'Slow down. *You* right?'

His question wormed into her pain. She leaned against him and breathed softly.

'*Wia*. That Mullett, he's too cheeky, he hurts me and Fisher, she belts us.' Tears seeped down her face. Colin grew cold, felt the hairs on his neck and head rise as he struggled to breathe. He took her hand, understanding immediately about Mullett.

'We're goin' home to Mum,' he murmured. 'I run away from Moore River. Bad place. I ain't goin' back. Can ya leave tonight?' As he spoke he gripped her hand, working hard to conceal his anger. He didn't doubt her for one minute. He was equally angry with the Fisher bitch. *Call 'emselves bloody church people. They don't know shit from clay! Liars more like, flat out liars.* He was thinking hard and asked again, 'Tonight?'

'Colin, I'm scared. They'll miss me straight away and get the cops.'

Lucy had scarcely finished speaking when the back door banged open and Matron Fisher appeared. Lucy flinched involuntarily.

'Fox! Lucy Fox! I know you're out there. Come inside this minute.' Colin could hear the anger in her shrill voice.

Lucy's fear was tangible and Colin felt her shaking. '*Nyigiwa*. Church at three,' she whispered and melted into the darkness.

'*Yuwii,*' he murmured.

As she moved across the garden, Colin found himself wondering. *Had he been moved to Moore River because of Mullett's attacks on Lucy? How often had he done it?* Dimly he recalled Miss Brigette swearing at Mullett when he'd pounced on Lucy years ago at Turkey Creek. *Could she possibly help?* While he didn't know the answers to these questions he did know that his intention to get home was unbreakable.

As he moved towards the garden shed where he would camp for the night, he could hear Fisher harshly abusing Lucy for being outdoors.

On Saturday afternoon at three, Colin crept to the back door of the church and found it unlocked. Entering the gloomy light he was aware of a snuffling, grunting sound ahead and to his right. Creeping slowly forward, he drew level with the nave of the church and stopped, stricken. On the floor Mullett was astride Lucy groaning, his withered arse writhing, trousers to his knees, hands around her throat. Lucy, on her back, dress up, legs askew, was not moving.

Overpowering rage engulfed Colin. A polished candle stick lay some distance from Lucy's feet. He grabbed it and, with a piercing scream, bounded towards Mullett who looked around only to feel the full force of the heavy brass stick across his face. There was a satisfying, bone crunching squelch as Mullett's nose and teeth disintegrated. Without pause and with all his strength, Colin hammered Mullett twice more before dropping the candlestick. He dragged Mullett off Lucy and knelt by his little sister. He knew immediately she was dead and, as he took in the blood around her legs, the frailty of her young frame, he was consumed by grief and howled with pain and despair.

And that was how the Reverend Ian McManus found them. Colin curled into a tight ball, uncontrollably weeping. Mullett, in a bloody pool on his side, head caved in. Lucy on her back, her young body exposed.

At the police station, Colin sat numbly with a young policewoman in the interview room. Having been briefed on the murder scene, her heart had opened to the boy. He was still softly whimpering. A ten-year-old child, inconsolable in his grief, shattered and unable to talk sensibly. It was five o'clock and Colin had gone with police to tell them his story. The door opened to admit Detective Dean Wildman. He gave the policewoman a sour look and crossed to the boy.

'Shut up you snivelling little prick. D'you hear me? Shut up!' Blade sharp, icy with disdain, his tone penetrated Fox's anguish. 'We've been doing some checking. Seems your sister was not little Miss Innocent after all. Matron Fisher tells us she had a "thing" for Mullett. She'd let him play with her before. Egged him on in fact. Matron had to wash her mouth out trying to stop her nasty habits. This may not be as simple as you'd like us to believe. Your sister gave herself to Mullett.'

'Are you sure that's right Sarge?' asked the policewoman.

'Who asked you to speak? Keep your mouth shut or get out.'

The policewoman turned scarlet. 'I'm not leaving you alone with this boy and you don't have the authority to order me out. And if you do, I'm going straight to the Inspector.'

'Coon lover are ya?' Wildman switched his attention to Fox and ignored the woman. 'Well? What have you got to say for yourself?'

'She was good. Today she was seven. Matron Fisher's a lyin' bitch and if ya believe her, ya sick.'

'So why'd you belt Mullett?'

''E was hurtin' my sister. I saw 'im.' The policewoman looked at the floor and coloured again.

'She was giving it to him, like all gins,' Wildman sniped.

Though still dazed, Colin felt some sort of strength begin to quietly settle over him. He was young and out of his depth, not yet initiated into his *Gija* law but he knew he possessed a power far greater than this ignorant *kartiya*. He knew the truth.

'When ya talk to other girls,' he said tonelessly, 'Mullett was cheeky with lots of 'em. 'E killed my sister. Fisher's lyin'. You're the cop, find out.'

Wildman leaned across the table and slapped Fox's head heavily.

'You're a smart arse, kid. You know that? You can spend the night in the cells here and we'll see what happens tomorrow.' He rose and left the room.

Caroline Connors, the policewoman said, 'Are you alright? He had no right to hit you.'

'You 'ave to be jokin'. Fox laughed at her. 'You 'eard 'im, I'm black. We don't have no rights. If you wanna help, speak to Miss Brigitte … the Anglican Mission. You'll see then.'

By Monday afternoon it was clear that Wildman could not shift the blame from Mullett to Colin for Lucy's death. Too many things didn't fit. Mullett's semen was inside Lucy and bruises on her neck matched his hands and finger spacing. Apart from Fisher's disparaging comments about Lucy's alleged behaviour, Wildman had no factual or corroborative evidence of her promiscuity. And if other girls had been victims, they were too intimidated to speak out. Brigitte Murphy would say nothing in support of Colin or anything derogatory about Mullett. And while he wouldn't openly admit it, Wildman knew Murphy's position was important and she wanted to keep a lid on things. He would help her do so. Colin had never denied hitting Mullett and was vehement about protecting Lucy. Many within the force were sympathetic towards the boy. Given Lucy's age and the nature of her injuries prior to death, consent was irrelevant. Wildman had run into a brick wall and could not lay a charge.

On the following Friday, Colin Fox was transferred into the Catholic system and conveyed to Mount Barker, a mission with the harshest of reputations.

CHAPTER 4

1966

At thirteen, Fox stood five feet seven inches tall in a body as lean and hard as whipstick mallee. Daily shovelling shit in the vegetable gardens and stables, baling hay and grooming horses had toughened him. His reputation for gentleness with horses and ability to quieten even the most intractable steed extended well beyond the mission. And, when he could, he was in the mission pool swimming — lap after lap after lap. It was a peaceful and beautiful means of escape. Without any conscious effort and through his own intrinsic qualities, Colin Fox had changed incrementally to become an informal leader.

It had not been so when he arrived. The Brothers had been ruthless. On the first day his head was shaved and his few possessions burned. To all and sundry he was labelled a "white" killer and his little sister a slut. Henceforth, he was to be known only as Fox.

That same afternoon he encountered the viciousness of Brother John, a hulking man with thick black hair. His frequent slandering of Lucy prompted Fox to glare at him and mutter, 'Ya wrong.' Brother John had grabbed Fox by the shirtfront and dragged him to the meeting hall where, in no time flat, a "line" was assembled. Sixty boys formed two rows facing each other about a pace apart and, while Fox did not know what was coming, he experienced deep fear. The atmosphere was electric — suppressed excitement, resentment, apprehension and resignation. It swirled around him like a poisonous cloud. Suddenly, with a mighty shove, Brother John sent Fox sprawling into the maw of "the line." A fury of ugliness erupted as the terrified boy picked himself up and struggled between the two rows of boys — punched, knuckled, slapped, kicked and jeered from both sides. Anyone failing to deliver this treatment was subjected to the same experience. Several times Fox fell, dazed by the blows. Tears flowed, pain mushroomed but not one sound escaped his lips. By the end of the line his nose was bloodied, his teeth chipped, chunks of skin were missing and one eye was rapidly swelling shut. His silence infuriated the Brothers. Afterwards, his dogged determination to seek no help won support from several of the older boys. It was Fox's second act of defiance in one day.

Two months after arriving at Mount Barker he appeared before the Children's Court in Perth for stealing the bike he used to reach Lucy. Being his first court appearance, he received a warning. Back at the Mount, he was treated to a whipping for thieving. Brother John delighted in vigorously wielding the belt in the name of Christ. After that, Fox spent a week in the Tower. Four small, barred rooms above the granary were used to imprison boys deemed in need of discipline. There, Fox began dreaming at nights. At first, his dreams were nothing more than images of country presented in striking colours of rich ochre. But gradually, they presented messages. One night he was visited by a powerful ancestor from his mother's family. By the time he left the Tower he felt able to focus upon achieving right outcomes from any adversity.

Seven months later, Fox attended the Coroner's Court; this time as a witness regarding Mullett's death. Mullett's rape and murder of Lucy was indisputable and the body of evidence fell in Fox's favour — he *had* been trying to save his sister. In that respect, the Reverend McManus was at least supportive. Eventually too,

Brigitte Murphy broke her silence concerning Mullet's behaviour towards Lucy and other children at Turkey Creek. No charges would be levelled against Fox.

After this hearing, Fox was deemed wild and uncontrollable and sent to the Tower for three months. This, the Brothers believed, was appropriate given the Court's failure to exact justice. The truth, more likely, was their abhorrence of his regular incantations for illness to befall Brother John, a practice not unnoticed by the boys. And later, when Brother John experienced a paralysing stroke that halted his delivery of brutal beatings, Fox was regarded as someone special. Brother John's replacement on the belt, Brother Mark, was much less vitriolic and a mere shadow of the former's fury.

Over time, the Tower became a place of retreat, growth and nourishment for Fox. It was no longer a place to be feared. He exercised and dreamed expansively and vividly. His dreams revealed knowledge, brought comfort and enabled profound spiritual connection to his *Gija* family. In the Tower he recalled stories and experiences involving his mother, his country and his family. Slowly he devised and mastered a form of meditation which facilitated his entry to this realm of dreaming at will. Above all, time in the Tower began sharpening his desire for escape.

Over the next two years he worked hard, immersed himself in the available schooling and extended his already proficient use of code-switching (the transfer of linguistic items from one dialect to another). Fox discovered that he was naturally curious and thirsted for knowledge. He learned patience, kept his counsel and scoured the library for stories about the first and second world wars, particularly those of escape. One day he chanced across a battered paperback by Lobsang Rampa called *The Third Eye*. It contained a phrase that resonated deeply and would become central to his life: *"the strong can afford to be gentle, the weak and unsure brag and boast."* Every day he found some way to make the phrase work for him. He despised bullies and befriended the smaller, younger boys set upon by sexual predators at the mission: some of them Brothers, some of them older Aboriginal boys. He talked to the young kids, listened to them, shared their fears, reassured them, told them his story and encouraged them not to lose hope. And never did Fox stop believing he would return home.

Over the months and years at Mount Barker, life became a treadmill of hard labour, privation, prayer and joylessness made bearable only by Fox's personal quest for survival. The one hypocrisy that always made him laugh was the six monthly welfare inspection. On this day the boys dressed in white shirts, clean trousers and black shoes without socks. Unruly locks were trimmed and every dormitory was neatened and straightened. The day after inspection, normalcy resumed as the white shirts, trousers and shoes were put away until the next assessment.

Throughout his tenure, Fox had come to hate the Brothers' embargo upon his traditional language. Every boy heard speaking in his own language not only received a thrashing, but was bullied to believe he was white. And white people didn't speak "gibberish." Despite many a beating for breaching these rules, Fox would be an adult before he fully appreciated the calculated harshness of this policy and its legacy of deprivation, a deprivation that he learned constituted one of the several elements of genocide.

One day in the stables, Fox heard a whimpering cry from a stall at the far end of the run. Quietly, he went to investigate and found sixteen-year-old Dan Lovett sitting on top of eight-year-old Charlie Dyar, a friend of Fox's. Charlie's pants were halfway down his legs.

'What's goin' on Dan?' queried Fox.

'Mind yer bisness and fuck off,' said Lovett.

'You right Charlie?' Fox asked.

Before he could answer, Lovett grabbed a handful of Dyar's hair and twisted it hard. 'I told ya, fuck off. He's orlright.'

'Can't do that. Get off 'im.'

'Make me.' Lovett laughed.

'Dan, leave 'im alone. If you don't, I'm gonna beat the shit out of ya. And there'll be more. Same as 'appened to Brother John.'

Lovett blanched but, being bigger, older, stronger and unwilling to lose face said, 'You and what army Fox? Yer too bloody big for yer boots. Think just 'cos you killed a *wadjella* I oughta be scared – *fuck off!*'

As Fox opened the stall gate, Lovett rose. He was just on six feet tall and a good two stone heavier than Fox – pudgy. Little Charlie Dyar rolled over and Fox watched him scuttle out of the way. Fox stood holding the gate open.

'What are ya waitin' for Dan? Ya piss weak!'

Lovett bellowed at the taunt and charged at Fox, arms whirling. At the last moment, Fox stepped aside and viciously swung the heavy half gate shut. Winded and stunned, Lovett fell to the ground in a heap. Fox stepped into the stall and delivered three well-placed kicks to Lovett's abdomen. When he curled into a ball to protect himself, Fox grabbed a riding crop from a hook outside and laid into Lovett, thrashing all parts of his body except his face.

'Had enough?' Fox enquired breathlessly.

'Yeah, yeah,' sobbed Lovett.

'Leave Charlie and his mates alone. If ever I hear ya touched one of 'em again, ya for it. Ya hear me?'

'Yes,' blubbered Lovett.

'Good. Other big kids here think same as me. I'll be tellin' 'em about ya. Today. So ya won't only have me to worry about. I know there's more of your lot 'ere too, so give 'em the message.'

'Okay, okay,' said Lovett.

'So get. But before ya do, tell Charlie here you're sorry for what ya done. Oh, and don't tell the Brothers, otherwise you'll be walkin' the line – *my* line.'

But two days later, Lovett told his special friend – the hulking Brother John. Late that evening, the "line" was assembled and Fox was dragged into the meeting hall by two brown robed Brothers. With a clutch of cassocked tormentors nearby, Brother John stood at the head of the line, huge, aroused and leering; right arm hanging uselessly.

'So Fox, not so clever now are we?' he mumbled, his speech affected by the stroke. 'After this, Tower for a month! Get down that line,' he bellowed. With that, Fox was hurled into "the line".

But Fox had his own ideas and the line was not among them. After the Brothers released him he dived to the floor in a forward roll smoothly rising to sprint to the end. He ran at Brother John, leapt, somersaulted and delivered a mighty kick to John's chest. Shocked, unable to defend himself, John thumped onto his arse and sprawled on his back.

Pandemonium erupted as the boys watched Fox's powerful and brazen defiance. They whooped and hollered, stomping their feet when Fox broke three of Brother John's fingers by viciously plunging his boot heel onto his scrabbling left hand. Fox turned and glared at the clustering, brown demons, staring them down, his own malevolence outgunning their resolve and anger. An uneasy silence fell.

'Lovett, you slimy bastard,' called Fox softly, 'I warned ya to tell your bum-fuckin' mates to leave us alone. Ya brought this down on yourself.' He gestured to the remnant line. 'You're dead. I'm sendin' your black soul to hell. And while that's happenin', don't think ya can be saved. No one's gonna' worry about ya. Ya head will be filled with snakes and you're gonna waste away. I warned ya.' Fox's quiet voice was menacing and unequivocal. He turned to Brother John. 'I'm *not* goin' to the Tower and you're joinin' Lovett.'

Stunned by Fox's audacity, no one tried to stop him as he stalked from the hall. Ten minutes later, when three brown vultures hunted for Fox to punish him, they found that he and his meagre possessions had vanished.

CHAPTER 5

1970

By the age of seventeen, Fox had worked for two years with Joe Darrigan's Boxing Troupe. He was lean, muscular and tough. At five feet ten and weighing eleven stone, Darrigan decreed Fox good enough to mix it with the suckers. On this afternoon, he was on the platform banging the old base drum: *ba – boom, ba – boom, ba – boom.* Behind him, a weathered mural portrayed long past pugs in a montage of combative postures. Tent boxing these days was a threatened activity. Whispers from government, as yet unconfirmed, hinted at new rules to control fight frequency. The do-gooders proclaimed: too brutal, too crude, too violent, too foul. Too uncomfortable.

'Bloody neo-religionists,' Darrigan had responded, 'too thick to realise one of Australia's best known pastors, Doug Nicholls, was a tent boxer.'

Ba – boom, ba – boom, ba – boom. Darrigan whistled through his fingers and bellowed, 'Holdah! Holdah! Holdah! C'mon boys – step right up and give it a go. Don't be lily-livered. Twenty dollars to go the round – fifty if youse last the full distance. Show us ya courage. Holdah! Holdah! Holdah! If youse have a score ta settle this is the place! Who's gunna take on "Killer" Conroy here? Me little firecracker from Tassy. Get up here "Killer".' Darrigan whistled again. "Killer" Conroy, a short, nuggety man in his early fifties climbed onto the platform, white towel around his neck, resplendent in a crimson satin robe.

"'Killer' here, ladies and gents, is a gun woodcutter from Tasmania. He's yusta felling big bluegums and mountain ash. Shearers, stockmen and miners are mere kindling to 'im.' The balding Conroy, whose original features had been generously reshaped by his many battles, scowled at the crowd.

One by one, showcased in spurious tales of pugilistic glory, Fox drummed Darrigan's team onto the platform – a colourful, pseudo belligerent, shockforce of warriors. And slowly too, the platform filled with volunteers as Darrigan conned them from the throng, challenging their manhood with his mixture of flattery, scorn and financial reward.

Fox paused as Darrigan continued his invocation. Indifferently, he scanned the crowd, wondering who next would step up to the mark. The mugs were all types: serious brawlers, bullies, brash kids, tough stockmen, half drunks chasing a quid and occasionally, the odd nervous one who wanted to boast later that he'd done it – mixed it with Darrigan's finest. Country boys loved a stoush, especially the Aboriginals. In the heat and dust of the outback, tensions could fester. The boxing tent brought legitimate and colourful relief, and men and women alike flocked to the spectacle when it hit town.

Fox's eye fell upon a lanky sun bronzed man with features as sharp as gibber rocks. *Skinny – bloody – Rogers!* That bloody copper bastard who, with that vile turd Mullett, had pinched him and Lucy! He raked Rogers with a cold glare. He hadn't seen him in more than ten years and instantly wanted to batter the shit out of him. Darrigan's policy wouldn't allow that, even if he could. He used the beat of the drum to calm his turbulent feelings. He remembered Rogers' iron fists and how they'd flattened the men of his camp. *Ba – boom, ba – boom, ba – boom.* Mentally, he began to challenge Rogers, to draw him near, every beat a blow upon his soul.

The transition to Darrigan's had not been easy. From conversations with old men at Moore River Fox learned of three girls who ran away from the place in 1931 to find their way home by following the rabbit proof fence. The old men also told him about Geoff Guest. Guest was an Aboriginal boy sent to a cattle property near Toowoomba in 1936. Aged only eleven, sometime during 1939 – 1940, Guest fled the station after its English overseer inflicted a serious flogging that left him badly scarred and stuttering. Guest had breached the Englishman's decree that no Aboriginal was to speak indoors. One afternoon, while alone with the overseer, Guest spoke. Enraged, the man grabbed his whip to deliver a hiding but Guest got in first and felled him with his own lead-tipped yard whip. Fearing he had killed the man, Guest shot through. The escape had been long planned for the right time and a horse and provisions were stashed in readiness. Fox filed this story in his memory bank and at Mount Barker, began hiding his own stores in the bush.

After upending Brother John, Fox dashed to his cubicle, grabbed his hat, stuffed Lobsang Rampa and his few clothes into a sugar bag and slipped silently into the night. Unlike Guest, he had no firearm or tools but he did take a horse and saddle and rode to his stores about a mile north of the mission. His plan was simple: live off the land and make his way to Turkey Creek via the Canning Stock Route. The "wallopers" would soon be after him so he needed to stay out of their way and make as much ground as possible.

Cantering under starlit skies Fox skirted the vineyards and worked his way deep into the bush, an ugly chapter of his life abandoned in idyllic surroundings. East lay the beautiful Porongurups, a ribbon of ancient hills first seen by white man in

1829, four years after convicts settled at Albany. North was the breathtaking Stirling Range. A spine rich with wildflowers, craggy peaks, heaths, woodlands, birds, animals and thick scrub. For Fox, it was a veritable supermarket. By dawn he had reached Kalgan River – forty-nine miles lay between himself and the mission.

His dreams informed him that he would be okay all the way to Turkey Creek, 1700 miles north. After that, he had to be patient.

Ten days out from the mission and 350 miles on, Fox veered east from Southern Cross to skirt Lake Deborah East. A tourist information board said the Lakes, settled in the 1890s, were surrounded by granite outcrops and fresh water wells. These days, the "Cross" was prominent because of its commercial wildflower crops and rich flora – delicate salmon gums and red barked gimlets. The board mentioned too that camels used during an 1891 Elder Scientific Expedition were troubled by lack of food. But Fox knew it was *kwongan* country – heathland – and that he and his horse, Bob, would be fine.

On his solitary moonlight journey Fox envisaged Lovett and Brother John beginning to waste with fear. On the screen in his head, he watched Lovett writhe; witnessed the remorseless pounding headaches, smelled the stench of his body odour and heard Lovett cry out as he grappled with the slithering knot of King Browns squirming in his mind. He observed Lovett slowly descend into madness. One by one, his mates stopped visiting and soon, Dan Lovett, who had lost more than half his body weight since being cursed, was dead.

Brother John, on the other hand, pretended nothing was happening. Yet Fox sensed the cold dread stalking him, the clammy, suffocating iciness he could neither deny nor shake. Forever looking over his shoulder, logic told Brother John it was nothing but imagination. Yet, when alone, dank, withering tentacles of claustrophobia reached out to strangle him. He became terrified of confession and experienced indescribable horror every time he entered the box. There, darkness weighed him down with such a palsy he felt unable to leave. His hair fell out, boils developed, his weight dropped away and he began talking in strange, nonsensical sing-song tones. Laughing and cackling, he wandered the mission corridors in preference to sleeping at night. Truth to tell, he was afraid of sleep because his ghosts magnified tenfold.

None of this was a mystery to Fox.

His journey home made him feel alive and of the earth again. The scent of gums, grasses, rain and dust seeped into his pores. Goanna, snake, bush potatoes, the odd fish, kantilli and lizards were all plentiful. But best of all, as the earth-spirit embraced his soul, there came a freedom as unencumbered as the sky, as rich as desert sunset and as sweet as wild honey. Nothing about this epic ride was anything other than fulfilling. His only sorrow was Lucy's absence – always he had planned for them to return together.

And then he rode into Turkey Creek, slap-bang into a mourning ceremony. Looking around the old camp, his heart contracted. His mother's shelter and possessions were nothing but a pile ash, burned to the ground as a shield to her spirit. He saw the scars of mourning wounds; witnessed the silent communication between women who dared not utter Rosie's name and understood. Spirits of the dead must be isolated and left undisturbed. These were ancient practices connected with death.

Sitting high up on Bob, Fox did not recognise the wail assaulting his ears was his own. Having been taken from his home, the dream of returning with Lucy had sustained him. Her death had deeply wounded him and were it not for the thought of his waiting Mum, he might have given up. Now he was alone.

The Aunties said when Rosie learned of Lucy's death, a flame had died. It had been her birth that helped with the loss of Duncan, her loving husband. Her big, strong stockman, a man proud of his Scottish roots, a man who had cherished them all. He had been taken by a mindless drunk-driver soon after Lucy's birth. After that, Rosie moved away from Leopold Downs and back to Turkey Creek. There, with her children and family, she had slowly become strong again.

And then came Mullett and Rogers and Brigette. Her children taken to join the ranks of the living dead. She had no rights, no news and no hope of seeing them. Gradually, Rosie declined. Three years later, word arrived of Lucy's murder. Rosie knew nothing of Colin, only that he was in a mission – *somewhere.* Rosie's world collapsed, depression accelerated and quietly, she wasted away. Fox's arrival coincided with the final phase of her mourning.

He stayed three months. He saw the end of the mourning and left with no great plans other than finding work. He decided to head for Noonkanbah, a huge cattle station on the Fitzroy River between Camballin and Fitzroy Crossing, some 360 kilometres east of Broome. There he could comfortably work with horses and cattle and be among the *Yungngora* community, traditional land owners who ran the station for its owners.

But, in 1968, there was trouble at Noonkanbah. The old station, a former Royal Australian Airforce base and staging post for the Netherlands East Indies Air Force during 1943-44, was rank with discontent. The *Yungngora* people were intensely dissatisfied with pay and conditions and highly suspicious of the insatiable minerals hunt in the Kimberly. As mining exploration forged ahead, conflict between Western Australia's Court government and *Yungngora* people grew. The issue at heart was whether sacred Aboriginal sites should be protected from vested interests wanting the mineral wealth. Later, this rancour would crystallise until its essence stood raw – mutual distrust and disrespect between traditional Aboriginal law and white western law.

Fox found the atmosphere toxic and moved to Broome. A willing and hard toiler, he had no trouble getting a job on the fishing boats. One quiet Saturday afternoon he visited Darrigan's Travelling Boxing Troupe with his mate Tommy Barker. The hype, the smell, the noise and the action instantly appealed and between shows, Fox presented himself to Darrigan and asked for a job. Darrigan thoughtfully sized up the slim young man.

'Come to the next show and I'll see how yer go in the ring. Ask me again after that.'

Two hours later, Fox volunteered for a bout with one of Darrigan's team, another Aboriginal named Danny Stocker. Stocker, about thirty-five, was experienced, muscular and skilled. While Darrigan's rules forbade the boxers from seriously hurting punters, they were still to look after themselves. At almost sixteen, Fox had no great strength to his punches but he out-paced, out-thought and out-boxed Danny Stocker.

And so it was he thumped the drum*: Ba – boom, ba – boom, ba – boom.* The steady rhythm throbbed. Rogers stared at him, a thoughtful, penetrating gaze. The drum pulsed louder: *ba – boom, ba – boom, ba – boom.* Silently, Fox called Rogers to him. Challenged him. Told him he would never win. Silently, Fox reeled him in. *I will humiliate, not retaliate. Take your pride, not your strength. Lance your arrogance and sear your soul.*

In the next pause, when Darrigan challenged the suckers to battle, Rogers' rough voice called, 'I'll take the young darkie.'

'Dunno about that mate, you look a bit too big and experienced to be takin' the boy on. He's for kids his own age and size.'

'Yeah? You're piss weak Darrigan. He's up there isn't he? Let him speak for himself.'

Fox grinned at Darrigan and nodded. *Ba – boom, ba – boom, ba – boom!*

Humiliate don't retaliate; humiliate don't retaliate; humiliate don't retaliate. Fox's grin spread slowly from ear to ear. His personal misery – Lucy's death, Rosie's death – all triggered by this man's intervention. Joe Darrigan would never know the satisfaction Fox was anticipating. He was unbeatable. As Fox's steely grey eyes bored into him, Rogers' memory stirred. Familiar eyes. He couldn't recall when, or where, or the circumstance, only that he remembered them. Fox laughed inwardly watching Rogers' face pucker in concentration, memory chafing, recall working overtime. Fox playing mind-games.

Ba – boom, ba – boom, ba – boom. Humiliate, don't retaliate!

CHAPTER 6

The crowd before Darrigan's platform swelled. Fitzroy Crossing in early July was warm and clear and people aplenty had come in off the stations for the annual rodeo. Many were Aboriginal people from the four main language groups and today the usual town population of about 1200 was almost 2000. It was an exciting time with the horses, the fights and a couple of nights of grog, dancing and good fun. This mid-afternoon, a good-sized mob had gathered for the fights and the dust was rising beneath impatient feet.

Start time was ten minutes away. Mardie, Joe's wife, opened up the ticket box and the noisy, cheerful crowd bustled into the tent. One of Darrigan's fighters marshalled the challengers off the platform and around to the back of the tent. There they had to sign consent forms and disclose if they were carrying injuries; it was also a final chance to withdraw. Darrigan was wary of the creeping tide of litigation.

Before they started, Darrigan spoke to the volunteers.

'Righto youse blokes, listen up. The rules are simple: fight fair. That means no hittin' below the belt, no hittin' anyone with their back to ya, no hittin' someone fallin' down and no bloody kickin' – this ain't a pub brawl. I mean it. Some bastards ferget where they are! Just to make sure ya don't ferget, Big Merv, me heavyweight here, will belt the livin' shit outa anyone who sinks the slipper. And, at minimum, there's twenty bucks fer youse all, whatever happens.' Naturally, Darrigan's unstated rule was: "never let the suckers win".

'Any questions?'

The eight men were silent.

'Anyone wanna change their minds?'

Again, no response.

'Okay. Shirts off, fight in bare tops or singlets. There's a bunch of runners and clean socks in them boxes. Get some that fit. If ya wanna fight barefoot, that's okay too. Five minutes we start. Lightweights first, workin' up ta heavies. Okay?'

Fox strolled around the corner of the tent. He watched Rogers find and don some runners. Rogers was tanned and sinewy, his flat belly rippled like washboard. He wouldn't be a pushover. Still, Fox had faith. Rogers looked up from tying his laces and nodded to Fox. Fox could see puzzlement lingering in his eyes. Inside the crowd roared and chanted as the fights kicked off. Fox went off for a leak. He closed his eyes: *humiliate don't retaliate, humiliate don't retaliate.* It was okay, his way was clear.

Soon enough, Big Merv stepped out and beckoned Fox and Rogers. They went in. It was a big tent, about thirty by twenty-five metres. In the centre, instead of a traditional ring of ropes and posts, there was a large tarpaulin painted with a blue square representing the ring. Anyone pushed or hit from the ring was thrown back again by willing and vocal spectators. A couple of light plastic chairs stood diagonally opposite each other in the ring corners – one red, one blue. The tarp, which measured about six by six metres, was tautly staked down over a spread of wood shavings some ten to fifteen centimetres deep, a surface that was firm but relatively soft. The shavings extended another metre beyond the tarp. Beyond the shavings, set back another couple of metres, tiered stands rose around all four sides of the tent. An aisle ran through the stand from the ticket box to the ring and then on from the opposite side of the ring out back where the fighters gathered. It was through this aisle that Fox and Rogers entered.

Inside, after watching three bouts, the crowd was good humoured, charged and clamorous. The tent, filled to capacity, was hot and steamy from the warm day. A potpourri of odours wafted around the tent space: stale sweat, pine shavings, perfume and tobacco smoke. Spontaneous raucous laughter bubbled up every so often like a geyser. Impeccably dressed in a white shirt, white cotton trousers and black sneakers, Joe Darrigan stood in the centre of the ring. Fox automatically went to the red corner. Rogers rolled his shoulders, whirled his arms, marched to the blue chair and sat. Each fighter's white clad attendant was there to provide water, a towel and styptic pencil to staunch blood from cuts or scrapes.

Fox was composed and remained standing. He danced lightly, one foot to the other, eyes closed, breathing slowly – in through his nose, out gently through his mouth. The noise of the crowd receded to a low hum. His focus intensified: anticipation was heightened, clarity was brilliant and movement slowed. He opened his eyes and fixed on Rogers who was caught as clearly as a rabbit in headlights.

Rogers felt uncomfortable. He'd come to watch the fights, not participate. His reputation was already lethal among the locals and he didn't need this to feel comfortable in his own skin. Yet, in some strange way he felt compelled to challenge this young kid. He didn't know why. And there was something familiar about him, something he couldn't pin down. He wasn't worried about the fight – he could knock anybody sideways on sixpence into next week. Yet his opponent made him uneasy. Although he was moving he seemed still amid the din. Something about him made Rogers' scalp crawl.

Darrigan waved them in. The chairs were whisked away. The crowd clapped and whistled and stamped. Rogers stalked to the centre, glowering at Fox. Fox seemed to glide across the tarp, so light was his step.

'Righto boys,' bawled Darrigan, 'ya know the rules, fight fair. It'll be three three minute rounds. If I say stop, stop! And step away. If either of youse get knocked down, I'll count to eight, whether ya hurt or not. They're me rules. Right, touch gloves.'

A bell clanged and they stepped forward to touch gloves. Before they'd even finished, a lightning left from Fox bloodied Rogers' nose. He danced back out of the way. Rogers shook his head, he hadn't even seen it coming. The crowd roared. This one was off to a good start. Rogers, a local hero was sure to retaliate. Rogers crouched, tucked his elbows in and went after Fox. He was at least fifteen centimetres taller with considerably longer reach; he was fit and much heavier than Fox. Bang, bang, left right combination to Fox's head – except Fox was not there. He had already swayed right, ducked and installed a solid left rip to Rogers' midriff and skipped away.

Fox circled Rogers. Everything Rogers did Fox saw in slow motion, even before it was initiated. Rogers whirled and shuffled towards Fox, eyes focussed keenly on his opponent, *This kid's good. I'd better watch him.* He moved rapidly after Fox, trying to crowd him out of the ring. Jab, jab with the left, looking to plant a right cross. None of his blows landed. Again, Rogers tried to press Fox out of the ring, all the while his dynamite left pumping piston-like. Fox was elusive. He seemed to float around the ring, to tie Rogers in knots, to confound his sense of place.

The bell clanged. As Rogers returned to his corner he was aware the crowd had quietened, they sensed something different about this fight. Even Darrigan was baffled. He'd never seen Fox fight like this. He'd landed only two blows, both telling, yet he was overwhelming Rogers. Rogers' approach was stolid, focussed and clearly professional. Fox was something else. He seemed ethereal.

Out again. Rogers decided to stay away from Fox, to draw him in, to make him box, not crowd him. Fox obliged. He entered Rogers' fire zone and immediately bloodied his nose again, launched an upper cut and belted his ribs just under the heart. Rogers reeled. He could not believe Fox's speed and dexterity. He'd had many fights but none like this. Fox was beginning to annoy him. He shook his head and charged at Fox, intending to clinch his neck and sink a hard right deep into his belly. Fox stood, waiting. Rogers cannoned into him, reached to imprison his head and was met by a straight left that sat him on his arse. The crowd roared and stomped their feet. This was something special. So far, although Rogers had swung many blows none had seemed to hit Fox. Rogers was purposeful and serious, Fox moved mischievously like thistledown. Rogers' blows were ferocious and powerful. Fox was controlled, conserved his energy and exerted just enough power. His speed was dazzling. And now, Rogers had the indignity of having to wait for the count of eight.

The round ended as Darrigan bellowed eight. Last round. Rogers decided to demolish Fox. He was angry and knew that angry was not clever. He rushed across to the red corner ready to down the lazily rising Fox with a looping right to the head followed by a body rip. But, like smoke, Fox just floated away. As Rogers passed, he poked a stinging left under his guard and into his jaw. Rogers whirled and swung a long right hook at Fox that glanced off his gloves. *Ha huh,* he thought, *he's not invincible.* Rogers stalked Fox. Left, left – left-right combination. Fox swayed, ducked and hammered Rogers' ribs. And then, with ninety seconds to go, Fox attacked. Delicate, stinging blows surgically placed assaulted Rogers' torso, head, arms and ears. It was not that the onslaught was brutal, just that it was fast and relentless. And Rogers could not escape. Before he knew it, he was on his back. Up again after the count of eight. Down again with his nose mashed for the third time. Up again after eight and down again with his head spinning from a cracking right cross.

The bell rang for the last time. For what seemed an eternity, the big tent was silent. Rogers, on his back, not hurt but embarrassed.

Fox loped back to his corner, took a long draft of water and walked back to the centre of the ring. There, Darrigan proudly raised Fox's arm as victor. He had never witnessed a bout like this before. He knew Fox was a great little fighter, but this … this was outstanding! The crowd yelled, whistled and bellowed their approval.

That night, Fox climbed the steps to his trailer.

'Fox!' A low voice called from the darkness. Fox waited, motionless; payback was known in the boxing-tent world. Rogers stepped into the light. 'Fox. I'd like to talk to you.'

'I've got nothing to say Rogers.'

'So you know me then. Well, I've got things to say to you. Do you want to hear me out? Want to go for a beer?'

'I don't drink. Come in but don't do anything stupid.'

'You're safe with me, but I'm not so sure I'm safe with you.' Rogers grinned ruefully and nodded.

They entered the trailer truck. The long caravan, divided into a series of tiny rooms, was towed by a prime mover. At the back of the trailer, off the drop down steps, was a small lounge area. It was Spartan-like and scrupulously clean. Darrigan style.

'Well, what do you want?'

'Like I said, I want to talk to you. First of all, I want you to know I didn't come here today looking for a bout. Meeting you was the last thing I expected. I thought you were familiar but I couldn't place you. It was only through the last half of the last round when you were whipping me that I remembered. It was your eyes. I remembered those grey eyes glaring at that bastard Mullett.'

'I'm glad you remembered. You caused a lot of harm.'

'I know. That's what I wanted to talk about. Look, I'm not proud of any of that. I was just doing my job and it never bothered me. But I heard about Mullett and what happened. It made me sick to think I'd been part of that. That I'd just gone along without question. So, I wanted to say I'm sorry. And I know sorry doesn't cut the mustard …'

'Too bloody right it doesn't.' Fox's eyes glittered, pain pummelled his face. 'Lucy was murdered by that vile piece of shit employed by the state. Me mum is dead after wasting away and you think "sorry" fixes things? *Piss off!* You saw what Mullett was doing. You coulda kicked him in the balls at the time, you coulda prosecuted him. But we're black. We aren't worth it, so ya did nuthin!'

Rogers moved to the door. 'Yes. It was wrong. After I heard about Lucy I quit the force. Couldn't stomach it any more. I always knew Mullett was sleazy and rough with kids but I never caught him doing anything indecent. He was a bit too cunning. I should have followed up my instincts, but I didn't do that either. I'm sorry about your mum, I didn't know she'd passed on. What happened today was proper. You gave me a lesson I won't forget. You had the skill and power to hurt me badly, but you didn't. You were controlled, you embarrassed me in front of a crowd, you hurt my pride, but, at the end of the day, that's nothing compared to what I did to you. I want you to know,' he said softly, 'I am deeply, deeply sorry.' Rogers turned and left the trailer.

When he'd gone, Fox slumped into a chair, anger turned to sadness. Sad for all of Rosie's losses, sad that Lucy's bright spirit had been extinguished and sad for Rogers. Rogers had seen wrong and done nothing; he had accepted bad law and bad policy. It was too easy to argue that Rogers was only one against many of his kind, that he was only doing his job – he *knew* it was wrong and failed to act. Fox had always acted. And copped the consequences! Beatings, confinement, bullying, isolation and starvation. None of it had ever stopped him speaking out against wrongdoing. He had stood against paedophiles, rapists, sadists and intimidators – both black and white. Predators who concealed their behaviour under the guise of "good works".

Grudgingly, he admitted Rogers was due some respect for coming to apologise. It changed nothing, but he had done it. Rogers would carry his demons about Lucy in his own way.

Fox rose and walked to his bunk. After today, he was done with Joe Darrigan. When they finished here they were off to Winnellie, in Darwin. He would leave Darrigan then.

CHAPTER 7

September, and the air huffed warm and salty from a mild onshore breeze. Fox entered the Esplanade from Hughes Avenue and loped along Darwin's beach front. The sun had relinquished its force to become a soft, orange-rich orb glowing from the brink of the Timor Sea. He had been running just over an hour from Frances Bay Drive, enjoying the sunset and a smooth, easy rhythm. His breathing was even, his strides metronomic, his runners tap-tapping softly on the pavement.

At Centennial Park near Knuckey Street, the path meandered towards a dense thatch of trees. Almost past them, Fox caught a flash of movement to his left and heard a muffled yell. He stopped abruptly, turning towards the sound. Then, a cry of anguish – a woman. He moved swiftly towards the sound and saw, closer to the beach, a knot of thrashing bodies. Moving silently, he saw three men with a woman in their grasp. One had an arm around her face and over her mouth, a second was tearing her skirt from flailing legs and a third was trying hard to hold her arms while ripping her blouse open. She was resisting fiercely.

As Fox stepped into the open, her face spasmed in horror. He raised a finger to his lips and before awareness dawned, delivered a mighty kick to the head of the man who had now pulled her skirt free. As he sank without sound, the mauler ripping her blouse whirled. Another withering kick, this time to the victim's crotch.

Roaring in pain, he doubled forward and received a crushing left-right from Fox's flashing fists. Felled, unconscious. The third man fled towards the beach. Fox overtook him in less than a dozen strides, leapt and smashed him to the ground. Effortlessly, he twisted the man's arm and snapped the shoulder joint leaving him to scream in agony.

He ran to the woman who, with her back to a tree, shoulders heaving, breath rasping, was trying desperately to pull her skirt up. Her racking sobs sliced at Fox's heart. In the failing light he could see her entire body violently shaking. Suddenly, she turned and vomited.

Standing back, he studied her quietly, knowing instinctively that any move to touch or comfort might accelerate her fear. When she recovered sufficiently he spoke gently.

'Eh, you're okay now. No one's gunna hurt you. You're safe.'

She seemed not to hear. Trembling, sobbing and occasionally retching, she continued to pull her skirt up.

Fox tried again. 'You're safe now. Can I help you? Is there someone I can take you to? Or get for you?' His quiet voice was husky with concern.

She paused, peering through the gloom – seeing, yet not seeing him.

'I … I … don't … know,' she stuttered. 'They just grabbed me. They punched me and dragged me down here.'

One of the men at her feet began to groan. Fox stepped forward, placed a foot on his neck and hissed, 'Shut up. Another squeak and I'll break your neck.' Heavy silence filled the air.

The woman was frantically trying to fasten her skirt with a zip that obviously had broken. Her torn blouse gaped revealing a white bra. In the distance, "Broken Shoulder" moaned. Gradually, the woman quietened.

'Are ya hurt at all?' Fox asked.

'No. They'd just got me here when you arrived.' She shuddered.

'I've got a massive headache from their punches though.'

Fox, from a metre or so, gazed at her intently. After a period of silence he said, 'I know you.'

Fear surged afresh. '*No!* What do you want? I've never seen you before.'

'Yeah, you have. I'm Colin Fox. You spoke up for me at the police station years ago when that prick Wildman hit me. He was investigating my sister Lucy's death. Lucy Fox. Connors isn't it?'

'Lucy's brother! Oh … oh … ' She slumped against the tree.

Gently, Fox said, 'You really are alright. I mean you no harm, but I'll damage these bastards if you want.'

Connors reached towards him, took a step and stumbled over the man on the ground. Fox caught her as she fell and steadied her. When she recovered, he stepped away.

'I can't believe it's you. So often I've thought about you. Wondered what happened to you. How can I ever thank you for this?' She gestured towards the two men on the ground in front of her.

'Yeah,' Fox rasped, 'they meant business alright. But they're not so tough now. What do you want to do with the bastards? I can wait with 'em till you bring the coppers back if you like.' He eyed her keenly. Even though trembling, her composure was returning.

'That'd be good. I'm staying at a pub on the Esplanade – it's not far. I'll be ten or fifteen minutes, twenty at most.'

'Go for it. I'll be 'ere when you get back.'

'Thanks, thanks again.'

Fox smiled in the dark. 'That's a change: a white sheila indebted to a black fella.' There was wry humour in his voice. 'Eh, ya shirt's buggered. Do you want a lend of mine? It's a bit sweaty but it was fresh tonight.'

She considered his offer, examined her own torn fabric then nodded. He removed his T shirt and watched as she pulled it on over her blouse.

At ten the next morning, Connors met Fox at the Darwin Police Station in Mitchell Street. The night before they had been interviewed and given copies of their statements. Connors and the offenders, three German tourists, had been medically examined and treated. The attackers were then locked up after being charged with abduction, attempted rape and assault. By the time they were through it was after midnight and the pair agreed to meet at the police station the following morning and go for lunch.

Connors arrived in a soft lime linen frock, her thick blonde hair wound into a knot on top of her head; she carried a cobalt blue shoulder bag and wore matching sandals. At thirty-eight, Caroline Connors was an attractive woman. Fox wore pressed moleskins, polished brown boots and a crimson shirt rolled to the elbows. His wavy black hair was brushed loosely. With his regular features, unusual grey eyes and smooth skin, he was a picture of vitality. Patiently, he waited in the foyer until Connors was finished and the best part of an hour later, they set off for lunch.

'How did you sleep?' he enquired

'Well, all things considered, not too bad. I ached a bit and found when I showered I was covered in bruises. They must have belted me more than I realised. Men,' she exclaimed with venom. 'Those idiots are here backpacking from Germany. Now they've buggered up their holiday, their lives and the lives of their families. Too much beer — straight to their balls!'

'Did ya call home?'

'Yes, I phoned John this morning. We decided not to tell the kids.'

'Ya lucky but I'm glad.' Fox was pensive, thinking of Lucy. 'I often wish Lucy 'ad your sort of luck.'

Immediately Connors placed a consoling hand on his arm. 'I know,' she said softly. 'That must have been a nightmare for you — you were only ten for God's sake. And poor little Lucy. What a tragedy.'

They walked in silence, Fox flushed with pain after vividly recalling the chapel at Sister Kate's.

'I'm pretty sure that's what killed Mum.' His voice was soft. 'They said she was depressed. But it was us – being taken. Utter crap it was. Mum thought she 'ad no one left and nothin' to live for. Dad was dead, Lucy was dead and I was missin'. What's to live for? She was a good person.'

Connors heard pain in his voice. She knew there was nothing she could do to reverse the harm. She said nothing and they continued in silence.

Eventually she spoke. 'In a strange way it's because of you I'm here in Darwin.' He peered at her quizzically. 'Lucy's death upset me so deeply I resigned. My old boss, who's dead unfortunately, said I was being too hasty. He'd spent a lot of time in the outback and reckoned there were things we *could* do to help Aboriginal people. He was a rare one. Not many thought his way and his views weren't popular. But he believed in doing the right thing and often that meant sidestepping policy.'

'So what are you doing 'ere? Did ya change police forces or somethin'?'

'No.' Connors smiled at him. 'You may not remember but you asked me to contact Brigitte Murphy. I did, and after a bloody big effort to convince her to tell what she knew, the result eventually was a whole new world for me. I now work in child protection. I'm still with the WA Police and I'm attending a child protection conference here.' She pulled a face. 'Most cops I know think this work's bullshit – not real police work. They reckon it's for "do-gooders" in welfare. But when I think of Lucy, they did her no good and neither of you fared well.' She smiled tautly. 'So, I'm in the vanguard of this field. It's new work and, over time, I hope to help lots of kids.'

'Yeah, well,' he paused, 'that bloody Wildman. I can see now ya stuck ya neck out. Didn't appreciate it then but I never forgot. *You* spoke for me!'

Connors nodded. 'You won't be surprised to learn that

Wildman's bad habits caught up with him. He belted someone once too often. That someone had influence and the Discipline Board sacked him. Last I heard, he was a hopeless alcoholic.'

'Yeah ... well, the grog's no good, but that's justice.'

Connors laughed, a soft warm sound. 'Enough of him. What are you doing here?' She didn't want to think any more about what could have happened the previous night had Fox not appeared. Having him talk kept that darkness at bay.

'Where do I start? Long journey.' As before, when he'd spoken of Lucy, Connors discerned an underlying sadness.

'Tell me about Darwin. When did you come here? Why did you come here? What do you do? From the look of you, you seem to be doing alright.'

Fox laughed aloud. 'Spoken like a true copper. Did ya think I was on the dole or somethin'?' He continued to smile, liking her warmth and interest in him. 'I've been 'ere a couple of years workin' in the Botanical Gardens. Before I used to work with Darrigan's Boxing Troupe. Done a bit of work on boats in Broome and with horses. But really, I'm on the run.' His dry tone and sparkling eyes suggested the contrary.

Connors gazed at him speculatively. 'I don't believe it, pull the other one! Let's go in here for lunch and you can tell me the real story.' They walked into the Bluebird Café on Knuckey Street, a place grounded in the fifties. It was long and narrow with comfortable, high backed, six-seater wooden booths. A short, dumpy, balding man with pencil-line moustache stepped forward to escort them to a seat. He had a happy lived-in sort of face and an impossible Greek accent. As they walked towards the back, Fox noted the cafe was close to full. Conversation and laughter mingled with the rich aroma of good food.

They settled into a booth and sank into the thick, padded blue cushions and slid towards the wall. As they moved, the high backed seats creaked and the scarred wooden tabletop rocked, small features confirming the café's popularity. They ordered hot coffee and waited for the menu.

'You first,' he said pre-emptively.

Connors smiled, knowing he was buying time before committing himself.

'Not much to tell really. I wasn't married when I first met you. I am now, to John McNulty, a wonderful man who is a doctor at Royal Perth Hospital. We have three children and live in South Perth. John and I both love swimming so we take our kids to the beach as often as possible. Cottesloe is our favourite. And, as I said, I'm helping develop a new field of police work in WA which is due mainly to you and Lucy. I'm happy, I love my husband, my kids and my work. That's me!' She smiled again, a gentle engaging expression of pleasure.

Fox gazed at her enviously. He would forever regard her as a considerate person genuinely interested in the welfare of others, and yet, by the mere colour of her skin, she was unlikely to experience the sorrow and pain inflicted upon him and so many like him. But that was not her fault. To the contrary, her compassion and good spirit were focussed on change, however limited it might be.

They both ordered barramundi, chips and a Greek salad. Slowly, over the meal, Fox recounted his life in the missions at Moore River and Mount Barker. He watched Connors pale as he described "the line", the sexual and other assaults by the Brothers and their favourite older boys, bouts of solitary confinement, poor meals, incessant lying about families and the constant repudiation of their culture. Brother John loomed as a gargantuan bully obsessed with young boys. His activities were overtly encouraged through the wilful blindness of his institution and by government indifference. Fox spoke softly of the violence he encountered for defending younger boys and the punishment he'd meted out to offenders in return. Eventually, he told Connors of his escape and the long ride home to Turkey Creek for a bitter and empty purpose.

Connors listened attentively, her stomach knotted, her meal forgotten. Mentally, she compared the life of the then ten-year-old Fox with her almost nine-year-old son Jason. She winced at the futility and malice of a government policy so short on standards, so bereft of consistency and so lacking in compassion. Yet beneath the horror, Fox's strength and character shone with integrity and a kind of wild purity. By any measure, he was an unqualified success. She certainly understood his streak of mongrel, evident not only from the way he defended her the previous night, but also from the fierce penalties dished out to Mount Barker's bullies. In a perverse way, she thought him principled. And there was no doubting his courage. Fox was a young man with presence and a dry laconic sense of humour in spite of his horrifying life's experience.

She truly liked him.

CHAPTER 8

Abruptly, Connors pushed back into the booth, white faced. 'Would you mind if we left now? I need some air.' As she paid the bill she glanced at Fox and said, 'Don't argue. Let's walk down to the beach.' They strolled slowly, not speaking, Connors unsettled.

'What you said in there made me realise just how hard it's going to be to change things. Your story is not only wretched, but horribly dispiriting for what I'm trying to do now. You are remarkable. Do you ...?' She stopped, an amalgam of sadness, softness and profound understanding washing over her face. 'Remarkable,' she said softly.

Fox, unused to praise felt a warm glow. 'Well, I always planned goin' back to Mum. After Lucy died, that's what kept me goin'.' His tone was subdued, thoughtful.

Walking through Centennial Park they again lapsed into silence – memories of the previous night haunting. On the sand, Connors shucked her sandals, stuffed them in her bag and walked in the warm frothy water.

Pensively, she said, 'I don't know how you survived those years and I had no idea it was that bad. Yes, I knew the policy was, to use your words, crap! I knew it was discriminatory. I knew it was harsh. But I didn't know it was so malicious, so calculated, so violent or ... so ... bloody horrible! It cannot continue like this. It just can't! Why don't you work to change things? Maybe even work with me?'

'What, ya mean like bein' out there? Like Gary Foley over east? Nah, that's not for me. Coulda got involved at Noonkanbah but chose not too. I'm happy helpin' others individually but I'm not into big causes. Too many politics, too much about power, too much back-stabbing. Not even our mob can get it right. Sure, there's lots of agreement, but when it comes down to it, the old power thing always rears its ugly 'ead, 'specially where money's involved. Nope. Up 'ere I work in the open, I enjoy the gardens, I've got special knowledge about the country, the plants, the birds and the animals – I know how it all fits together. I've even got respect. I like it 'ere. Don't get me wrong Caroline. I agree with you only, it's not me. Sorry.'

She smiled. 'You've got so much going for you. I don't know what sort of education you got in that maelstrom you experienced, but you're smart, you're resourceful and from where I stand, tenacious. You could do good things for Aboriginals without getting involved in a major cause.' Her deep brown eyes danced with the smile on her face.

Her expansive mood touched Fox. *Yeah, she is a good person.*

'What did you 'ave in mind?' he asked, piqued by her interest.

'Well, as I said, you've got some great skills – they would bring credit to anyone. But, being Aboriginal, the bonus could be even greater. Don't get me wrong, it'll still be tough. But … *I* think that's what you respond to. Helping others is what you're good at.' She paused and reflected a moment then, in a rush, 'You could join the army, become a Police Aid in the Territory, or a copper in one of the eastern states. You could even be a social worker.'

Fox roared with laughter. 'You didn't think about that one Caroline! Brigitte Murphy was a social worker. Mullett hung out with social workers and neither of 'em did us any good. You said so yourself.'

'I know,' she said with a rueful grin. 'Speaking of Mullett – even though he's dead – because of what I do now, I decided to look into his background. There's a lot to tell about him. Curiously, there are even parallels between his life and yours.'

'Bullshit! He was just a rotten, twisted, pommy bastard. There was nothing about his life similar to Lucy's or mine!' Disgust laced Fox's voice.

'Try this on for size then. What do you know about the Fairbridge boys and Pinjarra?'

Fox shrugged and shook his head.

'Quick history lesson.' Connors' face was animated. 'Back in 1618 the first child labourers from London were sent to Virginia. These kids were vagrants, today's street kids if you like. The subtext was they would help build a new nation, live in the fresh air, develop and grow and leave the slums behind. In truth however, they slaved for their very existence while their removal emptied London's streets of riff-raff. In January 1620, England's Privy Council approved the dispersal of unmanageable and delinquent children – *against their will* – to the Virginia Company in the Americas. It was the formal beginning of England's colonial child migration. The racket lasted 150 years as children were forcibly sent to populate and develop the British Empire. Kingsley Fairbridge, a mover and shaker of his day, was one of the first to use the plan in Australia. He got land at Pinjarra, south of Perth, in 1911. By then of course, the kidnapping was outlawed, but plenty of others were involved: the churches, Thomas Barnardo and William Booth of Salvation Army fame. Fairbridge's idea was to create farm schools where children could be placed with colonial farmers. The theory was sound, but reality ignored the violence and exploitation that came with it. The farmers were strict, canings were frequent, privileges were withheld and, you guessed it, sexual abuse was common. For some kids it was so bad they killed themselves. Mullett, the bastard child of a fifteen-year-old Birmingham prostitute was sent to Pinjarra at the age of twelve in 1921. I've spoken to a couple of men who were there with him. They said he was small, shy and, back then, an appealing little boy. He was a favourite of the supervisors and apparently endured systematic sexual abuse. We know now that behaviour patterns like this can repeat and manifest in the adult life of former victims. It seems that's what happened to Mullett.'

Fox was stunned. Never had he imagined that Mullett too might have been a victim. Motionless, he stood staring far out to sea – glassy eyed, unseeing, breathing shallowly. Eventually, in a voice thick with emotion he said, 'I'm sorry for the child but revile the man … 'e grew up, 'e 'ad choices, 'e knew right from wrong. 'e'd been through it, 'e was weak … 'e deserved what 'e got.'

The mood between them was sombre. Connors resumed walking along the shoreline, Fox lingered. After several minutes he jogged up to her.

'That was a real shock,' he said, 'Mullett is finished for me but never forgotten. Tell me more about what you think I could be doing instead of messing round in horse shit.'

Connors turned, smiling gently, accommodating his need to change a painful subject. Companionably, she took his arm and they continued walking.

'I accept what you say about working at the Botanical Gardens. I understand why you like it. But I think you have a lot to offer by way of example. What you said just now about Mullett is right – he did have choice. He chose his way and, under very similar influences, you made your choice. And look at you – poles apart. That says heaps about you and it could motivate others. Through lived experience you can show that rising above the heap is possible, that adversity doesn't automatically mean a life of booze and crime and wife bashing or dependence on government hand outs. Yes, the more I think about it, the more I like it. The army for you boyo. Just imagine: training, opportunity – there's enormous job variety in the army – travel, combat, responsibility. And, while I stand to be corrected, as far as I know, there aren't too many Aboriginals in the army these days. It'd be really good for you. Think about it.'

EVOLUTION

All growth is a leap in the dark, a spontaneous
unpremeditated act without the benefit of experience.

HENRY MILLER
(1891 – 1980)

CHAPTER 9

1981

'C'mon Fox, c'mon! You can do it man, c'mon!' Massed members of 16th Battalion Royal Western Australian Regiment's (16 RWAR) inter-service swimming team bellowed at Fox, willing him to fly the last one hundred of the 1500 metre freestyle final. He cruised three body lengths behind the navy swimmers, Letts and Dean. As they battled each other for supremacy, Fox, in a lane to the far right of the pool, was difficult to see.

Suddenly, navy's cheers outgunned 16 RWAR and almost lifted the roof. Letts turned fractionally ahead of Dean, Fox was two strokes behind. Yelling, stomping, clapping and whistling, navy were doing everything to inspire their men to victory.

Fox's reach lengthened, white water churned from his kick and his body lifted to a glide. With twenty-five metres to go, he headed Letts and touched a half body length in front. His swim had been superbly timed to strike during the final fifty metres.

The win moved army two points clear of navy and six points ahead of air force. For the first time in years, army were outright winners of the entire Inter-Service Sports Competition. And Fox had contributed handsomely: winner of his weight classification in the boxing, second in the equestrian contest, third in the 5000 metre track event and winner of this blue riband swimming race.

With nine years of army life behind him, Fox had changed. He felt part of a whole and considered he belonged. After basic training at Kapooka in New South Wales, he selected 51st Far North Queensland Regiment for his first posting. Fifty-one FNQR conducted reconnaissance and surveillance patrols in remote areas and worked with Indigenous communities. Overall, the regiment patrolled 640,000 square kilometres. While he enjoyed the work and fitted into local communities easily, he realised it was not enough. He wanted more.

In mid '79 he transferred from Cairns to 16 RWAR in Perth. In the Light Infantry Unit he had earned respect, made close friends and attended a range of internal and external courses. He even found time to occasionally date a girl from another unit.

Before joining the army, Fox had not realised the significance of sport in the services. He soon found that teamwork and competition brought great satisfaction and freedom. His boxing prowess boosted him to legendary status in 16 RWAR though he remained silent about his riding and swimming skills. Over time, these too were "sussed" by his mates who entered him in the annual Inter-Service Sports.

Although unappreciative of their skulduggery, his belief in honouring a commitment and his sense of pride compelled him to accept *their* pledge. Success in boxing, riding and swimming enticed him to enter the following year – including some track events.

His win today cemented a decision he'd been toying with for months – the challenge of the Special Air Services Regiment (SASR). Unexpectedly, his Commanding Officer, Captain Peter Flynn, himself a former SASR member, had suggested a move in this direction. Fox smiled to himself as he remembered the conversation in Flynn's office two months before the sports.

'Are you saying Fox that you haven't contemplated the SASR?'

'Well, not exactly sir. I've given it a lot of thought but didn't think I was quite ready yet.'

'Too modest, Fox.' Flynn smiled. 'What are you now, nearly thirty? Your age is right and you've had a bloody good grounding in the service. What's more, I don't think you've anywhere near reached your potential. The SASR will bloody soon test that. Your field craft will be a major asset, your knowledge of horses and animals is an advantage and you're damned fit. You've got talents they want – excellent judgement, self sufficiency and intense motivation.'

Fox shifted uncomfortably in his seat. He knew his strengths but, as usual, had trouble hearing them from others. He remained a private man.

'At what stage do you think you'll be ready?'

'I'm not quite sure sir, maybe another year or two.'

'Bullshit! Two more years with us will change nothing. You're as ready now as you'll ever be.' Flynn's eyes twinkled. 'I just happen to know SASR is advertising for recruits *soon,* think about it. Hard. I'm not trying to get rid of you, to the contrary. But, I do believe the SASR needs our best and you'd fit in well. Now, bugger off.'

Fox rose and snapped a salute. 'Yes sir, I appreciate your advice,' he said, not entirely convinced.

Flynn had winked as Fox departed.

A month after the Inter-Service Sports, the army doctor closed Fox's folder after making extensive notes.

'Well Fox, you're good for the next round – nothing wrong with your health. You'll be off to the shrink this afternoon. See the clerk on the way out for details.'

Fox allowed himself a tiny smile. His homework revealed that at least twenty per cent of applicants dropped out during this first stage of medical and psych tests. Having made it through an excoriating pre-selection panel of hardened veterans, Fox was unfazed by the next session. He was certain of surviving.

A fortnight later he presented with eighty-five others for

the second phase – a three day "barrier", or entry test. Another twenty per cent would fail this stage: endurance marches, push ups, swimming and sleep deprivation. The medical, psych and barrier tests determined whether candidates were suitable for the uncompromising, three week selection course. By the end of that course usually only a quarter of the applicants remained.

The selection course probed individual strengths, weaknesses and skill sets as well as evaluating resourcefulness and teamwork. The sociability index too was significant – the SASR wanted people who were neither too introverted nor too extroverted, people who were forthright, hard to fool and highly motivated. Resilience and personal toughness were critical qualities as was ordinariness. The capacity to blend with a crowd yet remain wary in the presence of strangers was highly desirable. What the SASR didn't want was drongos. To the contrary, they wanted men who were widely read, adaptable and could learn quickly; decisive men who could make bold, intelligent and reasoned decisions. They wanted the best.

Fifty-two men, including Fox, made it to selection. Over the next seventeen days Fox's brutal childhood and personal philosophy about life proved comprehensive preparation for the rigours of SASR selection. Nothing encountered on the course disturbed his balance, perspective or concern for others. The long distance runs, day/night marches, weight packs, swimming in temperatures of extreme cold, sleep and food deprivation, sit ups, push ups, mental games, starlight navigation, faulty maps and interrogation resistance – none of it could dent his steely determination to succeed. At the end, Fox and eleven others were successful: less than ten per cent of the 125 starters.

That night, Fox celebrated in the family home of Caroline Connors, her husband Dr John McNulty and their three children, Jason, Jennifer and Judith. He had renewed contact with Connors on returning to the west and now seemed part of their family.

Jason, only fifteen when he first met Fox, was inspired by the man's balanced outlook on life and his curious inner stillness. He thought these qualities at odds with army life, Fox's obviously competitive nature and his years in the boxing tent. Of particular interest to Jason – in his final year at high school and deeply interested in politics – were Fox's laconic yet incisive views about current affairs. His two sisters loved Fox dearly and Judith, who was only nine when he entered their lives seemed, from the beginning, to have some kind of soul-deep affinity with him.

The March evening with its soft sky and river-scented breeze was perfect for the gathering seated around the huge jarrah table on McNulty's wide veranda. Hunger was teasing as a result of the tantalising aromas from John's barbecued lamb chops, porterhouse steaks and onion rings. Stomachs were rumbling. Caroline and the girls had prepared a variety of salads, dessert and a dark rich fruitcake. Jason had mown the lawns, swept the paths and cleaned the barbecue and when Fox arrived with flowers, champagne and a huge box of chocolates, everything was ready.

After dinner, they bombarded him with questions about his new life in the SASR. Diminutive brown-eyed Judith was the most insistent.

'Come on Foxy, tell us, did you top the class?'

'I don't know Jude. They don't tell us. All I know from the debriefing is that I was in the top five. Where in the top five, I don't know.'

'I bet you were *numero uno,*' said the eleven-year-old, her eyes shining with pride. 'What's a debriefing?'

'It's a bit like your parent/teacher nights where Mum and Dad get to hear how brilliantly you're doing at school. In my case, the bosses speak to everyone who was successful, tell us how we went, what areas need improvement and finally, what we're doing next.'

Jenny started to laugh. 'More like how un-brilliantly she's doing! She's too mad keen on sport to be doing school work.'

Auburn curls bounced around her face like butterflies flirting with blossom.

'I am not,' said Judith pouting, 'and anyway, *un-brilliant* is not a real word!'

'Will you be shooting people?' intruded the serious-minded Jason.

'Hold up mate. That's not a fair question,' said his father. 'Fox can only say it's a possibility.'

'Give over Dad. I've read up on the SAS. I know they specialise in counter terrorism, rescue missions and deep reconnaissance in other countries. That's what they do! Dangerous stuff. And Fox just qualified for it.'

Fox responded with a quiet smile. 'You're both right but I have no idea what the future holds. If you have read up on these things Jason, you'll remember the SAS hostage rescue from Iran's Embassy in London last year. Five terrorists were killed, all hostages rescued. I understand it was that first shot from the SAS which saved the lives of fifteen people trapped in one room. So yes, it is a possibility. Believe me though, decisions like that are not lightly taken.'

Caroline winced; the nature of the conversation was depressing. She vividly recalled how willing Fox had been to hurt the men who attempted to rape her ten years earlier. Changing the subject, she said, 'Is there any likelihood you could be posted overseas for exchange purposes? You know, professional development?'

'As a matter of fact there is. At the debriefing they told us about postings in New Zealand, the UK and USA. I said I hoped to get to the UK. But look, that's years away. In the meantime, let's toast successful futures and maybe, even Judy could have a tiny glass of champagne. What do you think Mum and Dad?'

'Oh Foxy, that's a great idea,' bubbled Judy. 'And while you're here, could you please make me another grass wristlet? My last one wore out.'

Softly lit by fat mosquito candles, they sat well into the night, a temperate breeze stirring the peppermint gums, the moon, a jigsaw of silvery shards on the nearby Swan River. They laughed, joked and talked about school and politics, policing and movies, army life and good books. Caroline Connors watched them all, her heart swelling – these were the most special people in her life.

CHAPTER 10

Motionless, breathing controlled, Fox stood moulded to an ant hill. In the cold black July night, eyes closed, he focussed upon his stalkers. The three of them approached cautiously. Mentally, Fox acknowledged their stealth but as usual, he felt that someone or something was always looking out for him. These blokes had no chance.

Strung out with three to five metres between them, they were moving in a trailing formation, about thirty metres between first and last. Fox decided to let them pass, kill the last man, move up to the second and then on to the leader. Three kills would be good work. His mate, Scotty Neal, a skinny red-head from Waikowhai near Auckland, lay in wait about 500 metres ahead. If Fox didn't get them, Neal would.

Softly, the three men passed. Fox moved. Clamping a steely hand over the last man's mouth he hissed, 'You're dead mate. Don't make a sound.' He marked the man's back with a yellow slash then slipped after the other two. The "dead" soldier, an Indonesian, was dumbfounded. He had heard nothing until his jaw was gripped in a painful vice and a voice whispered in the darkness. Later, he reflected that his attacker had melted into the night like smoke – without noise, without substance. *'Mengancuk,'* he thought, *'bahwa manusia itu creepy!'*

Over the next twenty minutes Fox stalked their pursuers,

"killed" them and joined Neal. All were participants in the regular *Top End* military exercise which, this year, involved 1800 personnel and eighty aircraft from four countries. *Operation Tar Pot,* occurring over six weeks between July and August, involved the USA, New Zealand, Indonesia and Australia. In this part of the operation, Indonesia and USA were paired against Australia and New Zealand; the former defending Tindal RAAF Base, the latter charged with taking it. Rules of engagement were strictly enforced and any person declared dead was, to all intents and purposes, dead — unable to communicate with colleagues or participate further in the contest.

In their team of two Aussies and two Kiwis, Fox and Neal had hit it off immediately. Ten days earlier with six other teams, they had been dropped 360 kilometres east of Tindal at Port Roper in the Gulf of Carpentaria. Their journey south lay through country weathered by millions of years into hungry yellow, grey and red soils interrupted by tracts of sediment stitched with lacy tributaries padded by mangroves. These formations traversed the fat, green Roper River creating illusions of lushness. Inland, less than a kilometre from the coast, sandy beaches, mudflats and coastal she-oak changed rapidly to open eucalypt forests of woollybutt, ironwood and Darwin stringy-bark. Still further inland, the river country was replaced by undulating ranges, low rocky rises, unexpected gorges, stunted eucalypts and ancient she-oaks. This country, threaded by tussock and hummock grasses, extended all the way to Tindal broken only by occasional billabongs, freshwater mangroves, screw palms and paper barks. It was a landscape familiar to Fox, and one through which the attacking Australians and Kiwis ghosted to penetrate "enemy" lines.

Two days earlier, and fifty kilometres from target, Fox's team had been cleverly ambushed by six Kopassus fighters from Indonesia. One Kiwi and one Australian had been "killed" along with three Kopassus troops. Since then, Neal and Fox had pressed on, pursued by the Indonesians. Now wanting a clear run at Tindal, the pair had decoyed their opponents into territory where Fox held the advantage.

After dispatching the Indonesians, they held a whispered conversation.

'We've got the rest of tonight plus two clear nights to get back. Got any ideas about a final assault?' murmured Fox.

'Too bloody right,' said Neal through a broad grin, 'but we'll need to go like cut cats to get to the Katherine side of the base – about sixty to sixty-five ks. Can do?'

'Shit yeah,' retorted Fox, 'it's only a marathon and a bit. Lead on McDuff.'

They recovered their packs and weapons from a depression near Fox's anthill and set off at a steady lope. An hour before winter's sunrise, they were adjacent to, and roughly five kilometres east of the air base. Untroubled by "enemy invaders," they had travelled around fifty kilometres. Their plan was to watch traffic to and from the air base from their camp at the start of the Katherine–Tindal straight.

Shortly after eight, Neal handed Fox the binoculars. 'I think this guy could be our target.' Fox studied the two people in the car.

'Yep. If these characters return to Katherine this afternoon, I'd say you're right. See any other possibilities?'

'Yeah,' drawled Neal, 'one. He'd do at a pinch but wouldn't be as convincing.'

'What time did he go through?'

'Just before eight,' said Neal, 'but if we take him, we are going to have to be bloody slick. Let's get some sleep. I'll take first watch.'

'One more question,' said Fox scouring the road with the binoculars. 'How many vehicles between our primary and secondary targets?'

'None. But that's the risk. We don't have enough time left to assess patterns …' He left the sentence unfinished and grinned.

Fox nodded, made himself comfortable and straight away faded into a deep sleep.

Late in the afternoon, Fox gently nudged Neal awake. Both had snatched four and half hours sleep.

'Tucker time,' said Fox. 'It's about an hour till sunset and we might as well use the light. We can kip again tonight ready for tomorrow.'

'Agreed,' said Neal sitting up. 'What's happening?'

'Lots of civilians and a sprinkling of service personnel travelling towards Katherine between 1615 and 1700 hours. From then on, just a few service personnel. Not much in the opposite direction. Our primary target passed at 1725. I reckon it's a safe bet that most of the service folk get to work before or around eight. What do you reckon?'

Neal yawned and stretched. 'Well, there was bugger all going to Tindal after 0830; only what you'd call regulars, you know, tradies and deliveries.'

'In that case,' said Fox with a smile, 'let's finalise it.'

The following morning, after the bulk of traffic had passed, Fox and Neal watched their secondary target drive by. They moved into position. And then, in the cool crisp air where pale sunlight slashed the roadway with long shadows from short eucalypts, they waited.

Soon after, Colonel Winston S Holmes Jnr of the United States Marines and his driver approached the low bridge over the creek beneath the Katherine-Tindal straight.

'Slow down Roy. What's that on the road?'

'Looks like a body sir,' drawled Sergeant Roy Carmody as he braked.

They stopped about six metres from the body of a man, obviously a soldier, lying on his back. His raised right knee was gilded by a shaft of sunlight, his left arm outflung away from the car, head resting on his left shoulder, blurred by jagged shadow. From the car the man's face appeared battered and covered in blood.

'Looks to me sir as if this guy has been hit by a ve-hickle and dragged along the road a bit. His clothes seem shredded.'

Holmes nodded and said nothing. He eyed the scene before him, wound his window down and slowly scrutinised both sides of the road.

'I'm callin' this in. This is the final day of the joint exercise and I don't trust these Aussie bastards.'

'That's a real good call Colonel,' said Neal, sliding up from below the sill of the stationary car. He had been lying beside the crash rail ten metres west of Fox, rolled beneath it as soon as the car passed then, in a crouch, doubled to its rear.

'Git out Sergeant and put your hands in the air.' Neal put his M.4 Carbine to the side of Colonel Winston S Holmes's head to emphasise his point. As Sergeant Roy Carmody stepped from the car, Fox rose and advanced. Holmes and Carmody saw that Fox had been "made-up" to look injured: his clothes, sliced in many places, carried a liberal coating of dust and smeared rabbit guts.

Neal opened Holmes's door, drew his knife and held it to the Colonel's throat. He threw his carbine to Fox who deftly caught it and trained it on both men.

'Righto Sergeant,' said Neal, 'git your shirt and tie off and be bloody quick about it. Anything goes here. I'm in no mood to piss around. Your fuckwit Senators want to punish my country over your crap nuclear ships.' Neal's demeanour was savage – he meant what he said. Holmes was silent and inwardly seething. He could not believe he'd been caught by such a simple ruse.

'Put your gear on top of the car and step away,' said Fox to Carmody. As Carmody complied, Fox reached into the car and took the keys.

'Move back.' He motioned to Carmody with his weapon. As they moved to the rear of the car Fox opened the boot. 'Get in.' Carmody squeezed himself into the space and before slamming the lid Fox said, 'For the purpose of this exercise, you're wasted, dead as a maggot.' Joining Neal, he opened the back door and sat behind the Colonel placing the M4 at the back of his neck.

'Right sir,' said Fox softly, 'you are now an official hostage and under the rules of engagement, you are a pawn of some value. Just remember, I am here with this gun and need only say bang and you are dead. You dead, or alive, is of no consequence to us – we'll use you either way. Shut the door and put the window up.'

As soon as the door closed Neal raced to the driver's side, whipped his jacket off and donned Carmody's shirt and tie. Fox passed him the keys as he got into the car and a moment later they were underway. From start to finish, the abduction had lasted six risky minutes.

Ten minutes later, when the security gate at the RAAF Base came into view, Fox slid to the floor of the car.

'Colonel sir, my carbine is up your arse. Don't do anything stupid.' About ten metres from the guard house Holmes suddenly leaned towards Neal, chopped his left arm and grabbed him by the throat. The car lurched as Neal fought for control.

'Bang!' hissed Fox from the floor as the car came to a stop.

'What's going on?' said the guard peering at the two men in the front seat.

'The Colonel was demonstrating a yarn,' drawled Neal, 'only I didn't think it was funny.' Holmes remained mute: he was now dead.

'Where's Carmody today? And what's your name? I haven't seen you before.'

'Carmody's indisposed and my name's Cassidy.'

'What's wrong with the Colonel?' asked the guard, ever inquisitive.

'I think he's suffering apoplectic rosacea, the same kinda problem as Carmody. P'raps I should get him to a medic.' Neal's drawl was slow and sardonic.

'Doesn't sound good. Sooner than later I'd say by the look of him,' said the guard. 'Catch ya later.'

Fox and Neal breathed a collective sigh of relief and smiled as they rolled forward. 'I warned you Colonel. Now you have the ignominy of not only being taken hostage, but also of being returned dead. Eh Scotty, what's with the Cassidy bit?'

'Hop-along you idiot! First thing I thought of in present company.'

'So who the hell is Hop-along-Cassidy?'

'Kid stuff, don't worry about it.'

'Hang on, hang on. What the hell is apoplectic rosacea?'

Neal slid a wicked glance up to the rear view mirror and grinned. 'Buggered if I know – I made it up.' A quick laugh bubbled upwards. 'Come on, back to work. We've gotta manage this last bit right with these two "dead" bastards on our hands.'

Driving at the stipulated twenty kilometres per hour, they travelled inside the base for another kilometre, turned south and went to the base gymnasium.

'Colonel,' said Neal, 'you can either stay in the car or wait in the gym until we're finished. Don't mind which. Just remember, you and Carmody are dead.'

'Listen Sonny, you ain't heard the last of this,' said Holmes tersely. 'I've minced bastards bigger than you. Don't think this is the finish.'

'All I can say sir,' replied Neal with a crooked grin, 'is those bastards musta been dumb bastards. This is supposed to be war, and that's how we're playin' it. And you're dead! No point gettin' your knickers in a twist now. We'll just tell everybody you were outsmarted. Now,' said Neal, his voice icy, 'what's it to be? You and Carmody wanna go and wait in the gym?'

'Yeah, we'll go in,' Holmes grated. 'Get Carmody.'

Fox winked at Neal who threw the keys to Holmes. 'Your man, you get him.' They walked inside leaving Holmes to his incendiary mood.

In the change room they ratted various lockers and assembled a variety of sneakers, shorts and T-shirts for themselves then showered. As they were towelling off Carmody strolled in. He was relaxed and his eyes glittered. Without his shirt they could see he was well muscled and fit.

'Hey Coon, you're a piece o' no good shit. Ah'm gunna whup yo' ass. An when ah'm through with yo' ah'm gunna break yo buddy's arms.' Carmody continued to walk cat-like towards the showers.

'Hey, hey, here's Lazarus. You notice how these tin-tanks are always full of crap? You know Scotty, if bullshit was electricity, this prick could almost be a power station.'

Despite his levity, Fox was sizing up his opponent and respected what he saw. He would let Carmody make the first move – there was a tenuous advantage in the American's anger. That Carmody was ignoring contest rules bespoke his humiliation at being transported to base in a car boot. Fox tucked the towel around his naked frame and waited. This was going to have to be quick and dirty but without too much injury. Carmody stopped about a metre from Fox, his face pale and mask-like, another danger sign. Tuned in, Fox stared into Carmody's eyes, dense with concentration. Without warning, Carmody delivered a turning kick outwards and upwards at Fox's throat. Fox blocked and imprisoned Carmody's boot, stepped backwards and viciously yanked him off balance. Falling to the wet, slippery floor, Carmody twisted to break the fall with his hands. Before he could recover, Fox stamped on Carmody's other leg and gave the one he held a mighty upwards jerk. All three heard the clear snap of Carmody's adductor muscles as they tore from the pubic bone in his groin. A deep moan of anguish followed. Carmody lay still on the wet floor, immobilised by searing pain.

'I don't like being called a coon and I don't like people who can't stick to the rules. Next time, I'll break both your arms. Keep out of our way!'

Unhurriedly, Neal and Fox dressed in their purloined running gear and, taking three tennis balls found in one of the lockers, left the gym. Jogging at a steady pace, they headed in the opposite direction to the Command Centre, a room within the main administration block fronting the runway. Circling streets around the base, they chatted and bounced a ball back and forth between them as they ran. They drew little attention. Despite the current exercise, daily life at the base continued as usual.

Jogging past the ops centre, they drew cold, professional stares from marines guarding the three entrances. Continuing their circuit, they passed the guards a second time twenty minutes later. On their third circuit, they positioned themselves to pass within a pace of the two marines at the main entrance to the ops centre. Five paces from the marines, laughing and still bouncing the ball, Fox applied a spin that made it whizz between the heads of the marines. As they turned to see what had happened, they were savagely felled by Fox and Neal who leapt upon them. The two continued their charge at full pace through the door and left down a short corridor to the Command Centre. There, they bounced their remaining tennis balls into the midst of the Directing staff and bawled, 'Wipeout! You've all been blown up.'

CHAPTER 11

1985

'Come,' barked Major John Hoey to the soft knock at his door. Corporal Colin Fox entered and snapped to attention before his desk. 'At ease Fox. Sit.' Hoey, at fifty years of age, was a highly respected administrator and renowned as a fearless soldier. His personal credo was shaped by an oft repeated phrase: '*substance flows from action.*' His piercing blue eyes examined the world from a calm, strong face and his presence filled the room.

'Been going through your file, Fox. Impressive. Got a bit of "go" about you. I like that. And you're quiet with it. I note quite a few entries here concerning your contribution to our knowledge and understanding of Aboriginal food and customs. Bloody good! It builds on work by Elder Sam Woolagoodja and Major Les Hiddens. I must confess too – and Chatham House Rules apply here – I pissed myself laughing when you took out that snooty nosed Holmes in *Tar Pot* last year. Sometimes, the oldest and least complex strategies work best. Trouble with the bloody yanks is, they think they're God's gift to the world. If, as I have, you study their history in war, you'll find arrogance is their achilles.'

Fox sat quietly, wondering what was coming. This summons had come yesterday, during an exercise at Rottnest Island off the Western Australian coast. Being there depressed him. Between

1838 and 1931 Rottnest had held more than three thousand Aboriginal prisoners. Boys as young as eight were incarcerated with men in their seventies under brutal conditions. Taken from all over Western Australia, there was no common language, dialect or custom between them. Shackled at the neck and ankles by chains, 370 souls had perished and still, the Western Australian Government equivocated about properly recognising their burial place. It had been a period of unbridled and sadistic savagery and Fox found the government's lethargic attitude beyond belief. He was there because he had to be, but didn't like it.

He did, however, like Hoey. Hoey was a "straight-up" bloke who spoke the truth and pulled no punches.

Hoey peered at the file before him. 'I see when you joined us three years ago you said you hoped you might get to England for professional development one day. Would next month suit?'

Fox's even features cracked into a broad smile. 'Yes sir. It certainly would! Do you mind if I ask a question?'

'Speak,' smiled Hoey.

'Well, it's just … this is … unexpected. I mean … there's been nothing on the radar about professional development for any of us.'

'Bloody hell!' Hoey laughed. 'Don't tell me we've actually managed to keep a secret.' He laughed again. 'As you know Fox, we've been through trying times over the last couple of years. Army recruitment has been falling and our traditional recruitment base for the SASR is the army. We've just been authorised to raise another squad but, as you can imagine, finding the right people is bloody difficult. We've had modern equipment on order for so damn long it's nearly a memory. Now it looks as if direct public recruitment to the SASR will get the nod and, our new equipment is beginning to arrive. But that's not why you're here. Apart from telling you about the UK, there's something else I want to raise and I want you to indulge me a little. I know your training fully covers origins of terrorism. I, however, have a particular view of things that's not always appreciated and I believe you are the kind of person who can take it on board. I want you to think about these things when you are overseas.'

Fox was intrigued – he sensed an aspect of Hoey that perhaps was revealed only among trusted friends and felt honoured. Moreover, he sensed that Hoey was settling in for discussion of a subject dear to him.

Tilting his head, Hoey gazed reflectively at the ceiling. Patiently, Fox waited.

'Terrorism,' started Hoey in a quiet, matter-of-fact tone, 'has been around a bloody long time – at least from the first century when zealots tried to annihilate the Romans. It will never go away. We all know, or think we do, the reasons for terrorism: destruction of governments, nullifying opponents, polarising unity, subjugating by fear and popularising the terrorist cause. Motivating all of that is the toxic and heady cocktail of ideology and politics. That's how it's been since the days of the French Revolution. And, as you know, any means is used to effect terror – bombings, hostage taking, arson, rape, armed attacks and horrendous forms of murder.' He paused, a wry smile upon his lips. 'Even we, in Australia, contributed to the terrorist arsenal. Did you know the pipe bomb used by so many of our mad friends is attributed to the Eureka rebellion at Ballarat in 1854? Strange how these things can bite you on the bum. But Fox, terrorism is an interesting term.'

'How do you mean sir? We don't seem to have too much difficulty understanding it.'

'I'm sure you don't because here, we are mainly concerned with action, not the origins of terrorism. And that's okay – action is our role. When we get involved, we are inevitably dealing with a situation demanding an immediate solution.'

'So what *do* you mean sir? I detect some equivocation,' Fox challenged.

'No. I am quite clear about our role, but, I do wonder about our political masters. For them, things *pirouette* on matters of convenience, power or politics, or all three. And let me tell you Fox, for your ears only, the older I get the more slimy I think politics is. Let me give you some examples. Yitzhak Shamir, twice Prime Minister of Israel, is reported to have written in 1943 that moral considerations were not part of the equation when pursuing a national identity. He said something like "...*first and foremost terror is for us a part of the political war and appropriate for the circumstances of the day.*" He was then a member of the Stern Gang seeking formation of a Jewish State. I see no difference between his statement then and the actions of Arabs today who repudiate a 1948 *political* decision. In another case, Harold Wilson's decision to send the SAS into Ireland in January 1976 was more about making a *political statement* than any considered military strategy. Indeed, when he announced his intention, as I understand it, he didn't even bother to advise his Ministry of Defence. He just put it out there.'

'So, one man's terrorist is another man's freedom fighter?' asked Fox, observing the Major sceptically.

'More or less,' said Hoey with a grin. 'Yassar Arafat, told the United Nations in 1974 that "... *whoever stands by a just cause and fights for freedom and liberation of his land from the invaders, the settlers and the colonialists cannot possibly be called a terrorist.*" Hoey paused and looked at Fox keenly. 'I venture to suggest that your warriors, Pemulwuy and Yagan, would have roundly endorsed Arafat's viewpoint.'

Fox nodded imperceptibly. Hoey's statement resonated far more deeply than he could have imagined – Mullett, Matron Fisher, Wildman, Brother John and his brown cronies all swirled to the fore.

'What I'm saying is this: our job is *always* clear – it is governed by operational imperative. Nevertheless, it is important not to lose sight of the big picture, to reflect not only on the now, but the history, the context, the politics and the purpose behind what we do. It won't change your role but it will help you maintain perspective and that is important for those occasions when the public reject *political* imperative.'

Fox nodded. 'What about the incidents we discuss in training, where do they fall?' asked Fox.

'Let's start with Hitler, Mussolini and Stalin,' said Hoey, warming to his subject. 'Unquestionably they used terrorism to quash opposition and rule by fear. They were leaders who used state might to repress their own people. In a quite different context, the Red Brigades kidnapped and murdered Italy's former Prime Minister Aldo Moro. Their goal was to destroy the Italian government by revolutionary action, to attack NATO installations and to "… *wage war on anti-imperialist multi-national corporations*". South Moluccans in the Netherlands, Hezbollah, the Armenian Secret Army, the Popular Front for Palestine, Basque Separatists, Abu Nidal. And so it goes. These groups believe their actions are rational and justifiable. Good leaders, Fox, should not ignore history. I've been in this caper a long time and terrorist patterns are changing. I worry about where they are heading.'

Fox straightened, his senses sharpened. From Hoey, this was significant. 'My concern was triggered by the Iranian hostage crisis of '79. Fifty-three yanks captured and held 444 days. Why did that happen? Oil. I'm not going to labour the point – you're smart enough to work it out. Oil, Iran and problems with Britain, Russia and the USA go back to at least 1901. At the time of that hostage crisis, the USA needed Iran's oil and backed the Shah. Superficially, Iran appeared stable but the Shah's people hated him, thought he was evil. By 1978 the plans of an underground Islamist fundamentalist movement to remove the Shah were well advanced. As his protector, America was Iran's enemy. In 1953 Britain and the CIA, with the Shah's support, engineered the overthrow of Iran's democratically elected leader, Dr Mohammed Mossadegh, a man of integrity. Mossadegh had nationalised Iran's oil supplies in a fight against what he called a "... *savage and dreadful system of international espionage and colonialism.*" His actions did not suit USA or British interests. In short, Iran had been ripped-off by Britain in every conceivable way through its oil agreement.'

Fox, thinking of Aboriginal history and the Rottnest Island debacle, gave Hoey a hard, penetrating look. 'I take it you are alluding to my people again.' The statement was blunt and flat-toned.

'I see definite parallels Fox – different times, different ways but parallels nevertheless. Anyway, since '79 we've seen the emergence of various Islamist groups around the world, attacks on and in numerous countries and the deaths of hundreds of people. My point is this: Ayatollah Khomeni's return to Iran parallels the rise in Muslim extremism, power, and aggression. Confrontation against the secular west is occurring on the basis of religious fundamentalism and democratic states around the world are being assaulted by it. *I* think *this* is a paradigm shift. History shows that wars fought on the basis of religion *always* contaminate "white hats" just as much as the "black hats". Where is this all heading? Who knows. But where do we live? Just below one of the most populous Muslim nations in the world.'

Hoey paused again and Fox thought: *Hoey's right – none of their instructors had presented this slant on terrorism.* Put in the context of Aboriginal history, Hoey's perspective had even more bite. Nothing, it seemed, was simple and straight forward. And with that, Mullett again flashed in and out of his mind – a tiny abused boy.

'Obviously Fox, you're familiar with Sydney's Hilton bombing in '78 and the Iranian Embassy siege in Britain. Before Hilton, Australia had no formal means of dealing with terrorist attacks. Between those two events, SACPAV – the Standing Advisory Committee on Commonwealth State Co-operation for Protection Against Violence – was created. Sir Robert Mark, former head of New Scotland Yard, was brought out by the Federal Government to talk about terrorism and training as part of SACPAV's initial development. His strong recommendation was, and I quote: *"close quarter battle is a task for the most experienced soldiery, not for the police whose role should be that of containment until the military arrives."* 'That message has now been understood. Increased numbers means we'll want bloody good leaders in the SASR. I expect you to be a sergeant by this time next year. You've got what it takes to get on Fox. In preparation for that, I want you, and others like you, to broaden your understanding of how things work in other places and cultures. We are still in our infancy in this field and have much to learn. Many countries have developed excellent anti-terrorist tactics but *I* think the Brits still hold the edge because of their experience in Northern Ireland. You requested the UK, you've got it. If you are wondering why you're getting this lecture, it is because Indonesia is Australia's largest and nearest Muslim neighbour. It is a pushy and aggressive nation as can be seen by its actions in East Timor and West Papua: rape, murder and massive population dislocation is par for the course. In the context of my concern about Islamic fundamentalism and because of Indonesia's proximity, you will be receiving some extra-curricular training that others on your course will not be getting. If the shit hits the fan with our neighbour down here, I want our strategies properly informed. Make ready Fox. I'll talk to you again before you go.'

Fox rose, snapped a sharp salute.

'Thank you sir. I'll be doing my best.' He left the office, feeling elated yet deeply thoughtful.

Two nights later, after finalising matters with Caroline, Fox arrived at the McNulty home on South Perth Esplanade. This time with a special treat. He rang the bell and waited, listening to the light step and happy whistle of Judy as she skipped down the hallway.

'Hi Foxy.' Eyes widening, her dimples embraced the huge smile that followed. 'What have you got there? Oh, he's beautiful.'

She reached up, hugged and kissed the grinning Fox and removed a squirming bundle of yellow fur from his arms. 'What's his name?'

'She Jude, she. And I've been calling her Lucy, after my little sister.'

'I thought you guys couldn't speak the names of dead people,' she said.

He smiled but said nothing.

'Oh, I love her Foxy, and Lucy's a great name. What about Mum and Dad? What will they say? And what about Belle? Belle's not going to like competition. And whose dog is she? Mine, Jen's or Jason's? Or does she belong to all of us?'

'Hey, what's with the twenty questions?' Fox stepped inside, still smiling. 'First of all, Belle is getting old and might like a companion. Secondly, Mum and Dad have okayed this …'

'And to think they never said a word,' Judy interrupted, managing to pout and giggle at the same time while the puppy licked her face.

'… Because Lucy belongs to you all. I thought it might also be a good idea to leave something here for you to remember me by while I'm overseas — out of your hearts and out of your minds.'

'As if,' grinned the light-hearted Judy who, privately, was already beginning to miss Fox. 'Mum! Look what I've got!' They walked into a warm kitchen filled with tantalising cooking aromas.

Caroline, bending to close the oven door straightened and turned. She had a smudge of flour on her cheek and a lick of thick blonde hair clinging to her forehead. She held her arms out to embrace Fox.

'Hi Col, you look disgustingly happy and healthy. Welcome. John's in the study just finishing a phone call. He won't be long. Would you like a stubby?'

'Yep, just one. Dinner smells great. What's on?' said Fox as he stepped forward and swept Caroline into his arms with a giant bear hug.

'Garlic bread, lamb and apple cider stew, minted peas, baby carrots and spuds in their jackets followed by home-made apple crumble and cream. So … this is Lucy is it? Put her down a minute love, I want to see what she does.'

Judy placed Lucy on the floor and they all laughed as she yipped in her puppy bark and ran about madly sniffing this and bumping that.

'How old did you say she was Col?'

'Fourteen weeks with all her first round jabs complete. Here's the papers.' He passed across a thick envelope. 'Her next immunisation is due in two weeks and, they've been paid for. Pedigree papers are there too, pure bred golden Labrador.'

Then, as if by magic, Belle, the family's antique black Labrador, entered the kitchen, stopped and gave a single deep bark. Lucy darted across the floor and began leaping and dancing around her, yipping and nipping in delight. Stoically, Belle stood her ground and eyed Caroline with a look that said, 'How could you do this to me! At my age. What an upstart!'

'Put the dogs out the back will you please Judy. Belle can show Lucy the ropes.'

'Oh Mum, she's only just arrived. Can't she have permission on her first night?'

'NO! That's what I mean about learning the ropes.'

Judy looked imploringly at Fox who shrugged and grinned. 'Don't look at me mate, your mum's the boss here.'

'Thank you very much *Mr* Fox! And here was I thinking I'd trained this house to run exactly as I needed.' John McNulty walked into the kitchen, hand extended, smiling. 'Good to see you Fox. I see Caro's got you a beer. So, this is the new addition to the family, eh? She looks pretty lively.'

'G'day John. Yep, this is Lucy. Jason and Jenny in too?'

'No, Jason's still in the eastern states at Melbourne uni but Jenny should be home in the next ten minutes. She's been out on the water all day as part of her studies. Said she'd be home at seven.'

'Dad, can we leave Lucy inside until Jen's home?'

'What did your mother say?' he asked, catching Caroline's sly wink.

Suddenly, there was more high pitched barking as footsteps came down the hallway and Jennifer entered the kitchen. A flurry of golden fur launched itself into the air yapping and licking the new arrival, stopping only to piddle with excitement.

'And who is this?' asked the lissom, auburn haired girl in her well-modulated voice.

'Jenny, meet Lucy,' said Fox stepping forward to give the beautiful girl a warm hug and kiss. 'She's your new play thing and Belle's nightmare.'

When they'd finished laughing at the antics of the little dog Caroline said, 'Sorry Judy, just joking Poppet. Of course you can have her inside, Belle's here most of the time why not Lucy. But do please clean up that puddle. Tea will be about ten minutes.'

Fox walked off to the bathroom to wash before tea and heard Jenny ask, 'What happened to your car Mum?' Caroline's response was lost in the hiss of splashing water.

Over dinner, conversation bubbled backwards and forwards between Fox's impending journey overseas and family activities: a medical professorship, the children's studies and Caroline's recent promotion to Senior Sergeant sub-charge at Fremantle. During a lull in conversation Fox asked, 'Did I hear Jenny suggest there's something wrong with your car, Caroline?'

'Oh some ratbag ran a key or something all along the passenger side and gouged the duco. Don't know when it happened. I noticed it when I was shopping at Booragoon this afternoon. It wasn't there at the weekend because Judy and I washed the car so it's happened some time in the last three days.'

'Yes, and I think that's strange,' said Judy, 'when I got my bike to ride home from school this afternoon both brake cables were disconnected. Fortunately they weren't broken and Tory Stephenson fixed them for me.'

'You should have mentioned that earlier, Judy,' said Caroline frowning, 'that's dangerous. Were they alright when you went to school this morning?'

'Yeah, they were fine.'

'I'll have a word to the headmaster. We can't have students doing stuff like that, it's irresponsible.'

'What about the car?' asked John, 'insurance?'

'No, it's not worth losing the no-claim bonus. I'll get a price from a couple of local repair shops in Freo.'

At ten, on the grounds of a follow-up exercise at Rottnest Island, Fox excused himself with a promise to attend a final dinner before leaving for the UK.

CHAPTER 12

He sat brooding, scowling sullenly, fidgeting on the eighth floor balcony. The tremors wouldn't stop and heat coursed through his veins like a bleve. In the darkness, Perth city glimmered, showering the surface of the Swan River with a myriad of animated crystals. Yet none of this lively energy registered. The only thing that mattered was the immediacy of events in the McNulty household.

He raised the glasses to his eyes again. Except for the son, they were all there – *Toffy nosed creeps! And look at her, Bitchface, holding court like Queen-fuckin'-Victoria. We'll soon see how bloody good you are,* he thought. *Soon see how fucking tough you are.* 'B-i-i-i-t-c-h!!' he screamed, silently into the night.

He had told himself a million times that she was the one. She had caused him to lose his job, to get the sickness, to live like shit for so long. Well, now she would pay. It had taken three tortuous years to claw back from the abyss. To recover from the black void of alcoholism. To beat the squalid, mind numbing, undignified vagrant's life. To spurn the cheesy stink of unwashed body, pissed-in-clothes, greasy hair, matted beard and fucked up boots. To be able to reject other people's fag ends and White Lady, the el-cheapo blast of water and meths or, on a good day, Fanta and meths. But he had come back from the edge. The Salvos and AA had extended the hand of friendship and he had made it. Even so, the craving was always close.

So now she would pay. *They* would pay.

The Salvos said he needed a purpose to survive. Purpose was good. Once he began to get his head right he found it: white hot, pure, untarnished revenge. That's what he lived for. The McNultys were not aware that he had been manipulating them for more than nine months, practising that revenge. Living that purpose. Little things causing them to puzzle but not dwell upon. Little things that ebbed and flowed in frequency. Little things that could be rotated around the five of them to make his actions less noticeable. Little things that gave him great pleasure and undeniable power.

Sheer luck that he'd run into his old mate Garry McLune after he scrambled back onto the true path. He told McLune he had been away, working over east. To explain his incessant tremors, he said he had been diagnosed with Duchenne's disease, a form of gradually worsening muscular dystrophy. McLune didn't know he had been living in the gutter as a boozy, fuckin' alky. And then, wonder of all wonders, because of past favours, McLune asked him to house-sit his unit on South Perth Esplanade for two years. TWO FUCKIN' YEARS! Rent free. Just look after the joint, he'd said. He was off to Europe to work for Reuters and wouldn't need it. Keep it clean, water his plants, feed the birds. And no rent! What a gift.

He watched them again and began plotting his next move. He wondered if Bitchface had discovered the duco yet. He had been into their house half a dozen times in the last nine months. His trophies were mounting: knickers from the women, John's expensive fountain pen, an important assignment of Jason's on a CD. He'd laughed over that one. He could clearly see into his room and had watched Jason tear it apart looking for something, something he guessed he had, a university assignment on the "Ethics of Business Takeovers". He had even taken the young one's birth certificate and Bitchface's bankbook. And no one was aware that he had even been in their house. That was the best part. He had learned heaps by pinching their mail. He was more selective about that, didn't want it to become too obvious. But he knew how much Dr John and Bitchface had in the bank, when the car rego was due, how much it cost for Jason's and Jennifer's uni fees, how much electricity they used, what their health fund cost and lots more interesting things. Yeah, pinching the mail was a bloody good source of knowledge.

Time I went in again, he thought. He'd have to watch out for the new dog though. She wasn't like that other bloody antique – unable to do anything but fart. The black bastard had brought it, the new dog. And that thought stopped him short – he actually wasn't sure which one he hated more: Bitchface or Midnight. They both deserved to die. And they would. It was just a matter of time.

CHAPTER 13

The plane droned on through the night, the cabin lights hosting a pale gloom.

Fox squirmed restlessly in his seat. While those around him snored, sleep evaded him. For the *Gija* boy from Turkey Creek, separation from country, culture and tradition was a major wrench. He could feel pain. The very core of his being felt scoured by every minute of progress towards England. In some strange way, even his "belief systems" seemed to be leaching from his soul. Logically, he knew it was nonsense to feel this way. He had made his choice and there would be new people to meet, sights to see and experiences to encounter. He might even get to Scotland, to Pittenweem where his grandfather was born. He knew all that. Yet somehow, he felt plundered.

His country enfolded a past laid down long ago through *Ngarrangkarni* stories from the Ancestors. The very essence of the land brought an invigorating pleasure to be savoured through its vastness: the soft red sands of dune country, the unique smell of the desert and the seductive, captivating moods of dawn, dusk, darkness and starlight. The forms and shapes of country charted ancestral journeys which nurtured the law, language and culture of his *Gija* people.

Fox believed that most white people failed to understand this holy trinity and saw much of it as fable. That belief explained why the gulf between black and white people over the importance of country had occurred virtually from settlement in 1788. These differing perspectives about the value of land triggered the first major conflict between the two peoples on the Hawkesbury River in New South Wales in 1795. Constantly clashing black and white opinions over land eventually spawned the Aboriginal Land Rights Movement which was immortalised by skirmishes at Noonkanbah, Wave Hill and Wreck Bay; had prompted the Canberra Tent Embassy; and eventually resulted in the return of Uluru to traditional owners. His own *Gija* family endured a past florid with massacres and poisonings, like those at Moola Boola, at the hands of pastoralists during the 1800s. White settlers then believed their right to farm land *usefully* was superior to its "wasteful" occupation by Aboriginals who did "nothing" with it. In truth, they simply did not comprehend the profound importance and power of country to traditional owners.

But there was more, something vague and amorphous niggled at Fox, something that directly involved Caroline, a sense of foreboding. Normally, he would ask for guidance, but up here, high in the sky, that did not feel right. Fox's thoughts drifted to his rousing farewell in Perth at the International Airport. Not only had the bulk of his unit arrived to deliver a boisterous goodbye, but so too had the entire McNulty clan. And within that crowd, he noticed the spontaneous attraction between Jennifer and Courtney Dalgleish, his unit's young signals specialist. He reckoned "Kurt" would waste no time beating a path to the McNulty front door. Jennifer had grown into a beautiful young woman whose steady blue eyes and calm, mellow voice were arresting. Her deep, rich, auburn hair too was magnetically attractive. Beneath these obvious physical attributes lay a quiet, impish sense of humour, a tiger on the basketball court and a young woman whose great love was the wellbeing of the world's oceans.

In the semi-darkness, Fox smiled as he then thought of Judy.

Now fifteen, she possessed a refreshing naiveté and infectious zest for life. In his heart, Judy was his favourite.

Never was she without one of his grass wristlets, even though he had shown her how to make them. They were not the same as the ones he made, she said. For that reason she always demanded a supply so that when one wore out there was an instant replacement.

And she adored his paintings. He had explained, and she had understood, that the planes of black, white and brown ochre with the yellow, white and black dots were maps of his country and *Gija* culture. Three of his paintings hung in her bedroom. There were qualities about Judy strongly reminiscent of Lucy, and this, more than anything, made the presence of his nebulous concern profoundly unsettling.

And lastly there was Jason, forever in search of truth and the pursuit of justice. At sixteen, when he was all height and no muscle, he worried over two boys hassling him at school for being a "clever bastard." He implored Fox to give him boxing lessons. After discussion with his parents, Fox began sparring with him in the garage.

Fox grinned, remembering that first lesson. Within ten minutes Jason had stopped and said earnestly, 'Fox, hit me. You're treating me like a girl. I want to be able to do this. It's not just about me you know, they're picking on other kids too and I want it to end. Let's get into it.' Fox had instantly bloodied his nose.

'That's more like it,' Jason responded blinking back tears, 'I didn't even see that coming. That's what *I* want to be able to do.'

Several months later Jason calmly announced to Fox and his family over one Sunday night tea that on Friday, he had knocked Bob Harley out for the count in an unofficial grudge match organised by the sports teacher in their school gymnasium. Word spread rapidly that McNulty was a dangerous, ballsy bastard: he'd ko'd the school bully. To be certain he and others would not be picked on again, Jason wasted no time tracking down Harry Smith,

Harley's co-partner, and warned him the bullying was to stop – or else. To reach that point, Jason had taken a pummelling from Fox but gutsily stuck at it to earn Fox's deep respect. *He should*, thought Fox, *make a damn fine lawyer.*

From earliest days, when Jason was much younger, the pair of them had enjoyed many weekends in the bush. Under Fox's patient guidance, young Jason had become skilful in finding and preparing a wide range of bush-tucker foods from seemingly empty country. They were special times and the pair had bonded closely.

Yep. They were all likeable kids with different qualities yet the same sense of goodness. He had grown to love them all. Along with John McNulty, or Doc, as Fox mostly called him, and Caroline, they had become his surrogate family. And, in the years following his return to Western Australia, they had all shared scores of happy days. Leaving them was heart wrenching.

With these thoughts in mind, Fox slipped into deep sleep. Some time later he awoke to a muffled ping signifying an announcement. He looked out the window and realised that as they descended into the grey day beneath him, they were flying over the Thames and city of London. A new chapter of his life was about to begin.

CHAPTER 14

The SAS Barracks at Hereford were not to be found on the general locality maps. In fact, there were no public directions to the barracks at all. And, while locals knew generally of the doings there, they maintained a collective and respectful silence about this special group of people.

Collected from Heathrow, Fox was driven south to the base where he met the Officer Commanding, Colonel Adam Chartres. With formal niceties dispatched, the Colonel outlined the content of Fox's twelve month stay including, at Hoey's request, additional specialist training in Germany, Holland and France. Chartres concluded their meeting by telling Fox he was expected to join the fifteen mile training run at eleven that morning. He would be shown his billet, have time to unpack, eat if he wanted and be on parade at the appointed time.

Fox found the barracks austere but well equipped and conceded that equipment and facilities at home were more rudimentary. Not so the training. Although his first week at Hereford was no cakewalk, the intensity and quality of training was little different to that at home.

That first week morphed into a blur of names, places, faces, training runs, close quarter battle routines, lectures, interrogation exercises, weapons practice and orienteering on the Brecon Beacons in Wales. Although comfortable with the work, Fox found adjustment from the southern to northern hemisphere timezone trying. But, as he was reminded by his peers, this too was just another facet of training.

A month later, Fox's rhythm was attuned to the local pulse, some solid friendships had been established and letters were arriving from the McNulty mob along with some cheeky insults from Scotty Neal in New Zealand. Next Tuesday, he and seven others were off to Northern Ireland. Fox and his new Welsh mate, Davey Gordon, would be there for a month, the others for three months. In the meantime, they all had three days pre-departure leave.

Gordon had invited Fox and another of their squaddies, Alex McPhie from Kircaldy, a town not far from Edinburgh and close to Pittenweem, to a fund raising afternoon tea at Kilmore Castle. The castle was just outside Blaenavon in Wales, about an hour from Hereford on the A465.

'After-bloody-noon tea? What are you – a bloody wuss?' Fox had quipped in response to Gordon's invitation.

'No,' Gordon responded warmly, 'Me and Alex are pretty fond of these, to use your idiom, two army "sheilas" – they invited us. We're really going to see them.'

'So you want me to chaperone you wild men?'

'In a pig's eye,' said Gordon, 'you'll not only meet some nice girls but also get to see how the aristocracy live. I used to sometimes visit the hall with my parents as a boy. Old Lord Ravenscroft is big on charity do's, especially if they're health related. We went to quite a few of his special afternoons. Fabulous bloody spot.'

Now, as Fox was polishing his shoes in readiness that sunny Sunday morning, he found himself pondering the McNultys. His thoughts about them had been hazy, as though distance had generated static, something he had never encountered before. Perhaps he was doing too much but, whatever the reason, he felt troubled by the presence of some vague threat to his friends. Yet it was elusive and too indecipherable to commit to paper. He huffed on the toes and heels of his shoes, rubbed hard with the cloth and, well satisfied with their sheen, put them on.

Fox was gobsmacked. He could not think of a better word to describe his feelings.

'Christ Davey, do you mean to tell me that *one* family actually lives here?'

Gordon grinned. 'They do. But it's a business for them. One family lives here with quite a few others as well. I don't know the figures now but Ravenscrofts used to employ about 150 local people here. The grounds and castle are used for weddings, anniversaries, special occasions and holidays. Lord John, Earl of Kilmore, spends most of his time in London at the House of Lords while his son and daughter-in-law run this business. The girls tell us today's function is all about children's cancer.'

The object of Fox's awe stood before them: a solid, red-brick rectangle at least seventy metres across with soaring hexagonal turrets at each corner. An enormous deep, pale pillared archway stood at its centre while a broad expanse of stone steps led from the driveway to a portico beneath the arch. To Fox, the castle appeared to have about six levels. And the grounds! A twenty-five hectare lake was within easy walking distance of the castle which was surrounded by at least ten or more hectares of elegantly manicured gardens. To reach their present location they had driven through some 100 hectares of verdant oak and pine forest and passed several paddocks of fat Hereford cattle.

'What do you know about this place?' Fox asked.

'It's a fully functioning farm of about 1200 acres – something like 480 hectares in your terms. The castle was built around 1590 and is full of magnificent rooms adorned with ancient furniture, silks, carvings, paintings and gilt. Beautiful ornamentation! The general style of the building is gothic with lots of marble, fireplaces and stained glass. It's a stunning place Fox.'

'It would be too claustrophobic for me,' muttered Fox. 'Even so Davey, I agree, it's a bloody swanky joint. I'm sure Caroline and her girls would love it!'

They scrunched along the white pebble drive towards men in eighteenth century court garb directing cars to a park at the western side of the building.

'Where are we meeting the lassies?' McPhie asked Gordon.

'They said they'd be at the top of the steps at the front entrance at thirteen hundred hours, and, 'he threw a quick glance at his watch, 'we'll be right on time.'

The three casually, but sharply dressed men made their way to the main entrance among the swelling crowd. Soft spring sunlight painted the day with a warming golden hue. It was the perfect afternoon for a function. At the top of the steps, Gordon and McPhie waved to two women standing aside from the surging mass flooding into the castle.

'Fox, this is my good friend Heather Maddox, otherwise known as Maddie, and this is Lex's friend Rebecca Baine. They're both from 16 Medical Regiment at Cardiff.'

Fox shook hands with Heather, an attractive blonde slightly taller than himself and Rebecca, a much shorter and generously proportioned girl. Both were English and bubbled with good humour and instant acceptance of Fox. Their pleasure in seeing Gordon and McPhie was obvious.

'Did you line someone up for our Aussie mate here, Maddie?' asked Gordon.

'No, but we could introduce him to the boss, she's here.' She cast an arch look at her friend Rebecca and raised one eyebrow slightly.

Rebecca shook her head gently and said in a low voice, 'I don't think so. I think Fox is too nice for that.'

'Ho ho,' said McPhie, 'what are you not tellin' us about her?'

Rebecca smiled innocently. 'She's our boss and we are not going to put her down – let's just say we think, on reflection, she's not Fox's type.'

'How do you know what Fox's type is?' asked Gordon.

'I'd say someone who is very caring, someone attractive and someone who is totally honest,' said Rebecca. Heather nodded in agreement.

'You've only just met him. How can you say that?' McPhie asked.

Feeling rather like a spectator, Fox stood on the sidelines smiling.

'Easy,' said Maddie, 'women's intuition – a skill we have that you wouldn't understand.'

McPhie grinned wryly. 'Rubbish. Let's have a look aboot. I'm with Fox, this joint's amazing.'

They moved inside and crossed a long, broad hallway running east and west across the front of the building. To their left, wide, polished and ornately carved timber stairs led upwards, while to both right and left, a series of archways stretching the length of the broad hall gave haven to suits of armour, coats of arms and access to various rooms. The lofty, off-white rococo ceiling was richly decorated above soft salmon coloured walls holding numerous gilt framed paintings of long dead nobles and ancestors. Along the length of shining parquetry floor, several large, colourful Persian rugs lay randomly scattered. In either direction, the most spectacular crystal chandeliers blazed.

And on they went, part of the throng until at last they arrived at the rear terrace, a place more to Fox's liking. Here, the ground below sloped gently to the lake providing an expansive view of water and sky. To left and right, like sheltering arms, groves of ancient oaks stretched away from the castle. Between the terrace and lake an intricately patterned geometric hedge of clipped knee-high box and yew set in verdant lawn provided a stunning mosaic of shadows, shapes and shades of green. Although not his style, Fox appreciated the handcrafted beauty.

At the bottom of the steps bejewelled courtesans relieved everybody of £20 per head and directed people to the lakeside where marquees, music and other forms of entertainment were in full flight.

People drifted and swirled as the crowd continued to grow.

'I can smell food over that way. Let's get something to eat,' shouted Rebecca, who clung to McPhie's arm pointing right. They meandered through the laughing, chattering masses and arrived at a huge, open sided marquee bursting with tables and chairs. At one end of the pale diaphanous shelter long bench tables groaned under the weight of sumptuous cakes, gourmet sandwiches, salads, seafood and assorted cuts of hot lamb, beef and venison.

Babble in the marquee was at fever pitch. Music from medieval drums, lutes, pipes, tambourines and whistles floated in from outside making normal conversation impossible. Fox felt himself sliding into a bubble of disembodiment – this was so left-field for him.

He became aware of Maddie shouting to him and pointing over his shoulder. He turned and gazed along her extended finger. Slowly, making her way towards them was a stunning beauty with coal black hair and a clear, pale, flawless complexion.

'Who is she?'

'Our boss.'

Fox turned and looked again, as did Gordon and McPhie. About 175 centimetres tall, the woman was elegantly dressed in a beige linen frock with a generous white silk collar. Large amber buttons extended from the collar down the front to mid thigh. The sleeves were gathered just below the elbow. Chatting at various tables, she flashed a brilliant smile here while offering an easy hand shake there. Fox thought her manner both charming and poised. She was a jewel!

The three men looked enquiringly at the two women.

'How come you didn't tell us about this beauty?' asked Gordon.

'What? And allow you to lose your chance with me?' Maddie laughed.

'Well, who is she?' asked McPhie.

'Doctor Heidi Ravenscroft. Youngest granddaughter of old Lord John, Captain of 16 Medical Regiment, Cardiff if you please,' Maddie responded.

'Shite. What's a looker like her doing in the army? She ought to be on the cat walk,' quipped McPhie.

Rebecca jabbed him in the ribs. 'Watch yourself sunshine. Anyway, I've got better tits.'

While they all laughed, Fox felt uncomfortable. Although he was no saint he was not used to women being so forthright. He figured it was a hangover from his past and told himself to get over it.

They had resumed their meal when suddenly Rebecca stood.

'Hello, Heidi. Fabulous day, are you pleased with the turn out?'

'We are,' she responded in a voice husky from talking over crowd noise. 'Mother and father are thrilled and at this rate, we could take over £5,000 for the North East Cancer children. Not only that, Grandfather has promised that if we exceed £4,000 he will make a one for one donation. And who are these fine gentlemen?'

'This man,' said Rebecca, 'is the closest thing I have to a boyfriend. His name is Lex McPhie and he's based at Hereford.'

Lex stood and extended a hand, not surprised by the cool firm grip he encountered.

'Pleasure to meet you, Heidi.'

'Maddie?' Heidi enquired.

'This is my friend, Davey Gordon and while I can't claim he's my boyfriend, I am working on it. He's also from Hereford.' Gordon grinned broadly and shook Heidi's hand.

'And who is this?' Heidi asked, beaming a lighthouse smile at Fox.

Fox, also standing, smiled back, a warm and pleasant greeting.

'Colin Fox, just known as Fox. Also from Hereford.'

'Well, just-known-as-Fox, do I detect an Aussie accent there?' Heidi's eyes sparkled.

'Yep. I'm here for a while to learn from the professionals. Today they thought I should come and see how the other half live.'

'And what do you think Fox? Is this a lifestyle for you?'

'Nah. Deserts are my go.' While Fox's tone was teasing, he spoke the truth. Heidi turned incandescent blue eyes upon him and smiled winningly, at the same time extending her hand.

'An interesting challenge. In the meantime, have a lovely day. There's plenty to do and see, all the gardens are open, boats are on the lake and lots of things around the pile to sample. I expect I'll see you again … soon,' she said looking directly at Fox.

She continued on from table to table without a backward glance, Fox staring after her.

'Shite Fox, if that wasn't an invitation I don't know me arse from me elbow,' said McPhie.

'Indeed,' said Gordon, 'go for it man!'

Fox turned and mildly surveilled his friends, a quiet smile twitching his lips. Despite their enthusiasm, he had not missed the veiled look passing between Rebecca and Maddie as he said ambiguously, 'We'll see, we'll see.'

CHAPTER 15

He knocked on the McNulty's front door at 1:00 pm knowing the house was empty. Caroline and John were both at work, Judith at school, Jason away somewhere and Jennifer at university. Still, he went through the motions – you never knew who was watching. In the next breath, he was inside, his actions practiced and smooth from intimate knowledge of the house.

Today, he would return items taken months ago. He laughed quietly at the thought of their bafflement when they discovered each thing in turn: John's fountain pen, Jason's assignment, Caroline's cheque book and Jennifer's "Walkman". From his vantage point at the flats he'd chuckled over the silent movie of family members searching for their things. He could read their body language, saw anger and accusation, frustration and despair. And, in the end, bewilderment and resignation. What was happening? Where could things be?

As he replaced Caroline's cheque book in the kitchen dresser he froze – noise from another part of the house. He grabbed the carving knife from its rack and moved quietly to the kitchen door … silence … he waited, head pounding at the threat of discovery. Nothing. He decided to keep the knife and leave.

Halfway down the hall to the front door came a low growl and the scrabble of claws. He turned as Lucy, the golden Labrador, launched herself from the floor, fangs bared, jaws open. Instinctively, he took a short step back then lunged with the long blade. Lucy yelped and shuddered as the knife went deep into her throat, blood spattering the walls, floor and his clothes. She fell with a thump, legs thrashing. Enraged, he stabbed her again, and again and again.

Panting with exertion he stood up. *Jesus that felt good!* They would really know he meant business now. *Funny,* he mused, *the dog is always locked outside during the day, she's never been inside before. Still, one less problem to think about. And the other old crock has passed ... there won't be any dogs to worry about when the time comes.*

He went to the bathroom, washed his face and hands, undressed then padded into the adult's bedroom and helped himself to a shirt and trousers from John's wardrobe. For good measure he took a pair of Caroline's knickers and a bra and left her underwear drawer gaping. Now they might begin to understand events over the last twelve months. Change of plans. Full scale intimidation. He sniggered to himself. He knew what would follow and was confident he could handle it. He held the power.

Fuckin' bitch. And he was making the boldest of statements to confirm it. He found a plastic bag in the kitchen, stuffed his bloody clothes inside and left, locking up behind him. He wanted to get back to his flat so he could watch their reaction. He whistled as he walked down the Esplanade peeling off his rubber gloves. This would really be good.

CHAPTER 16

Judy raced into the driveway and laid a skidding broadside in front of the garage. Exhilarated, she had ridden from school at break-neck speed to phone her mother with some good news – selection for the school interstate athletic team. She lifted the garage door and swung her bike onto its hook, hefted her school bag and went to the letter box. More joy! A letter from Fox.

She loved his dry, humorous notes which, in so few words, painted graphic pictures of his mates, training, the English countryside and the "pommie" lifestyle. They had all laughed over his comparison of Kilmore Castle with the beauty and simplicity of Turkey Creek, the latter, according to Fox, light years ahead. The letter meant he was back from Ireland where he had not been able to do more than send a couple of post cards. From them, the family had gained an impression of long hours, little sleep, constant vigilance and a sense of unreality. His last card had promised a letter on return to Hereford.

Pausing on the top step she looked out across the Swan. Bright sunshine and a good stiff breeze beckoned for a fast and exhilarating sail in their Moth. She skipped across the veranda, opened the front door and was removing her schoolbag when she saw a lump in the centre of the hall. As the horrific scene of blood and fur registered, she fell to her knees sobbing as she beheld their beautiful Lucy.

It felt like she stayed on the floor crying, numb and nauseous for hours. Eventually, she rang her mum. After several false starts, she reached Caroline at Fremantle Police Station.

'Mum.' She wept. 'Mum, come home. It's Lucy dog.'

Instantly concerned, Caroline said gently, 'Calm down darling, calm down. Tell me what's happened.'

'I've just come in from school.' Judy's voice faltered as she choked on her tears. 'It's Lucy … she's dead in the hall with … with … there's blood everywhere … she's been murdered!' Judy's voice dropped to a whisper as the shock of articulating what she was seeing sank in.

Sharp, commanding and controlling her own fear, Caroline said, 'Where are you now?'

'In the kitchen.'

'I want you to go straight to Linda's place and don't touch anything.'

'Who would do this Mum? Lucy dog. How?' Judy's voice, cracking, rose in fear.

'I don't know sweetheart but go to Linda's *now!* I'll contact the local police. Hang up now and go. *Go!'*

Judy put the phone back and left the kitchen via the double glass doors and rushed around the side of the house to Linda Allen's. That way she didn't have to look at Lucy again.

Hammering on the door she fell sobbing into Linda's arms. Linda drew Judy inside and closed the door. With an arm around her shoulders, murmuring words of comfort, she led Judy to the kitchen where gradually she learned the cause of the young girl's distress.

'Was the house locked when you came home, Judy?'

'Yes, it was,' she sniffed.

'Did you look through the house yourself?'

'No. Mum said to come straight here. She said she would get the local police.'

Immediately grasping the implications of Judy's discovery,

Linda was chilled by endless possibilities.

'Did you hear anyone inside dear?'

'No, Linda. I just saw Lucy in the hall and went to our kitchen to ring Mum. Then I came straight here like she said.' Slow, racking sobs punctuated her words.

When the doorbell rang a minute or so later, they both jumped.

'Stay here while I see who it is,' said Linda tiptoeing to the front. Observing police uniforms through the peephole, Linda opened up to a male and female police officer.

'Mrs Allen? I'm Sergeant John Danby and this is Senior Constable Shirley Summers. We're from the Mends Street Station. Caroline Connors said we'd find young Judy here. Is she okay?'

'Yes, but she's had a nasty shock. Please, come in.'

Judy was pale and shaking when they walked into the kitchen.

'Hello Judy, I'm John Danby. Your mum sent Shirley and me to see how you are. She said to tell you she's on her way home. Would you tell me what happened please.'

In a faltering voice, Judy told Danby what she had found. Tears seeped as she described Lucy.

'Did everything look normal when you arrived home?' Summers asked gently. 'I mean, was there anything to suggest someone had been inside your house?'

'Nothing,' said Judy in puzzlement. 'I went to the mailbox first, unlocked the front door and was a couple of steps inside before I realised there was something on the floor.'

'Do you always leave Lucy inside?' asked Danby.

'No, we don't. Mum just started doing it recently and I don't really know why. I thought she was being super kind to Lucy, 'cos that's how Mum is.'

'Before you came to Mrs. Allen's, did you unlock your back door?' Danby asked.

Judy thought for a moment. 'Yes. It has bolts top and bottom and I had to undo them to come to Linda's.'

'So, at this stage, you don't know how, or where, someone got into your house? Is that right?'

'That's right.' Judy shivered, her voice hushed.

'One last question,' said Danby, 'what time did you get back from school?'

'Probably 3:30 or 3:35. I rode quicker than usual because I had some news to tell Mum.'

'Okay, stay here with Mrs Allen while we search your house. I'd say there's small chance of finding anyone there but we might discover how they got in. Your mum will be here soon so just sit tight.' Danby smiled encouragingly and left after a nod to Linda Allen.

Ten minutes later the doorbell rang again and, from the kitchen, Judy heard her mother and Linda talking.

The mood in the McNulty household over dinner was tense and sad. No one could fathom who or why anyone would break in and kill Lucy. And, to further complicate matters, when Caroline searched the house with Danby and Summers, several previously missing items were, inexplicably, found. Conversely, she also realised that numerous items of John's and her clothing were now missing.

After a fruitless and circular discussion, Jason asked the inevitable question: 'Mum, why was Lucy inside anyway? I don't understand that.'

'Well,' said Caroline slowly, 'over the last three weeks I realised that certain items of mail hadn't arrived. I made enquiries and confirmed they'd definitely been posted. I asked both Linda and the Grabowski's next door if they had lost any mail. Neither of them had. I started to think of all the things that were mysteriously "misplaced" over the last twelve months, quite a few of which turned up in weird places sometimes weeks or months later. Because there was no sane explanation for it, I wondered if we had a stalker, a stalker who obviously was entering our house. But when I looked for evidence of forced entry, there was nothing, absolutely nothing. The house was always locked, none of the windows were tampered with and there was no damage to the roof. Apart from the missing items, nothing inside was ever out of place. I conducted fingerprint tests and discreetly made enquiries along The Esplanade. No one had seen anybody strange or heard anything suspicious. The grounds for my belief seemed … I don't know … weird … unrealistic. Your dad and I talked about it and although he was sceptical, we decided to leave Lucy inside in case I was right. We didn't want to mention it to any of you because we had nothing concrete. Now I realise it was a dreadful mistake and we should have done things differently.'

'I was the sceptical one and I was wrong,' John said with a catch in his voice. 'We could have hired one of those sound activated film recorders but I just wasn't convinced. We compromised and I thought that, at the very least, if we left Lucy inside it would be some form of deterrence.' He dashed a tear away from his face. 'I'm really sorry kids. We all loved her and I would never have thought in my wildest dreams this could happen.'

They continued toying with their meals, despondency and gloom deepening.

'Alright, listen up,' Caroline said firmly. 'What's happened changes everything. I don't want either of you girls coming home to an empty house. You are to go to Linda's if Jason, your father or I am not here. Judy, you are not to go sailing, running or riding on your own any more. If you can't find someone to train with, you'll just have to miss out. Until we find out what this is about, all of us have to be careful. I don't want *anyone* taking risks.'

CHAPTER 17

'Jesus H Christ. I thought I left yu' fuckin' nigras at home,' drawled a lazy American voice.

Fox, who had been stashing some gear in his locker, looked around while Davey Gordon, who was kneeling at his floor locker, stood and turned. A two metre tall man in an American Special Forces uniform stood at the doorway of the change room. He wore the usual US Army buzz cut: a spiky circle of dark hair atop an otherwise bald dome. His face was sour and he crackled with hostility.

'What's yo' problem Arrogance?' drawled Fox in perfect imitation of the visitor's accent.

'Yo' presence nigra, that's the problem. Why don't yu'all just fuck off.'

Davey Gordon leaned against the lockers, a lopsided smile on his face, hands in his pockets.

'Why don't you sod off with your head up your arse. This is my mate. Insult him, insult me.'

The Yank swaggered forward. 'I'll pretend I didn't hear that remark whereas I heard everythin' shit features here said.' He nodded at Fox.

'Better wash yo' mouth out boy,' Fox drawled, 'otherwise, yo' ain't gonna fit in here.'

The American continued to swagger forward and stuck his

face about two inches away from Fox. 'We'll jus' see about that, nigra.' He turned and strutted out.

Fox and Gordon shook their heads and looked at each other.

'What the fuck was that about?' asked the big Welshman. 'What sort of rock did he crawl out from? Hope he hasn't joined our lot.'

'Dunno,' said Fox, 'I've never seen him before. Have you?'

'Nope, but I think I'll sniff out his story. The CO sure as hell won't tolerate that attitude.'

They left together and soon peeled off in different directions: Fox to his bunk, Gordon to the admin centre. The American was nowhere to be seen.

After a gruelling run over parts of the Brecon Beacons in the morning, the squad was enjoying a two hour break before a solid unarmed combat session. Given his hostile confrontation with the American, Fox thought he would meditate. He had been slack about it of late and felt out of touch. The encounter with the American reminded him that he needed to practise regularly to achieve the state of serenity he desired.

Entering his room he found a letter tucked under the door – the handwriting was unfamiliar. After opening the heavy cream envelope, he smiled to himself – Heidi Ravenscroft.

> *Hello, just Fox,*
>
> *I did say I expected to see you again. I've checked your schedule for the next couple of weeks and see you have the weekend after next rostered as a stand-down. As it happens, so have I. I'll pick you up at the barracks gates, 2000 hours on that Friday night. Have your toothbrush ready. You won't be needing pyjamas. And don't try saying no. I'll be offended.*
>
> *See you then,*
>
> *Heidi.*
>
> *1/10/85*

He chuckled aloud and wondered. No doubt about it, Heidi was a bloody mystery. Why had she set her sights on him, a pretty average bloke from Oz? He was definitely not in her league. He recalled the visitor's day at Kilmore Castle – he had neither seen nor heard from her in the weeks since. He also remembered the veiled looks between Rebecca and Maddie as Heidi had walked away. Maybe this invitation was what those looks had been about. Maybe there was … history?

Dressed in tracksuits, the men met in the gym for their afternoon routines. Fox and Gordon saw the American straight away – he stood aside from the team making no effort to join them. They looked at each other and then at the American, curiosity burning in their eyes. Gordon's enquiries had yielded nothing. Captain John Arbuthnott, or "Ropey" to his men, chief PT trainer, bustled in.

'Righto men, gather round. I've got a special treat over the next ten days. Sergeant Saul Carmody here is from the US of A Special Forces. He's going to teach us some new unarmed combat drills. I'm not detailing his history other than to say he's been around and is classed as their best instructor. In short, his reputation is formidable. There'll be a fifteen minute warm-up after which Carmody will start on the new routines. Right, get to it.'

Fox, Gordon and the others, paired off for exercises involving rolls, break falls, stretching and rope climbing followed by a set of drills: twists, hops, break-holds, leg locks and parries. They finished the warm-up concentrating on the work ahead through some centring and breathing techniques.

Carmody walked to the large mat in the middle of the gym and bellowed.

'Right, listen up. Circle round. There's a lot to learn and perfect in ten days. I'll be working with yu'all individually, in pairs and at times, in threes. There are only two rules: the learning phase, where yu' will all be observant, thorough and careful. Next, the *applied phase*. Here there are no rules, just full scale hostilities. I will assess and advise each of you when you are okay to exit the learning phase for each routine at every session. Any questions?'

Carmody was all business: sharp, engaged, impersonal and in command.

Over the next several days, he did almost exactly as proclaimed. The exception was Fox. Carmody ignored Fox; individually, in pairs and with the exit phase. The pattern was obvious. At the end of the sixth day, Ropey called Carmody into his office and closed the door. Fifteen minutes later, Carmody stalked out, murder on his face.

'Yu. Tomorrow,' he hissed at Fox. In that instant, Fox recalled *Operation Tar Pot* and the marine, Sergeant Roy Carmody. Everything clicked into place. Somehow, Carmody had placed him with *Tar Pot* and wanted revenge. *Shit!*

As an instructor and competitor, Carmody was impressive: lightning fast, superbly fit, incredibly streetwise and very knowledgeable. He was taller and heavier than Fox and possessed a chilling technical and tactical armoury. And Carmody's hatred of Fox was as evident as his desire to hurt him … seriously.

But Fox too was skilful and fast. He knew his best chance lay through speed. Before it came to that however, the sensible thing would be an open and frank discussion about the other Carmody – brother, cousin, uncle, or whatever hell relation he was.

Later that evening, Fox acknowledged a soft knock on his door. Davey Gordon entered, a good natured smile on his face.

'Fancy a pint before turning in?' he enquired.

'No, not tonight,' responded Fox, 'I need a good kip instead.'

'Thought you might say that. You know we're all with you don't you?' He pulled Fox's chair from the desk and sat.

'Yeah,' said Fox wryly, 'like rats at cheese.' He grinned at

Gordon. 'It's nice of you to tell me.'

'What we can't work out,' Gordon replied thoughtfully, 'is Carmody's aggro. I mean, I was with you the day he arrived. I could see you didn't know him. Although that didn't stop you handing it straight back.' He grinned. 'What's his fuckin' problem?'

'Me,' laughed Fox. 'It came to me today when he fumed out of Ropey's office. I'd seen that look before.' Fox told Gordon about *Operation Tar Pot,* Holmes's kidnapping, Roy Carmody and the confrontation in the showers.

By the end of the story, Gordon was chuckling.

'So, *this* Carmody is some kind of prick relation who wants to settle scores?'

'That's my guess.'

'Worried about him?'

'No, not worried … cautious. We've all seen his ability,' Fox said slowly. 'I've learned never to take things for granted, so … I'm cautious.'

'Anything I, or we can do?'

'No mate, but thanks.'

'Listen Fox, the only reason we almost like you is because your team can shit on the English at rugby.' Gordon was smiling again.

'Speaking of liking things, what do you think of this?' Fox rose from his bunk, took Heidi's letter from the small dresser and handed it to Gordon. 'Reckon this is a good enough reason to be cautious?' A slow smile cracked his face and his grey eyes shone with mischief.

Davey Gordon read the letter in silence then looked into Fox's grinning face.

'You tinny bastard! I bloody knew she took a shine to you. I knew it! You might as well know, I am immediately entering "covet mode". Wait till I tell Maddie about this, she'll pop her cork.'

'Tell you what Davey,' said Fox, more seriously, 'that day at the castle – Maddie and Rebecca were more informative about the young Ms Ravenscrosft in what they *didn't* say rather than what they did say. Can you find out from Maddie what her reservations are? I don't want to be making an ass of myself with a bloody Lord's granddaughter. Oh, one more thing, not a word to anyone but Lex.'

Gordon shook his head in disbelief and laughed. 'You'll be as safe as the Bank of England with a letter like this mate. Just get on with it.'

CHAPTER 18

By 6:15 the following morning Fox had swum hard for two kilometres then enjoyed a profound meditation. He was prepared for anything.

The morning lectures were spent unravelling jungle warfare problems and alternatives to various complexities encountered in Vietnam. A visitor from MI6 spoke on terrorism and the politics behind it, including some of the stuff Hoey had referred to. After lunch, the squad assembled for their unarmed combat session. The twenty men were alert and expectant, most had given Fox a pat on the shoulder or a gentle nudge. After five months in their company he'd forged some warm and solid friendships.

When Carmody appeared he was loose, relaxed and poised. Gone was the acetous hostility; present was a man whose mission had come. An involuntary quiver ran through Fox as he assessed his opponent. Even though standing among his peers, he knew that he, and he alone would be selected for combat. He had a brief moment of de ja vu as the image of Skinny Rogers flashed through his mind and then, he was ready.

'Fox,' said Carmody softly, 'it has been suggested I'm biased against yu', that I've neglected your training and treated yu' unfairly. So … let's redress that shall we? Are yu' up for it, or just a wet pussy?'

'What are the ground rules?' responded Fox calmly.

'Oh, I think that after all yu've seen in the past six days yu'll be ready for the applied phase. Don't yu'? So get your black arse up here.'

'How do you intend to signal submission?' Fox did not move. Unblinking, Carmody stared at Fox for several seconds.

'Yu' won't need a signal Fox, yu'll know when to submit.' He then moved to the centre of the mat.

From his office, Arbuthnott watched the manoeuvring, determined to hang back but ready to intervene. He too, like the men of this team, liked Fox. He saw him as a man who could absorb information and knowledge, who worked and trained hard and could take plenty of good natured joshing. The main difference he'd seen between Fox and the rest was that Fox didn't much care for booze. He was always careful.

Fox moved to the centre of the mat. In a scornful parody of civility, Carmody bowed from the waist. On the instant of completion, Fox slid forward and delivered a smashing straight left to Carmody's nose. He felt and heard it break, saw blood pour down Carmody's shirtfront. With that, his tactics were launched: he would crowd Carmody, be the aggressor, inflict maximum damage, move at speed and, where possible, surprise.

Carmody grunted and responded with a sharp foot sweep to the side of Fox's knee and a vicious chop at his throat. Before they could connect, Fox had leapt vertically and delivered a driving side kick to Carmody's sternum, a kick that triggered the solar plexus nerve and left him winded.

Like a tiger, Fox attacked with a combination choke, strangle and joint lock. Carmody escaped Fox's holds and countered with a searing leg and ankle lock that caused Fox serious pain. Fox shifted focus, applied a shoulder lock and leveraged until Carmody was hurting. They released holds and sprang up from the floor.

The men were enthralled. They all knew Carmody was talented, but compared to Fox's grace and lightning speed, he seemed lumbering. Fox was combining speed and power in a way they had not seen. Many wondered if he could sustain the pace because the duel was deadly. There would be no breaks and though the contest was only minutes long, Fox had been exceptionally energetic.

But Fox had entered a plane of acute awareness – he could anticipate Carmody's moves from minutely telegraphed body signals before their execution. To Fox, Carmody's actions were as sluggish as treacle on a frosty morning. Conversely, his own holds, throws, parries, punches and locks were applied with ferocious certainty, pinpoint accuracy and maximum impact. Even so, Carmody's strength and some of his feints surprised Fox and resulted in damage. While Fox showed superior speed, the battle was far from uneven.

At the six minute mark, the pace had not slackened – both combatants carried injury and seemed close to spent. Fox, gashed on the left side of his face, was heavily favouring his left arm. Carmody, with a broken nose and closed left eye, was seriously limping. Still they battled on, more slowly, more deliberately. Grunting, heaving, throwing, sweeping, blocking and locking. Suddenly, Fox unleashed an ungainly frontal assault. He grabbed Carmody's belt, applied a hip throw, swivelled then dropped his knee into Carmody's rib cage at the same time hauling on an elbow lock.

Everyone heard Carmody's ribs crack.

'Submit, or I'll break your arm,' Fox ground as he applied pressure.' Carmody paled and stilled. 'Submit!'

Arbuthnott appeared. 'Fox, release him. You've made your point.'

'I'm sorry sir I can't. He's fighting Sombo style. He won't stop just because you say. He either submits or takes a broken arm.'

'Carmody, submit. You could be permanently damaged by that lock.'

'With great respect sir, get fucked. Arrghh!'

With the ease of breaking eggshells, Fox snapped Carmody's arm and became the victor. He stood and looked at Carmody who had passed out. He then addressed Arbuthnott.

'Sir, he's a prick but he was also a worthy opponent. I respect his ability. He can always claim no submission but, if we'd been in the field now, he'd be dead.'

Arbuthnott glared at Fox then barked, 'Gordon, see these two clowns get down to the hospital. Jamieson – take the rest out on another five mile run and be back in thirty-five minutes. After that, call it a day. Dismissed.'

CHAPTER 19

Throughout the following week Ropey and his fellow instructors ensured Fox was overloaded. Disagreement between soldiers was not uncommon, but to encounter what could easily have been an ugly outcome between two overseas visitors on foreign turf would, to say the least, have been unusual and unwelcome.

From Ropey's perspective the matter was finished. After interviewing various members of Fox's squad he reported adversely to Carmody's superiors citing provocative and unprofessional conduct. Whilst he admired Fox's principles, he didn't want him thinking he approved of his behaviour. He needn't have worried. Fox was simply responding to a bully. So, with his bruises, cuts, aches, sprains and a doubled workload, he copped it sweet.

Early Friday morning, Gordon and McPhie joined Fox in the pool.

'So bonnie lad,' said McPhie, 'tonight's the night? Are you sure you don't want a stand-in with those bloody bruises all over your body?'

'I was worried about his good looks,' Gordon chimed in, 'I thought that since his mug was so mashed I'd offer mine instead.'

'Piss off you pair of bastards,' laughed Fox. 'You're too fond of Maddie, Davey and I see that since our visit to Kilmore Castle Lex, Becky has you wrapped around her little finger. Just imagine what those two women soldiers would do to the pair of you, not to mention me, if one of you stood in for me. Sorry guys, I just have to do this by myself.'

'Damn,' muttered Gordon.

Friday evening at precisely 2000 hours, Heidi Ravenscroft stopped in front of the barracks in her trendy black Porsche 928S.

'Hello there Fox,' she called, 'throw your gear in the back and hop in.'

'I thought that being a Lord's granddaughter you'd be driving a phaeton and four,' Fox laughed.

'No, I prefer my 300 horses instead – much more exciting. But I can show you our phaeton. Grandfather has a collection of early transportation and farm implements dating from around 1600. It's actually pretty interesting stuff.'

'Fine. Be happy to see it. Any chance of a gallop over the weekend?'

'Of course, but you surprise me – I didn't think you'd be the riding type. We've got a few nags and I quite like a canter myself.'

'So where are we off to now?'

She looked at him sideways and grinned wickedly.

'I thought we could go clubbing and dancing in Cardiff. My flat's there. Tomorrow, if you like, we could go to the manor for lunch and either stay overnight or go back to my flat. What do you think?'

'If we go to the castle won't your folks ask questions … you know … about us … being together?'

'God no,' she laughed, 'I've been shagging since I was fourteen. All Mummy asked was that I be careful. So I am. Anyway, hard for my oldies to point the finger, they were goers themselves. When he's in his cups, Grandfather tells the story about coming home late one night to find them at it on top of the billiard table. Mummy was about eighteen. No, they won't mind, they think it's healthy.'

Fox was dumbfounded. Heidi's candour was way outside his

experience and so different from his perception of her at their first encounter. Unexpectedly, he felt a twinge of concern. Still, he wasn't going to knock back the experience because that's all it was, experience – the urge to merge.

'Okay, clubbing it is,' he replied. 'Now, do tell – why me?'

'You interest me, Fox. You're a spunk, I know you don't talk much about yourself and that gives you an air of mystery. Apart from that, you fight like a thrashing machine. That American, Saul Carmody – he was in my care for a couple of days so I've seen the results. I'm not sure his elbow will ever fully recover. And you … you look relatively unharmed.'

'Don't believe it,' he grinned, 'You might get to see my bruises later.'

'Bet on it,' said Heidi chuckling, 'don't think I'm going to behave.' She changed down, accelerated through a left hand bend onto the A49 towards Redhill then suddenly slipped her hand deep into Fox's crotch. He jumped. After a few moments she removed it to change gears again. She laughed aloud and said innocently, 'Had dinner yet, Fox?'

'No,' he said, still feeling the warmth of her hand and his own rising response. 'As your note was so cryptic I thought I'd wait in case you had something planned.'

'I do indeed. I've made a tasty lasagne and salad and organised a nice Australian red to drink. I thought we could get acquainted over dinner before we go dancing. That suit you?'

'Absolutely, though I'm not a great one for drinking. My dad was killed by a drunk driver and booze doesn't interest me much.'

'I'm sure there are other interesting things we can do, like, skipping lasagne and just getting acquainted.'

Two can play this game, he thought.

'Why wait for Cardiff, let's get acquainted at the next lay-by then, by the time we get to Cardiff, lasagne will be looking really good.' Heidi's laughter was warm and sensual.

Zooming up a long, steep rise they both saw the blue sign indicating a truck stop. Heidi slowed, indicated and pulled left. Slowly she drove past two parked lorries to the far end of the lay-by where it was empty and dark. Even before they had stopped, Fox felt his seat beginning to recline beneath him. After parking, Heidi released her seat belt and glanced at the laid back Fox.

'This soon enough, Mr Fox? I don't know why we're waiting either.'

She wriggled out of her seat belt, climbed over the gear stick and rolled onto him, cradling his head, searching for his mouth. He pressed her slim body to him, a body soft and firm in all the right places. Heidi kissed him hungrily, crushing his lips. Fox responded vigorously. He was intensely aware of her delicate perfume, thick silky hair and skin as soft as swan's down. She kissed with frenetic urgency, inflaming his desire.

'Ahh, Fox,' she sighed, 'this is nice … so … nice.'

Her breath, he noticed, was sweet and minty. She kissed him again, less urgently, more deeply and with tenderness. Fox responded. Although boiling, he caressed her face softly, then, slowly … raggedly … dragged his thumb down her spine to the top of her buttocks. She shivered gently.

Unhurriedly, Heidi sat up and straddled him, knees either side of his hips, hands on his shoulders. Fox could feel his heart pounding and thought she must be able to hear it too. In the pale green light of the dashboard clock, he could see only her dark outline and an occasional glint from her eyes.

'So Mr Fox, are we becoming nicely acquainted?' she asked quietly in a husky, teasing voice.

'The nicest kind of acquaintance I'd say,' he replied hoarsely.

'Well then, let me see what you're made of.' She chuckled, raised herself, rearranged her skirt and unzipped Fox to expose his rampant manhood. Slowly, she lowered herself, engulfed him and began to gyrate. He groaned with pleasure, amazed to find that not only was she without knickers, but hot and deliciously wet.

Their sex was boisterous, lubricously noisy and satisfying. After regaining their composure Fox, euphoric, heart still thumping said, 'Jesus, you're dynamite.'

'That's because you've got such a bloody good fuse,' she laughed and kissed him again, long and hard.

They adjusted themselves and drove on. To Fox, the interlude seemed only seconds but the dashboard clock boasted fifteen minutes: longer than he had imagined and more than enough to know the promise of a luridly raunchy weekend. Sated, he sank into the seat and watched the darkened country side flash by, a companionable smile on his lips.

CHAPTER 20

'Don't be a bloody piker man,' railed McPhie, 'tell us what she's like.' Gordon and McPhie had waited for Fox late into Sunday night and were itching to know all about Heidi the Hot, Heidi the Stunner, Heidi the Bold. Fox wasn't having it.

'Listen, do I badger you buggers about Maddie or Rebecca? Of course not. And why? Good taste and respect: for them and, God forgive me, for you ratbags. That's my rule, like it or lump it.'

'Yeah, but in this case,' chuckled McPhie, 'we're dealing with a gorgeous bloody aristocrat. That puts her in a different league. Knobs *are* fair game.'

'Well,' laughed Fox, far from offended, 'not from me lads. Sorry, but that's the way it is. The only thing I can tell you is she's a bloody good horsewoman, her parents seem okay and when you get away from the "pile", as Heidi calls the castle, the woods and grounds are beautiful. I had a bonza weekend.'

Although disappointed, they respected his stance.

For his part, Fox was glad to be back on "home turf". Mixing with Heidi's parents had been hard work. Pleasant enough, they had still presented an air of condescension and aloofness. Status and wealth were the only things of meaning to them, a belief Fox considered superficial. He acknowledged their generous fund raising and their considerable local employment but, at a deeper level, they evinced an unspoken superiority grounded in that quality McPhie had once mentioned – ancient aristocracy. So, Fox played the game. He was polite, respectful and charming while underneath, he was ill at ease and on guard.

Heidi, on the other hand, was free flowing, gregarious, funny, natural and insatiable. He had never had so much sex in such a short time, experienced so many different positions, done it in so many strange places or, with such abandon. Yet, he was relieved the weekend was over.

Over the next six weeks Heidi blitzed Fox with phone calls, impromptu visits, passionate weekends and an avalanche of cards. And, though he was a receptive and ardent partner in their steamy sexual games, at times he found the depth of Heidi's possessiveness overwhelming. Fox was a free spirit, Heidi's single-mindedness was a strait-jacket. That this beautiful, sexy creature had even selected him was a puzzle. It was not as if their relationship would go anywhere. She would probably marry someone of equivalent station and he, most definitely, was returning to Australia, a place he knew would be a social desert for her.

Again, he wondered if Maddie or Rebecca could tell him more. They worked with her, had known her for ages and, from their first meeting at the castle, caused Fox to suspect they knew a lot more about Heidi than they were saying. As usual however, he kept his thoughts to himself.

The following day, Fox rang the McNulty's in Perth. This was only the third time he had phoned because of their regular exchange of post cards, letters and photos.

'Hi Caro, how's things?'

'Colin my dear, how good to hear you. How are you?'

'Absolutely fine but I needed to hear an Aussie voice and find out what's happening.'

'Ah, a bit home sick then. Tell me what you've been up to. Met any nice girls over there?'

'Yes and no. Remember I wrote to you about Kilmore Castle some time ago?'

'I do. Your comparison between the castle and Turkey Creek made us all laugh. What about it?'

'Yeah … well … Turkey Creek is always a blast. What I didn't tell you though was that I met the Lord's granddaughter that day too. Now, this woman is beautiful. Out of ten she's a twelve and, for whatever reason, she seems to have taken a shine to me and we've been out a few times since.'

'Good for you.' Caroline chuckled warmly, 'Knowing how little you talk about such matters, I can imagine your entire regiment would trade places with you. But I'm not surprised. You're a handsome young man Colin.'

'C'mon Caro, this is me – don't bullshit a bullshitter.'

'Of course you are. Both my girls love you to bits.'

'Yeah, but that's different. I love them too, you know that. They're my sisters. At the moment though, I am enjoying what I can only call a pretty full-on dalliance. Now, what about the rest of the gang, how are they?'

'John's working too hard. Judy's training like a mad thing for an interstate athletics competition. Jason is loving this semester on prosecution tactics and Jenny is spending so much time at sea these days I'm sure one night she'll come home with gills. And, speaking of Jenny, I should tell you that she and young Courtney Dalgleish seem hopelessly in love. I'm really happy with the way he treats her. He's very considerate and respectful towards her. I like that.'

'Yeah, he's a good colt, young Kurt.'

'Now Col, what else is happening? Anything I can pass on to the others? Unfortunately, they've all gone to the Subiaco market.'

'Just tell 'em I love 'em all. Also, I've got some special training at Greenwich in London in a couple of weeks. Should be good. It combines army, navy, airforce and police and various odd-bods from the Home Office. We don't have all the details yet but it's some kind of joint terrorism exercise. I understand the police contingent is coming from a joint called Bramshill, wherever that is.'

'I know about Bramshill. One of my colleagues here has twice applied for a gig there but the Commissioner knocked it back. It's a top notch police training college in the Hampshire region. It runs courses for aspiring Assistant Chief Constables, overseas students, sergeant ranks and some very sophisticated crime management training. I understand it was built around the twelfth century. Sounds like you'll have a bit of "class" around you.' Caroline laughed softly.

'What? Are you suggesting I'm mixing with drongos over here?'

Caroline continued laughing. 'No, just that the boys in blue will show you up.'

He grinned down the phone, happy to be talking with a good mate.

'Yeah, I'm looking forward to it. Goes for a couple of days and, if it's not super secret, I'll tell you about it afterwards.'

'Good. If that means another phone call, we accept. But, on another note, I'm glad you rang.' Her light hearted tone changed. 'We didn't quite know how to tell you this so we put it off. A couple of months ago, it must have been just after you got back from Ireland, the house was broken into. Whoever it was killed Lucy dog and poor Judy found her after school – a horrid, gory mess. My little poppet was absolutely heartbroken and had nightmares for weeks afterwards. Even now she still has the occasional bad dream. It really shook her up.'

Instantly, Fox felt an almighty kick to the stomach. He *knew* things there were not right but he had not tried hard enough to identify the cause. Too busy bonking Heidi was the truth. And though aware he could not have prevented what happened, with greater diligence he might have been able to warn them. The intensity of Judy's anguish seared him.

He was silent as a hurricane of thoughts and feelings somersaulted within. He chose his next words carefully.

'Caroline, I am really sorry about what happened, especially since it involved Judy. I'm sure you know she's my favourite. I will try to make amends when I get back.' He paused before continuing. 'I've been reluctant to mention this before now and I don't want to sound melodramatic but, there is something going on around you. I don't know what it is, but something is not right. Be very careful. Whatever is happening, it's *not* finished.'

CHAPTER 21

'Fox, I *am* coming to see you this weekend. I have to.' Heidi was not only emphatic but pissed off.

'Heidi … look, I'm sorry, but we're on a training exercise in the Brecons. You know how it works. This game is not nine to five Mondays to Fridays. We'll be out overnight and all weekend.' Fox did his best to sound placatory.

'Perhaps I could sneak into your hutch at night.' Heidi started to laugh. 'That'd be good … bonking under canvas with the troops listening in. They'd all start wanking and we could have a collective climax.' She giggled at her own description. 'That reminds me of a line from the Eton boating song: "We'll all swing together, our bodies between our knees."' She laughed aloud.

Fox, fully attuned to her quirky humour, suspected she was only half jesting.

'Sorry Heidi, this weekend is out. I know you've got contacts down here, so check it out. You'll see we leave at 0600 Friday and get back at 1800 Monday.'

'Yes, I know how it works. I'm just feeling hungry for you Fox. I don't recall ever having such good sex before. So, when will you be available? What about next weekend?'

His mind raced. Heidi's company was always good fun and full of abandon but lately she had become suffocating. In his time on the course Fox had cemented several strong friendships. Before she appeared he had regularly managed weekends at the homes of different blokes from the course. Post Heidi, these weekends had dried up. He was mindful that his time at Hereford was diminishing and he had not yet completed his exploration of London. Those enjoyable forays were slowly providing gifts for home.

'Sorry Heidi, I've got next weekend booked with Alex. We're both flying up to Scotland. I remember telling you that some of my family came from a place called Pittenweem. Alex is from Kirkcaldy, near Pittenweem and we're going to check out my dad's roots.'

'Well I'll just have to come to Kirkcaldy for a shag. I'll see you there.' The phone crashed down.

Bloody hell! What had started out as good fun was becoming not only claustrophobic but annoying. Fox wondered what her reaction might be if he gave her the flick. Although not quite ready to do that, he was beginning to think it could be a good idea. After seeing each other for just over two months, most of it in bed, he quickly discovered that Heidi could be spiteful and ill tempered when she didn't get her way. He had heard several exchanges between Heidi and her parents which revealed her obvious pampering as an "only" child. Good fortune had blessed her with a sharp intellect together with an education at England's finest schools and universities. Yet once, when Fox asked why she had joined the army, she was evasive. Knowing her demanding sexual appetite, he thought the rumours of her numerous paramours, though muted, had something to do with it. He was thinking too that perhaps the reason Maddie and Rebecca were reluctant to speak openly about her was because they knew *too* much.

Her reputation as a doctor was sound. She was renowned for amazing diagnostic skills and although cool with her patients, she was sufficiently caring to be remembered for more than her good looks. Good looks which concealed a short fuse. Fox had witnessed Heidi's impatience with staff and her arrogance with people she disliked. Paradoxically, he had also seen her generosity, good humour and sparkle. He suspected that if her dark side should ever be fully aroused, she would be intense trouble.

He quickly decided he'd better put substance to his lie and organise the weekend away with McPhie. It had been a long standing invitation by Lex that was yet to be fulfilled and Fox did not think Heidi would be so crass to visit Kircaldy.

He heard the loud Australian voice well before he found its source. With Davey Gordon and four colleagues, Fox was looking around the Old Royal Naval College at Greenwich, London. They were there for two days on exercise with a formal Mess Dinner in between. Having arrived with an hour to fill before the exercise commenced, they were walking towards a knot of men standing beside the antique *Cutty Sark* moored on the Thames's south bank near the college.

'Is that one of your Aussie mates I can hear?' Gordon asked Fox.

'Sounds like it. Loud bastard.'

Gordon grinned at him as they kept walking. Closer to the group they saw the speaker, a huge man in police uniform. His voice was jovial and blaring as he talked about the *Cutty Sark* and a recent visit to Portsmouth. Fox and Gordon stopped to watch.

'Hey, you bloody great kangaroo, come and meet my little Aussie mate,' Gordon suddenly bellowed.

Fox shot an ascerbic look at Gordon as the big man stopped mid-sentence, grinned, and ambled over.

'Well clearly Taffy, that's not you. Spencer Johnson, Australian Federal Police. I'm at the Embassy here in London.' He thrust out a huge hand to Gordon, then to Fox. 'Here for the ex are you?'

'We are. We're from Hereford. I'm Davey Gordon and my little mate here is Colin Fox from Perth.'

'G'day,' said Fox, shaking an iron-like grip. 'How come you're here?'

'The Embassy sent me down to Bramshill to do their MOSSC course and I was lucky enough to get a guernsey in this as an add-on. Oh, sorry – MOSSC is the Brit's Management of Series and Serious Crime Course.'

'Yeah, I heard about it from a friend of mine at home. What's your role?' asked Fox.

'Observer. What about you? Hereford's the home of the SAS – are you one of them?'

'Yes and no,' responded Fox, through a wry grin. 'Same bunch at home, here for twelve months. Done nine, so close to stumps.'

Davey Gordon was eyeing Johnson up and down as the pair talked.

'You ought to think about switching jobs and joining us, you're big enough and ugly enough. No fat on you.'

Johnson let go a booming laugh. 'I'm a body builder in my spare time so I eat like a horse, work-out like a bastard and swim like a fish to avoid getting fat. But I'm not far off entering veterans class now, age is mowing me down. Bloody hard to keep looking like this. I'd be no good in your caper. You buggers'd be too agile for me.'

Johnson evidently possessed an amiable good humour and showed no sign of rancour. Certainly none of Gordon's insults affected him.

'What do you do at the Embassy?' Gordon queried.

'Bit of this, bit of that, nothing important. Well, you know: help out Aussies in trouble from time to time, see there's nothing amiss with security, ride shotgun over difficult patrons, liaise occasionally with some of your spooks, the police and such like. Run of the mill stuff. Irregular investigations – all that.'

'Sounds pretty laid back to me, when do you do the other stuff, the body building?'

'Pretty much every day – got to keep at it you know.' Johnson glanced at his watch. 'Better move in I guess. Do you blokes know where to go?'

When they both shook their heads Johnson said, 'Okay, tag along with us. I've been down here a couple of times before.'

As they walked towards the college, Fox admired its classical appearance.

'How old is this joint?' he asked Gordon.

'I understand most of the buildings here were designed by Christopher Wren as a hospital in the late 1600s. Some time in the 1870s it became the Royal Naval College. I've got a vague idea the site was originally a palace and that the first Queen Elizabeth was born here.'

'Ho, ho,' said Johnson, 'showing off our primary school knowledge are we?' He laughed heartily, happy to have a lash at Gordon. 'As a matter of fact Mr Fox, it was Queen Mary II in 1692 who converted the King Charles wing of her palace to a naval hospital for sailors wounded at the Battle of La Hogue. Christopher Wren helped with the re-design but Mary ordered the avenue between buildings because his original design buggered up her view of the river.'

'How come you know so much?'

Johnson laughed again. 'I told you Fox: I've been down here before. When you bring others, they ask questions, just like you. Because I didn't know the answers, I found out. Simple.'

Fox smiled. He liked Johnson.

CHAPTER 22

Judy sauntered through Mends Street mall after buying the milk and Saturday morning papers for her mother. For her, this was an enjoyable, but irregular ritual reserved for non-competition days: no running, no cycling, no basket ball. What made it special was a hot chocolate at the Plaza Café. She always ordered a large mug with double chocolate in piping hot milk.

She liked to get there early when it was not too busy and generally, she managed to snare her favourite seat near the coffee machine. She loved the smell of coffee but found the drink too bitter. With the newspapers and three litres of milk beside her, she sipped her steaming chocolate and scanned *The Weekend Australian*.

Four tables away, he watched her. He had discovered her little ritual quite by accident a couple of months earlier. Returning on successive Saturdays he found she didn't come every week but when she was there, it was enough just to watch her. Over the past six months the "little girl" had almost disappeared. She was now much taller, trim and shapely and her face more finely chiselled.

What promise! Too bad, so sad. From behind his own newspaper he peered discreetly. She was enjoying her drink and reading intently. Well, his plans were finalised … wouldn't be long now.

He had been forced to wait after killing the dog. Bitchface and her clan immediately raced into security over-drive. A thrilling result. It meant he was pulling their strings, controlling them and they didn't have a clue who, or where he was. And the fuckin' local coppers – useless. Eventually they clocked him, just like everyone else in the units. He had given them a crock, including a bodgy name. Unfortunately, he had said, he could not help them, he had been asleep. He even showed them his medication. And the good thing was, none of the coppers recognised him.

He sneaked another look. She was smiling at something in the paper. Pretty girl and getting more so. Quite different from her red-haired sister. Now, she was a looker by God! But she was hardly around any more. If she wasn't doin' uni stuff she was out with that friggin' soldier bastard. Probably one of Midnight's mates. Speaking of Midnight, he hadn't seen the prick for months. He wondered where he was. After the dog episode he had reluctantly suspended his stalking pleasures. He hadn't even pinched their mail. For a while he worried over that because it was a prime source of information.

Never mind, preparations for the final stage caused those worries to fade. Readying for that day was exciting, daring and completely absorbing. It was only now with everything almost set that he had again begun to think about their mail and other matters. He peered at her again. She was packing up to leave, completely oblivious. Well … pretty soon … she wouldn't be.

CHAPTER 23

On the other side of the world, seven and a half hours after Judy had enjoyed her hot chocolate, Fox and McPhie drove slowly into Pittenweem. Kissing the coastline of Fife's East Neuk, the tiny village of white painted stone cottages with their red tiled roofs bloomed as a hamlet of pride and beauty. Inexplicably, Fox felt as comfortable as if he were back in Turkey Creek. And yet, it was an alien place. It had been shaped by trade with the low countries five centuries earlier. An anchorage where glittering white homes were beacons of succour to fishermen at sea. But in some strange nostalgic way, it was as cosy and familiar to Fox as his favourite jacket.

'Crackerjack spot, Lex,' commented Fox as he wound the window down to sniff the sea air. 'When were you last here?'

'Two months back. Me Mam likes the fresh fish from here. Brought her up here last time I was home.'

'That's a thought. Could I take some back to her?'

'Aye. I'll call her and check though. Since me auld Dad died she's become a bit quaint and has funny ideas about keeping too much food in the house. You know … like … somehow it's wasteful. It's easiest to humour her.'

'Fair enough. What are your thoughts about finding my relos?'

'Finding what?'

'Family, relations, kinfolk – you nutter.'

McPhie laughed. 'Just kidding laddie. Anstruther is next town on, aboot ten minutes. The post office for this region is there so that's where we should start. If we strike oil we'll come back and dig 'em oot. We'll do that anyway because you need to look aboot. No point being all this way from Aus and not getting a feel for your roots. In fact, before we go on, I'll show you the harbour.'

He turned right off the A917 into Charles Street and headed down towards the sea. On the way, Fox couldn't help thinking that McPhie's accent had become more pronounced since returning home.

The harbour was buzzing. Fishermen were plentiful in searing yellow and orange waterproofs lifting, loading, yelling, swearing. Bobbing at the dockside, they worked from blue, black and white painted boats, masts and spars reaching to the heavens. Fish. Boxes of fish, treasure from the sea moving onwards, upwards, into vans, away to processors, out to shops and onto tables. White fish, pink fish, prawns and lobsters, tipping and flipping from black plastic baskets into thick, square, styro-foam caskets. Overhead, razor eyed gulls wheeled and screeched, dipping and diving, hungry for a feed. And throughout it all, the onlookers – talking, walking, bidding and haggling. Fox drank it all in, contented, transported to Broome and the luggers. It was wonderfully familiar.

'What are you grinning at?'

Fox's smile broadened as he turned to McPhie.

'Reminds me of when I was a kid. I worked on fishing boats around Broome for a time. Interesting to see it's not much different on this side of the world. It's nice.'

They left the clamour and salty air to head back to the A917. In less than ten minutes McPhie turned right onto East Shore Road in Anstruther. Saturday morning shopping was in full swing and finding a park was tricky. In the end, they found an empty spot reserved for boat owners and walked back past the Anstruther Fish Bar to the post office.

Inside, the old building exuded efficiency, bees wax and

purpose. Behind the polished counter a young woman and older man were weighing letters and filling out forms. The room was otherwise empty. McPhie headed for the man. Fox thought he was in his sixties. Stooped, balding and wearing thick, heavy glasses, he had an owlish look. His crisp white shirt and Argyle pattern cardigan bespoke pride and attention to detail.

'Hello, I wonder if you could help us?'

'Depends what you're after.'

'I'm Lex McPhie from Kirkcaldy. My friend, Fox here, is from Australia. He believes some long distant relatives may live in Pittenweem, people he's never met. Since he's only here a short time I thought we might try to find them. I was wondering if you know of any Foxs living there.'

'Aye. Happens I do. There's three. Louisa in her eighties and two nephews. Andrew and Duncan. What's the connection Mr Fox? You look a tad dark for Scottish ancestry.'

'My grandfather sailed to Australia from there. As best I understand, he was just a small child. Don't know much more than that. There was a rumour he had a sister in Scotland. I'm keen to see if I can learn more about the family while I'm here.'

'John Cameron's my name and I'm not usually in the habit of giving oot people's addresses. What do you do?' He peered at Fox intently.

'Army,' Fox responded, 'here for special training. Be gone in a few months.'

Cameron was silent as he deliberated – his huge, magnified, unblinking blue eyes examined Fox. Eventually, he said, 'Well, you look alright and if you're a dud, I'll be sure to hear from Louisa. I think she's your best bet. South Loan, small stone cottage – number twenty-six.'

'Thanks mate, I'm really grateful.' Fox stepped forward and shook Cameron's hand firmly. Within, his pulse surged, a spike of excitement he could not explain.

CHAPTER 24

Number twenty-six was a narrow, weathered, two storey grey-stone cottage with white wooden dormers in a red tiled roof. Wide white sills at ground level anchored robust flower boxes clutching a few dried stalks from summer. Entry through a thick, panelled door was straight off the street.

As they left the car, McPhie nodded to Fox. 'You first, this could be gold.'

Fox rapped on the door, a bold, authoritative knock guaranteed to be heard at the back of the house. After a few minutes, silently, and without warning, the door swung inwards. A slight woman of late years stood before them, hair, a braided silver halo. Warm grey eyes danced behind shining gold rimmed glasses, her longish face bearing the faintest of smiles.

'You must be the Australian,' her voice, warm and mellow, was much younger than her years. 'John Cameron thought he should warn me. Do come in. I'm Louisa Fox."

'I'm Fox too, Colin Fox and this is my friend Lex McPhie.' Fox, nervous, concealed his anticipation with a broad smile.

They stepped into a weather lobby of comfortable size. On the right, ancient black metal coat hooks and several umbrellas clung to a polished wooden transverse. On the left, a simple splay-legged oak bench was the perfect companion for shoe changing. Large, worn, flagstones paved the floor and supported a glowing oak and glass palladian barrier, sentry against icy winter winds. Sunlight from the rear gentled what might otherwise have been a gloomy and foreboding entrance.

They followed Louisa along a short, buttery coloured hallway and into the kitchen, a gleaming, airy space of light and warmth. From an oaken carcass burnished by decades of waxing, the heartbeat of an ancient Ansonia wall clock measured their visit in a slow, calm, pulse. A simple room, it was spotless and comfortable – the very soul of homeliness.

'Well lads, before we start, a cup of tea?'

Both murmured their agreement. Louisa moved an old black kettle off the hob and onto the centre of the Aga.

'It'll only be a few minutes. I made fresh pikelets this morning, would you like some wi' your tea?' Moving about her kitchen with authority and grace, Fox observed that although Louisa was slender, her years had not brought frailty. To the contrary, she possessed a vitality and sprightliness which Fox found appealing.

'I'm here from Australia for some special army training,' Fox offered, 'and my friend Lex is from Kirkcaldy. He brought me here because I believed I had relations from here.' He stopped, not quite certain what to say next.

'Aye, it's possible.' Louisa turned from the stove, eyes glowing. 'A long time ago my older brother, Colin Joshua Fox went to Australia. He was killed in the first war. Sit at the table lads while I finish this and then we'll talk.'

From an ancient and gleaming pine dresser she fetched cups, saucers, plates, knives and paper serviettes. From the fridge came whipped cream and pots of strawberry and blackberry jam swiftly joined by a large plate piled high with pikelets.

'Well boys, tuck in. Now, Colin, the very first thing I noticed was your silver grey eyes and then your colour. A curious combination but I can say with certainty that your eyes are just as I remember my brother Colin's. So, let me hear a little aboot yourself.'

Lex, contented with the fare in front of him, smiled. He held Fox in high regard but knew little of him. Fox rarely revealed anything of his past beyond army life so McPhie was keen to learn more.

Always uncomfortable when asked this question, Fox usually fudged a non-committal response. But not this time. Intuitively, he knew this woman was someone to respect. Family.

'I'll give you the short version because I really want to hear about this side of the family. My dad was Duncan Fox. My mum was Rosie, nee Harris, an Aboriginal. Dad was killed by a drunk driver a few days after the birth of my sister Lucy in 1957, I was four. Up to then he'd been a stockman, fencer and musterer and had met Mum in Wyndham, Western Australia. My memory of him is hazy but Mum always said he was a very kind, hard working and courteous man who loved us dearly. When he died he was foreman of a big cattle station called Leopold Downs in Western Australia. Mum often referred to him as her big Scottish husband because his dad was Scottish, but, as far as I know, my dad was born in Australia. After his death we all went back to Turkey Creek to live with the mob.'

Quietly, with sadness and eloquent power, Fox told of his removal from Turkey Creek, Lucy's death, life in the church institutions, escape, Rosie's death and his relationship with Caroline Connors and her family. He concluded by saying, 'Caroline is the reason I joined the army. So, Louisa, I'm here today to find out if we might be related. The only reason I think we could be is that my mum used to laugh at the name of my grandfather's town: Pittenweem. There was just something about it that tickled her fancy. I know it's a loose connection, but that's it.'

McPhie had stopped eating and was staring at Fox, dumbstruck by his early life. Louisa, scarcely breathing, eyes rimmed with tears, sat in silence.

After a few moments Louisa rose and went to Fox. 'You are

FOX

indeed my great nephew, grandson of my brother, Colin Joshua, and I can fill in some gaps for you. I am truly sorry that life has been so cruel to you.' She embraced Fox, gently kissed his cheek and stroked his hair. She resumed her seat, eyes searching Fox's face. 'I'll show you some photos of my brother later. But looking at you now, you are so like him. You even walk like him. I saw the resemblance the moment I opened the door. Our parents, Gordon Charles and Katherine Mary Fox, were born here in Pittenweem during the 1860s. In fact, my father was born in this house. He was a fisherman, as was our grandfather who built this house. Your grandfather, my brother, was born on April 21, 1895 and I was born on January 26, 1897 – that makes me eighty-eight. In 1900, my parents decided to migrate to Australia. My father's younger brother, James, came to live in this house. I was only three at the time and don't remember too much aboot things but I do recall the boat journey seemed to take years. Colin was five. We went to a place called Renmark, in South Australia – a very new settlement. Father was keen to take up the new practice of grape growing there, an industry started by people called Chaffey whom I think were Americans. Because Mother was a school teacher she had no trouble getting work in the settlement. Then, in 1911, we received a cable from Uncle James saying that grandfather was dying and wanted my father to take over the family fishing business. Colin was then about sixteen and flatly refused to return. I remember there was a huge row about it and I'm not sure that he and Father didn't come to blows. Anyway, Colin kissed Mother and me good- bye and rode away on horseback. That was the last I saw of him. Sometime in 1913 he wrote home telling us he was going to marry a Margaret Lucy Ryall. They were both only eighteen but madly in love. Your father, Duncan, was born in late 1916 after Colin had gone to the war in France. Colin died there from wounds without ever seeing your father. Over the next few years Mother and Father received letters from Margaret, or Maggie as she was commonly called, but eventually, they stopped. The last news we had was that she'd become a governess somewhere in Queensland but we never knew what became of her or your father, Duncan.'

Fox sat silently, spellbound. While he always knew he had white blood, he had only ever considered himself Aboriginal. He could hunt and track like few others, could still speak his language and was tied to country. And yet, here was another facet of his life's prism. Here was a history of travel, romance, adventure, military service and sadness. A history about which he knew nothing. *His* history. He felt a wave of disorientation.

He realised suddenly that both Louisa and McPhie were staring at him expectantly.

'I'm sorry, I'm just trying to take it all in. Tell me about my grandfather. You said you last saw him when he was sixteen and he was killed in the war. What kind of man was he?'

'I always remember him as looking out for me – a protector. He was ramrod straight and afraid of nothing. He was affectionate towards our mother and me and always respectful to our father until the day he was told to return to Scotland. He'd decided by then that Australia was the place for him. It was a young country with huge opportunity and he was prepared to work hard and succeed. He mixed well with people and he loved animals, especially horses.'

At this, Fox smiled and said quietly, 'Funny, me too. I've always had a knack with horses. Perhaps it comes from him.'

'Aye, perhaps it does. He was a very proper person too. Although he fell out with Father, by the time we got back home, and remember, Colin was only very young, there was a cable of kind and loving words to heal the rift. When he was killed it broke Father's heart and he never fully recovered. He died in 1920

'Mother and I were both teachers and we lived in this house and taught in Pittenweem from that point on. I never married and in due course, this house will go to Uncle James's oldest son, Dougal. He lives here in the village so if you have the time, perhaps you could meet him.' Louisa stood, lightly placed her hand on Fox's shoulder and said, 'I have some things for you that I have cherished ever since they were passed to me. When Colin was killed Maggie received several letters: one from his Officer Commanding, one from an American nurse who cared for him, and one from a subordinate. They are wonderful letters and I would like you to have them and his medals. Maggie grieved terribly over his death and wanted no reminders of that terrible war so she bundled everything up and sent them to Father. I'll fetch them.'

In her absence McPhie said, 'How are you feeling mate? You look like you've been hit by a train.'

'Lex, I can't even begin to explain how I feel. It's like being split in two. I had no idea of all this family history, only the vaguest of hints. I've always, always, considered myself *Gija*. Now I feel a bit … well … I dunno … I have to think about it. It's the weirdest feeling. Anyway, one thing's for certain, I like Louisa and will be keeping in touch with her. Actually, I can't wait to tell Caroline and John about her. They'll be really chuffed for me. I think I'll call them tonight.'

Louisa returned with a small wooden box and placed it on the table.

'You wouldn't have known Colin, but your grandfather was a recipient of the Military Medal for bravery. Have a look through these while I make fresh tea.'

McPhie watched Fox tentatively reach for the box and withdraw some worn and faded papers, papers exuding the musty tang of antiquity. Louisa busied herself at the stove. After some minutes, Fox silently handed McPhie the first letter, his face a maze of emotions.

U.S.Army
Base Hospital No. 5
France.

My Dear Mrs. Fox,

Although I am an entire stranger to you, I feel that I must write you a few lines because your husband, Sergt. Fox, was my patient and I was with him when he died. You will, long ere this, have had word from the War Office, and doubtless you will have received a letter from the Padre, who took charge of your husband's belongings to forward them to you.

I thought so often of you, in those few days your husband was in the ward: he had shown me the picture of you with your son and the other one of the little fellow on his own. 'That's why I am anxious to keep this arm,' he said.

He was quite a sick man from the time he reached us, but we did hope to see him pull through. His wound was in the shoulder and a very bad one. He was a bit delirious at times and was always back with his men, going over the fighting and trying to do something or other in the attack.

He was so cheerful and courteous, so nice to us all, and so appreciative of everything we did for him. I couldn't bear the thought that he had to go.

Wednesday, the day he died, I was with him a great deal of the time. Although he always said, 'No, no pain,' when I asked him, he was restless and uneasy but would quiet down and talk quite rationally if I stayed with him. He looked up once and smiled and said, 'Oh well, Sister, it's all right. God's in his heaven; all's right with the world.'

Sometimes he seemed to think he was going back home again, he said, 'I've done my last fighting.'

Towards the last he went to sleep and passed away very

quietly and peacefully. I told him I would write you, and he seemed to wish me to do so. I think it must mean a great deal to have a word direct from the one who was with him. The Padre said he was allowed to tell you where he is buried.

I have been there and can tell you what the cemetery is like: a slope down towards the sea, with big hills back of it and sand dunes and pine groves beside it. When I went there, a few weeks ago, it was a blaze of color — all the pretty, old-fashioned flowers in bloom — marigolds, nasturtiums, forget-me-nots, asters and many others. How many brave men are lying in just such little cemeteries in France today!

Please accept my very sincere sympathy in your sorrow: I'm glad to have known Sergt. Fox even for so short a time: certainly we see so few such gallant spirits as his. It brings a feeling of personal loss to have to say farewell to such a man.

Believe me, dear Mrs. Fox.

Very sincerely yours,

Rose N. Butler
Sister in Charge, Wd. A3)

Saturday, October sixth,
Nineteen seventeen.

McPhie too was powerfully moved and looked across to see Fox stoically reading another letter. Quietly, the Ansonia ticked. Even more quietly, Louisa filled the kettle and gently stoked the fire. McPhie was transported to another age, another land, courtesy of people he didn't know. He could scarcely begin to imagine how Fox was feeling about a grandfather he had only just discovered.

Again, Fox passed the letter to McPhie.

Head Quarters, Aus. Corps
B.E.F. France
Jan. 24th. 1918

Dear Mr. Fox,

I so fully enter into your feelings, which prompted you to write to me about your brave boy, in whose loss, I sympathise with you and his mother very deeply.

It is indeed sad that so much sacrifice has been made necessary by these Germans, and though I know there is nothing that can compensate you for the loss of your son, yet I trust it will afford you some consolation to know how gallantly he gave his life in the service of his country – which no man can do more.

Your boy took part with his battalion in the attack on Polygon Wood, on the ridges east of Ypres, in the early morning of 26th Sept. During the same evening, when your boy's company was in the support trenches, the enemy put down a heavy artillery barrage, preparatory to, and during their counter attack on the front line, causing considerable damage to our trenches.

It was particularly at this stage that your boy distinguished himself. Throughout the bombardment he moved about freely, regardless of all personal risk, and his courage and coolness under very trying conditions were invaluable in setting a fine example to his men. He rendered splendid service in reorganising the company, when the enemy counter attacked and failed, and displayed great initiative in leading his men forward to meet the enemy.

It was while doing this, that to my great regret he was wounded. His commanding officer informs me that he was very shocked to receive the news that his wounds had proved

*fatal, for though he appeared to be badly shaken, he was
as cheery when going down to the ambulance station, that
those who saw him were deceived as to the seriousness of his
condition.*

*Those who were with him cannot speak too highly of the
fine soldierly qualities he displayed during the critical time I
have mentioned, and I was so glad to have the opportunity
of awarding him the Military Medal which he so thoroughly
deserved for his good and gallant work. You may well be
proud of your boy, and believe me, I do feel for you both so
very much in your irreparable loss.*

*With kind regards
Yours sincerely*

*W.H.BIRDWOOD.
COLONEL, C.S.L, CLE., D.S.O.*

Gently, the kettle began to whisper – sibilant counterpoint to
the soft tick-ticking of the clock. Louisa had returned to the
table so quietly that neither man was aware of it. She rose to
make tea and Fox, his face damp, passed the third and final letter
to McPhie. A sensation of weightlessness and then, unstoppable
falling overwhelmed Fox. At the same time, he was mystified.
How could a man completely unknown to him from the other side
of the world evoke such powerful feelings? Yet even in turmoil,
he glimpsed shadows of his own likeness to this man. Clearly, the
bond of blood and genes traversed not only time and space, but
race and culture too. It was something he had never contemplated.

He faced Louisa and said thickly, 'Are you certain you want
to give me these? I mean, they've been in your family for so long.
They must be very special to you.'

'It is *because* they are special, Colin that I want you to have them. Your presence here today completes a chapter in my life that has been missing for such a long, long, time and I am grateful to be able to close it. We are your family too. My brother was a good man and he was your grandfather. I know he would want you to have them. You'll find his medals in there too. Now, what about a spot of lunch? It's well after midday and experiences like this are draining. Yes?'

They both nodded.

'Louisa, would you mind if I call me Mam?' asked McPhie. 'Fox here wants to take some fish back to her but I need to check first. Could I use your phone please?'

'Of course Lex. Through there, in the dining room.' She pointed the way.

As Louisa heated chicken broth and made fresh sandwiches, she and Fox chatted about their lives. After ten minutes or so, McPhie returned, his face like a thunderstorm.

'What's up?' enquired Fox.

'Heidi's arrived at Mam's and is making a fuss. I don't wish to be rude Louisa but I think we should leave straight away.'

'Whoa, whoa. Hang about. Why so quickly?' asked Fox. 'Surely we can eat our lunch.'

'Me Mam. She doesn't handle grief at all well. Heidi appears to be dishing it out in ocean loads.'

'Who's Heidi?' asked Louisa.

Fox smiled, an apologetic look on his face.

'A lady I'm seeing at the moment – Lord Ravenscroft's granddaughter. She's obviously come here from Cardiff. I told her I was busy this weekend and wouldn't be seeing her. Evidently there is some part of no she does not understand.'

Louisa's eyes creased with amusement at his remark. 'Well, that's a great shame. I was going to ask if you'd like to stay the night. Plenty of room. You could have met cousins you didn't know you had.'

'I'm really sorry about this Louisa, especially after the trouble you've taken. Perhaps I could come back before I go home, but really, I don't want to cause problems for Mrs McPhie.'

'Of course, I understand. At least take the sandwiches and eat them on the way. I'm sure we'll catch up again before you go home Colin.'

CHAPTER 25

The McPhie kitchen was crackling with tension when they walked in. Mrs McPhie sat frostily at one end of the table, Heidi at the other, pouting. Neither talking.

'Surprise, surprise Heidi,' said Fox pleasantly, 'I told you I was looking up my family this weekend. How come you're here?'

Heidi rose gracefully and blazed her perfect smile, first upon McPhie and then Fox. She ignored Mrs McPhie.

'How lovely to see you boys,' her low and sugary response, acid laced, ignored Fox's question. 'Please excuse Colin and me while we go for a walk.'

Mrs McPhie, clearly puzzled by Heidi's sudden change, gawped. Fox, glancing at McPhie, raised his eyebrows slightly and received a slow wink in return.

'Good idea Heidi, there's a lovely park not far from here. Let's take a stroll.' His face was unreadable, his voice neutral as he reached for Heidi's hand. She jerked away. Fox's eyes glinted as he nodded apologetically to Mrs. McPhie.

Outside, in the afternoon sunshine, Heidi turned to Fox.

'You bastard,' she spat. 'I told you I was coming yet you pissed off and left me in the lurch with that daft old biddy. Do you think you can treat me like some cheap tart from Soho?'

Fox leaned casually against the gate post and gazed at her coolly.

'How did you get here?'

'Borrowed grandfather's helicopter. Why?' she grated.

He studied her before responding. He saw a beautiful face scrunched with resentment, eyes like lasers, svelte body prickle-stiff with anger.

'Heidi, I told you what I was doing this weekend. I didn't invite you here. McPhie didn't invite you here. I didn't give you McPhie's address and if I recall correctly, you said something about coming up here for a shag. The only difference between you and a cheap tart from Soho is that you don't come from Soho. I am not your "toy-boy" nor am I at your beck and call simply because your grandfather is a Lord. Where I come from, that just means he's a shit in a bowtie. Do yourself a favour – get back on your broomstick and fly home.'

Transfixed, Heidi glared at him, vituperation rising like bile. Nobody spoke to her like that.

'You piece of shit. You have just made the biggest fucking mistake of your life Fox,' she snarled. She stalked past him to a shiny red Mini and, without a backward glance, got inside, slammed the door and roared down Buchanan Court towards Links Road.

Fox watched with mild disappointment. He had ended many relationships, always amicably, never in spite. He had often glimpsed Heidi's dark side during their tempestuous months together so a finale of this tenor was not surprising. With a sigh, he walked inside. They had enjoyed some wonderful times and he had seen and been to places beyond his imagining, places that would never have been open to him without Heidi's influence. And the audacious, rollicking sex! Certainly he would miss that.

McPhie met him at the door. 'What's happening?

'Gone back to Wales in her grandfather's chopper. Said I'd just made a huge mistake, or, to quote accurately, "the biggest fucking mistake of my life."'

'Why don't we wander down to the local for a wee natter.'

'Fine with me. What about your mum? She okay? I'm

really sorry about Heidi. I've seen her in "abuse mode" and she is seriously intimidating.'

'Aye, she's braw. She's not easily intimidated but she doesn't like being sworn at and abused. She said Heidi laid it on thick.'

Fox nodded thoughtfully. 'She's a chameleon is Heidi. Most of the time she's charming but man, she has one hell of a mean streak. Still, nothing between us was ever going to be permanent.'

'Better watch out then Fox.'

They went to *Harbour Bar* on the High Street – one of the town's old traditional pubs – and settled into a corner just off the main bar: McPhie with a heavy, Fox with a squash. A ricochet of chatter pummelled the room and provided the two men with a balloon of noisy privacy.

'Big day Fox. Heidi, Louisa. Especially Louisa. Powerful stuff. Not sure how I'd cope in your shoes.'

'I'm not sure about anything Lex. I mean, I always knew I had a white father and grandfather, but … it was another world, one I knew nothing about. It wasn't real to me. Dad died when I was so young and being raised at Turkey Creek I was, as I said earlier, a *Gija* boy. Regrettably, much of my early life was spent with people who tried – unsuccessfully – to convince me, and others like me, that I wasn't Aboriginal. Government people, church people and all kinds of "do-gooders". Now … here … in this place, in *this* history …' His voice trailed off as he sat reflecting for a few moments. 'After meeting Aunt Louisa today, a woman who is every bit as kind and gracious as my old mum, every bit as genuine as the members of my adopted white family in Perth, things *are* different. But how different, I don't yet know. One thing Lex – I'd appreciate you not telling the others what we talked about today. You know, my childhood and all that. Not even Davey. It's been hard putting all that crap behind me and Caroline Connors has been key to it. Today was special and it needed to be said, but otherwise, forget you ever heard it.'

'Sure. I can understand that, but when I see the man before me and how he conducts himself, shit Fox, you've abso-bloody-lutely nothing to be ashamed of. To the contrary, you've everything to be proud of.'

'It's not about shame Lex. It's about horror, degradation, loss and a battery of things. I don't like being reminded of all that stuff because none of it is good. Good things only started happening when I kicked Brother John onto his arse. From then on, life changed and later still, when I caught up with Caroline and her mob, good became wonderful. I'm here because of them.'

'I accept all that Fox but the real point is, you are here because of your own intrinsic qualities. I suspect that's what this Caroline sees. What I'm interested in is how you reconcile what you say is your Aboriginality with your white side. I'll say it Fox, and I don't mean to offend, but, you don't look like the pictures of Australian Aborigines I've seen.'

Fox grinned wryly. 'Yeah, I know. Genes I guess.'

'So, how do you feel aboot your white side?'

Fox stared silently into the middle distance, his eyes lustrous as molten pewter … fathomless. He was calm and still.

'I don't know. I really don't know. It's been white people who committed the worst injustices and abuses on so many Aboriginal people. Some of that harshness flows in my veins. On the other hand, through Caroline and her family, much of my life has been turned around for the better. Now, I'm not one who believes in accepting responsibility for the past sins of others. Things past matched standards of the time and no one can change that. Yet even today, huge improvements for indigenous people are desperately needed on so many fronts. What disconcerts me about today is the thought that probably I'm closer to the "inflictors" of some of those problems than I realised. I've never had reason to give it any thought before. I'm still trying to nut it out.'

After a period of silence he spoke again, his voice tinged with sadness. 'You heard only a fraction of my story today Lex, there's a much bigger one: the whole issue of white settlement and the idea that no one owned Australia before English occupation. A crap idea. Australia was occupied by Aboriginals for at least 40,000 years before 1788. White settlement brought poverty, massacres, land theft, abuse of power, poor education and appalling health care. The list goes on. Much of that still remains. The pain is not forgotten nor can it be ignored. I try to bury it. For me, achievement comes by accepting personal responsibility and setting goals. It doesn't come from sitting on your arse looking for hand-outs and whingeing about the past. But after today … I feel kinda bushwhacked.'

They sat quietly, the pub noise a companionable envelope around them. McPhie sucked slowly on his beer.

'Fox, I'm the first to admit I know bugger all aboot black and white Australian relationships. I know even less aboot most of the things you've mentioned. I think the *real* question is: who are you? I agree, you can't change history, you can't right the wrongs of others, but what you do have is something unique – a rich, proud and ancient indigenous culture with an equally fine Celtic background. You merely need to continue being who you are. The respect you've generated here has nothing to do with your origins, it comes from you, the man. Reading those letters and talking with Louisa has shown that you can be as proud of your white heritage as you are of your black. And what I see is a bloody fine mixture of both. My advice Fox is not to get too intellectual aboot it all. Just keep on being you.'

CHAPTER 26

Fox pounded along the old River Wye tow path towards Fiddler's Green. It was Saturday afternoon and he was running into a stiff westerly breeze in cool wintry sunlight. Christmas was approaching and the temperature hovered in the low fifties.

A solitary leisure run, this location evoked memories of home – sweet air, damp leaves, moist earth and the river's muddy tang. And birdsong. From song thrushes, Scandinavian wax wings, robins and wrens. Fox drank in the elegance and simplicity of nature's beauty.

A laughing young couple in a bright red canoe were trying valiantly to best the blustery wind and, as Fox had often seen them before, he waved as he passed. By mid-afternoon he was an hour and twenty minutes from home, time to turn back. Evening would settle by four o'clock and he would be arriving at the barracks in the dark.

Heidi Ravenscroft and her final words weighed heavily on his mind. He found himself frowning as he ran. He wondered if Heidi could be stalking him. On Thursday evening he got some scuttlebutt that her car had been seen several times outside the barracks at odd hours. He'd received phone calls but no one had spoken and recently some of his clothes had gone missing. He couldn't imagine what Heidi expected to gain from such behaviour although Maddie and Rebecca told Gordon and McPhie their Major was currently alternating between iciness and vindictiveness towards them. Thoroughly familiar with her moods, they said they had never seen her quite like this before.

Fox ran on swiftly through the dimming light and switched his focus to letters he'd received from Louisa following his Pittenweem visit. Each one was packed with detail about his grandfather or the larger Scottish family. He loved her writing and supposed, as befitted a teacher, that years of experience had refined her skills. She wrote with an old fashioned eloquence, economy and penetrating wit. Often he chuckled aloud at tales about the family's doings from years past. Clearly she had loved her brother deeply and remembered him with great tenderness. Again, he was moved when she sent him a long letter penned by his grandfather in 1915. He marvelled at how some things at home were seemingly changeless – drought, fluctuating agricultural prices, bickering between states and the simplicity of country life. So often had he read this particular letter he knew every word and nuance, could almost touch his grandfather's sense of country and love for the land. Parts of the letter flashed through his mind as he ran.

My Dear Father,

Love and greetings to you and Mother dear and my delightful Louisa for the New Year. On this first day of 1915, the weather is fine and clear and a lovely 79 degrees.

Well, we are glad to see the end of a black year with drought, wars and all sorts of black events happening. Food prices are rising culminating in bread at ten pence per large loaf. I was making good money at 10/- per day but living is taking nearly all and saving propensities seem awfully low ...

The River Murray has stopped flowing here as damming is occurring up at Mildura, Nyah, Cullawah, Wentworth, Merbein and stopping at Renmark ...

1914 saw the opening of a railway line to Paringa which saved Renmark a lot on account of the cartage fee from Morgan ... £8:00 per ton in 1913. Boats are still running from the wharf to Paringa rail station however ...

... the wheat market is 5/3 a bushel in New South Wales and 6/1 in Victoria and the different States are squabbling about exporting their own wheat and axing the importation of wheat from other States. The NSW government (Labor) are bringing in a bill for compulsory buying of wheat at 5/4 for Sydney and 5/- in the country. Farmers are kicking as they are the only ones who have any wheat. At the same time, the NSW government is trying its best to get them to put as much land under wheat as they can ...

... currant crops have set badly and rain has cracked more. Ours were not hurt either way which we put down to cultivation. Other people's gordos, especially in the high ground, have set badly with some even going as far as cincturing them on spec. of their setting; but it was no good ...

... we are both very happy here together and, as you can see, there are many things to do and a busy season coming up. We hope that your year is prosperous and send our love to you Father, Mother and Little Louisa.

Your loving son,

Colin.

And then there was the McNulty clan, his most loved friends on earth. According to Caroline's last letter, most of them were moving into transit mode. On Boxing Day, John was commencing a three month stint at Beijing's Jishuitan Hospital teaching the latest methods for treating and managing burns, Jennifer and Kurt were off to Nepal and Jason, after finishing his honours year at university, was moving east to Sydney in the first week of January. Caroline and Judy would be home by themselves for several weeks.

That situation bothered Fox. He still had not been able to shake the feeling of misfortune pooling around the family. He and Caroline had had several phone conversations about it and each time their discussion ended the same way: he was vague about an unspecified threat, she was adamant they were alert to anything untoward. Nothing unusual had happened since Lucy dog was killed in September, Caroline had said.

Less than a mile from home Fox slowed to a jog, then an easy walk to cool down. Entering the complex he strolled past the security gatehouse and was stopped by an MP's restraining hand.

'Corporal Fox.'

'Yes Sergeant, what can I do for you?'

'I must advise you Corporal that I am placing you under arrest for rape. Please come with me and don't make a fuss.'

Fox twigged three more MPs emerging from the shadows to flank him.

'I haven't got a clue what you're on about but I haven't raped anybody. Can we talk about this?' Fox was nonplussed.

'Yes Corporal, at a formal interview. In the meantime, keep your mouth shut.' The Sergeant's tone was not unfriendly and Fox interpreted his comment as advice rather than insult. For all he knew, this was another training test. He remained silent.

CHAPTER 27

'Right Fox, where's your room?'

'Has the Officer Commanding been informed of this allegation?' parried Fox.

'Can't say at this stage. My instructions are to search your room and then take you to Campion Lines at Bulford. The Special Investigation Branch want to talk to you. I doubt that could happen without your OC's knowledge.'

'And who am I supposed to have raped?'

'All in good time Fox. Let's get to your room.'

Fox knew, even as he asked the question, that Heidi was involved. Knowing how vindictive she could be, and her influence, he was instantly watchful.

'For the record,' said Fox coolly, 'I want you to inform Colonel Chartres of your accusations about me and confirm with me when he has informed Major John Hoey back in Australia. For the record, I am here for special training, I am not one of yours. By the way, I didn't catch your name.'

'Dickins, Royal Military Police. That's all you need to know.'

Fox and the four MPs moved off to the dormitory wing. No sooner were they out of sight than the gatehouse Corporal rang McPhie.

'Lex, Josh Cardin here at the gatehouse. Four MPs just arrested your mate Fox. I heard the Sergeant say it was rape. They're all goin' up to the dorms to search the joint.'

'Fuck,' said McPhie savagely, 'it'll be that bitch Ravenscroft. I'll get Gordon. Would you give Ropey the heads up too? Thanks Josh.'

'Right,' said Dickins when they arrived at Fox's room, 'stay out here with Rankin while we search. If we want you, we'll call.'

'Sorry mate,' said Fox evenly, 'doesn't work like that. I'm entitled to be in my room while you search. Remember, you asked me not to make a fuss? I haven't and I won't, provided you follow correct procedure. Fuck me around and I'll break Rankin's arms and legs quicker than you can say your name.'

Fox was perfectly still, perfectly balanced, arms loose at his sides. His arctic stare jarred with his mild tone and Dickins sensed serious menace. As he weighed the odds Dickins knew that even though he had the numbers, if push came to shove, procedurally, he'd be up shit creek.

'Ok. Stand in here and don't move.' Dickins and two corporals entered Fox's room. Rankin remained outside watching Fox who leaned casually against the door jamb in his room.

The small space which had been spartan before Fox moved in now bordered on sterile. Dickins started with the narrow clothing locker and flicked through the hanging garments. He took nothing. He looked in the shoe compartment at the base of the locker and removed a pair of worn and mud spattered runners. Next he searched a small dresser, scrupulously examining the neatly stacked underwear and T-shirts. He removed a green and gold T-shirt with a bold white outline of Australia on the back.

'Where's your other track suit Fox, the pale blue one?'

'Don't answer that,' roared Ropey, breathless after thundering down the hallway like a Pamplona bull. 'Sergeant, have you cautioned this man?

'No sir.'

'Why not?'

'Because we haven't charged him with anything at this stage,' Dickins replied.

'I understand he's under arrest. He should have been cautioned. Why have you arrested him? ' said Ropey acidly.

'Orders from SIB sir. We know his reputation. If he cocks up under arrest, he makes life more difficult for himself.'

'What? Practising entrapment are you? Listen sonny, I'm not as green as I am cabbage looking. I don't know where you did your training, but that is a crap response. If you haven't got an arrest warrant you'd better start again.'

Fox watched the interchange with mild amusement.

'I'll ask you again Sergeant. Who am I supposed to have raped?' Fox enquired

'Major Ravenscroft,' Dickins responded tightly, resenting Ropey's presence.

'Sir,' said Fox turning to Ropey, 'I have absolutely nothing to fear from that quarter. I am prepared to comply with whatever these blokes want. Ravenscroft has been out of my life for some time now and I've not seen her since McPhie and I were in Scotland several weeks ago.'

'Are you sure Fox?'

'Quite sir. But, I would like Major Hoey informed of this.'

'Okay Dickins. You heard what Fox said. Conduct your search but show me your arrest and search warrant.'

'I don't have it with me sir, but it exists.'

'Poor form Dickins. Expect a kick in the arse when you get back to base. In the meantime, Fox will accompany you … voluntarily. He is not under arrest. Clear?'

'Sir,' said Dickins uncomfortably.

'Fox this had better be bullshit. Neither Chartres nor Hoey are going to be impressed,' Ropey barked.

'Sir, I appreciate your support. I assure you, this is "A" grade bullshit.'

Gordon and McPhie bustled up throwing murderous looks at the MPs.

'Ok Fox?' asked Gordon.

He nodded.

'Ravenscroft?' enquired McPhie.

'Yeah. Haven't seen her since Pittenweem.'

'What's the story then?' queried Gordon staring bleakly at the tight-lipped Dickins.

'Don't know. They allege I raped Heidi,' responded Fox.

Gordon coughed.

Fox threw him a warning glance.

'I know Fox, I know,' said Gordon quietly, 'but Maddie's told me a few things. Women find out stuff.'

Ropey listened quietly. He was aware that Fox had been seeing Ravenscroft but, not one for gossip, was ignorant of her reputation. On the other hand, he believed he knew Fox well, he was not an attacker of women.

'Fox, I'm off. I'll make sure the CO knows what's going on. If you need anything, holler.'

'Thank you sir. I will.'

'So what happens now?' asked McPhie.

'Have to see the Special Investigation Branch at some joint called Bulford,' replied Fox.

'Shit, that's right on Ravenscroft's bloody doorstep,' said Gordon. 'I don't like it.'

Fox grinned. 'Nothing better than stepping into enemy territory.'

'Fox!' called Dickins harshly. 'This is no joke. Where's your sky blue track suit?'

'I pitched it. I got this new one I'm wearing. The other one wore out.'

'Bullshit. Where are the red and black runners you were using?'

'Pitched them too. Got these new English ones,' he said, lifting his right foot.

'Too convenient for my liking Fox. I don't like coincidences.'

'What are you suggesting? That I knew you were coming and ditched them? Wake up to yourself. Do you have any idea how many miles a week we run? They were worn out, I replaced them.'

'Yeah. Well I smell a rat Fox and it closely resembles you.'

'Would you rather I told you the truth and said that some unknown person stole my things from my room? How does that look for coincidence?'

'Ok lads. Corporal Fox here seems to have disposed of the evidence. We'll see how clever he is when he gets to Bulford. Pack your toothbrush Fox, you won't be back tonight.'

McPhie and Gordon looked at each other. 'You know how to reach us if shit happens,' said McPhie, 'don't hesitate.'

Fox nodded. 'I do, but I'll be ok.'

CHAPTER 28

At Bulford they went straight to the Duty Officer's room. There, Captain David Fanshaw introduced himself. A slender man of medium height and clipped fair hair, he wore rimless glasses with gold coloured arms. His uniform was immaculate – trousers creased sharply enough to cut a finger. To Fox he seemed a mirthless and studious man.

'Ah Fox. I've had a call from Captain Arbuthnott. Sorry about the confusion. Everything will be clear shortly. Cup of tea?' His voice seemed to issue as much from his nose as his mouth and arrived in high, exaggerated syllables. Except he was for real, Fanshaw, to Fox, could have stepped from a PG Wodehouse novel.

'No thanks. What do you mean: "everything will be clear shortly?" Either you are or you aren't investigating me for rape. If you're not, take me back to Hereford.'

'Not so simple Fox. The police are involved and they'll be taking over.'

'What do you mean? Your men said this was an army problem, specifically one for SIB. What's going on?'

'All in good time Fox.'

'On what authority are you holding me here? Show me your warrant.'

'Don't need one Fox. I can hold you for assaulting a senior army officer while I conduct the investigation. That's what I'm doing. Sit tight and wait.'

Fanshaw walked from the office to leave Dickins with Fox. Neither spoke. Fifteen minutes later Fanshaw returned with a ranking, uniformed police officer and a man in plain clothes.

'This is Superintendent Cyril Early and Detective Inspector Jonas Lyons. You'll be going with them Fox.'

'Going where?'

'Colin Fox,' said Lyons, 'I'm arresting you for the unlawful assault and sexual penetration of one Heidi Ravenscroft on Saturday the ninth of December, 1985. You do not have to say anything in answer to the charge but whatever you do say may be taken down in writing and used in evidence. Do you understand that? I am now executing this arrest warrant upon you for that and other offences. Do you have anything to say?'

'No, but I have a question. How come you guys are taking over? I thought this was an army investigation.'

'The SIB has assisted us with our enquiries,' Early responded. 'We've been investigating an ugly criminal assault on the Wye River tow path about five miles east of Hereford. That's not army land, which makes these offences civil matters. We are the investigating authority. It just happens the case involves army personnel. That's neither here nor there as far as we're concerned.' His tone brooked no contradiction.

'And how come wonder boy Dickins here couldn't tell me that?'

'Because I instructed him not to,' responded Fanshaw.

'And why was that?'

'Because Fox,' said Early acidly, 'this is a sensitive matter involving important people and I wanted the matter handled with discretion.'

Fox studied Early in silence. A tall, cadaverous looking man with prominent front teeth and a receding chin, his pink skull shone through thin, grey hair. A clipped moustache lent no strength to weak features.

'This is all bullshit. What you are really saying Early is that Lord Ravenscroft leaned on you and now you're so far up his arse your shoe laces can barely be seen.' Fox's insolence conveyed his anger. Lyons smirked.

'You're distasteful remarks do not enhance your position. Our evidence is overwhelming. I suggest you own up to it and let us get on with it.' Early looked and sounded pompous.

Fox was furious. He knew this was a set up. The one thing of which he was certain was that Heidi, and possibly her family, had contrived this situation. His guess was they were colluding with this weedy prick to make it happen. Suddenly, her words reverberated in his ears: *"You have just made the biggest fucking mistake of your life Fox."*

'Cuff him Lyons. Tight. And get that smirk off your face,' growled Early.

'Just a minute,' interrupted Fanshaw. 'Fox came here voluntarily. He has been co-operative from the jump. I don't think cuffs are necessary.'

Early glanced at Fanshaw icily, the trace of a smile on his lips.

'My responsibility Captain Fanshaw, my call. Cuff him Lyons.'

Fox stuck his arms towards Lyons, looked at Early and laughed.

'I bet you don't walk down dark lanes at night Early. You probably even jump at your own shadow.'

Lyons clicked the handcuffs shut, adjusted them so they wouldn't pinch and discreetly winked at Fox.

'Captain Fanshaw, one last thing,' said Fox, 'Captain Arbuthnott appears not to know the police are involved. Please inform him of this development.'

Fanshaw said nothing as Fox was taken from the room.

CHAPTER 29

In the last week before Christmas he had been watching McNulty's closely. Their busy home was more active than usual. He was curious. Something was brewing and he didn't want to miss it.

And then, on Christmas eve, around lunch-time, some sort of bad news arrived. The women were weeping and he could see the men were sombre. It was both fascinating and frustrating as he had no way of discovering the source of their unhappiness.

Not like when he killed their fuckin' dog. Their behaviour then was the same. And he knew the reason for it. *Shit, that had been a good day.* He wondered if he should feel pleased with their present misfortune.

Then, quite late in the afternoon, he saw a slim, commanding and well dressed man arrive in an army car. This event resulted in the women crying even more, especially the youngest. On speck he wondered if it had anything to do with that black prick, Midnight. He hadn't seen the bastard for months and knew he was overseas. *P'raps the fucker is dead. Christ, wouldn't that be good.*

Yeah … that's it. Fuckin' Midnight's dead. Halle-fuckin'-luja. What a stroke of luck. Not that Midnight could have prevented his plans for Bitchface. His plans! Soon he would be home free. No one would suspect him and by the time the deed was done he'd be long gone. It was close.

CHAPTER 30

After Hoey's departure they sat glumly around the kitchen table. Fox in custody on a charge of rape! None of them believed it. Caroline especially knew that such an act was inimical to Fox's personality.

She had known from the absence of a Christmas card or letter that something was amiss. Institutional life had made Christmas very special to Fox and he loved to celebrate and spoil their kids. The silence was so unlike him.

And then, the terrible midday phone call. A Major Hoey wanted to visit and talk about Fox. On the phone he was polite but circumspect and refused to be drawn into details. The girls quickly concluded that Fox had either been killed or seriously injured. And their distress triggered tears from Caroline.

With Hoey's arrival, the bombshell. Rape!

They had all clamoured as one in their defence of Fox. Hoey attempted to placate them and make clear that neither he nor his English counterpart believed Fox guilty of the crime. The police, on the other hand, maintained they had a water-tight case. As a result, Fox was in prison, a hearing was set for early in the new year and bail had been refused because he was regarded as a flight risk. Neither army monitoring nor passport confiscation was consdered strong enough to anchor Fox in the UK.

Caroline pressed Hoey for details but he apologised and said that he and his English counterpart had little information. All his Hereford shadow could say was that Fox's conduct had been exemplary – the police were simply not talking.

While they took heart from Hoey's belief in Fox, it altered nothing. Christmas day was tomorrow and three of the family would soon be leaving home. Fox's predicament chilled all thoughts of celebration. The only upside was how much this news reinforced Fox's place in their family. They had to support him.

It was Judy who hit on a solution.

'Mum,' she said thoughtfully, 'why don't you and I go to England? Everyone else will be away, I've got school hols and you've got six weeks leave. I think we should get over there. Quick smart.'

'What a fantastic idea, Jude,' responded her father. He paused before continuing, 'it'll be tricky though getting a flight to the UK just now. But why not? We should have a go. I suspect the reason we've not heard from Fox himself is prison rules. But ... if you guys turn up fresh from Oz to see him, they'd hardly be likely to say no. Let's give it a crack. I'll check for flights.'

They all nodded and felt some gloom lift. They were doing something.

'John,' said Caroline quietly, 'when you've finished on the phone I think I'll try contacting the Australian Embassy in London. I want to know if I can learn more about this because what we've got so far is not good enough.'

'Sure.'

Twenty minutes later McNulty emerged from his study smiling.

'I've managed to get you both on a Qantas flight leaving Perth at 5:30 am for Sydney direct on Saturday January 4. The same day you continue on to Heathrow and leave at 3:50 pm. Compassionate grounds! Your flight home is booked for Saturday February 8. You'll have to take a little extra leave though Caro. And ... ta daa ... business class both ways. How's that?'

Caroline and Judy hugged him.

'I always knew you had magic powers Dad,' said Judy, 'now you've just proved you're a wizard.'

Caroline smiled gently as she walked into the study and shut the door. She didn't want to be distracted.

'Good Morning. Australian Embassy London, Kate Fischer speaking.'

'Hello Kate. This is Senior Sergeant Caroline Connors from Perth calling. I want to make some enquiries about a Colin Fox. He's in the UK on SAS training and I've learned this afternoon that he's been remanded in custody somewhere in Cardiff on a charge of rape. Can you tell me anything about this or put me through to someone who can please?'

'May I ask the nature of your interest? Is he connected to similar matters in Australia?'

'Good heavens no! He's like a son to us. I've known him since he was ten years old.' *Not quite true*, thought Caroline as she said it, but close enough. She wasn't in a mood to care, she wanted to discover what the hell was going on.

'It's just that being Christmas,' she continued. 'we can't find out anything. My daughter and I have just booked a flight to London on January 4. We know so little about the case or where he is and we want to see him.'

'Yes, of course. Things are closing down here for the Christmas break too, just like home, but I'll see what I can do. I'll put you through to Spencer Johnson, he generally handles matters like this. Just a moment.'

After a couple of clicks a loud cheery voice boomed in Caroline's ear.

'Spencer Johnson, how can I help?'

Caroline explained who she was and the situation as she understood it. Johnson listened.

'Senior Sergeant eh. Where are you stationed?'

'Freo,' said Caroline, wishing he'd just get on with it.

'Know it well. Many happy memories of the place. Well, as it happens, I know this Fox. Met him earlier this year in London. Haven't got much on him and I haven't seen him yet. I only got advice about his case yesterday although I see the arrest was ten days ago – a bit sloppy. Knew it was him straight away. There aren't too many Aboriginal Fox's here on SAS training. What's your interest?'

Caroline was uncertain of how much to tell Johnson and decided to play safe.

'I've known him since he was a boy of ten,' she said. 'Both his parents and little sister are dead and, to us, and our children, he's one of our family.'

'Yeah … I remember him well,' said Johnson reflectively. 'Quiet bloke.'

'Spot on,' said Caroline softly. 'What can you tell me?'

'Not much. The pommy coppers seem to be treating it with kid gloves. Everything is hush hush. Outward and inward communication is deeply muffled and so far, it's been impossible to penetrate the bullshit. But … the guts of it seems to be that he's charged with raping an army major named Heidi Ravenscroft.'

'That's utter crap,' Caroline replied, bristling. 'They used to be an item. I think he said she was some Lord's granddaughter or something.'

'Ah,' retorted Johnson knowingly, 'old aristocracy protecting itself perhaps? What would you like me to do?'

'Saturday week my daughter and I are flying to London. If you could tell us where he is, how to get there and suggest somewhere decent to stay, that would be really helpful.'

'He's tucked away in the Knox Road remand centre in Cardiff, a centre for local males. We can find some good digs down there for you, no worries. What's your flight number? Are you on Qantas?'

'Yes. Not sure of the flight number but it leaves Sydney mid-afternoon.'

'Okay. We've got all the tick-tack here for arrivals so I'll meet you when you come out of customs. Look for a sign with Connors on it. I'm happy to get you down to Cardiff straight away but you might want to stay in London and catch a few hours sleep. You land here pretty early in the morning and probably you'll be rat-shit.'

'You're a gem. But look, if it's alright with you, I'd like to shoot straight down to Cardiff and find out what we have to do to see Colin.'

'Ok Caroline. I'll set things up and see if I can learn more about the case in the meantime. Let's have your phone number, home and work, in case something develops. If I learn anything important I'll let you know.'

CHAPTER 31

In Her Majesty's Prison Remand Centre at Cardiff, Fox was encountering near isolation. No visitors, no phone calls and practically no letters – only two encouraging cards from Maddie and Rebecca, McPhie and Gordon. And although he did mix with other prisoners, he had less yard time than anybody else. Depressing, bleak and powerful memories of Mount Barker surged like a phoenix. Without wanting to seem paranoid, Fox believed his circumstances reflected the influence of the Ravenscrofts.

He was confident Heidi would be exposed. He had never assaulted her – belting women was taboo. The most influential people in his life had been women: Lucy, Rosie and Caroline Connors. Most recently, Louisa, his great Aunt. All these women had, one way or another, exerted positive and powerful influences upon his life.

Christmas had come and gone and Fox knew John McNulty would be in China. Whether the family, or Hoey, knew of his circumstances was uncertain. Thus far, there had been no evidence of Australian Government action so he had to assume Hoey was ignorant of his situation. And that *was* frustrating. The thought of Hoey being in the dark did not fit with his understanding of Hereford's culture. Someone surely would have contacted him. There had to be protocols for cases like his.

As in the granary years before, Fox honed his fitness. The

vague threat he had glimpsed hanging around Caroline for so long was taking a harder edge, though it still remained formless. He saw it as a tentacled black mist oozing from units near the McNulty home. Somebody wished Caroline deadly harm and Fox, pressed by a sense of urgency, was powerless.

Locked up, a black offender charged with rape, segregated, little rapport with other prisoners and no prospect of communication with prison staff, his impotence was maddening. The *only* thing he could do was will a warning to Caroline and Judy and hope they were receptive.

On this morning he was peremptorily marched from a rare period in the exercise yard to an office within the prison labyrinth. There had been no warning about what was to happen. On being ushered into the room, he was stunned to see Spencer Johnson.

'G'day Fox,' grinned Johnson, 'not as salubrious as the Naval College eh?' He stuck out a huge paw then gestured to a chair opposite. 'I've got an hour only and quite some ground to cover. Excuse me mate,' said Johnson when the warder positioned himself by the door, 'this is private. Outside if you don't mind.' He jerked his thumb at the door.

'Guv'nor's instructions, sir,' said the warder.

'Is that right?' Johnson rose, pulled some documents from a folder on the table before him and took them to the warder. Fox, who had not yet uttered a word, was curious.

'Now listen mate,' said Johnson reasonably, 'I know you're only doing as you're told, but read this document of agreement between your Home Secretary, who's in charge of prisons, and my government. You'll see that in international matters involving Embassy staff and people in custody that I, as the Embassy representative, shall have *private* discussions with the incarcerated. Private excludes you earwigging. Scarper back to your Governor and check it out.' He handed the document to the warder and waited while he read it then said, 'Any part of that unclear to you?'

'No sir.'

'Right, you can leave now because this is eating up my time.'

'Sorry sir, the Guv'nor says to stay.'

Johnson's demeanour changed instantly – he looked murderous. Fox smiled. He liked this bloke. Johnson towered over the warder, reached over his shoulder and hit the panic button, all the time muttering and glaring at the man who was beginning to look worried. Within minutes two warders burst into the room, batons and capsicum spray at the ready.

Johnson lashed them with a flinty stare.

'Get your Governor down here now or his arse will be superannuated faster than you can say bullshit,' he growled.

They both looked at the escorting warder and said in unison, 'What's going on?'

'This character,' said the man, 'says he's from the Australian Embassy and wants to talk to the prisoner in private but the Guv'nor said I was to stay here.' The escort glared at Johnson. 'He doesn't like it. He showed me some paper what says he can do it, but the Guv'nor said stay.'

The older of the two newcomers looked at Fox then at the bear-like and wrathful Johnson.

'The Embassy rep is right,' he said, 'step outside and leave 'em be. I'll deal with the Governor … if that's necessary.'

'Time starts now,' Johnson barked as they departed. 'You've just chewed up ten of my minutes.' He returned to the table and sat, a warm smile on his face.

'Impressive,' said Fox.

'Mate, you've no idea the flak I've had to run to see you. You've got some serious bloody enemies. When I eventually got to the Governor he basically told me to go play in the traffic. I had to threaten him with an "international incident" that would show his face and intransigence on the front page of every major newspaper in the UK and Australia before he caved in. Finally, he got it – he would be number one scapegoat. He was not a happy chappy. That little episode evidently was his last card. Now, first things first. Caroline Connors and her daughter Judy are flying out tomorrow to see you. I would have been down here eventually, but at this point, I'm here because she rang the Embassy yesterday. She says you've been hard done by. After what I've encountered today, I agree. Since she phoned I've discovered that, for whatever reason, you have the Establishment on your back. They are quietly pulling strings to ensure you go down for rape. In this country, that's an average of five to seven years with a maximum of life.'

'Wait up,' interrupted Fox, 'can you get a message directly to Caroline?'

'Of course, I've got her home and work phone numbers.'

'Thank Christ!' Fox was focussed, his tone urgent. 'I won't go into detail but trust me on what I am about to say. Caroline and I have talked of this over recent weeks. I am certain there is an imminent threat to her life from someone very near to them. I know it sounds weird, but believe me, I have never been more serious.'

'Are you for real?' Johnson sat back in his chair and studied Fox sceptically. 'Are you clairvoyant or what?'

Composed, Fox eyeballed Johnson with an unflinching stare.

'Trust me,' he said quietly, 'I am telling you – this threat is real. I need you to tell Caroline and Judy to move out of their house until they leave. At the moment, that's all I can tell you but you must promise me you'll do it.'

Johnson was perplexed. Fox appeared genuine and Connors spoke of him with enormous affection and respect. Hereford said he was an outstanding warrior and yet here was a bullshit request out of thin air. In the end, Fox's earnestness convinced him.

'Okay, I'll do it as soon as I get back to London.'

Relieved, Fox nodded. At last, direct communication to

Caroline. He held up a finger and his eyes bored into Johnson. 'Thank you, but I must know they have moved out.'

Johnson returned Fox's gaze. 'I'll make sure you are told. Now, let's cut to the chase: did you rape Heidi Ravenscroft?' Johnson was business-like.

'No. I ditched her. She didn't get her own way. That's what this is about. Heidi is fun loving and intelligent but she is also spoilt and has a streak of malice.' Fox shrugged and raised his palms upwards as if to say, this is what happens if you don't play by *her* rules.

'Figured as much. Tell me about Ravenscroft. And don't give me any "that's private" crap. Caroline told me what you're like. Get this into your skull very bloody clearly: you are fighting for your liberty here. You are dealing with a medical doctor who's alleging rape. She *knows* how to make that stick evidentially. She belongs to the entrenched aristocracy of this country, she has powerful parents and on top of that, her grandfather has pull from here to Melbourne. So let's be clear about what's going down here: they want you buried lad. Got that?'

Fox stared at Johnson for what seemed an eternity, puzzlement, pain and sadness etched upon his face. If Caroline had spoken so bluntly to Johnson, it was for his own good.

'Alright,' he said resignedly, 'no bullshit.'

'Good. Now tell me what sort of person she is. How she thinks, how she behaves, how she analyses things, what her life philosophy is.'

Fox cornered his thoughts before responding.

'As you already know, she's well educated but she's also streetwise. Her "crowd" clubs, drinks and does drugs on a big scale. A few of them have come unstuck with the law and she's learned a lot about the shifty side of life because of that, so yeah … rat cunning. Big ego, loves compliments and adoration. Thrives on it. Spats often with her mother but is the apple of her father's eye. To be honest, I couldn't quite work her out. She kind of goes through the motions but I never felt any genuine warmth from her. For instance, we had lots of sex, I mean, seriously, lots of sex. And yes, the sex was pleasurable, but there was no real affection, no intimacy – just lust. I don't know if Heidi ever thought about that. She often wanted to do it in places that were on the edge; more than risqué, NQR. Believe me, the most important person in Heidi's life is Heidi. Her sharp and caustic tongue can be unleashed in a flash and although it was never directed at me, until the very end, I've heard her speak to her staff and her mother in ways that would fracture an iceberg.'

Johnson's pen raced over the pages. He paused and looked up. 'Would you say she's a narcissist?'

'Yes,' Fox replied thoughtfully, he paused, 'yes I would. She has a huge sense of self importance. And, she's a bloody good chameleon. Mind you, not all these qualities are initially apparent – it took me a long time to discover them. For instance, if she walked in here right now you would be gob-smacked. You would see an attractive, bright, engaging woman – a cracking good sort. And most of the time she is absolutely all of those things. But there's an under-side that's cold, calculating, distant, and ruthless. To be honest with you Johnson, I think it was this aspect that began to change my feelings about her because even before she chased me up to Scotland, I was planning to end the relationship. Apart from that, I was going home soon.'

'Yeah, well at the minute that's a definite maybe.' Johnson grinned raggedly. He paused. 'Why do you think she made this allegation of rape?'

'Anger, revenge, a desire to hurt. Spite. I can't imagine she's used to being dumped, that would mean a loss of control and big loss of face. She would hate that.'

'Let's talk technical. There are several ingredients to the offence of rape and I want to briefly run over them. First there must be the *acteus reus,* the wrongful act which constitutes the crime. This means tangible physical actions or omissions – not just bad thoughts. Bad thoughts however, combined with bad or wrongful acts will constitute a crime. So, in a charge of rape, the lack of consent is crucial. Consent must be actual, not necessarily spoken but, by willing and compliant actions, granted. Clear?'

'Perfectly,' said Fox nodding.

'Consent cannot be implied or "apparent", such as consent in response to actual or threatened violence. Sex with someone who is drunk, drugged or asleep can never be consensual. And consent can't be obtained by fraud or impersonation. For instance, if you were the husband's twin and the wife thought she was having intercourse with her husband. Consent must always be freely and voluntarily given. In short, if force, fear or fraud is involved it is rape.'

Fox nodded again. 'I've always understood that. In this case, there was no consent because there was no sex at the time she is alleging.'

'Let's move on,' said Johnson after scratching more notes. 'The prosecution has to prove both the sex and the intention of having it. Did they question you about that?'

'They did. They also told me I did it and said the injuries I inflicted on Heidi proved both intent and lack of consent. And, I am telling you I would never hurt a woman. Caroline will tell you, I saved her from certain rape. I killed a man who was raping my baby sister when I was only ten. I do not harm women! There was no rape and no injuries were ever inflicted upon Heidi by me.'

Johnson was astonished by these revelations and thought they might provide solid character evidence. He said nothing but instead quietly asked, 'Did you tell Heidi about these incidents?'

'Of course not,' said Fox.

'Are you implying that somebody else raped Heidi?'

'Who knows? She's a forceful pursuer of sex, a predator even, and as I said, she likes it in ways and places that are dangerous and exciting. And to be candid, it was just that with her, dangerous and exciting. I wouldn't be surprised if something went too far with someone else and later she decided to use whatever it was to thump me.'

'Okay, change of subject. I've tried talking to the police at Cwmbran but it was like pulling bloody teeth. No help. All I heard was they have a fool-proof case. They wouldn't tell me who the investigator was, where the offence occurred, when, or exactly what happened. But of course, if rape did not occur, I can understand their reluctance. Oh, another thing, Cwmbran, as the crow flies, is just down the track from Kilmore Castle.'

Fox nodded, immediately grasping the implications.

'Interestingly, a day or so after I'd been throwing my weight around, I discovered a short message on my answering machine from a detective called Lyons. He suggested I check the relationship between Early and Lord Ravenscroft. Know anything about that Fox?'

'Nope. I'd never heard of Early until they took me to Bulford. I remember Lyons though. My impression was that Early gave him the shits.'

'I haven't had time to check Lyons suggestion yet but it's worth following up. So … give me some history.'

Fox began by telling Johnson when and how he met Heidi, what they did and how often they met. He outlined the unpleasant scene at Pittenweem and her very specific threat. He mentioned his lack of direct contact with her after Pittenweem but explained how he had seen her on some of his Saturday runs. There had also been a "heads-up" from the Hereford security blokes about sighting her at odd times of the day and night, not because they knew the pair were no longer an "item" but because they believed the contrary.

Johnson listened without interruption and scrawled rapidly.

'Let's take the day in question Fox, December 9. What do you remember?'

'I've had a lot of time to think about that since I've been here. In the morning, Davey Gordon and I swam together between nine and ten o'clock, I did my washing, cleaned my kit and wrote home. About midday, Lex McPhie dropped in and asked me to join him and Davey with the girls for a pub dinner and movies that night. I agreed.'

'The girls? Who are they?'

'Rebecca Baine and Heather Maddox – Maddie. They knock about with McPhie and Gordon. They're nurses in Heidi's Medical Unit at Cardiff.'

'Go on.'

'We all teamed up not long after I got to the UK and I regard them as friends. Anyway, in the afternoon I went for a run along the old tow path beside the Wye River. I generally travel about an hour and a half to two hours out, turn around and come back.'

'Do you always use the same route?'

'No, I alternate. East one week, west the next. On that Saturday I went east.'

'How do you know? The cross examining barrister will claim you're lying, that you are confused between east and west or anything else he can invent. What confirms you ran east?'

Fox ruminated. 'Occasionally I've seen a young couple on the river in a red canoe. We wave to each other, exchange words about the weather and a couple of times we've chatted as they paddled and I jogged. They are only ever on the east side … and they're foreigners. That day was unusual because even though it is winter, the sun was shining, the air was like ice but everything was sparkling. I saw the canoe couple and remember they were having trouble with their boat in the wind. I waved to them and they waved back.'

'Do you know their names?'

'No.'

Do you know where they come from?'

'No.'

'When you say they are foreigners, what do you mean?'

'They have accents. I'm not sure but I think they could be French.'

'Do you know what time you saw them?'

'Not with any certainty. Roughly about forty-five to fifty minutes after I started, so, around 2:15 pm. To be safe say between 2:15 and 2:30 pm. But generally I see them around about the same stretch of river.'

'Anything prominent to mark the spot? A bridge, a tree, a ford, a cottage? Something like that?'

'Well there's an old elm just to the north of the tow path. One of the boughs has taken a lightning strike. The branch stump is charred. Looks to me like it occurred years ago but it's distinctive because it makes the tree look unbalanced.'

'Can you drive there?'

'Not to that spot, no, but about a half mile further east there's an old pub called the *White Duck* – it's on the water's edge. You can drive there and get onto the tow path.'

'How often would you see these people?'

'Hard to say, just intermittently. Possibly every five to six weeks.'

'Have you told any one about them?'

'No-one. I hadn't even thought of them until you asked the question.'

'What were you wearing that day?'

'Pale blue track pants and my green and gold Aussie top.'

Here was something, thought Johnson. The copper he'd spoken to mentioned Fox disposed of clothing after the attack.

'Any reason for the clothing mix? I mean, aren't you blokes kitted up to be uniform?' asked Johnson frowning.

'Yeah, we are. But I don't run in that clobber at the weekends unless it's official. My own track suit was old. I love pale blue and often wore the blue top to relax in. It wore out so I kept the bottoms for running in and wore my gold top. But then the duds went missing from my room and I bought a new track suit in Hereford.'

'When did you get the new togs?' Johnson's frown deepened.

Fox reflected. 'The top would have gone mid to late October and the pants only a couple of weeks ago. I might still have the receipt from the sports store in Hereford. I bought new runners there too.'

'Did you report the fact that the track suit pants went missing?'

'No. I really didn't worry about it because they were pretty clapped out. Now though, I can see that a different connotation could be placed upon their disappearance.'

'Ok, just so I am sure. On the 9th of December, you were running in your off-duty gear, is that right?'

'Yep.'

'Sorry to labour the point Fox, but barristers are tricky bastards and they can make a cloud passing over sun appear to be a total eclipse. Did the coppers press you on this?'

'Interestingly, both the MP Dickins and later the police hammered me about it. The police especially accused me of disposing of my gear after the rape – concealment of evidence they said.'

Johnson paused and studied Fox. 'I want you to put yourself back in the cop shop and recall as much as you can of their line of questioning about the rape. How did the interview commence?'

'They told me I had sent a note to Heidi, saying I wanted to patch things up and asked if she could meet me.'

'Did they show you the note?'

'Yes and no. They waved a piece of paper around that had what looked like my writing on it but they didn't give it to me to read. I wrote quite a few notes to Heidi over time and some of them would definitely have been invitations to meet somewhere.'

'Where were you supposed to meet?'

'According to the note it was a spot near Ruckhall. There's a straight stretch of river there and farm roads wind in off the B439. It's on my western run along the river.'

'Obvious question: have you ever met her there?'

'Yes, once. She brought a picnic lunch and I ran there from the barracks. It would have been in the first few weeks of going out together.'

'And did you write to her about this spot?'

'Possibly,' said Fox, his forehead wrinkling with recall, 'we exchanged quite a few notes in those early days so it's more than likely.'

'Why there?'

'Heidi was keen to see me as much as possible, and vicky verka, and I knew the spot from my runs. It's about twelve miles from base, easy to get to by car and the river is very pretty there. It seemed like a good thing. We had a nice lunch, a very active afternoon and then Heidi drove me back to barracks.'

'Well, the trick will be to locate the canoeists. Clearly you couldn't be in two places at once that day. Ok, what next?'

'They said I got into Heidi's car, we started kissing then I'm supposed to have started groping her and when she didn't co-operate, I smacked her around and raped her.'

'Have you had sex in her car before?'

'Plenty of times. We'd be out driving somewhere and Heidi would say, "Let's do it here." She picked the most bizarre places, like the motorway in an emergency lane. She thought that was funny – emergency sex. Things like that.'

'What sort of car is it? Make and colour?'

'A black Porsche 928S. What else?' Fox grinned.

'Fox, understand where I'm heading with these questions. I

don't have any particular interest in your sex life but if scientific officers examine her car and find evidence confirming sex there, it's potentially a knot in the noose around your neck.'

'I do understand that,' replied Fox quietly, 'and they will find evidence. We must have bonked twelve or fifteen times in her car. Christ, the very first time I went out with her she came prepared. She had no knickers on and we decided to pull into a lay-by on the way to Cardiff. There'll be plenty of evidence.'

Johnson scribbled furiously and made several asterisks beside what he'd written.

'You said the police accused you of smacking her around. Did they show you photographs of her injuries or describe them to you? How did they cover that?'

'They didn't show me photos. What they said was that I had hit her once in the face, several times on the breasts and scratched and bruised her inner thighs around the vagina. They made it sound pretty ghastly but I didn't see photos.'

'Did you and Heidi ever have rough sex?'

'No. I am not into that.'

'Ok, so all this frenzied activity took place in Heidi's car?'

Fox smiled at Johnson's quizzical tone. 'No. It supposedly started in her car and then I dragged her outside to finish her off on the ground beside the car. Because it had rained a couple of days earlier she got mud all over her clothes – a skirt, blouse and cardigan. Oh, and that's another thing, I'm alleged to have literally torn her knickers apart in my desire to get at her.'

'Really? Have you ever tried to tear a pair of knickers apart, Fox? That's rubbish.'

'Not quite. She told me once she started having sex when she was fourteen. She has these weird duds that just seem to come apart at the crotch. Christ knows where she gets them but she uses them quite a bit.'

Johnson understood why the police believed their case was

strong. There would be plenty of supportive evidence for Heidi. On any points of divergence it would be argued that Fox was lying. He had met her where she claimed and physical evidence from the site and her car proved it. He wondered too about the new process of DNA "fingerprinting" that UK police had begun to apply the previous year. Still in its infancy, the use of DNA appeared to be a promising new tool. In discussions with senior police at Bramshill, Johnson was told that hair, blood, saliva and semen could be comparatively tested for DNA and would confirm the identity of an offender beyond doubt. It was miraculous they said.

DNA could conclusively and unequivocally establish a link between the person alleged to have committed a crime and their victim or the place where the crime was committed. Equally, it could just as powerfully *exclude* someone wrongly accused of a crime. While DNA testing was not universally accepted and still awaiting definitive court rulings, Johnson suspected that if it stood to benefit Lord Ravenscroft's granddaughter, all stops would be cleared to place Fox among the guinea pigs.

'OK, a couple more things about the interview. Was it taped?'

'I can't say. There was definitely a tape system in the room but it wasn't activated in my presence.'

'Are you sure of that?' Johnson asked incredulously.

'Positive.'

'Alright. Did they give you a copy of the interview or any notes?'

'No. They took notes but I didn't get a copy.'

'These blokes are idiots,' Johnson muttered softly shaking his head in disbelief. 'So tell me about the court hearing that put you in here.' He looked upwards and rotated his head.

'It was really simple: you and I would call it a kangaroo court. I went into a back room at the court, two justices of the peace sat on the bench. The whole thing took about ten minutes.'

Johnson nodded and smiled to himself. As a copper, he was familiar with the tactic.

'Tell me what happened.'

'A police prosecutor said he was seeking remand because they had not finished preparing their case. They requested refusal of bail and said I was a flight risk. They said I had committed the horrendous crime of rape on a defenceless woman, inflicted serious injuries and asked for a remand to early February when they would proceed with a committal hearing.'

'Were you given the opportunity to speak? Did the JPs ask you any questions?'

'No to both. To be candid, they looked like a couple of hayseeds to me. My impression was that they were a bit naïve and I couldn't help feeling they had been picked for the job. One JP was named Lexton but I didn't catch the name of the other.' Fox's jaw clenched at the memory.

'Did you have any legal representation?'

Fox laughed. 'Representation? Are you serious? Yeah, they sent some bandicoot from legal aid who was about as useful as a black-out curtain in a mine shaft. He barely took notes, asked no questions and instantly agreed to a remand and no bail.'

Johnson paused, flexed his arm and rotated his wrist. He was onto his ninth page of notes.

'Alright Fox. If what you say about the interview is correct then there are some serious technical flaws in the investigation. You are, however, dealing with a very old, very powerful and highly respected family. Whether or not Lord Ravenscroft knows the truth remains to be seen, but at this stage, it's probably fair to assume he believes his granddaughter was monstered by some bastard from the Antipodes. He may be using his influence to see you punished. Make no mistake, it will be an uphill battle thwarting that power but you've given me more than enough to get started. Ok, I'll be off. I'll ring Caroline as soon as I get back to London.'

'Thanks,' replied Fox smiling, 'I appreciate that. And thanks for coming too. I suppose this is one of your "irregular investigations" is it?' he asked, remembering Johnson's comments on their first meeting at the Royal Naval College.

'Yep.' Johnson nodded and gathered his papers. 'I'll be in touch soon.' They rose and shook hands. As Johnson left the office he turned and gave Fox the thumbs up.

CHAPTER 32

McPhie stood before the front door of the weathered grey-stone cottage. After a long discussion with the girls and Davey Gordon, he had agreed to personally inform Louisa of Fox's plight. He was not looking forward to it. He liked the old lady and thought she would be distressed by the news – she had taken an instant liking to Fox.

He rapped on the door and waited. Without warning, as before, the door suddenly and silently swung inwards. The old house seemed thoroughly soundproof. Louisa looked at McPhie then peered expectantly behind him before smiling warmly.

'Hello Lex, this is a nice surprise. Do come in.'

They walked into the warm kitchen.

'To what do I owe the pleasure of this visit? Cup of tea?'

McPhie succinctly explained Fox's situation, including *his* opinion of Heidi's allegation and concluded by outlining Fox's restricted visiting rights. In essence, he opined, he was unsure how Fox was coping.

'I remembered you saying,' he said, 'that one of your relations is a lawyer. We, that is, the people who knock about with Fox, were wondering if there was any chance of him helping Fox. We're all happy to club in for his fees.' Expectation hung heavy.

Quietly and deep in thought, Louisa busied herself with the teas before she sat. Only then did she speak.

'Do you think Colin has done what he's accused of?' she asked, the merest hint of a smile on her lips.

'Of course not. If we thought that I wouldn't be here. None of us have any truck for rape.'

Louisa nodded, more to herself than McPhie. 'I consider myself a very good judge of character. I share your opinion. I also suspect that even the police don't fully know the truth. As it happens my great nephew, Callum, is a criminal lawyer who works a lot with the United Nations. Presently he's in America but will be home in ten days or less. Naturally, I shall speak to his father Dougal first, but I am sure Callum won't mind helping out. That means we must now get those visiting rights sorted. Where is he?'

'Cardiff,' said McPhie with a grimace. 'Down in the lair of the villain so to speak.'

'Good God,' retorted Louisa, 'until you said that I was thinking of going myself but I'm not so sure. Cardiff, you say! It's a lifetime away.'

'Not as far as Australia,' he smiled. 'Aunt Louisa,' he said warmly, embracing Fox's kinship with her, 'you won't know this, but Fox and I had a long talk after we left here. Your impact upon him was immense and he is profoundly grateful to you for illuminating his father's side of the family.'

'I understand Lex. Now … what can you tell me that would help Callum?' She peered at him quizzically, gently but unconsciously wringing her hands in her lap, concern evident.

'Very little. He's in a remand prison in Knox Road Cardiff and, as I said, he's alleged to have committed rape. That's all I know. We've written to him a couple of times but nothing has come back to us. It's like he's been swallowed up by a black hole.'

Louisa drank her tea quietly staring into space. After a time she smiled gently.

'It won't be easy.' She paused before continuing. 'I perceive there are powerful forces aligned against him but, he will be released. He has not done what he is accused of.' Her statement was delivered calmly with the force of fact. McPhie was both surprised and reassured but knew she had no substance for her statement.

'You want to believe me Lex but you're not certain. You also feel I should be concerned but I am not. All I can tell you is, there will be some surprises. Let's wait and see.' She smiled warmly.

The day before Caroline and Judy were due to fly out, Perth experienced a blistering forty-three degrees. Footpaths and roadways simmered, trees were listless and even the cooling wind known as the "Fremantle doctor" failed to materialise. For Judy, the sweltering heat did not matter because tomorrow, they were flying out to see Fox. Nothing could stifle her happiness.

Whistling bursts of John Farnham's song, You're the Voice, still top of the charts after seven weeks, she entered their garage from the internal door of the house. Furnace-like after being shut all day, she opened the tilt door to release the viscous heat. Outside, soft shades of a purple dusk were descending and beginning to cool the sky, even so, few people walked the Swan.

At the back of the garage she lowered the loft ladder – she needed a small travel-bag for their shoes. The plan was to take only three bags: one each for clothes and personal effects and one for their footwear. Everything was packed ready, bar the shoes.

Standing midway up the ladder with half her body in the loft space, she easily reached the stored bags and needed only to make her selection. Humming Farnham's song with gusto, she jigged on the rungs while moving the luggage to enable the right choice.

Dean Wildman silently slipped into the garage. From his eyrie he had seen the house was empty. Only Bitchface and her daughter remained. He looked at the door into the house, listened, then moved to within a pace of the ladder. Had Judy looked down, he would have been out of her sight. He gazed up at the slim, shapely bronzed legs and trim bottom encased in brief white shorts. The little girl had indeed become an attractive young woman. She had no right to be so cheerful in this rotten heat and her humming was egregious.

He moved swiftly. Stepping forward he grasped her ankles and with great force pulled her legs out, away from the ladder and down. At the same time he took a half step backwards, twisted the young body in his hands and in a whip-like movement, cracked Judy's head on the concrete floor. The sudden and unexpected force on her unresisting body broke her neck and split her skull. He smiled, eyes glittering, as blood oozed slowly from the limp body. He felt enormous … powerful … unstoppable.

'One down, one to go,' he whispered.

Ghostlike, he entered the house: a sinister, noiseless shadow. He heard Caroline in their bedroom. He was intimately familiar with that room, her dressing table, her underwear, her perfumes, her creams and her toiletries. This had been a long time coming. Bitchface was going to get her just rewards for betraying him. The long, honed, kitchen knife slid smoothly from his trousers, his breathing was ragged with anticipation. *By God this would be good!*

He peered around the door. She was fussing over some clothes near the head of the bed. Damn, he wanted total surprise. She would see him straight away. He drew back. Soon, he heard her move and a wardrobe door open. He looked again. She was riffling through some dresses in the cupboard, her back to him. Perfect. Wraithlike, he crept into the room, knife poised to strike.

So intent was he upon the figure before him, he didn't see the case he kicked at the foot of the bed. Caroline turned at the noise and recoiled at the apparition before her: a wild eyed, heavily bearded man brandishing a knife. In the same moment his repulsive body odour registered – sour and penetrating. Her adrenalin charged concentration noted the creature's thin shaking frame and greyish colouring.

He leapt at her screaming, 'Ya fuckin' bitch, ya fuckin' traitorous whore, ya fuckin finished now. I've got ya!'

Caroline jumped sideways onto the bed and threw a dress over him. She bent, raised a bedside lamp and smashed it in his face. But nothing could stop the mad thing before her. Dragging the dress from his head, bleeding from the nose, he made a looping slash with the knife deeply slicing her calf. She screamed in agony. He pounced again and drove the knife fully into her belly. She sank to the covers and moaned softly.

'Hit me will ya? Ya fuckin' bitch. Hit me eh? I'll fuckin' show ya what I think of that.' He plunged the knife into her left and right thighs, then, grabbing her hair, drove the blade deep into her neck. 'Ya slut. Ya slutty fuckin' whore. Stick up for coons, dob me in to the brass, do me out of a job. Well how do you like this? Not so flash now are we?' He slashed at her in a frenzy.

Spent, he left the gory mess, showered, dressed in John's clothes and walked boldly through the front door. *I am Superman,* he thought, *and there is no Kryptonite around to bring me down.*

It was eight o'clock.

In Cardiff, alone again in his cell, a blinding flash exploded in Fox's head. Eviscerating pain ripped through his belly. He roared, anguish and despair overwhelmed him. He knew instantly that Caroline was dead.

Back in London after a frustratingly slow journey, Johnson rang Caroline Connors. There was no answer. He knew it was only early evening in Perth and wondered if they had gone out for dinner, enjoying an easy night before departure. He decided to try again in an hour. When there was no answer the second time, a spike of concern prickled. He could not forget how cogently Fox had made his plea. Johnson began ringing at ten minute intervals and after no success, decided to try Caroline's work number.

Eventually, he spoke to Sergeant Graham Mummery at Fremantle and after convincing him his call was not a hoax, left his number and asked to be called immediately on confirmation of the status of the Connors/McNulty household. Twenty-five minutes later, Sergeant John Danby of Mends Street Police Station telephoned Johnson. Struggling to remain composed, Danby told Johnson what he'd found. The house was wide open with Judith McNulty and Caroline Connors dead inside. The murder scenes were grisly and Caroline's wounds horrific. Her throat was cut and she'd been repeatedly stabbed and horribly mutilated. He explained to Johnson that he'd only met Judy the previous year when she had come home from school to find their dog butchered in the house. It too had been knifed.

Johnson's feelings were in turmoil. How could Fox have known something like this might be coming? How would he react when he heard the details? What could he do to ease Fox's circumstances? He decided to contact the Governor of the Remand Centre and explain he was returning for very special reasons and there had better not be any opposition.

After the usual delays he was put through to the Governor.

'Spencer Johnson from the Embassy again Mr Smith. I need to make an emergency compassionate visit to Fox and I'll be leaving in ten minutes.'

Smith was guarded. 'Why?' he asked.

'Because I've just had news from Australia that two very close family friends of his have been found murdered. They were flying out of Perth tomorrow to see him. This news will seriously distress him.'

'Too late.'

'What do you mean?'

'Well, I don't know what's going on with this character, but near one o'clock this afternoon he suddenly became immensely disturbed and wrecked his cell. We had to sedate him. The curious thing is, his rage was not directed at my men. But fuck me, what's left of his cell looks like match sticks. I've never seen anyone do so much damage with his bare hands. Could he have known about this?'

'I don't know Mr Smith, today was only the second time I'd met him. All I can tell you is, he is a most unusual man. Now, am I going to be copping any grief?'

'No,' said Smith quietly.

CHAPTER 33

Fox stirred at the insistent voice. He had been having the most horrible nightmare: Judy and Caroline were dead.

'Fox. Wake up man, wake up for Christ's sake.' Johnson was exasperated. He'd been sitting with Fox in the prison hospital ward for forty minutes. Even though sedated, Fox was thrashing violently, pain gouged his face despite the medication.

'Fox, wake up!' The deep voice rumbled.

Grey eyes opened, misty, unfocussed, staring at the ceiling. Johnson watched memory return followed by the dark spectre of grief. He leaned forward and put a friendly hand on Fox's shoulder. He knew without speaking that somehow, Fox was aware of the terrible truth concerning his friends.

Fox closed his eyes and struggled to sit up.

'Want a hand mate?' Johnson enquired. He stood, slid his arm beneath Fox's shoulders and helped him sit.

Fox's head rested on the wall behind him. Slowly, his eyes opened.

'You know too,' he said thickly. 'Tell me what happened.'

As Johnson recounted what Danby had told him, he watched tears slowly trickle down Fox's cheeks. Johnson began to understand how deeply this man cared for these people. With a jolt, he recalled Caroline's comment on Wednesday that Fox was one of their family. Johnson agonised for him. Fox closed his eyes again.

'Did you try to warn them?'

Johnson related the sequence of events from his end.

'I am really sorry Fox, but considering the time difference, I believe the act had occurred before I got back to the office.'

'Yes,' said Fox in a flat, tired voice, 'I felt an urgency but didn't know when it would happen.'

'Are you saying you knew this would occur before it actually did? That you know who did it? How do you know this?' Johnson's voice was rising in unison with his eyebrows.

'You wouldn't understand Johnson. This whole thing with Caroline started when I left Australia nearly a year ago but it was extremely vague. Over time my concern strengthened and I told Caroline to be careful. Things began happening to them – they had a stalker, items were stolen from their home, their dog was killed, things stolen were returned. It was all very scary. Caroline spoke to the local cops and they put on extra patrols but nothing happened. For weeks after Lucy dog was killed everything went quiet. Since I've been in gaol, my initial perception about this event has become clearer and I felt a powerful sense of immediacy. That's all I can tell you. Don't ask me to speak of it again.'

As Fox uttered the last his eyes cleared and a cold, intimidating hardness settled.

'Do you know who did this Fox?'

'Other than a man, no, I don't. But I will find him.' He lapsed into silence.

Johnson was perplexed. Fox seemed unworried by his imprisonment.

'We've got to beat this,' Johnson gestured to the room around him, 'before you can return home to find him.'

'No,' Fox said slowly, turning his gaze upon Johnson, 'I can start that process from here and I assure you … the outcome will be one hundred times worse than the harm inflicted on my precious friends.'

Johnson flinched before the power of Fox's glacial stare. He decided right then that never did he want to become Fox's enemy. Simultaneously, he realised how much restraint Fox had shown concerning Heidi's allegations. He wondered if that moderation would be out the window now that Caroline and Judy had been murdered.

'So tell me Fox, what can I do to help with this?' He turned his palms upwards and spread his hands slightly.

'You've got access to an international communications network that is probably more sophisticated and speedy than anything the police have and at the moment, the family is spread far and wide. I'd like you to track down and inform John McNulty, Caroline's husband. He's working in a burns hospital in Jishuitan, China. Then I'd like you to contact my Officer Commanding, Major John Hoey at Swanbourne in Western Australia. Young Courtney Dalgleish, an SAS colleague, and Caroline's other daughter, Jenny, are on a trek together in Nepal. Hoey will quite likely have their itinerary and be able to tell you where they can be located and informed. And lastly, Jason, their son is doing his articles with Mendelsohn, Ryder and Colebatch, one of Sydney's most prestigious law firms. He needs to be told. They all know where I am. I'd like you to tell them I am, and will continue to be, with them in spirit and that justice *will* prevail.'

The clear, simple briefing impressed Johnson. There would be no problems actioning Fox's requests.

'Oh, one more thing if you don't mind. I have a great aunt in Scotland – Pittenweem – her name is Louisa Fox. I would really appreciate you talking to her personally. Just to let her know what's happened. Although I've only just met her, I respect her greatly. Lex McPhie at the Barracks can give you her details.'

CHAPTER 34

Fox's circumstances weighed upon on Johnson. He'd had minimal contact with the man: a joint police/armed services exercise months earlier, two prison visits; brief discussions with a woman now dead and a hasty conversation with his PT instructor at Hereford Barracks. It wasn't much. He was an experienced copper used to making decisions about people in strange and difficult circumstances. He'd done it many times in many countries involving many cases – pornographers, slave traders, drug smugglers, gun runners, crooked cops and others. With slight reservation, he thought Fox odd but solid.

His situation was unusual: arrested for an alleged rape, seemingly a dupe to string-pulling by the invisible hand of English aristocracy, a great aunt in Scotland and now, the death of two people exceptionally close to him. And bizarrely, not only had Fox warned them of impending trouble, but knew precisely when their deaths occurred. Such prescience was enough to push anyone over the edge. His rampage confirmed that. Fox was definitely unusual and Johnson knew he hadn't even scratched the surface.

In the meantime, he had lots to do. Back in London, he contacted the Heads of Mission at the Australian Embassies in Beijing and Nepal as well as his old mate Superintendent Larry Craig at Australian Federal Police Headquarters in Sydney. The horror of his request was implicit and he knew it would be relayed speedily and tactfully. He next set up an appointment with Colonel

Chartres at Hereford. He wanted to learn more about Fox and his performance under pressure. Additionally, he needed to find the Scottish aunt through Fox's mate McPhie. Lastly, he made enquiries about the *White Duck* and booked a reservation for lunch the next day. Investigations like this one involving Fox were far more preferable to humdrum Embassy duties.

Johnson was an imposing man. At 183 centimetres and 95 kilos, he was superbly built, strong as an ox and the holder of many body sculpting prizes. His affable nature tended to soften his intimidating size and over the years he had cultivated these qualities to portray himself as a simple, uncomplicated, good natured bloke. Little wonder, he had grown up on Amberley Airforce Base in Ipswich, Queensland, played rugby with the local copper's son and mixed freely with the local Aboriginal kids. People warmed to his charm and often found themselves confiding their most intimate secrets to him. As a result, Johnson had become a warehouse of useful and sometimes devastating knowledge, an asset he occasionally and skilfully deployed.

For Fox, he would exploit this skill to its utmost. He began planning infiltration of the closed community at Kilmore Castle and its surrounding hamlets. Lyons cryptic telephone call suggested there was information to be had and used to advantage. Additionally, Fox's initial court appearance implied several pathways for exploration but, for the moment, he would give the coppers at Cwmbran a wide berth.

The *White Duck,* built around 1480, was one of England's oldest remaining riverside pubs. With its skewed brick chimneys, high, distinctively patterned thatched roof and small-paned leadlight casement windows, the old white pub and its darkened framing timbers was "chocolate box" charming. Discreet window canisters and dormant rose bushes coyly veiled the promise of picturesque appeal through spring and summer. Outside the pub, large rustic benches and tables suggested warm summer evenings and cheerful companionship. Expansive, yet impeccable lawns dipped gently to the River Wye. Johnson was impressed.

At lunchtime he stooped and entered the front door to a warm and friendly atmosphere. Blackened oak beams barely above his head reached across the low-ceilinged main room above worn flagstones. A crackling fire burned in a huge fieldstone fireplace on the far wall. Old fashioned and welcoming, Johnson hoped he would have not only an enjoyable meal but find the information he was after.

A young woman with dark curly hair in smart, well fitting jeans and a crisp white shirt greeted him. After confirming his luncheon reservation, he was shown to a seat overlooking the river and ordered minestrone, roast pheasant and baked vegetables. A local ale seemed appropriate while he waited.

'Could you tell me if the owners of the pub are here today? I'm Spencer Johnson, I spoke to Claude yesterday.'

'Of course. Claude's in the cellar at present and Maggie's upstairs. I'll let them know.'

Johnson nodded and smiled.

Ten minutes later he was tucking into minestrone and fresh bread rolls when Maggie Collins arrived. In her late sixties, she had few facial lines, a broad smile and matronly appearance. A handsome woman, Johnson liked her immediately.

'Mr Johnson, pleased to meet you. It's not often we see someone from the Australian Embassy, especially when they sound a little mysterious in their quest.'

Johnson stood and Maggie offered him a firm handshake. He gestured to the chair opposite.

'Will your husband be joining us?'

'He's busy changing barrels and taps at the moment. How can we help you? Claude mentioned something about canoeists.'

Without naming him, Johnson succinctly explained Fox's

situation concluding with a reference to a young couple in a canoe. When he finished Maggie was smiling.

'I think we may be able to help. My husband's name is actually Jean-Claude. During World War Two his mother was evacuated from France as a child. She came here. Eventually she married the owner's son and Claude is their son. So … we have French connections.'

'Well, the sixty-four dollar question from me Maggie is: can you give me an address or telephone number for those connections?'

'I'm sure we can but I'll leave that to Claude. In the meantime, enjoy your meal. We'll come back when you've finished.'

Thirty-five minutes later Maggie returned with a tall, bespectacled man whose white hair, though neat, was thin and wispy. His features were craggy and tanned from time outdoors. Piercing blue eyes sparkled behind spectacles and a rather long, angular nose accentuated the ruggedness of his face. He carried a bottle of cognac and three glasses.

'You must be Spencer,' he said smiling, 'I'm Jean-Claude, but everybody calls me Claude. Enjoy your meal?'

'Perfect,' said Johnson scrambling to his feet. He waited for Claude to put the bottle and glasses down before extending his hand in greeting. 'You've got a beautiful spot here and your food and staff are superb.'

Maggie and Claude nodded, graciously accepting the compliment before sitting. Claude looked at Johnson, raised his eyebrows and lifted the brandy slightly.

'Don't mind if I do,' Johnson responded, chuckling. 'Given your origins I am sure you will know the best, so yes, thank you.'

'My supplier is based in Poitou-Charentes, a beautiful region of France and home to the town of Cognac. I doubt you'll taste better than this.' Claude poured for them as Maggie and Johnson watched quietly.

'I thought you didn't drink on duty,' Johnson said to Maggie, smiling.

'Well, I did say rarely,' she replied evenly, 'and as we are about to have a serious discussion, this will be a good fortifier.'

Johnson studied them both, more questions in his eyes. He waited.

Claude settled himself, sipped his brandy and then fixed Johnson with a candid, unwavering gaze.

'I find it curious that the day you ring to enquire about some canoeists, a senior policeman from Wales comes knocking on my door to ask about a black jogger whom he says is connected to a serious crime on the Wye a month ago. Even more curious, you tell Maggie that not only are you interested in canoeists, but that they have something to do with a man wrongly accused of rape, a rape I presume has something to do with the river and or this location and the policeman yesterday. Now Spencer, I am a cautious man and I was truly unable to help the policeman, but you, a man from an Embassy who links the jogger, the crime and the canoeists, you cause me some concern. You have made a link different to that of the policeman so, before I play ball, perhaps you would like to explain in a little more detail.'

Johnson had not bargained on news that someone, possibly Early, from Cwmbran was snooping this far afield. He knew Fox had not mentioned the canoeists and wondered if the police had come across them some other way: luck, accident or diligent investigation. He was inclined to dismiss the last as he still believed that Early was working to sink Fox for old Lord Ravenscroft.

He looked at them both with an equally candid gaze.

'Right. No bullshit. The accused man is an Aboriginal SAS soldier from Australia. That he's here at Hereford speaks volumes. To cut to the chase, he developed a liaison with a female army captain who is a medical doctor and deeply connected to your aristocracy. At this point, I don't think you need to know either of their names. Anyway, the young woman, as a consequence of her background I believe, was used to getting her own way. Our SAS man gave her the boot. Unhappy with that, she accused him of rape. From my early enquiries I believe her family has been pulling strings to ensure our man is convicted. In my view, there are too many unanswered questions about this rape. As an Australian embassy rep, part of my role is to assist with matters like this. I spoke to our man in prison the other day and he gave me a perfect alibi. On the day and time the rape is alleged, he says he was jogging downstream of your establishment and waved a greeting to a young couple in a red canoe. The rape, on the other hand, is said to have been committed on the riverbank about the same distance from Hereford as your pub, but in the opposite direction. This puts the rape and the canoeists about fifteen to twenty miles apart at more or less the same time. Our man could not have been both here and there.' Johnson could see the cogs meshing in Claude's mind. He waited.

After a short silence Claude shot a quizzical look at Maggie who nodded slightly.

'I have cousins in France and every couple of months or so the son of one of them, Henri, and his girlfriend Mirelle, come to visit. Henri is connected with the London stock exchange and has to spend a week there every so often. If there is nothing pressing at home they usually come down here and we exchange family gossip. If the weather is right, they will often take our canoe for a spin. Not every time mind you, but often enough. They were here that weekend, it's in our diary, but whether or not they took the canoe out, I don't know. It was damned cold then.'

'Yes it was,' chimed in Maggie, 'but also beautifully clear, so they could have taken it. I mean, they don't come and tell us they're going out. We like them to feel at home.'

'Well,' said Johnson beaming, 'that's a good start. Do you have their contact details?'

CHAPTER 35

Over the next three days, Dr John McNulty, Jason and Jenny returned home. It was their first time together since the death of Caroline and Judy and they clung to each other – their pain visceral. Unable to face the house, John had moved swiftly to rent a unit on The Esplanade and there they sat in the tiny rear yard.

'What do we know Dad?' stuttered Jenny, 'have the police arrested anyone? Did Linda see anybody or hear anything?'

John shook his head. 'Darling, we know very little. The police have no suspects but they are trawling through all the arrests Mum made over the last few years to see if there are any leads there. They feel strongly that whoever was stalking her is the most likely suspect. But they are baffled. No one saw this stalker and he was very cunning when he entered the house — he left no trace of himself.'

Jennifer's last shred of reserve crumbled and she dissolved into racking sobs. Courtney Dalgleish drew her close and held her until composure returned. Numb, they sat silently, not knowing what to say to each other.

Eventually, John said, 'I do have some news. I've had a couple of phone calls from a bloke named Spencer Johnson. He's a federal police officer from the London Embassy – the bloke who had us notified about Mum and Judy. Mum had wanted to know more about Fox's arrest and she got onto this Johnson at the Embassy. As it turns out, he saw Fox twice after he spoke to your mother. On the first occasion Fox convinced Johnson that Mum and Judy were in danger and Fox wanted them to know that. Johnson had taken Mum's work and home numbers and when he couldn't contact her, he rang the Fremantle police station. That's how they were discovered. When Johnson received that news he went straight back down to Cardiff to see Fox only to find that somehow, Fox already knew. He had wrecked his cell in despair.'

Emotion gripped McNulty again and he wiped away some tears. Hoarsely, he continued. 'Fox was so distraught he had to be sedated and when Johnson saw him again he was in the gaol infirmary. When he got a grip, Fox asked Johnson to give us a message: "he would see justice done." I don't understand how Fox could know all this when he's locked up over there, but that's what he said.'

'Well, I'll hazard a guess,' said Jason, 'If he identifies the killer, I reckon he'll be "singin'" the bastard. And if that's the case, Mum's killer's got no chance.'

CHAPTER 36

Johnson knew instantly that the Director was seriously pissed off when he strolled into his office.

Carlisle Edwards' agitation had induced near hyperventilation.

'What the fuck have you been up to? I've had a police Superintendent from Wales on the line bitching about you interfering with his investigation. I've had the Cardiff Prison Governor complaining about your demands for visiting rights after hours and, for good measure, Lord Fucking Ravenscroft's son is bellyaching about you snooping around Kilmore and spying on his family. Well?'

Edwards wasn't the sort of man to be on the wrong side of. He had real power. A little man, barely five and a half feet tall, slender, fair haired and rosy cheeked, he was the archetypal political octopus – extensive reach and the ability to change colour at will. He could be genuinely charming and warm yet equally tough, blunt and coarse. Even so, his outburst had not in the least ruffled Johnson. To the contrary, it merely confirmed Johnson's view that Fox was pawn to conspiracy.

'Listen up, Carlisle old son. What I've been doing is taking care of a fellow Australian's interests. An Australian who's been set up by the filthy rich Ravenscroft family. You should have known because I gave you briefing notes on it. Rather than bleating, you should bloody well have been doing something. Instead, you've been sitting here with your head under your armpit sucking up to the English-bloody-aristocracy.'

'You friggin' great oaf, I'll not have you playing Poirot with the Ravenscroft family. They're off limits. Understood? And just to be sure, tomorrow morning at ten you'll be reporting to the Dublin Embassy. Our Foreign Minister is visiting in six weeks and I want security as tight as a hangman's noose. Now fuck off, get that organised and forget about that prick in Cardiff.'

'Is this your way of taking an interest in the well-being of overseas Australians? I'm sure the Foreign Minister will be thrilled to learn how you do your job. And since I'm going to Ireland, I'll tell him. Do you realise how significant it is to have this bloke Fox here on SAS training? He's special – the first Indigenous soldier to be doing this kind of stuff. That's why he's here. Don't you get that?'

'What I get Johnson is your insolence. I couldn't give a rat's arse if he was the first man on the moon. I'm recommending your demotion and when you're done in Ireland, you'll be back to Canberra faster than you can blink. I don't give a shit what you tell the Minister because by the time I've finished, your credibility's gunna be lower than a gnat's dick. Now piss off.'

Johnson smiled slowly at Edwards, took a step forward and snapped to attention. He raised his arm in a sardonic salute.

'Aye aye captain. One more thing. You've assigned me to escort the new Canadian Ambassador on a trip around Australian haunts in London tomorrow. Are you going to do that now?'

'I bloody well am not. Blythe can do it.'

'Blythe's off to Rome tonight to discuss security for the G7 Conference. What are you on old son? You don't seem quite yourself.'

'You heard what I said. Piss off. Be in Dublin tomorrow by ten or else.'

Johnson walked from the office in a contemplative mood,

dismissing Edwards' rant before even reaching the door. He had a day to organise matters and many things to do. His focus was solely upon Fox. From Ireland, his help would be limited.

Returning to the office Johnson fished around in his credenza for a Scottish telephone directory. He hadn't yet spoken to McPhie. After trawling through a column and a half of Fox's, he found most of the Pittenweem clan located within the same two inches of column space and, among them, one L Fox. He rang and knew instantly he was at the right place when a well modulated, elderly female voice answered.

'Louisa Fox speaking.'

Johnson explained who he was and why he was ringing. 'Do you have the time to talk for a few minutes?' he asked,

'Of course.' A hint of reservation, nothing volunteered.

'I recently spoke to Colin and he told me about you. Part of my role is assisting people in his situation and, even though my investigation is young, I am already certain Fox could not have committed the crime he's accused of. I still have numerous loose ends to tie up but now I have a slight problem. I've been dispatched to Dublin from tomorrow and don't know how long I'll be there. I don't want Fox thinking he's been abandoned. It's apparent to me that Fox holds you in high regard and he wanted you to know what was going on.'

'Aye. This is a terrible thing and I am glad you're helping him. I'm also pleased you've confirmed my own thoughts. I know people, Mr Johnson. Colin could never have done what he's been accused of. I did speak to Colin's soldier friend, Lex McPhie, a little while ago and I think we, his Scottish family, will be able to help. My nephew Callum is a lawyer and has just returned from the USA – he's agreed to take up Colin's case. I think the simplest thing you can do is speak with him. I have more than sufficient faith in his ability. Tell me Mr Johnson, why are you so sure of Colin's innocence?'

'Unless he's kin to Apollonius of Tyana, the explanation is very simple: he could not have been in two places at once.'

Johnson listened to the silence as Louisa digested the information.

'I don't think that small fact matters to this girl. She has money, influence and power and I feel she'll stop at nothing to contrive his conviction. Don't underestimate her. Even so, I think she'll find her match in Callum.'

CHAPTER 37

'Callum Fox?'

'Aye. Who is this?' Johnson analysed the voice: transatlantic, very slight Scottish burr, warm, deep, rich. A thoughtful kind of voice.

'Spencer Johnson, Australian Embassy. Your Aunt Louisa suggested I call you.'

'You'd be calling about Colin then?'

'I am. Look, if you don't mind, I'll get straight to the point because I'm rather pushed for time. I don't know what you know, so, if I cover stuff you're familiar with, I apologise in advance.'

'No need for that. I've never met Colin Fox so anything you say will be helpful.'

'Short hand version then.' Johnson concisely outlined Fox's circumstances. 'The thing is Callum, being a medical doctor, Heidi Ravenscroft is savvy and apparently exhibited all the right signs and symptoms for a rape victim. Additionally, there'll be plenty of physical evidence confirming sex in her car because they screwed in it so often. I think her very powerful family is pulling strings to make life hard for Fox. For instance, a court appearance that was worse than a farce and a legal representative who was a complete joke. These and other unfortunate mishaps appear to me to have been orchestrated. Not sure by whom other than her family.'

'I must say it sounds rather like a fruity melodrama even though the allegation is serious,' commented Callum drily. 'Aunt Lou said that Colin isn't guilty of the crime because he couldn't be in two places at once. What does she mean?'

Johnson explained what he'd learned from the Collins at the *White Duck*.

'Callum, I now have a particular problem. I've offended my boss here because of my interest in Fox. He likes all things aristocratic and I wouldn't put it past the bastard to be shagging Ms Bloody Ravenscroft as well. Not really, but he is blind to toffs. Anyway, for whatever reason, the little prick is sending me to Ireland tomorrow and I don't know when I'll be back. This means I can't investigate any more. What I really want to know is: will you take up Fox's cause.'

'Aye. I've had a long chat with Aunt Lou and she says Colin is solid. And he's family. That's enough for me. What you've just told me cements her view. I'm here in the UK for the next three months and that should be long enough to sort this out.'

'Well mate, you haven't got that long. The committal hearing is in two weeks. Now, there's one more thing you really need to know. I refrained from telling your aunt this. Did she happen to mention Fox's relationship with the McNulty family in Australia, particularly the wife, Caroline Connors?'

'Aye, she did. Why?'

'Caroline and her youngest daughter Judy were coming to England to support Fox ... they were murdered the night before they were due to leave. Fox went apeshit. Had to be sedated and put in the prison hospital. He could still be there. Now, I don't know much about this relationship other than it was deep. They loved him as a family member. I feel you need to be aware of this in case Fox is difficult.'

There was a short silence. 'Thanks for that. Tell me, if you were not going to Ireland, what would your next step be?'

Thoughtful, Callum replaced the phone slowly. After his conversations with Aunt Lou, Johnson's information further rounded his impressions of Fox. He wanted to meet him as soon as possible. He reviewed the cryptic shorthand taken during his discussion with Johnson. There was no doubting his diligence on Fox's behalf and, at least superficially, it did appear as though Johnson was being shunted aside. On the other hand, Dublin could simply be an innocent posting for all the right and proper reasons. Yet, the suddenness of it in conjunction with everything else happening to Fox seemed off.

He rose from the desk and took his coffee to stand looking over Claremont Gardens. Winter in Edinburgh could be miserable and today, the bare trees glistened in light but continuous rain. Street lights cast shimmering slivers of gold onto the wet footpath but did little to lift the gloom. He saw only two pedestrians in The Crescent and both were rugged to the hilt. It was bitter outside.

Almost thirty-three years old, Dr Callum Fox was a highly successful lawyer. Ten years earlier he had graduated with honours from Edinburgh Law School, become an articled clerk to Dalkeith and Sinclair and continued his studies. His stellar progress established a formidable reputation in broad scale human rights issues. His doctorate was the result of comprehensive research into barriers besetting countries striving for democracy under corrupt and despotic rulers. As a result, he had been catapulted first hand into many desperate and frightening situations in several third world countries, experiences that hardened his resolve against oppression and brought him to the United Nations.

A quiet and considered man, Callum was renowned in the legal sphere for his intellect, piercing analytical skills and prodigious work ethic. Between 1979 and 1985 after joining the UN's Human Rights Commission, along with others, he became deeply involved in the formulation of four important declarations. Among them, a *Declaration on the Inadmissibility of Intervention and Interference in the*

Internal Affairs of States and a Convention Against Torture and Other Cruel, Inhuman or Degrading Treatment or Punishment. At the same time, he experienced significant prosecutorial exposure at the International Criminal Court of The Hague.

Callum found it intriguing to think that on the other side of the world, resulting from family adventures long past, he had an Aboriginal cousin. He was acutely aware of a push within Australia to atone for past policies and legislation resulting in discrimination against Aborigines. In particular, the thorny matter of young children removed from their families. He wondered if Fox was such a person, he was about the right age. He made a mental note to ask Aunt Lou about it.

Callum wanted to know this cousin. Aunt Lou said he was a man of principle; she had seen silver shining from his soul. He knew her words were romantic and not based on any known fact but, they eloquently captured her powerful ability to understand people, a quality for which she was well known in Pittenweem.

Callum went to the kitchen, refreshed his coffee and returned to the desk. He sat and began formulating his attack. He re-read Johnson's plan and thought it a comprehensive beginning. Indeed, the only shortcoming he observed was that it that lacked depth on some of the legal aspects. Importantly, Callum had an ace up his sleeve. He had met Lord Ravenscroft on three occasions in different countries and they'd gotten along well. He intended using this twist of fate to advantage.

As keen as he was to meet Fox however, that needed to wait. His busy schedule required some serious re-prioritising.

Fox was under suicide watch in a new cell after his stint in the prison hospital. And that … that was funny. He was not in the least suicidal – it was vengeance that dominated his thinking, not taking his life. He had only ever gone off-line like that once before – the time he found Mullett raping Lucy. This time his rage erupted from the senseless deaths of Caroline and Judy. He could not shake the feeling that he should have done more to protect them. It was a crazy self accusation. He knew that. Nevertheless, guilt gnawed like acid.

In his lonely cell he had thought long and hard about the future and reached an important decision: he would quit the army. It was a practical decision – he could never pursue the kind of justice *he* wanted for Caroline from inside the army. More to the point, he couldn't do it from gaol. He accepted that his present circumstances would be temporary, but just how they would be resolved was still a mystery. Johnson, he knew, was working hard for him and while nothing had come from Gordon or McPhie, he was certain of their continuing support. They were not the sort of blokes to walk out on a mate.

All that aside, he had begun to reappraise his life. Right back to the beginning. Little of his early years had been positive apart from time with his mum, Lucy and the Mob. Christ! Turkey Creek was light years gone. He had worked hard against feeling sorry for himself: everyone had to live with the hand they'd been dealt. But, he had thought a lot about power: who had it, who didn't and how it was used for good and bad outcomes. He had seen bastards on both sides of the colour-pole use and abuse power for personal, selfish, greedy and manipulative reasons … some politicians especially.

He vividly remembered the Liberal Party's dirty tricks during Western Australia's 1980 State election. They had ferried forty-four gallons of plonk up to Turkey Creek in the hope that people would be so pissed on election day they'd be unable to vote. This, on top of their 1977 swifty of trying to disenfranchise Aboriginal voters. They'd come a gutser on that one. Their underhand tactics landed them in the Court of Disputed Returns where their victory was thrown out. Justice had truly prevailed when a black man became the sitting member for the region.

Years later Fox tasted bile when he came across a newspaper article about that particular election. The Liberal candidate, seemingly devoid of sensitivity and smug in his arrogance, was reported saying of the contest that it "…*was a degrading experience to have to campaign amongst the Aboriginals to the extent that I did. It offended me to know that whilst I was concentrating my efforts on these simple people over the last couple of weeks, I was neglecting a more informed and intelligent section of the community.*" Yeah, well … he got his just desserts. Beaten. Indeed, shat upon from great height because the black man who won the seat spent the next twenty-plus years in Parliament.

Yes, he thought, *I've got to get away from this. I'm only going to be satisfied when this bastard is exterminated. Have to leave the army otherwise I'll disgrace my colleagues and the outfit. Too much respect to do that … and anyway, joining them was a gift from Caroline. And there's Hoey and Flynn … good men I would totally offend. Don't want that. But this bastard's damage has to be punished and it can't be anything less than an eye for an eye. And stuff the consequences! I know Caroline would say leave it to the police and the courts, but I've seen how people like Ravenscrofts manipulate that system. How can anyone have faith in the courts? No … must be an eye for an eye.*

That evening Lex McPhie replaced the community phone contemplatively and went in search of Davey Gordon. He found him in the gym lifting weights.

'Hey Davey. Take a break?'

Gordon placed the heavily laden bar on its cradle. 'What's up?'

'I just had a phone call from a guy called Callum Fox. He's a lawyer. Fox's Aunt Louisa put him onto us. He wants to meet us and Ropey and even mentioned Colonel Chartres. He's back from America and wants a comprehensive picture of Fox's character. You know – work ethic, integrity and all that shit. Don't know aboot you, but I think we should also give him the intel the girls have been feeding us. That could help Fox too.'

'Totally agree. When's he coming?'

'Day after tomorrow. He's catching a train from Edinburgh tonight. He'll have to get his bloody skates on though. Fox's arraignment is only aboot ten days away.'

CHAPTER 38

The coffee shop, *A Shot in the Dark,* was located on City Road, Cardiff. Seated at a table farthest from the street, Callum Fox waited for Detective Inspector Jonas Lyons of Cwmbran. Contemplating the information he hoped to elicit from Lyons he smiled at the irony of the café's title, for a shot in the dark was all this exercise might be. The premises resonated with warmth and friendliness and Callum saw patrons reading or working on documents were left well alone by the staff. A good sign. He had checked the menu and thought the food a little pricey but, on the other hand, an interesting selection was offered. Additionally, he had already drunk one cup of coffee and found it exactly to his taste – rich, thick and aromatic.

Two days earlier at the Hereford SAS Barracks, he had spoken with Fox's Officer Commanding, Colonel Chartres. While Chartres had been suitably circumspect, Callum learned that Fox was a man of integrity, good judgement, flexibility, and interestingly, empathy. The PT instructor, John Arbuthnott, spoke highly of Fox's work ethic, his endurance and team spirit and mentioned that several times he had seen Fox unobtrusively helping others who sometimes lagged a little. Fox was also tough. He related an incident involving Fox and an American Special Forces trainer, Saul Carmody. In his view, while the outcome was brutal, he believed that Fox, under the circumstances, had exercised restraint. And when he and the other instructors heaped retribution on Fox for going almost too far with Carmody, Fox had not uttered a murmur. He had, afterall, disobeyed Ropey's direction to cease.

Fox's mates, Gordon and McPhie, were illuminating about Heidi Ravenscroft. They told how Fox, always the gentleman, was nothing but discreet about their relationship – even after the bust up. Callum learned that it was Heidi who had been the pursuer and initiated contact with Fox. While the relationship lasted, it had been full-on with Fox taking every moment to be with her. That is, until towards the end. He had mildly implied to McPhie one day that Heidi was becoming too controlling and possessive. Both men mentioned their own girls had taken an instant liking to Fox who treated them like royalty and with utmost respect.

Gordon went on to say that his girlfriend, Maddie, said she'd heard Heidi was currently dating an American. She was almost certain it was Carmody, the man Fox had put into hospital at Hereford. Furthermore, she understood the relationship was well underway before Fox ditched Heidi. Callum asked if Maddie would meet him. 'That's a no-brainer' Gordon had responded, 'anything to help Fox.' Consequently, Callum met both Maddie and Rebecca in Cardiff that morning before they commenced afternoon shift.

They talked generally of Fox and spoke of his good manners and consideration towards them. Callum was interested to learn that on the base, Heidi was a renowned man-eater, never happy unless she had at least two men on the go at once. Idly, Callum wondered if she might be a stalker. Another snippet Maddie offered was that recently she and Rebecca had, more than once, seen Heidi talking earnestly to a ranking uniformed policeman. While this would be expected considering the circumstances, Rebecca insisted there was something more to it. She had perceived a sense of intimacy between the pair, something she could only say she thought was not quite right. This was a pearl Callum wanted to polish.

Just after four o'clock a balding, stocky man with a drooping moustache and rumpled appearance entered the café. His dark eyes scoured the premises and stopped at Callum. He raised his eyebrows, Callum nodded. Jonas Lyons threaded his way to the back table.

Callum stood and extended his hand.

'Callum Fox. Glad you could come. What can I get you to drink?'

'Jonas Lyons. Pleased to meet you. A beer would be fine.'

They sat. Callum beckoned a waitress and ordered a black coffee and beer.

'So, Jonas, I understand from an Australian colleague you thought the relationship between Superintendent Early and the Ravenscrofts should be examined. Is that right?' The soft Scottish accent was gently beguiling, non-threatening.

'It is. That big bugger from the Embassy … er … Johnson. He came down here asking questions. Wrong ones mind. He set the hares off. Trouble was, he didn't know what he was looking for.'

'I don't know,' said Callum with a smile, 'I'm here. And I'm talking to the right person. Tell me, what's your beef with Early?'

'Who says I have one?'

'Everyone has an angle. You wouldn't have rung Spencer Johnson without reason. Especially since he got so little co-operation from people at your nick.'

'Fair enough. Early's a manipulator, a social climber, a bully but smart and streetwise. Sees himself as an up and coming Chief Constable. He's comfortable with bendin' the truth. I'm not. I just straight out don't like him. Apart from that, I loved the way that SAS bloke Fox took the piss out of him when we were at Bulford. Described him beautifully I thought. Early hated it. Anything *he* doesn't like, I do. Bloody pratt.'

'That's not the sort of information that's particularly helpful in a trial. What facts do you have?'

'Plenty.'

'In that case Jonas, I'd like to take some notes if you don't mind and I'd also like to get to the point. The committal hearing is only a week away and I still have plenty of ground to cover. As Fox's lawyer, if this is a fit-up, I need to be able to blow the case out of the water. But, if it's genuine, I have to provide him with the best defence I can.'

'Right boyo. Let's start with my wife. Evelyn's a Kilmore Castle lass. Her folks worked and lived in a cottage at the Manor all their lives. Still do. Old Lord Ravenscroft is generous. Anyway, my Evelyn is about three or four years younger than Heidi. When she was about ten she was in the stables one summer afternoon and Heidi arrives. Evelyn swears to this day she doesn't know why she did what she did but, she hid. They're big stables with stalls both sides of a central laneway and a platform for hay storage over the stalls. Heidi was on one side of the lane in the storage area and my Evelyn on the other. Anyway, Heidi stretches out on some bales, lifts her skirt and starts to rub herself. Not long after, Cyril Early appears. He would have been about twenty then and Heidi about thirteen or fourteen.'

'Stop. Why would Cyril have been there?'

'Because he lived there. His Da was head gamekeeper and old Lord R was payin' Cyril's way through university. During summer break, Cyril worked on the property as payback.' Jonas's dark eyes bored into Callum's blue ones. It was as though he'd heard the story many times and didn't want to miss a single element in relating it.

'What year was this?' asked Callum.

'Approximately 1969 I reckon, give or take a year. Anyway, Evelyn says Heidi whistled and Cyril climbed up to her. He stood watching and next minute, down came his trousers and he's givin' her one. Evelyn says Heidi was moanin' and groanin' and lovin' it. Looking back, Evelyn is certain this wasn't the first time. But here's the thing. My Evelyn saw this happen at least half a dozen times over that summer. Think about it. The age difference. It was a crime. Mind you, Evelyn said Cyril was much better looking then. He had all his hair and he was a bloody good footballer. I guess he appealed to a young girl.'

'How many people has your wife told about this?'

'As far as I know, I'm still the only one. As a child she was too frightened to tell her parents and more to the point, she was too afraid of being ridiculed by her school friends. You know, accused of makin' up lies. So, she never told anyone. She didn't even tell me until a year or so after we were married. And that was only after I'd had a run in with Early who was a Detective Sergeant then. I was still a Constable. I came home so mad one night sounding off about the pratt and Evelyn said, "Don't worry about him, he's a man of straw". When I asked what she meant she told me the story.'

'And are you from the Manor too?'

'Not me boyo. I'm a coal miner's son from Llanhilleth. Our pit closed in '69. There wasn't much going on around the village so I moved on and decided to become a copper.'

'Alright. So you're suggesting Heidi has a hold over Early because of this sexual behaviour?'

'Not suggesting, tellin' you. There's been plenty of times she's been in scrapes for drinkin', drugs and wild behaviour. She calls him up to cut her loose. Now, I don't know this for sure, but what I suspect is that she threatens to blow the whistle because he was bonkin' her when she was a minor. She'd do it too, schemin' bitch. He can't afford that. He's married, got kids, appears respectable and is working his way up the police ladder.'

Callum began to feel a small sense of comfort about Fox's case. The genesis of an explanation for Early's behaviour and the appalling judicial process surrounding Fox was beginning to emerge. It was good information and quite independent of the *White Duck* evidence. Useful.

'Okay. What about this rape? The rape of Heidi Ravenscroft by Colin Fox. Is that genuine?'

'You'll have to work that out for yourself. All I can tell you is that this entire matter has been pretty much handled by Early. He's kept all the information to himself closer than a vest. That's unusual. The two JPs are personal friends of his and at various times they worked at the Manor. That stinks. The legal aid lawyer is the son of a friend of Early's and has only just got his practising certificate. Green as grass! Chain of evidence is wonky and I can't be certain the proper procedures were followed.'

'If what you say is true, isn't there a huge risk for Early in all this? You just said he can't afford to be exposed and he's got career aspirations. If what you've said emerges during committal, he's going to be up that well known creek.'

Lyons sat back in his chair and took a long draft from the pint that had quietly arrived as they talked.

'Listen. I don't think you're hearin' me. You're dealing with the Ravenscrofts. That means big time power and serious political influence.'

'Hang on,' said Callum, 'I want to be clear about this. Are you telling me that Lord Ravenscroft is complicit in manufacturing an alleged rape?'

'Not for one minute. The Old Man is a genuine good guy, but his son and daughter-in-law, they're a different story. And make no mistake, between you and me, they have as much pull as the Old Man around here.'

'Enough "pull," as you say, to keep visitors and mail from getting to Fox in prison?'

'Piece of piss. They probably offered the Governor a fully paid holiday in Majorca or Australia or China – anywhere he wants to go. No problem, no record, no surprise.'

'Okay. What about Bulford where you collected Fox. How was it the Captain simply handed Fox over to Early?'

Lyons cocked his head to one side. 'Easy. Fanshaw and Ravenscroft are polo buddies. Have been for years. Early told me that on the drive down. They arranged for Fox to be collected from Hereford on the pretext of assaulting a senior officer, dropped the charge and handed Fox to us for the rape.'

'But surely that would be a risk to Fanshaw if this information came out in the court case?'

'Maybe, maybe not. I got the impression from Early that Ravenscroft influence well and truly extends to the armed services.'

'Do you know if Early has been seeing Heidi recently?'

'No I don't. He comes and goes but never says what he's doin'. And listen boyo, I am not his bloody keeper.'

'Do you know anything about a fight between Fox and some American Heidi might be seeing at the moment?'

'No. But there are plenty of Americans around this area. Is it important?'

'I don't know yet. Did you know Fox had been hospitalised?'

'No. Why?'

'Some very close friends in Australia were murdered and, to borrow Johnson's terminology, Fox went "apeshit". He was sedated and put into hospital. I formed the impression that since then, the Governor has viewed Fox a little more kindly.'

'Well, I didn't know about that. Early's said nothing. As for the Governor,' Lyons chuckled slyly, 'if what you say is true, it would be an aberration. He's in Ravenscroft's pocket. Make no mistake. Whatever they've agreed to do to Fox will happen. Nothin's goin' to change that.'

Callum smiled lazily. 'Don't be too sure. One last question. What's the best way to get to see Early?'

CHAPTER 39

Callum pulled into the car park of the gun club at Mynyiddslwyn near Blackwood, Gwent. It was a little over six miles from Cwmbran. *Convenient to Early's home*, he thought. According to Lyons, Early, an avid shooter, would be here for his weekly competition at 4:00 pm.

In the two days since his meeting at *A Shot In the Dark*, Callum had obtained a sworn statement from Lyon's wife Evelyn detailing Early's conduct with Heidi Ravenscroft, the child. Evelyn's memory was so clear she could even describe the clothes they wore. Although this was an aspect open to ferocious testing in court, the one fact impossible to dispute was the existence of a large port-wine mark on Early's right buttock. What her affidavit described was clearly consensual sex between the two parties and although she was then unaware, as an adult now, Evelyn could say they were not only practised but innovative.

Callum had also obtained a comprehensive statement from Jonas Lyons about Early's treatment of Fox throughout the investigation. It was damning. To cap it off, he had spoken to Spencer Johnson in Ireland and obtained copies of affidavits from Claude and Maggie Collins and their nephew Henri Rouquefort. They confirmed Fox's proximity to the *White Duck* at the time of the alleged rape.

To ensure Callum made no mistake about Early's identity, Lyons had given Evelyn a photograph of him from a police magazine which she handed over at her interview.

Just before four o'clock Callum entered the gun club and was met by a chubby woman with short, jet black hair and a welcoming smile.

'Hello, you seem a bit lost. Are you looking for someone in particular?'

Callum smiled back. 'Yes. I was wondering if Cyril Early had arrived yet?'

'Yes, I saw him go into the change room about five minutes ago. He likes to get here with time to spare and get ready *early.*' She grinned as she emphasised the word and turned pointing. 'Go through those double doors over there. They will take you to the change rooms. Can't miss them.'

Callum thanked her and began walking towards the doors. As he did so he tuned in to a sense of bustle and expectancy. A quick look around revealed the presence of at least fifty people. He slowed when he caught sight of a large notice board. It seemed that today was the final elimination shoot before club championships the following week. Early's name appeared in the top draw and he would be among the first round of finalists. Callum smiled wickedly to himself.

He pushed through the doors and angled left in the direction of a sign to the men's change rooms. Inside Cyril Early was seated on a bench tying up his boots. He was clad in khaki trousers, a bone coloured shirt and a shooting jacket littered with pockets. A peaked cap perched rakishly on the back of his head.

Callum paused to study him. Early was a picture of concentration as he tied the boots slowly and with precision. The look upon his face was intense. Callum perceived that Early was mentally reviewing his drills in preparation for the competition. Quietly, he walked up to him and said sharply, 'Cyril.'

Early's head snapped upwards, his concentration interrupted.

'What?' he said tersely.

'I'm the lawyer representing Colin Fox. I want to talk to you.'

'For God's sake man. Not here, not now, I'm getting ready for a competition.'

'I know,' said Callum acidly and leaned close, 'with me. Superintendent,' he softened his voice, 'if you want any shred of reputation left over this bogus rape, you'll talk to me now, and you'll talk to me truthfully.'

'Are you threatening me you pratt? I don't know who the hell you are and I certainly don't know what you're talking about.' Early's voice was beginning to rise. 'But I'll tell you this – if you don't leave here right now I'll have you removed.' Early had risen to his feet, a dark look upon his face. He shaded Callum by a few centimetres in height and was icily angry.

Callum dropped his voice further and smiled gently.

'Let's begin with the port wine stain on your arse shall we? Then let's go on to the repeated carnal knowledge of a minor by you in 1969. That's just for starters. Care to comment?'

Early turned ashen.

'Rubbish!' he roared. 'You are talking absolute rubbish. Get out of here.' Quivering, Early's previous composure was fractured and with it, any shred of power he might have had.

'Superintendent, believe me when I say that what you have done to Fox will pale to insignificance by the time I'm finished with you. Meet me in the car park in five minutes or suffer the consequences.' His stride, as he walked out, was measured and assured.

Behind him, Early, his usual control and authority in tatters, slumped to the bench. Two members ready for the competition approached.

'What's going on Cyril?' enquired Owen Fenna. 'Who was that?'

'Are you going to be able to compete Cyril? Only you look a bit shaken.' Aled Evans smiled, a fierce rival of Early and not particularly enamoured of him.

'For fuck's sake,' said Fenna, 'of course he's going to compete. He'll beat you blind Aled.'

Numbed by the blatant revelation of his youthful adventures, adventures Early believed that only he and Heidi knew of, he was too stunned to think clearly. Warning bells sounded. He tried to pull his thoughts together as Fenna and Evans yabbered at him.

'Listen boys,' Early said beckoning the two men close, 'I can't talk about it. Could you see the Captain and ask him to change me to the last draw today. I have to get something organised urgently. That's all I can say. Give him my apologies. I'll be inside for the last shoot.' He rose abruptly and hurried from the change room.

In the car park he looked around and saw the stranger standing by a black BMW sedan. Thinking furiously, Early decided to tough it out. The only person who could have given him this information was Heidi and he was too important to her to be ratted on. It couldn't be her. But that begged the question as to how this fellow had come by this knowledge. He slowed, breathed deeply and walked towards the car.

'You seem to have the advantage over me sir,' said Early extending his hand. 'You know me but I don't know you. Who are you?'

'Callum Fox,' came the reply, the outstretched hand ignored, 'here is my card. As I said before, I am representing Colin Fox whom you have unlawfully imprisoned.'

Early opened his mouth to protest. Callum silenced him with a raised hand.

'Now listen to me Superintendent, this is going to be your one and only opportunity to put things right with minimal damage to your personal reputation. I understand you want to reach Assistant Chief Constable rank, if not better. Unless you co-operate, four things are going to happen with such speed you won't know what hit you. The most probable result will be that you'll have no job at all. Do we understand each other?'

Early controlled his desire to thump Callum Fox. He swallowed hard and attempted to speak authoritatively, instead, his voice was strangled.

'Before I agree to anything with a complete stranger who is talking utter rubbish, let me hear it.'

Callum smiled. 'Fair point. I'll be succinct. First, I have a sworn affidavit from a witness about your sexual activities with a minor occurring throughout the summer of 1969. Second, I have sworn affidavits from witnesses placing Colin Fox some miles from the scene of the alleged rape of Heidi Ravenscroft on the day and at the time it is said to have occurred. Third, I have evidence of your personal friendships with the Clerk of Courts, the two justices who committed Fox without bail, the inexperienced junior Counsel engaged for Fox at that hearing, your collusion with Captain Fanshaw at SIB and your long running relationship with Heidi Ravenscroft. Fourth, I have a sworn affidavit from a witness prepared to assert that you deliberately ignored proper police procedures regarding the investigation of this alleged crime. And finally, I am aware of your friendship with the Governor of the Cardiff Remand Centre. Whilst I've not yet met him, I don't think it will take long for him to reveal that the denial of privileges to Fox was at the request of yourself and Heidi's father. It will be your decision as to whether I send a full package of this information to your Chief Constable, the press in Cardiff, to Lord Ravenscroft and, finally, to the BBC News Division. And that, Superintendent, is only the beginning. The civil and punitive damages claim I will run for what you have done to Fox will be substantial. The outcome of that combined with a fiercely contested criminal trial, which you will inevitably lose, is likely to render employment prospects for you anywhere remarkably slender. And regrettably, that will hurt your wife and family. Need I go on?'

Callum watched Early wilt before him. Callum felt no pity. For all he knew, Early might have been blackmailed into doing what he had done but it was no excuse. He had sworn to uphold the law and to dispense justice without fear or favour. He had failed.

'Get in my car,' directed Callum.

'Where are we going?' asked Early quietly.

'Nowhere. We are going to talk.'

After they had settled Callum said, 'I understand you have been manipulated by a woman who wanted revenge, a woman whom you could describe as a predator, a woman who uses sex as currency to buy and sell favours. A woman who can and does hit back if she feels slighted. I understand all that. What I want to know is how you came to this.'

Early looked at Callum, fear and loathing in his eyes.

'You think you are so bloody smart don't you. I remember you now. The hot-shot lawyer mixed up with the UN and justice for victims of crime. The Home Office made a big fuss about it earlier this year. You really have no idea about Heidi. She's like heroin – dangerous and addictive. Every time she was in trouble I'd bail her out and keep it quiet. Then she'd be mine for a week or a month of heaven then … bang! The bliss would stop like nothing had ever happened. Excruciating.' Pain was engraved on Early's thin features, a tear trickled from one eye.

'Tell me about the summer of '69,' Callum said, unmoved.

Early was quiet, a range of expressions flitting over his face: guilt, remorse, resentment, fear, disgust. He was trapped. Callum reached for his brief case in the back seat.

'Would you like me to read from some of the affidavits to refresh your memory?'

With growing resignation Early replied, 'Not necessary. Everything is etched into my mind.' Agonising, he gulped some air. 'It all started when she was twelve. Bloody twelve. I was eighteen. In the spring of '67 I went to the stables for a horse one day. Heidi had matured early and was quite the well built young woman. She was swinging on a rail over the stalls wearing a dress and no underwear. I was embarrassed and couldn't look at her. She could see that and started laughing and doing splits and scissor movements in the air. I walked out. Jesus, she was only a bloody child! After that it seemed as though she followed me and every time I went to get a horse she was there doing the same thing. In the end, it got to be that I could only go horse riding when she was physically not on the property. Then, one day late in '69 when she was almost fourteen, I thought she was away. I went to the stables believing all was clear. I saddled my horse and when I was leading him out I heard a moaning sound from a couple of stalls along. I looked in and there she was, no knickers, legs wide apart rubbing like crazy. I couldn't stop watching. That happened several more times and then one day she said straight out, "Come on for Christ's sake, fuck me." To my eternal shame and regret, I did. After that we began meeting in the loft over the stalls to have at it. From then on I was hers. I both hated and wanted her. I tried to get her out of my system by getting married but it didn't work and my wife, Isobel, who is a good woman, has always suspected that Heidi and I were once involved. She doesn't know I still see her. But now, Heidi, just like you, threatens to tell the world. I've tried to manage it all but … this thing with Fox … it's … it's the worst I've ever done for her.' Early's deeply anguished face had taken on a greyish pallor.

'Tell me about it,' said Callum.

'She came to me just before Christmas and said she'd been raped by this SAS bloke she'd been seeing. I knew she was lying, that there was more to it, but she showed me some pretty serious bruises and cuts on her arms and legs and insisted it was for real. I made some discreet enquiries and discovered this bloke Fox had been going out with her and he'd dumped her. Heidi doesn't do being dumped. Fox didn't know she was already playing around with some American soldier before he got rid of her. Heidi being Heidi wanted revenge. Anyway, I began the investigation. Her father was bleating for justice, Heidi was carrying on like a pork chop about what a bastard Fox had been and how cruel he was and how badly she'd been attacked. As I got into it, there seemed to be a *prima facie* case. Certainly there was injury and sufficient semen traces in her car to support her claim. So I went for Fox. It still didn't seem right but the family was insistent and then they began to threaten me saying I wasn't doing enough and they would report me to the Chief Constable. Beneath that, Heidi was threatening my exposure for what we had done when she was a kid. The family said that if I made the rape stick, they would ease my way to an Assistant Chief Constable's position. So I pulled out all stops. Then, one night after Fox had been committed and Heidi was wrapped around me, she tells me she planned the whole thing. She and the American. They'd had some really rough sex and when the bruises developed and were so ugly, she got the idea of hurting Fox for dumping her. The American helped her get it all together. Seems he had an axe to grind with Fox too. I was beggared after that. In too deep, at my wits end and dreading this day. It had to come. She, on the other hand, has done nothing but gloat. Believe me, I wish it were different.'

Callum was silent for what seemed an eternity. He did not doubt Early's desire for Fox's plight to disappear, nor did he doubt Heidi's machinations, but he was not convinced that Early's motives were honourable.

'Clearly your actions must be aired publicly. You are a servant of the law and you de-railed justice.' Callum, his tone cutting, was stony faced. 'You will accept the consequences, whatever they are. I will be in touch with you again but leave you with this counsel: do not try to avoid what is coming. In the meantime, I want you to ring the prison Governor and make certain that until I can get Fox out of there, he is to receive all privileges to which he is entitled. Goodbye Superintendent.'

CHAPTER 40

The day after his meeting with Cyril Early, Callum attended the Cardiff Remand Centre. He had two goals. The first to meet Governor Terry Smith, the second to meet Colin Fox. Around 9:45 am he was shown into the Governor's office. It was large, square, austere and starkly lit through a huge set of south-facing windows. Smith was of average build and appearance. *In a crowd, Callum thought, he would have looked so unassuming as to be almost invisible.* He rose from his desk when Callum entered.

'Mr Fox,' he said, 'pleased to meet you. I'm a busy man and I've squeezed you in at short notice. I understand you want to talk to me about Colin Fox. Do sit down.' No handshake, a cool, superior tone of voice.

Callum studied Smith and observed that at first glance while he might be "ordinary looking", his suit was exquisitely tailored. No off-the-peg clothing for Governor Smith.

Callum opened his briefcase and removed a legal pad and slim envelope.

'I believe you already know I am Colin Fox's legal representative and today I anticipate he will be leaving your custody after a hearing at Cardiff Magistrates' Court, a properly conducted and constituted court. Unlike the fiasco that placed him in your care, this afternoon's Special Sitting is before a Magistrate not from the Cardiff circuit.'

Callum's tone was neutral yet his presence seemed to expand and command Smith's entire office. Smith's countenance darkened with displeasure.

He examined Callum before speaking. He resented this jumped-up, international lawyer-twat taking over his office. He knew of his reputation and was pissed-off before they'd even met as a consequence of that fucking limp-wristed Early and his bloody phone call about restoring Fox's rights. He tried but failed to stare Callum down.

'You're implying that Fox's hearing was illegal. As far as I'm concerned, all the *paperwork* that sent him here is one hundred per cent correct. He's staying until I'm directed otherwise.'

'No Mr Smith, not implying. Your paperwork may be correct but that does not mean it is legal. So, if you don't mind, I'd now like to see my client. Oh, and this is a piece of paper which I assure you is both legal and correct.' Callum picked up the slim envelope and handed it to Smith.

'This court document directs you to do two things: one, allow me to see my client and two, ensure he is at the court by two o'clock today.' He rose and nodded to Smith. 'Now, I'd like an escort Mr Smith. Thank you for your time.'

Callum was skilled in knowing when and how to play hard-ball – this was one of those times. Smith had barely uttered a word before he found himself pressing a buzzer for Callum Fox to be seen out.

'Take Mr Fox to Number One Detail,' Smith said irritably to the woman who entered his office, 'and have someone accompany him to Colin Fox's cell. He has one hour, no more.' As soon as the door closed Smith picked up the phone and rang Kilmore Castle.

When the cell door opened, Fox was on his bed meditating. He opened his eyes to see the guard usher in a stranger. The man was around two metres tall, slim, bespectacled and had what

Fox considered a regulation navy beard – full, rich and perfectly trimmed. Longish, chestnut coloured hair completed the picture. He was dressed in jeans, a pale pink check shirt, lambs-wool jacket and polished brown boots. Overall, Fox perceived a man who clearly took care of himself.

The man strode forward, hand outstretched and, in a warm Scottish burr said, 'I'm Callum Fox, your lawyer and relative.'

As he closed the distance Fox immediately saw his own thick wavy hair and grey eyes smiling at him. He grinned, got off the bed and shook Callum's hand warmly.

'Jeez mate, I thought you'd never get here.' His smile broadened further.

'Did you know I was coming?' Callum asked, head cocked to one side.

'No,' responded Fox with a grin, 'that was a joke. I did know someone was going to get me out of this joint, but not who. Here, pull up a bed.'

Callum sat on the bunk and examined Fox for a few moments before speaking. The prison escort quietly withdrew and closed the cell door.

'I am really pleased to meet you Colin. In the short time I've spent on your case I have spoken to many people about you – it's all good. For me, however, the most important person is Aunt Lou. If she says you're okay, that's it. So, let's get to it.'

'Just before we start, please call me Fox, everyone does and has since I was a little kid. It's easy that way.'

Callum smiled slowly. 'Do you think we should start trying to confuse people?"

'Bit tricky,' laughed Fox, 'I'm black, you're white.'

Callum smiled. 'Okay. At two this afternoon you'll be appearing at the Cardiff Magistrates' Court where I anticipate you'll be granted bail. On Wednesday next week your committal proceedings commence. I'll be immediately moving a motion to have the matter struck out. There may be a little residual friction from some quarters but, I believe we have an overwhelming argument to firstly quash the matter and secondly, pursue substantial compensation. I've just got a couple of loose ends to tidy up this weekend and after that, full speed ahead.'

Fox remained perfectly still taking in every word, every nuance, his face impassive. Relief flooded through.

'Aunt Lou sends her love and hopes you will see her before you return to Australia,' said Callum, intruding on Fox's thoughts. 'Spencer Johnson wishes you good luck. He put in some really solid work on your behalf yet, for his effort, seems to have been banished to Dublin. And Gordon and McPhie said I was to tell you to stop slacking. On a more serious note, I've spoken to Dr John McNulty. I was truly sorry to hear of your loss there and understand how prominent that family has been in your life. They send their love and support and can't wait to see you home again. John asked me a question I didn't understand and perhaps you'll enlighten me.'

Fox peered deeply into Callum's eyes and spoke before he could ask the question. 'Not yet, but possibly. When I get home.'

Callum appeared nonplussed.

Fox said, 'You were going to ask if I was "singing" the man who committed those ghastly crimes. The answer is no. I need to be there first.'

'Aunt Lou said you were unusual. Okay, any questions?'

'No, I'll see you at court this afternoon.'

CHAPTER 41

'Heidi, we have to meet and talk about Fox. Today!' Early's tone was terse and unequivocal.

'You're an old worry wart Cyril. Dad's got Fox covered.' Heidi's tone was bantering.

'I don't think so. I'm talking about the lawyer Fox, the one who knows what we did years ago. The one who knows about my birthmark. The one I'd never met before yesterday. We have to talk.' He sounded desperate.

There was a lengthy silence. 'Six tonight then, on the road to Mynyiddslwyn,' Heidi said quietly, 'there's a wooded area a mile shy of the gun club. Six sharp in the parking area.' The phone went down gently.

Superintendent Cyril Early could not remember ever feeling the way he felt right now. Not before any of the football finals he'd played, not on his wedding day, not at any of his serious criminal trials, not at the birth of his children. He was anxious, deeply ashamed and fearful. And the reason for this emotional hamburger-with-the-lot was Callum Fox.

Since their meeting, Early had been powerless to stop thinking of Callum's dire warning. His ambition had shrivelled, his dreams were scuttled and glaring, horrendous exposure loomed. Everyone would see him as a weak, sleazy, fornicating, advantage-taker. They'd laugh and jeer and revile him. Some would even think him a paedophile. His embarrassment would be monstrous. The shame for his wife and children was beyond calculation. But, he had not taken advantage. He had simply capitulated to Heidi's relentless pursuit – become prisoner to a child whose mind and body was worldly beyond her years. Agitated, Early was now consumed with discovering a way of making people understand that Heidi Ravenscroft – beautiful, wild and unquenchable as Aphrodite – was as hazardous and toxic as Britain's giant Lion's Mane jellyfish.

He thought about her reaction to his phone call. Different – calm. He wondered if she already knew of Callum Fox. He was expecting her usual tirade of gibes followed by rapid dismissal. But no, he sensed in her a recognition of the name and perceived her thoughtfulness during the short conversation. And that made him even more uneasy because he knew the kinds of callous stunts she could pull. God she was complex! In reflecting upon her assorted misdeeds and his pains over the years to extract her from trouble, his unease ballooned. She could not be trusted.

Early drove his boxy 1984 Landrover slowly into the wooded clearing. Fox was free. Callum had been masterful in court and clearly reserved his punishment of the police investigation for the committal on Wednesday. Even so, the newly formed Crown Prosecution Service was already asking difficult questions. The future looked bleak.

It was 5:30 pm and a shit of an evening. Blustery, showery and cold – six degrees the announcer had said a few minutes earlier on the radio. Outside, it was as black as the inside of a cow. Even though the heater was up full blast, he shivered. With headlights on full beam, he turned in a large, lazy circle to survey the location. He had passed this spot a zillion times on his way to the gun club but never driven into it.

With branches clutching and snapping in a buffeting wind, the old bare oaks, junipers, birches and larch clamoured at the edge of the clearing. The surface beneath the car was slushy though firm underneath. *Bugger!* He desperately wanted a slash and would have to step out into the shit. He stopped near the tree line after completing his circle. He was farthest from the road here and figured the ground would be firmer and kinder to his expensive shoes. He turned the headlights off, left the parkers and motor on and stepped into the cold. The wind was lacerating. He stood close to the car so his piss wouldn't blow back on him.

In the middle of it and above the racket of wind and trees, he heard a misfiring motor approaching. He finished and hopped back into the warmth of his car. A minute or so later, a lone headlight turned into the clearing, slowed then moved towards him. Early flicked his lights on. A red Suzuki 750 motor bike was approaching. The rider waved and turned the bike sideways to stop squarely in the headlights a short distance in front of the car. He dismounted and walked to Early's window.

Early wound his window down but made no move to get out.

'Boy am I glad to find you here,' boomed a friendly American voice from the helmet. 'I thought I was gunna have to hoof it to the nearest town but I just caught sight of your lights. This goddamn thing seems to have a problem with petrol flow or somethin'. Curtis Clapton by the way.' Clapton took off a heavy glove and stuck his hand towards Early who shook it. 'Don't 'spose you'd have a few tools and a torch in there would ya?' Early made out a broad smile inside the helmet.

'I do as it happens,' said Early, twitchy about the interruption.

'Can you give us hand then. I hired this machine up in London so I could tour Wales for the next week. Wrong time of the goddamn year. Big mistake. Bitch of a thing doesn't like the cold.'

Early sighed. He could hardly say no. He shrugged into a woollen jacket.

'Yeah, we'll see what we can do.' He wound up his window,

stepped outside, shut the door and walked to the back of his vehicle. Clapton was there waiting.

'Got a good torch?' Clapton drawled.

'Yep, got most things in the back here,' said Early leaning forward to open the hatch. He grunted with surprise and pain as Clapton's needle-like, twenty centimetre brochette slipped through his jacket, up under his ribs and into his heart. Turning, gasping and in searing pain, he raised his arm to ward off a second blow directed through his ear to his brain. He fell, dying as he crumpled into the mush.

Clapton wiped the brochette on Early's jacket and slipped it back up his sleeve. He used Early's headlights to adjust the motor bike's carburettor, put his glove back on, turned off the motor and lights of the car and shut the door. He started up and rode out of the clearing into another heavy shower of rain.

At six o'clock Heidi arrived, her headlights instantly picking out Early's darkened car on the far side of the clearing. She covered the distance slowly, expecting to see him respond to her arrival. Even after all these years and the terrible things she had done to him, he still was besotted by her. *Strange,* she thought. *No one in sight.* She pulled up by the front passenger door facing the back of the Landrover. Definitely no one in the car. She checked her rear view mirror, scanned the clearing left and right. Nothing. She stepped outside and walked to the front of the Landrover and felt the bonnet. Still warm. She opened the driver's door and peered inside. The interior light revealed an empty car. A hint of warmth remained, as though the heater had recently been on. She walked to the back of the vehicle and almost tripped over Early's body in the gloom. From the diffused illumination of her car's headlights, Early's absolute stillness screamed death.

Heidi was stunned. She stepped around him, went to her car and took a torch from the glove-box. When she ran its beam over his body she saw blood stains on his jacket near the heart. An ooze of blood had also mixed with rain on the side of his head. Early's body seemed to have folded onto the ground. His right hand was just below his heart, as though to staunch the bleeding, head canted on the left shoulder resting in black mud.

She stooped and touched his neck for pulse. Nothing. His skin was cold and wet. She slid her hand inside the right side of his jacket – still warm, even in this temperature. He was not long dead. Suddenly afraid, she stood and looked around again. There was nothing to be seen in the blackness beyond her headlights. She ran to her car, got inside and locked the doors. A blast of freezing rain hissed upon the windscreen as the car rocked in a fierce wind gust. *Who? Why?* From her phone she rang her father. He would know what to do.

CHAPTER 42

There had been no thought of contradiction – the venue was decided with quiet authority by Lord Ravenscroft. Sunday, four o'clock, *Boodles* at 28 St James Street, London. Callum, wanting to take the Old Man through Fox's release from prison and talk about those responsible for his arrest had telephoned him on Saturday to suggest the meeting. Lord Ravenscroft had agreed without hesitation.

Boodles, built in 1775 – an elite establishment for gentlemen – was not a surprise. It was a landscape from a different era, a place of privacy, a club totally in keeping with the taste of this exceedingly wealthy and influential man. *Boodles* still barred women from entry and, over time, had provided sanctuary to the rich and powerful, harboured intrigue and borne silent witness to the acquisition and loss of fortunes. *Yes,* thought Callum, *the aged brown building with its Tuscan porch projections, capacious leather chairs and discreet old world style was a logical choice.*

Now, escorted to Lord Ravenscroft by an impeccably liveried staff member, Callum noted the Old Man had aged markedly since South Africa two years earlier. The lines on his face were deeper and craggier, his complexion was pasty and the once thick white mane had thinned markedly. A whisky tumbler was beside him, his old clay pipe in an ashtray – his eyes closed. The attendant coughed discreetly.

'Yes Barnes, what is it?' His eyes remained closed.

'Your guest, my Lord.'

Blink, blink. Powerful blue lamps lasered Callum. 'Thank you Barnes. A Bacardi and coke for you Callum?' He smiled and slowly eased himself from the chair, extending his hand.

'Thank you, no ice.' Callum smiled back. *Nothing wrong with the Old Man's memory.*

Ravenscroft gestured to the chair opposite and sank down again. At eighty-one, Callum could see he had slowed since their last meeting.

'So, young Callum, you want to regale me with the evil doings of my granddaughter Heidi? Nothing much you say will surprise me you know. I love her dearly. I'm guilty of being wrapped around her little finger even though I know she has the same streak of capricious malevolence as my mother. It's in the genes you know. Always on the women's side. Fire away.' He relaxed deeply into his chair, face composed, unreadable – eyes boring into Callum's.

It was not quite the opening Callum expected.

'I take it you know of Heidi's alleged rape and the arrest of an SAS soldier for it?'

'Yes.'

'Do you know also that the whole thing was a fabrication? Made up by Heidi with some help from a policeman named Early.'

'Not originally. It was always presented to me as a real and traumatic assault. Why did she make this claim?'

'She and the soldier were an item for a time and he gave her the boot. She wanted to hit back.'

Ravenscroft smiled sadly. 'Of course. What did I say before – capricious malevolence. She's used to always getting her own way.'

'I'm told you know Early.'

'Used to. He was murdered Friday night.'

Callum was gobsmacked.

'What? How? Where?' He leaned forward in his chair, mind

spinning, wondering what was behind the death. Immediately, he thought of Heidi.

'No, not Heidi,' said Ravenscroft intuitively. 'She has a legitimate alibi and actually discovered his body. Seems she and Early were to meet for a discussion about Fox's release.' Again, the Old Man smiled sadly. 'I understand he's a relative of yours.'

Callum nodded. Silent, his mind continued to race over possible consequences from Early's death. Ravenscroft scrutinised Callum, aware the cogs were churning.

'I'll save you the trouble,' said Ravenscroft authoritatively. 'Since learning of Cyril's death I have organised the following: first, Heidi has been posted to Canada and departs tomorrow evening. Second, she understands she is not to return to England until she has either completed her secondment – two years – or left the army and established her own business over there. She is not welcome here until she redeems herself. Third, my son, who runs Kilmore Castle, is on notice of total disinheritance. There have been difficulties with him before but this time his behaviour has been utterly disgraceful — inimical to our family reputation and to me personally. This is his last chance. I have nieces and nephews who are far more deserving and accomplished. Fourth, the Early family will not go wanting. Cyril was a good man but too weak to resist Heidi. I knew she used and abused him. I don't know what lies behind his death but I will not see his wife and children suffer. Finally, I have made arrangements for a £ 75,000 trust fund to be established for Colin Fox. You and he can decide what to do with it but until then it will stay in trust drawing damn good interest. I fully expect to be told to stick it up my nose but I hope he doesn't take that approach. When I initially heard about Heidi's alleged rape I had some research done so know a little of this Fox's background and while this will not compensate for what happened, he can use it any way he chooses.'

Lord Ravenscroft's actions, revealed at whip-cracking pace,

brooked no demur. For a second time that afternoon, Callum was gobsmacked. Without going into detail the Old Man had revealed a depth of knowledge about the incident and its key players which Callum found remarkable. He had thought the Old Man too far removed from everything to have little more than an inkling of the event. He had underestimated Ravenscroft, something to remember.

'I really don't know how Fox will react to your proposal but we will properly consider it. Early's death ... well ... as you can see, I didn't know about it and, as unfortunate as it may be, it will save many people a lot of embarrassment. The matter can be withdrawn ...'

Before he could finish Ravenscroft winked, lightly tapped the side of his nose and smiled.

'I've had a word there too, Callum. Don't worry – the Crown Prosecutor will handle it. Well young man, I think our business is concluded. Thank you for coming to see me.' He waved his hand and Barnes silently appeared.

'See Mr Fox out would you please Barnes.' He leaned forward, shook Callum's hand and nodded. Their meeting was over.

METAMORPHOSIS

All things must change to something new,
something strange.

HENRY WADSWORTH
LONGFELLOW

(1807 – 1882)

CHAPTER 43

He had covered his tracks well. The cops were unaware of him and more than two years had passed since knocking off that traitorous bloody Connors and her daughter. After a bumpy start in Melbourne, Wildman's life had more or less evened out. His health had settled down, his tremors were under control and he'd been off the booze for just on three and a half years – forty-two months or 1277 days – but who was counting? He still had to wrestle the urge though – strong as ever. He sat there, smiling to himself having just finalised arrangements with a West Australian contact. Four more pit-bulls, aka Staffordshire Terriers, arriving in two weeks from the good ol' US of A. Few people could tell the two breeds of dog apart, especially with forged documents so … in they came. Quarantine and then collection. As Western Australia was the best route, he eased more through there than other states. Best of all though, he didn't have to sling bribes to the crooked customs blokes. Sammy took care of it.

Sammy was Top Dog of the Blades. *Ha ha, Top Dog, joke.* Except – you didn't joke with the Blades. More especially, you didn't joke with Sammy Milosevic. One of the new young bikie gangs evolving in Australia, they were tough, fearless and ultra-violent. Brutally active in creating new ethnic divisions from the old established bikie culture, their aim was to seize the lion's share of Australia's billion dollar illicit drug industry. Membership required every last

FOX

one of them to have "offed" or seriously and permanently disabled someone in face to face confrontation. And someone didn't mean ordinary Joe Citizen – no, that'd be like squashing eggs in a chook yard. Someone meant some bastard from another biker gang, or a dude from an underworld mob. And, they had to prove it. Not only that, but the injury or death had to be inflicted by knife. Any pussy could use a gun, the knife was a challenge.

Milosevic began using Wildman after giving him a terrible thrashing for "dissing" him. Wildman couldn't remember what he'd said but now it didn't matter, it was past. After the beating Milosevic learned Wildman was an ex-copper and "sort of" recruited him. The arrangement was simple – "shut the fuck up, help me and live, or …" Milosevic soon twigged that Wildman had contacts in every state and territory – bent and serving, or sacked and disgraced cops. Useful tools.

Apart from Milosevic's remorseless drive to become an international force in the field of drug and money moving throughout Africa, Italy, Canada, Asia and several old Russian states, his team had other diverse interests. They cooked and distributed drugs, sucked in young kids as dependant agents, grew cannabis, imported firearms, scammed casinos throughout the country, revelled in armed hold-ups, held public fucking contests, and invested time, energy and thought in illegal gambling. Their specialism in the latter was the kind that would cause most folks to vomit – dog fights, cockfights and bare-knuckle brawling. And it was the dog fights that Wildman was thinking of now.

His broad array of associates had strong links with dog fighters in the UK, Japan, Ireland, Europe, South America, Philippines, USA, Canada, Spain, South Africa and the Triads of Malaysia. Using private planes, boats, subterfuge, healthy payouts and the dark encouragement of murder, Wildman, sheltered by Milosevic's muscle, smuggled outlawed dog varieties into the country for breeding purposes. Among them the *Tosa* from Japan, *Dogo*

Argentino from Latin America and the *Presa Canario* from Spain. These, crossed with fierce and brutal pit-bulls bred by Wildman, were producing some of the most ferocious and relentless fighting dogs seen in Australia.

The new breeds were tested for ability and fighting instinct at an early age. The endless supply of bait necessary for these fighters was arranged through Wildman's contacts who stole dogs from city and country regions all over Australia. Recently, Wildman was narked because the Hunter Valley cops in New South Wales were concentrating on the high numbers of dogs disappearing from their patch. Wildman had to scale back, an action that earned him another beating by Milosevic.

But Wildman used other techniques too. His team scoured media advertisements seeking "good homes for free dogs" and visited the odd lost dog centre keen to receive clandestine monies. Cash for "dogs in care" boosted business incomes, maintained animal turnover and reduced costs. It was a field where Wildman performed at his innovative best and amoral worst. Cruelty, manipulation and callousness were stock-in-trade tools for getting things done. And, so long as Sammy was happy, Wildman sought to ingratiate himself deeper into the Blades and their culture ever mindful of his tenuous employment conditions: "… help me and live or …"

Belatedly, Wildman found he possessed a nose for property acquisition. The isolated kind that often was wild, abandoned and not easy to find. Mostly these were farms, but occasionally, there was the odd suburban warehouse in a lonely industrial park. Sammy had purchased seven such places of which Wildman's favourite was at Flowerdale.

Roughly north east of Melbourne, yet not far from the capital, the Flowerdale property was buried in dense forest and devoid of neighbours for a seven kilometre radius. It had become the Blades' fight HQ and principal dog breeding and training ground.

Surrounding paddocks had mostly succumbed to wild fern, dockweed, blackberries and 'roos but there was space aplenty for cars, an important feature on contest nights. The buildings were crude, large, weatherproof and blokey: vertical slab walls, stone fireplaces, verandas, tanks and plenty of fallen timber for cooking and warmth. Sheilas didn't have to like the conditions as they came for one thing only – rooting money. What they thought didn't count. All that mattered was the Blades and of them, the only one to please was Sammy. If he said okay, everyone said okay.

The phone rang startling Wildman from his day-dreaming. He picked up.

'Everything set for next week, you sad little fuck?' asked a gravelly voice.

'Sure Sammy, everything.'

'How many bouts?'

'That depends ...'

'Don't tell me that arsehole, I want to know exactly,' Milosevic interrupted in chilling tones. 'Fancy your balls cut out? How many fucking bouts?'

'I've planned for six, got two extras in reserve, but if the fights are long we might only get in four.'

'Why didn't you say so the first time. Sounds good. Next time, don't fuck me around. Where are the dogs from?'

Wildman began to sweat furiously.

'Mostly Victoria but there's a champion coming from Queensland and another with a bloody good rep from South Aus. Two of the Vic dogs are bloody brutes that keep winning. They haven't fought each other yet and I was going to ask what you thought about puttin' them against the two interstaters. At the next contest, the two winners of those bouts could go against each other. We've talked about ...'

'Wildman shutup! I've warned you before – don't interrupt me when I'm thinking. I know what we've talked about.' The craggy voice was ominous, the ensuing silence brooding. Wildman waited nervously.

'Yeah, it's a start. Check WA and the Territory – see if they've got any willing potentials. You'll only get shit from Tassy. Although,' a sound somewhere between a bray and a cough assaulted Wildman's ear – Milosevic laughing. 'Although, some bright bastard down there might have crossed a Tassie devil with a Rotty. That'd be a sight.' He laughed some more then stopped abruptly. 'That only leaves New South.' More silence. 'Hook it up.'

CHAPTER 44

Murder was searing his mind. After returning from the UK, Fox patiently served out his contract time before making his move to leave the army. More than two years had elapsed since Caroline's and Judy's murders in January 1986. He had kept shtum about his intentions, performed to his best, imparted all he had learned and encountered a battle royal with Major Hoey when he finally submitted his papers.

'You've thought about this properly, have you Fox? I mean … really considered it?' Hoey was bleak, his gaze and tone flinty.

'I have sir. Seriously.'

'I am bitterly disappointed. Your training results, behaviour and demeanour both here and overseas are outstanding. You weathered all that shit in England and withstood more than anyone on that course. I personally know Colonel Chartres and old Ropey, and if you knew Chartres as I do, his level of personal support puts you in contention for some kind of bloody medal. Winkling praise out of him is nigh on impossible. But you did. And good old Ropey. He stuck with you all the way. He actually rang me about that idiot Carmody. Would rather it hadn't happened of course, but stuck like glue. You have to realise man you have more than enough potential to occupy *my* chair in a few years. You simply must not leave. It will be a huge waste of talent and investment.'

Fox, unaware of Ropey's and Chartres' views was stoked by the feedback, as well as by Hoey's comment about occupying *his* chair. For a fleeting moment, he faltered.

'Sir, I truly appreciate everything you have said. I have particularly valued your support and that of others. Even more, I will be eternally grateful for the opportunity of attending Hereford. I can honestly assure you that if matters had been different here, at home, I would not be leaving now. But, I have unfinished business to deal with and have waited patiently to get on with it. Now, my time is up. I can either renew my contract or leave and I have decided to finish the unfinished. I cannot do what I must by staying in the army.'

'I take it you are speaking of the double murder.'

'Yes sir.'

'What are your intentions?'

'To find the bastard who did it.'

'Well, I can tell you, I've kept an ear to the ground and the police have nothing, even after all this time.'

'They're not me,' Fox responded quietly.

Hoey allowed a tiny smile and softened his tone. 'I know that and, in your own best interest, that is the principle reason I want you to stay.'

Fox nodded and offered nothing further. There was a long silence as Hoey stared at Fox.

'Do you know who did it?'

'Sir, certain questions are better left unanswered. All I can say is: I know where to start looking. Resigning gives me the chance to do that.'

Hoey leaned back into his chair and steepled his fingers. His face was inscrutable and Fox had no idea of his thoughts.

'I don't like it one bit Fox,' he said after another lengthy silence. 'I think you are making a very big mistake. Having said that, you will be honourably discharged. I've got a rough idea of what you want to do and I wish you success. I just hope things don't backfire.'

Fox stood, saluted and walked to the door where he stopped.

'Sir, I cannot thank you enough – for everything. Whether I am successful or not, I anticipate that neither you nor anyone else will ever know.'

Hoey nodded. 'I know that too,' he said sombrely, his eyes glinting.

Fox could not explain to Hoey or anyone else the blistering pain and hollowness he experienced when finally he walked into the arms of the McNulty family. They were overjoyed to see him and plied him with a thousand questions but after the initial blush of greetings, there had been deep feelings of loss and anguish and interminable stretches of emptiness.

As part of their recovery they had sold their much loved home. They could neither escape nor endure the agony of bitter-sweet memories, the poignancy of all the good times.

In marking time to leave the army Fox had maintained regular contact with Aunt Louisa, Callum, Spencer Johnson and his mates Lex McPhie and Davy Gordon. Three months before his resignation took effect, Fox received a box of items from Callum concerning his grandfather's past. Among them was a letter from Aunt Louisa expressing her thoughts and feelings about her family's lives and her great pleasure at meeting Fox. It was a potted history of his Scottish family with names, places, dates, events and activities. The chronicle made Fox feel proud and connected and, as he read it, emotional. Now he knew his history not only from the time of "The Dreaming", but also his *kartiyah* side. Both were important and to be respected.

But now the time had come. There would be no peace for Fox until Caroline and Judy were avenged. As soon as he could after re-uniting with the family he had gone to their old home and stood in the driveway. There, he allowed his senses to explore every room before focussing intently upon the garage and Caroline's bedroom.

Next, he had gone to the highest point of King's Park overlooking the Swan River. He sat cross legged and, in a state of deep reverie perceived a misty image.

Soon after he caught a ferry to South Perth and viewed a large block of units just off Mends Street. He found his way inside and went to unit 8/2, a centre unit on the eighth floor of the sixteen storey block. Receiving no answer to his knocking, he checked the units on either side. Again, there was no answer at number one but unit three was a gold mine. There, the elderly Ms Doris Lavender told Fox that the owner of unit two, one Garry McLune, worked for the *West Australian* newspaper and was away working overseas. During his absence over the previous two years his unit had been occupied by a very strange man. Strange because he seemed unwell, had the shakes, was rake thin and wore a wild and heavy beard. Strange because he was secretive and rarely left the unit. Strange because he had an abnormally deathly pallor. When Fox pressed further she said that several times she had heard him shouting in a way she could only imagine was deranged. Not only that, but his language was the foulest she had ever heard. Did she know his name?

'Well dear,' Ms Lavender had said, 'he never told me and as I indicated, he was not friendly. Now, I am not normally an inquisitive soul but I did happen to see some letters sticking out of his mailbox one day. I thought I should put them in for him properly, just in case they got lost.' She smiled mischievously. 'The funny thing was, they were addressed to different people. Two were for a Mr Grant Edgeware and one was from a medical clinic in Melbourne addressed to a Mr Wildman. So really, I still don't know his name.'

But Fox knew. There would be no quarter until Wildman's death.

CHAPTER 45

Hay Street on Friday night was humming with late night shopping, dining, movie-goers and romance. Ecucina was one of Fox's favourite haunts – tasteful, low key, great food, attentive staff and a warm relaxed atmosphere. Here, the five of them sat around the table comfortable in each others company: Jenny, Kurt, John, Jason and Fox. Tonight, Fox was alive, vibrant and full of anticipation – tonight he would prepare them for his departure. For the moment though, he waited, sensing that Jenny was bursting with news of her own.

Having ordered drinks and dispensed with the small talk, Jenny turned to Fox.

'Foxy, why did you pick tonight? Here?'

He smiled gently at her use of Judy's pet name for him. He studied her before answering, feeling a swell of pride and affection. There was no denying it – the person before him had matured. She was an attractive, thoughtful, caring and intelligent young woman clear about what she wanted and made of the grit to get it. Her deep auburn hair, cut short in the latest fashion, lent an impish quality to her clear skinned beauty.

'I wanted to share some news and thought this was a good place to do it – my shout. However, I can see that your news is more important. If you don't hurry up and get it out, you'll explode.'

She threw a loving glance at Kurt and laughed, a warm, husky, comforting sound.

'I don't believe you Foxy, you always know things. Look!' With a flourish, she withdrew her left hand from beneath the table and rotated it several times. A gold and diamond ring flashed brilliantly under the lights. Dalgleish grinned broadly – proud. When the acclamation subsided, Jenny continued.

'Kurt popped the question a week ago after he saw this ring which he thought was just me. We had to get it adjusted and picked it up this afternoon. Believe you me, it's been bloody hard keeping quiet.'

'Can't say I'm surprised,' said her father, 'you two have been soul mates from the beginning. Your mother picked it straight away. Well done Kurt! Allow me to formally welcome you into our family.' He hugged Jenny and shook hands with Dalgleish.

Jason too was enthusiastic and as Fox watched them he was aware his own feelings were a mixture of pleasure and sadness. This was a celebration that both Caroline and Judy would have loved. Even so, he could see the family was healing slowly but surely.

'Your turn Fox. With that fantastic news, it has definitely become my shout,' Jason grinned.

'Well, as you know, I've finished my time in the army …'

'Much to the Boss's annoyance let me tell you,' chuckled Dalgleish.

'… and I'm heading off to Melbourne next week to meet up with Spencer Johnson,' continued Fox, nodding to Dalgleish. 'The Federal copper who helped me in England. So … new leaf, new job, new adventures. I'm leaving on Tuesday and for a while I expect to be out of circulation. Got to find somewhere to live, find some transport, get the hang of Melbourne and work out exactly what Spencer and I will do and so on. I don't want any of you to think I've forgotten you if you hear nothing for a few weeks. When I'm settled, I'll give you a contact number but, in the meantime, I'll keep in touch with the Doc.'

In truth, the only thing Fox had done was phone Johnson to tell him he was travelling to Melbourne.

As he talked, Jason studied Fox carefully. He heard the words but saw the merest hint of something else. Jason's regular appearances in court and plentiful dealings with people, good and bad, had sharpened his observation and analytical skills.

The others, unaware of Jason's scrutiny, plied Fox with endless questions about what he would be doing and whether he would like living in the eastern states. In the end, Fox threw up his hands.

'Enough! I don't have all the answers yet but when I do, you'll all be told. Now, Kurt, I'm stepping out of line here but I am going to ask if I can be best man.'

'Jeez mate,' replied Dalgleish with a broad grin, 'there was never any doubt. Jenny and I have already discussed and agreed on it.'

'I could be wrong Dad,' Jason said to his father on their way home, 'but I think Fox was not being entirely truthful with us tonight.'

'What makes you say that?'

'I can't quite put my finger on it … I just … know. I'm sure that whatever he's doing is connected to Mum and Judy and I reckon that's his real reason for leaving the army.'

John McNulty drove steadily in silence. Sworn to secrecy, Fox had told him there was new information about Caroline and Judy that he had to follow through. McNulty had no idea who or what Fox was chasing, or even if he was going to Melbourne. But whatever Fox was doing, he was not in the least conflicted about the possibility of an outcome that could contradict his own Hippocratic oath.

'We'll have to wait and see I guess,' he said non-committally.

CHAPTER 46

Fox had established Wildman's proximity to Caroline's home at the time of her death. From past dealings with him he had no doubt Wildman was his quarry. Where he had been and what he had done since leaving the force was anybody's guess. But Ms Lavender had been instructive: the man in unit 2 had attended a medical centre in Melbourne. Ms Lavender said she'd read of the terrible murders near her units and noticed that Wildman or Edgeware, whoever he was, had left the unit not long afterwards.

Fox contacted Spencer Johnson at Melbourne's Federal Police headquarters and during their conversation, casually enquired if he'd come across a bloke named either Wildman or Edgeware. This bloke, Fox said, had skipped town owing money to his buddy Dalgleish, the new fiancé of Caroline Connors daughter, Jenny. Johnson paused momentarily before asserting he didn't know anyone of either name. Though their conversation had been free flowing and amicable, Fox discerned that Johnson was hedging.

In Melbourne, Fox found himself a decent boarding house in Young Street, Fitzroy, midway between Kerr and Rose Streets. This placed him close to Brunswick and Johnston Streets in the midst of life and action – clubs, pubs, booze and drugs. It also grafted him into an urban Aboriginal community.

It was now Friday night and he had been two weeks in Melbourne. In that time he had informed Spencer Johnson of his arrival, made himself known to the Fitzroy Aboriginal Legal Service (ALS), met with a few of the young people, learned who the troubled ones were and offered his services to George Lucas, a thirty-something Aboriginal youth worker from Robinvale. George was good with kids – tough, forgiving, humorous, fair. Like Fox, he'd done a bit of boxing and was pretty good at football. In his early teen years he had snared a lot of grief from his local coppers for drinking, stealing, truanting, arson and fighting. There was practically no stunt the kids could pull that fooled him – he'd done it all. Except drugs. He hated the drug trade with a passion. Happy to help kids kick the habit, he couldn't abide growers, pedlars, cooks, enforcers or profiteers. He lumped the lot under the term "exploiters" and carried out constant warfare with any and all of them.

George's turn-around at sixteen resulted from a major arse-kicking for street fighting by Robinvale police Sergeant, Dan Kenneally. Afterwards, Kenneally had driven him to the local hospital and placed him in Matron Anne Bethany's iron-fisted clutches to help in the Casualty Ward.

For three months every Friday and Saturday night, Kenneally dragged George to the hospital where his job from seven until midnight was to clean up mess – blood, shit, piss and puke. He was compelled to observe what came in: horrific vehicle injuries, shooting victims, stabbings, brawl wounds, drunks too helpless even for arrest, domestic violence, child abuse and young overdose victims. He saw first hand the tirades and vicious bashings inflicted on nursing and medical staff by people he knew – people so crazed by dope they didn't know who they were, what they were doing or where they were. These days Kenneally's actions would be disallowed, but George was eternally grateful for what it had taught him about himself and others. Every year since he had exchanged Christmas cards with Kenneally and the now retired Matron Bethany.

On this Friday night, Fox and Lucas were doing a pub crawl to ensure that young black kids kept out of mischief. They had left the *Town Hall Hotel* in Johnston Street and were walking down towards the *Rochester Castle Hotel*. Some twenty metres away from the *Rochester* they saw a young man thrown bodily from the front door into Johnston Street. He hit the footpath with a bone jarring crunch, snapping his head onto the pavement. Next minute, a large, bearded man with tatts on his well muscled arms and neck stomped through the door. He was wearing a sleeveless leather vest, black T-shirt and black bandana with a silver motif. He hurled abuse at the youth and began kicking him. Fox could hear the sickening blows of his heavy boots over the traffic noise.

Simultaneously he and Lucas yelled, 'Oi!' and sprinted towards the pub. Beard looked up, saw them coming and continued kicking.

'Back off fuckwit,' yelled Lucas.

Beard grinned and delivered another savage blow to the young man's ribs.

'Fuck off chicken shit. This doesn't concern you.'

'Yeah, well it does now.' George stepped forward and delivered a long, looping blow to the Beard's solar plexus. The connection was solid and well executed. Beard scarcely blinked, rotated swiftly and launched a thigh high kick at Lucas which landed with a crippling, soggy thud. Lucas collapsed like a sack of spuds. Beard stomped on George's hand smashing his fingers.

'Oi. Shit for brains!' Fox barked.

The big man's lip curled at the sight of the slender man before him. He bustled over intending to crush Fox. But suddenly, Fox was behind him, and when Beard turned, Fox rammed the heel of his hand up into his face, breaking his nose and pushing the septum between his eyes. He fell screaming and Fox delivered a brutal kick to his balls. He screamed again and writhed in deep and shocking pain.

'Duck,' bawled Lucas from the pavement.

Fox dropped instantly, rolled, turned and sprang to his feet sideways. A clone of Beard, though slightly shorter and thicker, was lunging with a large bowie knife where Fox had been a second before. The adversaries circled. Beard Two said nothing, his face a mask torn by rage. He concentrated on Fox then swooped for the kill. But Fox, in combat mode, was well above the battle – everything seen clearly and in slow motion. As the knife rose upwards to gut him, he stepped in close, slammed down on the wrist, gripped hard, dropped to his knee for leverage and twisted wrist and arm savagely. Beard Two was powerful. He grunted, winced, dropped the knife and delivered a vicious, stiff, two-fingered stab at Fox's eyes with his free hand. Fox saw it coming. He twisted harder, turned his head and clamped his teeth on one of the jabbing fingers and bit hard. Excruciating pain electrified Beard Two who roared in agony. All the while, Fox's grip on the man's right wrist tightened, rotation increased and suddenly Beard Two was on his knees, his arm up his back. Fox was on his feet and shoved the arm all the way up until the shoulder popped. When Beard Two fell face-down screeching, Fox delivered a fearsome and sickening kick to his gonads.

With both men incapacitated, Fox helped Lucas who, with difficulty, was trying to stand. The young man thrown from the pub still lay unconscious on the footpath.

'Get an ambulance and the police or someone is going to die,' Fox growled at the patrons who now silently ringed them. No response. 'Didn't you hear me – someone is going to die!' As he advanced menacingly upon a man at the front of the group he heard a female voice say, 'I'll go,' and saw a slender blonde girl dart into the hotel.

CHAPTER 47

When police arrived they said Bobby Dawson – the youth thrown from the pub – was well known to them as a drug user and dealer. Not one of Lucas's favourite people. As for the attackers, they were bikies with long records and would be arrested but first, they needed a medical examination. One of the policemen told Fox that members of the gang always sought bail rapidly and that Beard One – Moses Barclay – had a violent history. Fox would need to keep his wits about him.

Four days after the *Rochester Castle* incident, Fox and Lucas went to St Vincent's Hospital. Bobby Dawson was on the ninth floor trussed up like a chicken. He had suffered concussion, four broken ribs, a fractured left arm and deep cuts to his face and head. When Fox and Lucas walked in he looked at them apprehensively but with no flicker of recognition. *Not surprising,* thought Fox.

Lucas took the lead, Fox content to watch.

'You were lucky we 'appened along the other night son,' said George.

'Yeah? Dunno. Can't remember.' Churlish.

'What's your name?'

'Whatta ya wanna know for? Anyway, who the fuck are ya?'

'Just interested since we got you out of trouble. Anyone you want us to notify you're 'ere?'

'Nah. Jus' fuck off will ya. Ya not doin' me any favours bein' 'ere.'

'Yeah? We thought you might like a bit of 'elp after what we saw the other night.'

'Did'n ya fuckin' hear what I jus' said? Ya not doin' me any favours so fuckin' disappear.'

'Look sunshine,' said Fox mildly, stepping forward to place a comforting hand on Dawson's left shoulder, 'we helped you the other night, we're here to help you now. So less attitude eh?' So saying he pressed a nerve beneath Dawson's clavicle causing him to shriek in surprise and pain. 'Do we understand each other?'

Dawson looked at Fox, then at Lucas and back to Fox, pain and apprehension etched upon his face. 'Whatta ya want?'

'Better,' said Lucas. 'What's your name? Where are you from and what was all that crap the other night?'

Dawson remained silent, sneering at Lucas. Fox placed his hand back on Dawson's shoulder.

'Orlright, orlright. Me name's Bobby Dawson, I'm from Framlingham down Warrnambool way. It was about drug money.'

Lucas glanced at Fox and then stared again at Dawson.

'Are you Aboriginal?'

'Yeah.'

Lucas was disbelieving. 'What's your clan?'

'*Girai* … *Girai wurrung*. Our mob is Framlingham.'

'Ow come I haven't seen you before?' queried Lucas.

'Have a look at me – I'm fuckin' white! Anyway, I know you're one of the dicks from ALS. I keep outa ya fuckin' way.'

'Well son, think of this as the start of a long relationship because if you keep goin' the way you are, you'll be part of the Dreamin' very bloody quick.'

'Fuckin' A gran'pa. Who gives a shit?'

'Attitude Bobby,' said Fox leaning forward, 'cut the language.'

Dawson winced anticipating more pain from Fox.

'So, who were the blokes givin' you a kickin'?' asked George.

'Ya don't wanna know.' Dawson started to tremble. 'They're bad bastards.'

'What did they want?'

'They call 'emselves the Blades. They're bikies.'

Fox leaned forward again.

'Now look Bobby,' his tone was soft and reasonable, 'we know that much already. We don't want to drag every single word out of you, just tell us what's going on. Otherwise, I promise you, the pain you felt at their hands will pale to nothing beside what I can do. Even here, in this hospital. You see sunshine, I happen to think you are a disgrace to your clan and your race. So have a little think. And before you speak again, understand we want all the information and we don't want to go through a three act play to get it. Comprende?'

Dawson paled further, trembled and nodded.

'Just as long as you know,' he said with a quaver, 'you'll be signin' me death warrant. Think about that!'

'Sometimes sunshine,' said Fox, his eyes hard, his face tight, 'sometimes that's the price you have to pay. Now, out with it.'

'The Blades kill people, mostly with knives, that's the symbol on their bandanas. They're heavy into drugs – makin' it and sellin' it. They recruit youngies like me to flog it around the pub scene, 'specially where there's entertainment. I trawl four of the eight pubs in Fitzroy for 'em. They never do it 'emselves, they always have runners like me. They hook us through free drugs and then work us to pay off the debt. An' of course, no one can pay it off – they keep jackin' up the interest. They own us. Anyway, I creamed 'em for some dosh. Not much, been doin' it for weeks. They musta found out because when I got to the Castle, they were waitin' for me. They said I could pay it all back right then with 100 per cent interest or take a lesson. I just finished tellin' 'em I didn' have the readies and you musta walked in on the rest.'

'Where do we find these Blades?' Lucas queried.

'Honest, I dunno. You musta come across 'em – they hang out in Fitz all the time. They're not that hard to find. They got lotsa joints I heard. Some in the city some in the country. I meet one of 'em every three or four days at the *Napier* because it's usually packed. I give 'em money, they give me drugs then I go to work. My pubs are the *Standard, Rochester Castle, Evelyn* and the *Napier.* They never ring me, I just rock up. If there's no one there on the third day I go back on the fourth. They mix it up. I get to keep a bit of the money an' they cut me some shit. That way they keep tracka the profit an' the amount of shit they give me. What I get usually lasts between meetings. Sometimes it doesn't an' it's hard but if I got greedy, they'd just knock me off. They probly woulda this time if youse hadn't turned up.'

'Who was beltin' you?'

'I jus' know 'em as Hawk and Moses. Moses was the one kickin' me.'

'So what do they deal?' said George with a frown.

'Everythin'. Illegal tobacco, hash, coke an' ice. They got the lot. I heard they do their own ice – on a farm somewhere. Dunno where. Might be jus' talk. Dunno.'

'What do you use?'

'Hash and a bit of ice.'

'Got a mobile?' asked Fox.

'Nah. Can't afford one.'

'I'll just check your little cupboard here then.'

'Hey, you can't fuckin' do that.'

'Watch me,' said Fox taking a new one kilogram Walkabout TM from the bedside cabinet. 'Nice one Bobby. Bit of heavy duty brass here eh?' Fox glanced across to George. 'He won't need this and since its worth about $5,000, I'll keep it safe. Apart from that, we don't want him calling any Blades, do we? Thank you Bobby, this is good stuff.'

Dawson watched helplessly as they walked from the ward.

'What are you thinking?' asked Lucas as they hit the street.

'Not entirely sure,' said Fox, absolutely clear of his next step.

'This little problem is incidental to the reason I'm here. I'll gather some info and give whatever I find – and maybe the phone – to a copper mate of mine. I'm sure they'd like a bit of help. A clarification though, Dawson asked if you'd come across these bikies. They sound entrenched.'

'Sure they are, and they terrify people. It's hard to get the kids to talk about 'em as you've just seen with Dawson.'

CHAPTER 48

Fox sat in a corner – well, as much of the corner he could garner – sipping lemon, lime and bitters. Friday night, nine o'clock and the *Napier* was jumping. He had arrived earlier and dined on their famous Bogan Burger – a feast the size of Sydney's Harbour Bridge foundations. A great wodge of steak with chicken schnitzel, bacon, egg, potato cake, cheese, pineapple, onion and beetroot cemented between generous slabs of Turkish bread. Salad and crispy, salted potato wedges on the side rounded the meal off. Fox was stonkered halfway through and thought that even Spencer Johnson, whose appetite was enormous, would be hard pressed to demolish one.

He hadn't shaved for over a week and looked on the rough side. His hair was long too. Simple camouflage. Before eating he'd been upstairs to check out the gallery and then outside to vet the beer garden. He hadn't seen anyone he recognised and certainly, no Blades. Now he sat enjoying the atmosphere of the old pub. Premiership posters of the 1913 and 1916 Fitzroy footy team, elegant stained glass windows, dark, worn, wooden floors and well loved furniture. Music wafted through the pub, voices rose and fell, laughter bellowed and tinkled here and there as the mass of people moved and breathed to the common pulse of pleasure. *It's a nice place, a happy place,* thought Fox. What a shame the Blades were using it as a clearing house for their business.

He got up, gently elbowed his way through the crowd to the

bar, bought a fresh drink then moved for a better view of the front door. At half nine, two Blades in their black bandanas slouched in. In their mid to late thirties, they were chunky, heavy and mean looking, like the two he'd encountered at the *Castle*. Fox stayed put and observed. They barged their way over to the 1916 poster and spoke to a well dressed man whom Fox judged to be in his early thirties.

Soon in deep conversation, Fox slowly angled towards the trio. Eventually he got to within a body or two of the threesome and, amid the raucous noise, managed to glean an occasional word. Three times he heard the words *pit bull'* and *Sammy*, twice the word *Lucas* was mentioned and then, unexpectedly, a gem, *Wildman.* A ripple of satisfaction shot through him.

Peering over the bikie's heads and feigning interest in a Lee Falk drawing from *The Phantom,* Fox realised one of the bikies was snarling at him.

'Hey, you black prick. Fuckin' answer when you're spoken to.'

Fox smiled, looked innocent and pointed to himself. 'Me?'

'You know fuckin' well you. What are you listening to us for you piece of shit? Want your fuckin' lights switched off?'

'No. Sorry mate. First time here. I was just reading the caption on the picture there.' He pointed to the wall. 'I'm going now. Didn't mean to offend.'

'Fuck off ya heap of shit.' The bikie stayed where he was and took matters no further. Fox smiled again, nodded and made his way to the door. The disjointed snippets of conversation were worrying – Lucas, Sammy and Wildman? And what was the go with pit-bulls? Puzzled, he went outside.

Using Dawson's phone he rang George.

'George, it's Fox. Got a minute?'

'No.' Lucas sounded breathless. 'I've just rocked up at the Legal Services office. It's been firebombed and she's out of control.'

'George – listen to me. I'm outside *The Napier.* Two of the

Blades are inside talking to some well-dressed cove. Your name came up. I don't know what's happening but it feels bad. I think you and your family should move out tonight – maybe for a few nights. Just in case, have a word to the cops too – about Dawson.'

'Too late. Dawson's scarpered – up and left. The 'ospital's worried because his concussion is more serious than first thought. He might 'ave a fractured skull.'

'George! Get home. I'm staying to watch the bikies. I'll fill you in when I see you next.' He cut the conversation and leant back against the Napier's ancient green wall tiles. From the sound of it, the pub was beginning to really buzz. The night was warm and still, the air punctuated by a regular clunk-clunk as new patrons entered the pub's front door. Few, it seemed to Fox, came out or left and he wondered how they all crammed in. *Booze, music, heat and drugs … a heady and potentially volatile cocktail,* he thought.

Clunk-clunk.

He looked around. The two Blades emerged with the younger bloke. Fox could not hear them and didn't want to attract their attention but he could see the bikies demurred to their younger companion. They split and went in opposite directions, the young bloke east on Moor Street, the bikies west towards Brunswick Street.

Fox followed the former. They turned north into George Street and crossed David Street. Not far from David Street Fox's quarry got into a deep green Jaguar XJS convertible. Fox took note of the number.

He watched it drive away. Who was this bloke? And what was he to the Blades? He seemed important. Fox looked at his watch – ten-thirty, not too late to call Spencer Johnson when he got back to his room.

CHAPTER 49

Early the following Sunday morning Fox paused on his 100th push-up as the phone rang. He let it go to message bank and then stopped to listen: 'Fox, can you make it to Faraday and Lygon Streets for breakfast by seven?' Johnson's tone had an edge to it – his message sounded more direction than request. Fox inferred the invitation was about something other than his own call the previous night. He finished his push-ups, showered and caught a taxi to the city.

He saw Johnson as the cab approached Faraday Street. Hard to miss him really, few people looked as much like the Incredible Hulk as Johnson did. As Fox stepped from the cab Johnson called out.

'Yo Fox. Hope you're hungry.' Johnson's face was expressionless and Fox instantly detected a mood, annoyance or perhaps suppressed anger. He wasn't quite sure. They shook hands and walked in silence to a café on the west side of Lygon Street.

'What gives?' Fox asked.

'You,' said Johnson unequivocally. 'Did you think I missed your not so subtle reference to Wildman when you rang from Perth? Or that I wouldn't hear of your stoush with the Blades? Or that the ALS fire didn't happen? Or that I *imagined* good old Georgie Lucas's house wasn't trashed last night? Just what the fuck are you up to? And while I'm at it, why did you ring last night?'

The big man was in full flight and Fox couldn't resist taking the piss.

'Jeez,' he drawled, 'not bad for a fed. I'm impressed,' he grinned wickedly, 'and it's not even your turf. This is state police stuff.' Then more seriously, 'I didn't know about George and his house though. Are he and his family okay?'

'No thanks to you. Now, give over. Just what are you up to?'

Fox sobered, a flinty look in his eyes. 'Classified information. Sorry Spence. But let me turn it around: why are you pissed off because I asked about a bloke named Wildman who owes my young mate Dalgleish money?'

Johnson studied Fox calmly before speaking.

'Let me tell you a story,' he commenced quietly. 'In another land at another time I met a hot-shot warrior bound up in grief and as close to despair as I've ever seen anyone. He looked and behaved like the walking dead. He was a bloke beset by a couple of nasty problems, not least of which was being locked up facing serious criminal charges. Was that a deterrent? Never. What kept him going? Innocence and revenge! His adopted family had been grievously wounded. He loved them and they him. So I understand the motivation behind certain actions. Do you like my story so far?'

Fox said nothing.

'Now here's where the story gets interesting. For some time the feds and Vicpol have had a thing going on a bikie gang called the Blades. Suddenly, out of the wide, wild west rides Sir Galahad in size fourteen bloody boots,' he inclined his head towards Fox, 'and guess what? In about three nano-seconds he manages to stir up a fucking hornet's nest. He attracts big-time scrutiny from both the Blades and the police but is oblivious to everything except his own goal. So listen up mate, while you're still able – *back off!*' Johnson's warning was unmistakable.

'Good try Spence. The only thing I've done is rescue young

Dawson and save George Lucas from a kicking. Nothing else. And … you didn't answer my question.'

Johnson smiled ignoring the dig. 'So … no eavesdropping on the Blades last night? No shadowing Sammy Milosevic down Moor Street?'

Fox was dumbfounded and it showed.

Johnson cracked a grin for the first time. 'Gotcha. You didn't know did you? Didn't have the faintest clue.'

Fox was silent, annoyed with himself. Clearly he had not used the skills he was so good at. He had been complacent. *That is not going to happen again*.

'So why the phone call last night?' Johnson asked.

'Believe it or not, it was to tell you I was at the *Napier* and to ask if you could get some car details for me. But now you've told me: the owner of the car is connected to the Blades.'

'Correct. Now look, I'm going to stick my neck out and tell you some things so you understand why you need to keep out of the way. Otherwise, you could end up arrested, seriously hurt or dead … or possibly all three. I couldn't say anything about Wildman because he's part of our focus. He works for a bloke called Sammy Milosevic, boss of the Blades … the one you dogged last night. Milosevic's thirty-three years old, lives in a top class home in South Yarra, is a chartered accountant and practising barrister and loves defending bikies. He's a pain in the government's arse on matters as diverse as human rights, the constitution – federal and state – discrimination, the right of association, tax, company, drug and gaming laws and anything connected to animal rights. He's a clever bastard with a smooth tongue and a vicious temper. He's every straight copper's nightmare. To cap it off, he holds black belts in a raft of martial arts. He's a very dangerous little man. We know he washes huge sums of cash from illegal gambling, vice and drugs. We also know that much of that money is laundered through the Macquarie Bank via shares, investment trusts, property portfolios, superannuation funds and similar schemes. We also believe he's mixed up with Triads in Japan and some heavy criminals in Vietnam. He's …'

'Whoa, whoa. Hold on Spence. If you know so much about him, how come he's not in the sin-bin?'

'Number one – he has no priors. He's never personally been caught for anything. He had two scrapes with the Children's Court for assault and both cases were dismissed. The victims, older and bigger, were said to be the aggressors despite being severely injured. He argued self defence. Number two – he has an army of helpers willing to take the rap. The bikies either love or totally fear him and will do as he bids. He has a habit of publicly "calling out" people who disagree with him and no one has beaten him in a fight. Most opponents become mincemeat. Basically, he's a talented, callous, lethal bully. He is not someone you want to mess with.'

Fox's mind was racing, wondering where and how Wildman fitted into this story. He also recognised this was protected information – Johnson was taking a *big* risk.

'Okay, a couple of questions.'

'Shoot,' said Johnson.

'How long has this operation been running?'

'Just under eighteen months.'

Fox nodded, more to himself than Johnson.

'And Wildman is mixed up in this?'

'Yes.'

'What if he were to disappear, let's say, got wind of the op and did a runner? How would that go down?'

'Very unfavourably – he's pivotal. My turn, do you think he's Caroline's and Judy's killer?'

'Don't know,' said Fox with a closed face.

'Bullshit Fox. You wouldn't be looking for him otherwise and I bloody well know what you said about Dalgleish is crap!"

'Honestly, I don't know. But … I do need to talk to him.'

'You can't, so stop looking. I'll say it again – back off. This is a big operation, parts of it are very delicate and we can't afford for it to go tits up because you want revenge. *If* Wildman is responsible for Caroline's death, he will be dealt with by the law. Otherwise, forget him.' Johnson glared at Fox, his warning clear.

Fox glared back. He understood Johnson's situation but would not be deterred. He stayed silent.

Throughout their conversation they had demolished large plates of scrambled eggs, bacon and tomatoes. When the plates were cleared, they ordered fresh coffee.

Johnson took a long swallow of a steaming flat white, re-settled and regarded Fox steadily. Fox liked this bloke and felt comfortable with him notwithstanding the previous brief tension. He still owed him big-time for all the spadework he'd undertaken on his behalf in the UK.

'Come on, out with it. What else?' asked Fox.

'Had a call from your cousin Callum yesterday.'

'Really?'

'He didn't know where or how to reach you. He tried John McNulty who said he hadn't heard from you recently. John thought of me – a wildcard try.'

Immediately, Fox felt guilty. He had promised John he would keep in touch. Instead, he'd immersed himself in his investigation.

'Guilty. I fluffed my promise to John. Unfortunately, life interferred.'

'Callum had news about Cyril Early's death. It seems there was a threat of disinheritance which loosened Heidi's tongue.'

'Go on,' he said huskily. Johnson had his full attention.

'I think you know Heidi's grandfather arranged to shunt her off to Canada before Early was even cold.' Fox nodded, thinking back to a conversation with Callum early in 1986. 'She's apparently done well for herself there as a doctor. Twelve months pass and your good friend, Saul Carmody, rocks up to profess his undying love for her. Things go nicely for a while and eventually he tells Heidi it was him who organised Early's death. He got a mate to do the job the same day Heidi told him she was meeting Early near that gun club. The guy who knocked him off only had a day left in England before returning to the USA. The job was done and next day Carmody's mate was gone – no leads, no witnesses. This was all too much for dear Heidi whose new morality – nurtured by the thought of disinheritance – kicked in. She blabbed to the Mounties. Eventually, they got their man, or men – the doer and the arranger – and helped the Brits organise extradition. Not an easy feat: Canada, US Army, Britain. Very tricky bit of footwork. Anyway, Carmody and his mate face the courts in the UK next week.'

Fox was astonished. He had worked hard to erase that experience from his mind and had pretty much closed the book on it. Not without scars though. He had become cynical, tougher and lost all respect for authority. He seriously doubted that Heidi was turning the page – she always played to her own endgame. What was it Callum said old Lord Ravenscroft had confided? Yes, "she possesses a streak of capricious malevolence."

Fox was quiet for so long Johnson asked, 'What are you thinking?'

'About that time – about all of it,' he said. 'I didn't like Early but he didn't deserve to be murdered. I think he was weak. Callum told me some time ago that Lord Ravenscroft was caring for Early's family because he considered Heidi responsible for him going off the rails. I don't believe Heidi will ever change, she's driven totally by self interest. She might have done some good things in Canada, but let's wait until the Old Man's dies. That's when we'll know if she continues to be a leopard or not.'

Johnson merely raised his eyebrows.

'Callum would like you to call him – here's his number.'

'Thanks. Did he mention a motive?'

'The old green-eyed monster. It seems Carmody had absolutely done his nuts over Heidi and couldn't stomach the thought of her bonking Early whenever she felt like it. He knew there were others, including you because he was part of your fit-up. He'd convinced himself that Heidi saw him as her god. In reality, he was too dumb to recognise that he was just another carriage in a train of lovers.'

Fox said nothing.

'Now … one last piece of news. I've submitted my resignation and I'll be out in three months. I'm starting up my own fitness and body sculpting gym – scads of competitions for the latter. I'm also commencing my own Private Enquiry Agent business here in Melbourne. I quite like the joint. I'm not going to press you on your immediate plans because, if you were truthful, I might have to take some strong action.' As before, the corners of Johnson's mouth twitched. 'But … I'd like you to think about coming in with me. I've already got several jobs involving some pollies and prominent business people lined up and I can assure you, my fees will be bloody healthy. Our work will involve,' he paused and grinned, 'flexible, unspecified action. Sometimes, some of the people who employ us will be,' he stopped to choose his words carefully, 'interesting, controversial, even unpopular. What do you say?'

Fox stared pensively into his coffee cup for what, to Johnson, seemed an eternity. 'I'll take that on notice if you don't mind.'

CHAPTER 50

In the early evening of that same Sunday, Milosevic rang Wildman. 'Everything set?'

'Yes Sammy. The first fight is in fifteen minutes and there's well over a hundred people here, including some from overseas. Latecomers are still trickling in. And heavy punters Sammy, heavy punters – just as you like it. People have been coming in all day. The sheilas have been here a couple of days and have been working hard. The booze and food is right – they're all primed.'

'Is Kransky there?'

'Yeah.'

'Who's handling the money?'

'Banker Stevens. Glendenning's got business in Warrnambool. But Stevens is used to it.' Stevens had been a bank teller before drugs, gambling, fraud and cops rearranged his life.

'What's the go with Dawson?'

'Dunno yet. That's why Glendenning's in Warrnambool. I'll let you know as soon as I do.'

'What about the other prick that was with Lucas? The black bastard. Where's he?'

'Nothing yet. Dunno who he is or where he's from.'

'Find out! Lean on Lucas.' Ominous.

'Sorry Sammy, Lucas and his family have shot through. I dunno where they are.'

There was a brief silence before Milosevic spoke softly into the phone, 'Listen you fuckin' moron, you're not paid to give me negatives. Find-fucking-out! Find someone close to Lucas and give 'em some real grief. Got that?' The soft voice was chillingly penetrating and laden with menace.

'G … g … got it,' stammered Wildman.

Milosevic slammed the phone down.

Wildman, tight as a coiled spring, slowly released his breath. In this mood, Milosevic put the fear of God into him and stress exacerbated his tremors. He didn't have a clue where Lucas was. The only positive thing he knew was that when they found this other mysterious black bastard, he would be vaporised.

He shuddered then forced his mind to the matters at hand. Dog fighting was not of particular interest to the police … yet. Enforcement was mainly handled by Local Government Rangers with the odd dollop of encouragement from do-gooders. With so many councils across Victoria, cohesion between them was patchy. A real plus. Experience had shown there were quite a few lethargic rangers hungry for a quid and willing to close their eyes to the contest scene. Some of them didn't even know what a restricted breed looked like! Wildman smiled to himself, perhaps he shouldn't blame them. The whole issue of restricted breeds was a regular source of tension between councils and professional dog judges. The good news was that such distractions provided opportunity. Opportunity built profit potential and that made Sammy happy.

His main headache was infiltrators. They could come from anywhere. The Royal Society for Prevention of Cruelty to Animals (RSPCA), the media, the cops, the council or even plain bloody dog lovers. And they were so bloody hard to suss. When Milosevic first put him on he was told to fix this problem once and for all. He ended up devising six simple rules:

No punters to attend without a Blade recommendation.

Dead or injured dogs retained on site for disposal.

Silence by attendees was brutally enforced by Blade members. Notification of contest venues was given as late as possible. Venues were generally limited to one fight per annum.

There could be no more than eight contests a year.

The rules had worked well and the loss of potential income caused by limited contests was thoroughly offset by cultivating discreet and wealthy clients.

Milosevic, intelligent and rat cunning had, over time, nurtured a broad range of these wealthy clients: internal and external allegiances from industry, commerce and the professional world including powerful Indonesian interests. The focus of the latter lay in mining, oil and timber but their importance to Sammy was their influence throughout Indonesia. For them, it was not so much that they were fond of dog fighting, rather it was their predilection for corruption and gambling. And Sammy's contests provided them with rich pickings for both.

Time to go. Tony Kransky, a Blade who boasted three murders, was MC. Wildman neither liked nor trusted Kransky. His copper's nose told him Kransky was more than just a bikie and he wouldn't have been surprised to learn Kransky was scheming to oust Milosevic. A tall man, Kransky, was all menace, muscle and meanness. He was afraid of nothing, including Milosevic, even though he deferred to him.

Kransky, as far as Wildman could see, clung to the edge of the Indonesians and other well heeled associates, constantly probing to learn more. Ever alert through fear, Wildman noticed that Sammy's ears sometimes pricked with curiosity when Kransky quietly asked questions of these businessmen about their infinite capacity to bribe or inflict injury, or to reach deep within Indonesian political circles, or the army, to foster their business ventures.

That Kransky was also abreast of Sammy's connections with the Australian Stock Exchange, Macquarie Bank and Melbourne's largest accounting firm, Leitch & McNabb, caused Wildman to be even more suspicious. Inadvertently, he had discovered Kransky possessed comprehensive knowledge of the Blade's property holdings – night clubs, factories, farms, brothels, houses – and their ever expanding gun-running caper. It was only Wildman's monstrous fear of yet another brutal bashing from Sammy that prevented him from conveying his deeply held suspicions about Kransky to the leader. Currently, Kransky seemed to be crawling all over Sammy's newest scheme to push "ice" onto a string of country kids between Bendigo and Mildura. He'd heard Kransky gloating about how, in double-quick-time, these kids would be sucked into the maw of the drug world as dependent "pushers".

Though he was only a shitkicker in the gang, Wildman knew he was a shrewd observer. One of the things he could not understand was that Glendenning, the Blade's Sergeant at Arms, Milosevic's closest confidante, seemed somehow to have a blind spot for Kransky's intrusive hovering. Kransky, in Wildman's opinion, was not to be trusted.

Right now the object of his dislike stood in the centre of the six metre circular pit with its one metre high wooden walls, walls scarred and stained with blood. Kransky exuded self-assurance as he raised both arms. The hubbub in the big shed died.

Packed together, the spectators were keen for the fight to start. None of them had bet in less than hundreds of dollars, many in thousands, all due to the re-appearance of an old favourite. The purse would be $75,000 for the winner, $25,000 to the loser.

'This first contest,' bawled Kransky, 'is between an old warrior – the bitch Brindle – and young Titan from Mount Gambier. Both, as you know are pitbull crossbreeds – Japanese Tosa in Titan and Fila Brasileiro in Brindle. Many of you will know that Brindle has been victorious in four previous long fought contests. This is Titan's first public appearance and he's considered by his owner to be Brindle's equal – has plenty of endurance. Both dogs have been trained with treadmills, neck weights, live bait and spring poles. To raise them to perfect pitch tonight, neither has been fed for forty-eight hours. Handlers, are you ready?'

The owners, with their dogs behind the scratch lines, nodded their assent. Their animals had been weighed and Titan, bigger than Brindle, was 500 grams heavier. The two dogs had been washed and cleaned to ensure neither carried a poisonous coating to sabotage their opponent. They were primed to kill.

Kransky stepped from the ring and called, *'Release!'*

Like two snarling bullets the dogs hurtled towards each other, crashing at ring centre with a sickening thump. Then, on hind legs attacking: tearing, biting, constantly seeking each other's throats, ripping and growling, exposing gristle, blood, spittle and bone. They fought with unflinching savagery.

And over the sound of this horrific combat, the roaring, stamping, cheering crowd of men. Men drawn by a ferocious, unyielding contest to death, men crazed by blood lust, seduced by the relentless fury of two bloodied animals puncturing and perforating without let. Men hoping to make a fortune from organised depravity – one life or the other. Bodies seared by bloody gashes, the pace slowed, the fury though, unabated. And inside the ring, behind their animals – the owners. With pieces of plastic piping they thrashed, separated and prodded, encouraging their dogs to fight harder, to release and re-fasten. Anything to win.

Thirty minutes. One hour. Two.

Explosively, Titan had Brindle's hind leg in a bone crushing grip. Her lower left leg, bitten through, flapped uselessly. Pain seemed not to register. Brindle's savagery rose. She fell, twisted and levered herself upwards to fasten onto Titan's snout. His blood misted the air – the crowd hushed. Titan's top jaw and snout was ground, shaken and sawn in a thorny vice until suddenly, it was torn from his head.

The effect was immediate. Titan fell, blood spewing over Brindle's face and chest. Then, her fangs ripped deep into Titan's throat, a gaping tear confirming a fate sealed.

Victorious, Brindle was taken from the ring and perfunctorily electrocuted. With her severed leg, she was of no further use. Her body was dragged outside and thrown next to her dead competitor. The two and a half hour duel had no winners and the combatants were oblivious to the night's final outcome – almost $900,000 wagered on fights and $250,000 creamed from drug sales. Whatever the prostitutes had generated was theirs to keep.

Surveying the scene at five next morning, Wildman was satisfied. It had been a good night even though he had been unable to run all six fights. The key thing, the gambling, had been solid and Sammy would be pleased. With military precision, the next contest rolled on.

And all the while, the lime pit devoured Brindle, Titan and the others.

CHAPTER 51

A week after his Lygon Street breakfast with Johnson, Fox arrived at the Melbourne Magistrates' Court in Russell Street, Melbourne. Milosevic was representing a Blade named Samuel Benson charged with bashing a jeweller and stealing his Porsche Boxster, diamonds and other jewels valued at more than $150,000. The jeweller, Ely Cohen, was still unconscious two months after the assault and remained in hospital on life support. Fox was keen to get a "feel" for Milosevic.

Fox had shaved, got a crew-cut, wore a pair of plain lens spectacles and dressed in a sharp, deep grey suit, white shirt and tie. He also carried a smart looking leather brief case. His appearance was greatly altered from the night he'd thumped the two Blades outside the *Rochester Castle*. Even so, he stooped and feigned a limp. Entering the small courtyard outside Number One Court he was assailed by a rumble of conversation from ten to fifteen Blades grouped near the court door. All wore bandanas and sported the obligatory tattoos, thick gold chains, earings, beards, pony tails and leather jackets or vests. Intimidation bounced around the small courtyard like storm waves belting a shoreline.

Fox skirted the group and entered the court. The raised witness box was on the left near the front of the court, a high-standing dock on the right led directly to a holding cell. The magistrate's position – behind an ornately carved, high wooden bench – was set between and behind these two structures providing clear observation of the court room. Directly below the magistrate was the clerk of courts and between the dock and witness box stood a long, broad, polished wooden table for the prosecution and defence. The room exuded an atmosphere of tradition and formality.

Fox took a seat mid-court, five rows back from the bar table. A female police sergeant sat on the right of the table near the dock facing the magistrate's bench. She rose to speak to a police officer who entered the dock from the holding area. Fox guessed the sergeant was in her early thirties. Her honey-blonde hair gleamed from a tightly coiled bun behind her head and she had dark-coloured eyes. Impeccably presented in her blue tunic and trousers, slender, tall and ramrod straight, her bearing radiated confidence and authority.

As she finished her conversation with the policeman, Milosevic stalked in with a bulging briefcase and clutch of papers under his arm. He set them down noisily at the opposite end of the bar table. He muttered something to the sergeant who reacted as though fresh dog shit had been shoved under her nose. Rampant hostility between the pair was visible.

As Milosevic arranged his papers, bikies trickled into the court room. With one exception, the Blades sat in two rows as close as possible to the prosecuting sergeant and began hissing a barrage of insults in her direction. Unfazed, she turned a withering stare upon them.

'If you babies can't behave yourselves I will have you ejected from the court,' she said in a loud, clear voice.

A venomous torrent of abuse fell upon her, Milosevic smirked. Undeterred, she raised her hand to the policeman on the court door and beckoned him across. They had a short whispered conversation and he left smiling.

Five minutes later, bang on ten o'clock, the clerk of courts bellowed, 'All rise,' as Deputy Chief Magistrate Kenneth J Smith entered the court and took his seat. Sixty-two years of age, silver haired, thirty years experience on the bench, Smith was renowned for a dry, tough, no-nonsense approach to his job. Slightly overweight, dressed in a light silvery-grey suit and ever the monarch of his court, Smith surveyed his domain through pale, icy blue eyes.

'Call Samuel Benson,' bawled the clerk.

'If it please your Worship, I am Samuel Milosevic and I appear for the defendant,' Milosevic had risen lazily to his feet and spoke in a dry, gravelly voice.

Smith studied Milosevic for a few seconds before saying, 'Yes Mr Milosevic. Sergeant?'

'Yes sir. Sergeant Claire King appearing for the Prosecution. Your Worship, in regard to Mr Benson who is in custody and was to appear before you seeking bail this morning, I was told only a short time ago that he is in the jail infirmary and unable to attend court.'

'Your Worship this is untenable,' Milosevic shot to his feet. 'Why wasn't I told about this? The prosecution and jail authorities are clearly in league over this. I demand an explanation.'

Dark and audible mutterings were heard from the bikies.

'Mr Milosevic,' said Smith quietly, 'your indignation is unwarranted and your assertion spurious. I am given to understand that Mr Benson is a member of a bikie gang. If I am not mistaken, these people clustered around Sergeant King are members of that same gang. I do not like their behaviour and will not tolerate their implied threats. If their interruption continues, I will have them removed from this court. Moreover, I regard the way they have surrounded the Sergeant as an act of intimidation. They have three choices: one, remove themselves from the court; two, spread themselves throughout the court away from Sergeant King and remain silent; or three, face incarceration for contempt of my court. Is that clear?'

Milosevic threw a poisonous glare at Smith then turned to face the Blades, a clear question on his face. They remained in their seats and turned up the hostility. King nodded to the court door officer and a few seconds later, a team of black-clad Special Operations Group police filed into the courtroom and lined up near the door. Milosevic stared venomously first at Smith then at King before turning to nod curtly to the Blades. The majority rose and one by one left the court, closely followed by the SOG officers.

'Mr Milosevic, we do not appear to have crossed paths too often and you obviously have much to learn about the way I run my court. For that reason, I advise you now I have decided this matter will not be relegated to any other Magistrate. I will be following it through to completion in this jurisdiction. Sergeant King, can you tell me why Mr Benson is in the infirmary?'

'Yes sir. Yesterday afternoon at around three o'clock I am told he attacked another inmate with a chair and inflicted serious injuries before several other inmates stopped him. I understand there is very clear CCTV footage of the incident from start to finish and I have requested a copy be brought to this court. As a result of inmate intervention, and before warders could reach him, Benson received a broken cheek bone, broken nose, three broken ribs and a dislocated knee. He is now in the infirmary and unable to walk or to breathe properly.'

'What do you have to say Mr Milosevic?'

'I am astonished sir. I have always found my client to be as meek as a lamb.'

'Do you wish to continue the bail application in his absence?'

'Yes sir, I do.'

'Sergeant King.'

'Sir the Prosecution continues to oppose bail. The victim, Mr Ely Cohen, remains in a coma. A medical report furnished on Friday last indicates his condition is deteriorating. I have copies for your worship and the defence. We believe that Mr Benson not only remains a flight risk but poses a grave threat to other witnesses. His attack on the inmate yesterday gives rise to further concern and appears to underpin Mr Benson's propensity for violence. For those reasons we strongly oppose his release into the community before the case is heard. It is our view that Mr Benson, on bail, poses an unacceptable risk.' King sat down.

Rising, Milosevic said obsequiously, 'Your worship, I submit that Sergeant King's comments are mere hyperbole. The very fact that my client is in a jail hospital is precisely why he should be released: he is not safe. The state has failed to exercise its duty of care towards my client as a result of which he now lies seriously injured. This matter has gone on for some weeks with bail denied to my client and no immediate prospect of the case proceeding. These decisions do not fall within the fundamental meaning of justice and are patently unfair to a man with family and children, a man who, as I said, I have found to be a model citizen. Because bail has been denied previously he now finds himself injured in hospital. Collectively, I submit the aggregate of these separate matters constitute exceptional circumstances under the Bail Act and therefore my client should be released. I therefore ask your Worship to set bail at $1,000 with a surety of $1,000 and a condition that Mr Benson report to the Broadmeadows police twice weekly.'

Smith considered Milosevic thoughtfully.

'Bail is denied – the application is dismissed. In my view exceptional circumstances do not prevail here and the heavy onus of proving those circumstances rests upon you and your client. That onus has not been met to my satisfaction. Indeed, I am persuaded by the events responsible for your client's non-appearance today that there is a high probability of him posing an unacceptable risk to other witnesses in this case, a case which, on the basis of the medical report received today, is becoming potentially more serious for your client. Oh, and Mr Milosevic … you are at liberty to appeal my decision.'

Fox's silvery grey eyes flicked randomly between the remaining bikies and the sergeant, Milosevic and the magistrate and around again. *I don't understand, Milosevic has behaved like a pratt, got the Magistrate offside and, in court, publicly demonstrated support for the Blades. What's his game? He is obviously not stupid. Spencer Johnson said as much. And what about Claire King? Obviously they've crossed swords before and not a skerrick of fear. To have the SOG on tap like that means she thought about a worst case scenario. Go girl!* Fox's thoughts were interrupted when he realised Milosevic was glaring at him, a sullen scowl on his face, contempt in his eyes. Fox eyeballed him straight back.

CHAPTER 52

Milosevic was fuming. Firstly, because he had been compelled to deal with that jumped-up twat King again, and secondly because he had been assured that Magistrate Linton Crozier would be the hearing officer. Instead, he had been ambushed by Smith's appearance. Crozier was a new young magistrate with a reputation for softness. But Smith? Umpteen appeals against his decisions had never been found wrong at law and none had been overturned. Shit! Shit! Shit!

He went to the nearest phone box outside the court and dialled a number.

'Yes,' said a guarded voice.

'Wildman!'

'Yes Sammy.'

'There was a prick here at court today. I want you to find out who he is. A darky. I can't be certain but he might have been at the *Napier* when I was there a couple of weeks ago. He kind of looked familiar … but that's all. Mid thirties, crew cut, snappy dresser. Don't know how tall because he sat the whole time. It's all I've got.'

'Nothing else Sammy?'

'No,' Milosevic snapped. Silence. 'Talk to the boys – they might remember something. Yes, now you mention it: grey eyes. He had silvery grey eyes. Bit unusual for an abo.'

Wildman shuddered. The only Aboriginal he had ever met

with eyes of that description was that fuckin' Midnight. Things fell into place: the two Blades thrashed by an abo outside the *Rochester Castle*, the disappearance of Bobby Dawson and the Lucas family, Sammy's sighting in the *Napier* and today, the prick at Melbourne Magistrates' Court. Fox was here! Had to be! An ice cold shiver ran through him from head to foot.

'Eh, Wildman you fucking shit. Have you gone to sleep?'

'No Sammy. Thinking. Sorry.'

'Leave the thinking to me. Just find out who this bastard is and where he lives. He looks like trouble.'

'Sure Sammy.' Wildman had no intention of telling Milosevic about Fox just yet. Any shit from his own past likely to bring grief to Milosevic would visit him tenfold – most probably put him in the lime pit. Somehow he had to establish whether or not it was Fox. If so, the Blades would handle him. But right now he had to keep his head down.

He lit a fag to calm his jangled nerves.

He was uncertain who posed the biggest threat: Midnight or Milosevic? Think, he told himself savagely, *think!* Several long, deep drags on his cigarette settled him and he began to smile.

He picked up his phone.

'Fitzroy Aboriginal Legal Service, Sharon speaking.'

'Yeah, g'day Sharon.' Smooth, charming. 'I'm Rolley Dawson, Bobby's cousin from Warrnambool. I was just wondering if Georgie Lucas is around.'

'Sorry Rolley, George is on leave. Can anyone else help you?'

'D'you know if his friend Colin Fox is in today?'

There was a pause. 'No, no-one of that name works here. Can we do anything for you?'

'Nah, she's right mate. I'll wait till Georgie gets back from leave, it's not urgent. Cheers.'

'George.' The tone was curt, wary.

'Sharon here George. You asked if anybody was looking for you or Colin Fox to let you know. Well this bloke just rang claiming to be Bobby Dawson's cousin Rolley from Warrnambool. I know the Dawson mob and there isn't a Rolley among 'em. I thought you'd wanta know ASAP.'

'Thanks Shazza, appreciate the call. It'll be one of the Blades I bet. What'd you tell him?'

'Said you were on leave and Fox didn't work here.'

'Thanks mate, grouse job.'

CHAPTER 53

Shortly before one, Spencer Johnson walked into a café tucked behind shops below the Warburton Highway. He was in the tiny village of Woori Yallock, about forty clicks east of Melbourne and well away from Blade territory. He was meeting Tony Kransky, an undercover colleague, for lunch. Kransky's present role as a member of the Blades was sustained by a dark and fabricated history that posed acute risks – one slip would bring certain death. With state cops leaking information to various Blade members and others, his existence was becoming increasingly tenuous. Johnson's job as Kransky's handler was to provide and receive information and ensure his safety.

Kransky had recently intimated to Johnson his distrust of a Victorian copper also working undercover, a man to whom he had naturally never divulged his own identity. This, and Fox's peripheral presence, was stretching Kransky's equilibrium to near fracture point. Not a good thing, especially as they were nearing the pointy end of their operation.

At one o'clock Kransky strolled into the café. Dressed in overalls and a beanie, tatts concealed, he could have been a farm labourer or chippy. He spied Johnson and walked over.

Johnson rose. The two men looked like a pair of goliaths. Today, however, Johnson's loud, cheerful, over-the-top persona was restrained and thoughtful. He was nearing the end of his police service and wanted this operation completed successfully, so … no noticeable behaviour. The two men shook hands.

'How are you?' said Johnson.

'Fine. Ready for lunch.'

They sat, checked the menu, beckoned the waitress and ordered.

'Our friend *M* was at court for the Benson matter today. He copped Smith instead of Crozier as well as that red-hot police prosecutor, Claire King. Kiddin' that didn't piss him off. He was barkin' grief all over the place. I think your mate Fox was in court too. *M* rang Wildman after and told him to find out who the abo was. He reckoned he'd seen him at the *Napier.*'

'That's something we need to talk about,' said Johnson. 'I told Fox about the court today. Keep an eye out for him. He's never said so, but I am bloody certain he believes it was Wildman who murdered two very close friends from Perth – a policewoman and her daughter. Long story short. Fox is ex-SAS and very accomplished. If Wildman is the man, Fox won't rest until he introduces him to his maker. I can't allow that to happen.'

'I remember the case,' interrupted Kransky. 'Most of the Blades cheered about the copper being offed but quite a few were seriously pissed about the young daughter. Mother and daughter was just too much for a few, copper or not. I never heard about an arrest.'

'No, and as I said, Fox has Wildman in his sights. But, we need Wildman for our cause. Thanks to you, we know that he knows a bunch of stuff about *M*. It's vital he's kept safe but … I don't want Fox hurt either.'

'Christ, why don't you give me something tricky!' Kransky grinned and tucked into the shepherd's pie and vegies on his plate. Johnson hoed into a lasagne and salad.

'I've no idea what Fox might do,' Johnson resumed, 'except it will be slippery. If you can, cover his back. Now … what about the Vicpol undercover, what's the go?'

'My feeling is they've turned him. His loyalties are confused and he's really enjoying hurting people. I know he's creaming dough from drugs that should be reaching *M*. That puts him directly under threat and potentially compromises us. It's quite possible the money he's stealing is being logged and accounted for … I can't be sure. If it is, sooner or later he's gunna become a statistic. I think you'd better have a chat with his bosses. It's going to end in tears otherwise.'

'Okay. I'll have a word. What else is going on?'

'A lot,' said Kransky with a wry smile. '*M*'s begun organising a small core of Blades to slide into the construction industry. He reckons developers and others are plum targets for his heavies: debt collection, "accidents," union control, drug pushing, stoppages, botched concrete pours and targeted violence, you know, the usual. He reckons he'll make millions by facilitating on-time job finishes, especially for big projects. His newest thing is illegal immigrants. He's been studying movement patterns in Europe, Canada and the USA and believes the next big target will be Australia. He's got a bunch of reasons for thinking that but *the* most important thing is our coastline. Huge … with fuck-all protection. For some reason he sees Indonesia becoming a regular conduit to Australia. He makes no bones about corruption in Indonesia and has been over there to do his homework. High fliers like police chiefs, judges and government ministers are very susceptible to graft, particularly if they're members of Suharto's inner circle.'

'Really? Shit. That sort of stuff needs to be shared with Immigration. I'll kick that upstairs. I can see big problems with that little scheme. What about the dogs?'

'That is seriously doing my head in. I've been able to identify dog supply sources in WA as well as the twisted customs guys there. Our friend Wildman is bagman for that lurk and he knows the money tree – how much, where it's hidden, how it gets there, who's involved, what companies, lawyers, institutions and so on. ... The one thing I cannot understand about Wildman is how in Christ's name he got into that position – he's such a weak, snivelling prick. On top of that, he's a bent ex-cop. But he's there and I 'spose that's why we have to keep him safe.'

'Correct. Anything I can do?'

'Nope, just get it wrapped up. And Jesus, get a move-on with the dog fights – I can't stress enough, they're bloody obscene. Here's your latest bunch of tapes.' Kransky handed Johnson a green and white plastic Harris Scarfe carry-bag. 'There's probably enough here to put *M* and the Blades away for a hundred years. With bastards like these it surprises me that governments haven't brought in USA's RICO laws[1] . It's bloody powerful stuff and has been tested to death over there for decades. All the legal wrinkles are known. I reckon legislation like that here would bust the pricks wide open.'

'Righto mate, I'll have a word to the Victorian Attorney General and order it for you next week.' Johnson grinned. 'Keep your chin up. From my side all the paperwork is in place. The legal eagles are poised and prosecutions are ready so we'll be good to go in the next two to three weeks. You'll be arrested and charged then disappear.'

'One last thing,' Kransky grimaced. 'Milosevic is becoming more and more unpredictable. I think he's big into 'roids at the minute. His mood swings are violent and typical of 'roid rage. It won't take much to tip him over the edge and he needs to be stopped before that happens because he becomes uncontrollable.'

---

1 Racketeer Influenced and Corrupt Organisations Act introduced in 1970.

CHAPTER 54

That same Monday afternoon, Fox was enjoying a large, seriously hot cappuccino in Bank Place at one of Melbourne's laneway cafes. Ensconced in the heart of the legal arena, Bank Place also harboured the *Mitre Tavern,* a genteel English-style pub believed to have originally been built during the 1850s.

Following court, Fox decided to reconnoitre Milosevic's home street of Cromwell Road, South Yarra where he fell foul of an intensely cold, wet and blustery autumn change. Drying out in the warm café with a hot drink and newspaper was a welcome distraction. Sipping his coffee he suddenly remembered he had not re-activated Dawson's mobile phone since court. He took the phone from his brief case and saw three missed calls from the same number in Queensland.

He listened to the first message.

'Hello Fox. It's George. Call me, it's important.' The other two messages were similar. Fox dialled the number.

'Yes,' said a cautious voice.

'Fox.'

'Jeez man, where 'ave you been? I've been tryin' to get you.'

'I can see that. How are you? I see you've gone north.'

'Thought it best. Collected the family after those bastards trashed our place. 'Ad a call – unexpectedly – from Dawson's mum and collected 'im too and 'ere we are.'

'Safe?'

'Yeah.'

'How's Bobby?'

'Still not good, but improvin'. 'E went 'ome to Warrnambool and 'ad a talk with 'is mum. Then 'e heard a bikie 'ad ridden into town and was askin' questions about 'im. 'Is mum said 'e oughta be thinkin' about pitchin' in with me. It was you that did the trick Fox, that's why 'e's with me. Anyway, 'e's been good as gold. Done cold turkey off the drugs, helpin' me wife and bein' good with the kids. 'E's talkin' about joinin' Noel Pearson's mob up 'ere. That'd be real good. Only thing is, 'e's still pissed about you havin' 'is phone.'

'Why did you ring George?'

'Someone rang ALS this mornin' lookin' for you by name. Sharon said you didn't work there. I reckon it was one of the Blades.'

'You're probably right. There's been a few calls on Bobby's phone.' He paused to think. *Milosevic scrutinising him in court, case concluded by 10:45, George's first call at 11:24. It fitted well enough.* 'I need some information from you George. Can you point me in the direction of a sacred Aboriginal site here in Melbourne? I need to check it out.'

'Why?'

'I have to do some thinking in the right place.'

'Just a tick, I'll ask the wife. She's from Melbourne.'

There was a muffled conversation and then, 'Marjie thinks Keilor. There's a spot near Dry Creek where our people go back centuries. It's pretty special. Marjie says it's near a quarry but she doesn't know what the access is like.'

'Perfect. Thanks for the heads-up. Tell Bobby he will get his phone back and there'll be a spare battery with it. Keep safe.'

CHAPTER 55

Fox parked the hired Vespa beside an ancient stone bridge over the Maribyrnong River. He was north of Keilor near Browns Road. By 10:00 am the temperature drop and rain of the previous two days had succumbed to a phoenix-like pulse of midsummer heat. It was thirty-six degrees. Yet, though the sky was a brilliant, cloudless blue, seemingly in defiance of the heat, the light was beginning to soften with seasonal change. Autumn was her fractious self.

After speaking to a woman at Melbourne's Aboriginal Affairs Office, Fox had learned more about the Keilor site. A sediment encrusted Aboriginal skull had been unearthed in a small quarry at the junction of Maribyrnong River and Dry Creek in 1940. Subsequent chemical analysis of the silt and carbonate encasing the skull suggested it was about 13,000 years old. Then, in 1971, archaeologist Anton Gallus found remnant Aboriginal stone tools and hearth charcoal in the same vicinity. Radiocarbon dating implied the artefacts were around 40,000 years old. These finds, she had said, suggested Aboriginal habitation of Keilor equalled the oldest known communities in Australia.

Fox's plan was to walk the north side of the river from the bridge until he came to Dry Creek. The need for this journey was vital – he had reached a cross-road demanding weighty decisions and he wanted just outcomes.

He found the junction between Dry Creek and the river on

the eastern side of a looping, southerly bend. Reedy banks hugged a good sized pondage nestling into the bend where several old gums stretched protectively across the water. The land beneath the gums, although overgrown, was relatively flat – possibly worn down by *Wurundjeri* people thousands of years earlier. Behind the flat rose a steep rock bastion through which the waters of Dry Creek had chiselled their way to the river. Overhead, the discordant yodelling of white cockatoos transported Fox instantly to bushland far from Keilor. Yet even this raucous cacophony was overborne by the frequency of jet engines whining into landing mode at Melbourne Airport, just north of the site.

Planes notwithstanding, Fox perceived subtle energies from ancient rites and ceremonies in what would have been a sheltering place. Softly, faintly, gently – from the whispering reeds, tinkling waters and pungent smell of eucalypts – there came to Fox echoes of a distant past. Women foraging for shellfish, trapping eels and yabbies and probing with their fire-hardened digging sticks for the sweet yams of springtime. *I am in the right place.*

He chose a comfortable space near the riverbank and sat with his back to a gum. He focussed on the natural sounds around him and slowly, the noise of descending aircraft receded. Closing his eyes Fox took several deep breaths, grateful for the faint, river-cooled breeze on his face. He relaxed and recalled an ancient *Gija* chant from childhood. Slowly, through the deep peace of an empty mind, campfires at Turkey Creek began to gleam as the click-click of clap-sticks and thrum of chanting began to murmur.

Proper thinking about the correct way of handling Wildman was required. Fox considered him a psychotic killer who had to atone for Caroline and Judy's deaths, yet a right outcome was necessary.

In this state, he heard Caroline oppose his intentions. She was an upholder of the law and argued strongly that Wildman must face court. Suddenly, Jason appeared to forcefully endorse his mother's perspective. But, Fox saw their advice steeped in a different culture, one belonging to an arcane legal system where sharp minds and silver tongues could somersault common sense into glib "new" principles far removed from what most would call justice. A culture he'd read that long ago was corrupted by judges wanting to conceal truth through maxims like "judicial discretion", a convention devised by Chief Justice Reading to shield evidence of his own guilt in the *Marconi* insider trading case. Continued over decades, this convention had been used to veil facts considered "prejudicial" to many people charged with horrendous crimes. Such a process could not, in Fox's opinion, deliver true justice.

Fox's dilemma lay in achieving justice for his friends without compromising Johnson's investigation of Wildman and the Blades. Wildman's disappearance would harm that investigation.

And then there was Milosevic. At court on Monday, Fox had seen nothing but malice and malevolence emanating from him. Without doubt Johnson's investigation would be thorough, but would it achieve the right result? Newspapers abounded with stories from Australia and overseas of heavyweight villains sustaining and enhancing their illegal empires from gaol cells. At court, Milosevic's demeanour implied that nothing other than death would stop him. So if both Milosevic and Wildman disappeared, how well, Fox pondered, would the police and public interest be served?

Fox "saw" that his future life would be coloured by the highs and lows of his past. Painfully, he recalled the brutal abduction of Lucy, himself and other kids from Turkey Creek, He heard again their grief-stricken mothers and mourning fathers. He felt their misery and powerlessness – their individuality heedlessly trampled by state might through callous ignorance and indifference. He thought of all the indignities he'd encountered until Joe Darrigan – a decent man and his first real opportunity. Limited though it might have been, after Joe, good things started happening. By chance he'd reconnected with his life-changing mentor – Caroline Connors. She had given him hope, respect, direction, love and her family. His impotence in preventing her death haunted him even though he was captive to yet another profane use of authority by the Ravenscrofts. That their invisible finessing of power, influence and money could discreetly manipulate people, systems and processes to protect their reputations was an obscenity. And even though old Lord Ravenscroft had paid a decent swag to assuage that abuse, Fox thought of it as nothing more than a bribe. He had not touched a penny.

From that point on while outwardly functioning normally, frequently Fox was wracked by feelings of pain, anger, emptiness and grief.

And yet, his UK experience had brought some amazing highs: the remarkable Spencer Johnson, Callum Fox and his treasured Aunt Louisa who opened doors to the unexpected and priceless gift of knowledge about his white ancestry. Additionally, he'd formed strong friendships at Hereford and was highly respected among SAS Officers and many army colleagues, both there and at home.

It was this complex tangle of emotions and events that brought him to this site for guidance. In this sacred place, Fox allowed himself to be transported to a place of quiet dignity and infinite knowledge, a place where he sought wisdom from the past to inform his present.

CHAPTER 56

That afternoon, Milosevic rang Wildman at Flowerdale.

'What are you doing?' he snapped.

'Checking the dogs – it's bloody hot and I wanted to see they were okay.'

'Forget it you soft bastard and get your arse into town.'

Wildman began to shake. 'What's up Sammy?'

'While you've been dicking around and failing to earn your excessive bloody keep, one of the Fitzroy users told Jaensch that our black man is possibly living in Fitzroy – somewhere near Young Street.'

Axel Jaensch was a Blade who often accompanied Milosevic to the *Napier Hotel* during cash and drug exchanges. He was short, wide and powerful. Noted for a quick and foul temper, he had a reputation for preferring to fight rather than fuck. His face and body bore many battle scars, the most garish being a wide, white slash beneath his right eye diagonally across his cheek to below the ear, product of a drunken brawl with another Blade who later disappeared into the lime pit. Wildman was very cautious around Jaensch.

'Go meet Jaensch at *Rochester Castle.* If this is the prick I think it is, he's going to pay big-time. I want you to work up a plan to grab him. Jaensch will expect you in forty-five minutes.' The phone went dead.

'Johnson.'

Fox spoke softly into the phone. 'I've decided to go back to Perth and then maybe Scotland for a bit. Spoke to Callum recently – Aunty Lou has become quite frail and hasn't been well. I thought I'd better see her before it's too late. I also want to talk to Kurt and Jenny about their wedding. I'll shove off soon and when I'm back, we'll talk about working together.'

'Great idea. Your departure at this point would be very helpful. When we meet next I'll tell you all about it. Let me know when you're back. And good luck with your aunt. If you happen to be near the *White Duck,* drop in and say g'day to the Collins for me will you. Bloody nice people.'

'Okay.' Fox turned the phone off.

'G'day Wildman. Wanna beer?'

'Lemon squash thanks.' Jaensch was unusually friendly. Wildman had made the journey in record time. The *Castle* was cool and dark inside and not too busy. It was a relief to be free of the heat. The two men took their drinks to a corner well away from the bar.

'What's the go Axe?'

'One of the local druggies, a sixteen-year-old sheila hangin' out for some extra crack, she saw me come in 'ere. She followed me in and goes, "if I can give 'er a bump up, she could help with the shit I was lookin' for." I said, "What shit would that be darlin'?" She goes, "I dunno his name. One of ya members showed me a pitcher of this black geyser. I seen him runnin' in Young street." I showed her the pitcher on me phone and she goes, "That's 'im. That's the one." I gave 'er a kick in the arse and told 'er to piss off and rang Sammy. 'E said to wait for you. So, to return the favour: what's the go?'

'We think he might be the bastard who hurt Hawk and Moses. Sammy wants us to grab him and find out. If it's not him, we just give him a kicking and chuck him in the Yarra.'

'Fuckin' A. I'll be in that. When's this happenin'?'

'Now. You and I are doing it, but we need a plan. How many pushers can you scramble in say, the next hour?'

'Probly about a dozen.'

'Can you get a transit van or something like that, something with closed-in sides?'

'No probs.'

'What about this sheila you spoke to – could we find her again?'

'Yeah, most likely she'll be gettin' rooted in the lane behind the pub – cash for crack, or crack for cash – same thing,' he sneered.

'My shout next time – let's go look for her. We need to ask a few more questions.'

Jaensch scowled but did not object as they went out into Johnston Street, turned west towards the city and walked up to Rochester Street. They turned left to access the laneway behind the pub and, as Jaensch predicted, the girl was backed up against the wall humping a young bloke while another two waited. All three males were in their late teens and scabby-looking.

'Fuck off you lot,' Jaensch bawled as he started down the laneway. The three youths turned aggressively towards Jaensch, inspected him looming towards them and rapidly retreated. The active one disengaged from the girl, zipped himself and quickly left the lane.

'C'mere darlin', I want to talk to you.'

Sullenly the girl fixed her skirt and sauntered towards them.

'What do you want? You pissed me off before.'

Wildman noticed she gave off a rank, sour smell. She looked unkempt and dirty but her clothes had been of good quality. Her speech was well modulated and clear, suggesting a good home. Now she was just another junkie.

'We'd like some information and I'll pay if you can help,' said

Wildman. Jaensch scowled again – she was vermin.

'What?' she sniffed.

'You told my friend here you'd seen a black guy in Young Street. I'm wondering if you can tell us a little more. You said you'd seen him running there, is that correct?' Wildman, the former policeman, had kicked in.

She sniffed again and dragged her sleeve under nose. 'Yeah, that's right.'

'How many times have you seen this man?'

'Probably half a dozen.'

'Always running?'

'Yes.'

'Any time pattern? I mean, if you saw him in the afternoons was there a regular timeframe? Or the evenings … same thing?'

'Yes. How much will you pay me?'

'Depends. You haven't told me anything I don't know yet.'

'Yes I have. You had no idea he's a runner or that he is regular about it. How much will you pay me?'

'Listen bitch, just answer the questions,' growled Jaensch as he lashed out to cuff her over the head.

She ducked and Jaensch missed. 'Fuck you mister. Find out your own information.'

Suddenly, the snarling figure of Milosevic sprang into Wildman's mind. He couldn't afford to screw up.

'Settle down, settle down. Look, this is important. This black man has hurt some very good people and we need to find him. If your info is okay I'll give you fifty bucks. What's your name?'

Jaensch glared at Wildman incredulously. 'Fuckin' mad,' he muttered.

'Much more civilised,' she said with an empty smile. 'I'm Candy.'

Again, Wildman discerned her present lifestyle had not always been so – her teeth were still perfect and under the grime and stench was a pretty young girl.

'If he runs in the afternoons it's mostly between three and five and he's generally out at least an hour. In the evenings he runs between seven and nine. He lives somewhere in the middle of Young Street and when he runs, I've only ever seen him turn left in Johnston Street towards Kew. That's about it.'

Wildman considered the information … remembered Fox had been in the SAS and thought her observations sounded about right. He nodded.

'Thanks, here's your fifty.' Again, a melancholy smile before she sauntered up towards Rochester Street leaving a swirling eddy of foetid air behind her.

'Let's go and have that beer,' said Wildman, 'we've got work to do. I reckon the prick will go for a run later today. It's too hot now and if he's already gone, it's too late to put people in place. My guess is he's running around the Kew Boulevard. Perfect for us.'

CHAPTER 57

Early that evening Wildman and Jaensch parked on the northern side of Johnston Street just east of Young Street. They were in a battered white Ford transit van. Along Young Street, Wildman had posted a pusher at each of the six intersections between Cecil and Johnston Streets. Armed with instructions, shown some rudimentary hand signals and offered a cash incentive, they were primed to contact him if Fox showed his face. Three more watchers were spaced between Wellington Street and Kew Boulevard, Fox's most probable destination. Wildman was confident these arrangements would result in Fox's capture, if not tonight then, within a couple of days.

'Don't fucking fail' was all Milosevic had snapped when Wildman reported back.

Although the sun had officially set at 7:32 pm, the hot cloudless day had faded slowly leaving a long, warm, lingering twilight. Proper darkness would not arrive until after eight and Wildman had death-warned his watchers to be alert for Fox who still had not been sighted.

It was fully dark when Fox slipped out of the boarding house and leaned into the shadows of the brick front fence. Statue-like, he observed the street for a full fifteen minutes. He saw a restless young man pacing at the intersection of Young and Leicester Streets to his north. South, at Rose Street, he observed another figure. Further south, way down at Kerr Street, he spied a woman standing under a streetlight. He continued his watch, sharpening his focus and eventually picked up a fourth shadowy figure leaning against a building at Westgarth Street. *It's worked out well.*

On returning from Keilor, Fox had packed his gear, taken it to Spencer Street station and consigned it to Perth. Back at the boarding house he settled his account and retained his room until the following day. From the few things he kept, he changed clothes, roughened his appearance and moved out to search some of Fitzroy's lanes. He was looking for street-kids. Eventually, in a small alley off a laneway between Greeves and David Streets he came across a young girl squatting in the shade smoking a joint.

'Want a fuck?' She didn't move and showed no fear.

'No thanks.' From several metres away Fox could smell her sour body odour.

'What do you want – a blow job? Ten bucks.'

'No, but I could use some help.' Fox could see that she had obviously enjoyed a better life. 'How old are you?'

'What's it to you? You like younger ones? Are you a paedo?'

'Just asking.'

She took a long drag on her joint and rocked on her haunches, her gaze losing focus. Silence.

'Stop gawking at me. What the fuck do you want?'

'Could you use some money?'

'Is the Pope a Catholic?' she jibed. 'Have a look at me; of course I could use some money.'

'What would you use it for?'

'Something better than this shit.' She waved her smoke aimlessly in the air.

'Where do you get it?'

'People.' She grinned mischievously.

'Why don't you clean up, have a good meal?'

'Crack's better.'

'I hear the Blades supply around here. Is that true?'

'Are you a fuckin' cop?' she asked guardedly. 'Look, what do you want? If you don't want sex then piss off and leave me alone. It's too bloody hot to be magging.'

'Okay, here's the deal. I need a small job done, there's a little bit of risk but not much … fifty dollars now and a hundred and fifty when it's done. But I have to know I can trust you. No goofing off and not doing what I pay for.'

She looked at him thoughtfully, silent for a long time.

'What do you want?'

Fox explained.

'Is that all? Piece of piss. Give us the fifty.'

'This is really important … I have to know I can trust you.'

'It mightn't look like it, but I do have principles. I used to be a prefect at my college … and athletics and basketball captain. I promise: no crack before the job's done.'

'Here's your money.' He took a fifty from his wallet, walked up and handed it to her. 'See that brick over there.' Fox pointed to a bluestone pitcher near the end of the alleyway. 'Come back later this evening, after dark, and the rest will be under it. Any questions?'

'Like I said, piece of piss.' She rose and proffered her hand to Fox. He shook it.

'You can trust me.'

'You should see a doctor, you're not well.'

'I know, but life is short and has to be enjoyed. You've just made mine a whole lot better. Under the rock … right?'

'Under the rock. Before I go, what's your name?'

She smiled lazily. 'These days I call myself Candy.'

Afterwards, Fox had thought about her – an attractive young girl whose life would undoubtedly soon end. Potentially, a great waste but he was not everybody's saviour. Nevertheless, he honoured his promise and put the one fifty beneath the pitcher as soon as she left the alleyway. From his observations of Young Street now, he knew Candy had kept her word.

He returned to his room, made final preparations, shouldered his pack and slipped into the backyard where he scaled the fence to land in a lane between Leicester and Rose Streets.

The lane's worn bluestone cobbles were reminders of Melbourne's first suburb – Fitzroy. In 1839, the town had primarily been working class but after the 1860s, experienced great change resulting in a mix of beautiful commercial buildings, terraces, mansions, narrow streets, lanes and alleys – the whole squashed into a mere 100 hectares. Years earlier this lumpy, dark and skinny lane was vital to the malodorous task of removing shit cans from backyard dunnies via horse and cart. Today, limited to a few vehicles and some occasional foot traffic, it was a collector for the detritus of modern life: graffiti, plastic bags and bottles, needles, cans and papers. Shit of a different kind.

Fox stood quietly nestled between a large steel sewage vent and the corner of Rose Street. To his left, the Young Street lookout was positioned near a No Entry sign – his head swivelling constantly. Keeping to the north side of Rose Street and hugging the buildings, Fox walked slowly west towards Brunswick Street. He looked back once only and saw no change in his observer. At Brunswick Street he turned north.

He crossed Brunswick Street, mingled with people drifting south and headed towards Johnston Street. There he crossed over, moved further south and waited five minutes near a Thai restaurant. He scanned for possible shadowers. Nothing. Crossing Brunswick Street he slowly sauntered along Johnston Street and, near Young Street, stepped into a doorway and waited. After several minutes he identified a solitary girl leaning against the wall of a building just shy of Johnston Street. Her stillness was contrary to the natural movement of people around her and, with her back to Johnston Street, she appeared focussed north along Young Street.

Not far from the girl, Fox spied a dirty old Ford transit van parked in Johnston Street. There was nothing unusual about it but now and then, its brake light flashed momentarily as though someone inside sat restlessly moving their feet. Fox moved until he was level with the van. As before, he stepped into a doorway, pulled his beanie well down, and watched. Two men sat in the front, windows down. The driver lit a cigarette and in the brief flame, Fox saw the distinctive bandana around his head. He could not see the second man clearly or discern if others were present.

Fox studied the landscape. Street lights at the corner of Young and Johnston Streets spilled enough light onto the van from behind to enable a limited view inside. To get that view, Fox needed to be on the van side of the street and approaching from the front. It was risky but he suspected the occupants might not anticipate his actions.

He looked down hill and saw the *Rochester Castle Hotel* where groups of young people milled about the entrance. He waited and watched. People regularly crossed back and forth over Johnston Street going to or from the pub. Small numbers also walked towards the city past the van. Fox left the doorway and merged with four people walking towards the pub.

Looking back at the van Fox saw the two occupants engaged in animated conversation. A crowd of about twenty young men and women spilled out of the pub, some the worse for wear. A staggering couple attempted to cross against the red light and were yanked back to the kerb. Fox mingled as they waited for the change of lights. They all crossed together and after more laughter, hugging, kissing and backslapping, a small group of about six split off and ambled towards the city, among them, two very drunken young women. Fox tagged along. At Napier Street, a man and one of the drunken girls turned and headed north while the others continued uphill towards Brunswick Street – noisy, happy, pissed.

As they closed on the van, Fox saw the occupants still engaged in vigorous discussion. Without taking his eyes off them, Fox moved closer to the group and nearer to the buildings. Illumination inside the van was poor but enough to show Fox that the pair in front were the only occupants. As his group passed the van Fox noted that neither occupant wore seat belts, both side windows were fully down and the passenger seemed rattled.

'I don't know where the bastard is,' Fox heard him yell.

'Your call,' said the driver contemptuously. They were definitely waiting for someone.

Fox passed them unnoticed. Drawing level with the back of the van he stopped. The group continued on. Fox knelt, ostensibly to tie a shoelace. Carefully, he looked around, removed his backpack and pulled out a pair of tough, latex gloves and readied some gaffer tape. He crabbed along the footpath to stop behind the passenger door.

'You were fuckin' mad givin' that filthy tart fifty bucks for bullshit information. Nuthin's come in from the observers. Nuthin'. You've fuckin' checked with all of 'em and not one has seen a fuckin' thing.' The voice was almost a snarl – ragged, coarse and angry.

'We'll give it till nine.' The passenger's tone conveyed exasperation. 'He could have gone out a different way. If nothing comes of it tonight, we'll try again tomorrow.'

Fox's concentration narrowed – Wildman. He would know that voice anywhere.

'Ya fuckin' mad. Find someone else. I'm not comin' tomorra.'

'Talk to Sammy about that Axe. He wants this black bastard real bad and I'd be turning up if I was you.'

'Fuck nine o'clock you arse-licker. If nuthin' happens in the next ten minutes I'm leavin'. Do what you fuckin' like.'

Fox rose, invisible behind the open window. He focussed intently on combining two of Miyamoto Mushashi's ancient warrior blows: the "blow of the single moment" and the "spark of the flint blow". Never was the SAS motto, "Who dares wins", more relevant. He required surprise, speed and force. In silence, at frightening pace and with enormous power and accuracy, he swarmed through the passenger window, clamped Wildman's head in his hands and with the impact of a pile-driver, smashed Wildman's skull into the other man's left temple. It was a brutal assault. Jaensch collapsed, unconscious and Wildman sagged, heavily concussed.

In the next three minutes Fox bound Wildman's wrists with tape, pulled his head back and bound it to the headrest covering his eyes and mouth. He moved to the driver's door, opened it and dropped the seat allowing Jaensch to fall back. Then, clambering through the rear doors, he pulled Jaensch's heavy body into the back, checked his pulse and listened to his ragged breathing. He would survive. Fox bound his wrists, eyes, mouth, knees and ankles. The next few minutes were spent searching the van.

Narrow shelves clung to both sides of the interior. Drawers and racks contained a variety of tools, fasteners and small cans of paint. Fox lashed the immobile Jaensch to the shelving struts. He searched him and removed a wallet and wickedly sharp, long-bladed bowie knife.

Fox then turned his attention to Wildman. He was barely conscious and breathing heavily. In the poor light, Fox noticed not only how much Wildman had aged, but how thin he had become. The bushy beard did little to improve his looks. He pulled the sprawling body properly into the seat, fastened the seat belt then wound several rounds of gaffer tape around Wildman's middle, wrists and ankles.

A phone on the floor in front of Wildman shrilled.

Fox answered, 'Yeah?'

'Who the fuck are *you?*' Milosevic asked.

'Jaydn Fiske.'

'Yeah, but who are you?'

'I work for Axe. Anyway, who the fuck are you asking me questions?'

'Never mind. Why are you using Wildman's phone?'

'I picked it up. The bloke with Axe dropped it when they went to the pub for a drink.'

'That'd be fuckin' right. Stupid bastard. Why are you with 'em?'

'I was doin' some scoutin' for Axe. He was after some black bloke but we haven't seen him.'

'What pub are they in?'

'The *Rochy,* here in Fitzroy.'

'Well Fiske, take the fucking thing to Wildman and tell him to ring me – I'm his boss.'

'It'll take a few minutes, traffic's got a bit thick.'

'Get on with it!' Contact was cut. Fox smiled and turned Wildman's phone off.

CHAPTER 58

Late that evening, Kransky phoned Spencer Johnson.

'I've just had a weird call from *M* and thought I should give you a bell. He says he spoke to a pusher named Jaydn Fiske this evening. Fiske reckons he was doing a job for Axel Jaensch but I've never heard Jaensch mention Fiske. It seems Wildman and Jaensch were setting up to grab your mate Fox near the *Rochester Castle* pub. Somehow Fiske got hold of Wildman's phone and answered when *M* rang. The point is, when *M* tried to contact Wildman soon after, his phone was dead – Jaensch's too. He sent a couple of Blades to check the *Rochy* – nothing. The publican said Jaensch had been there twice today but he hadn't seen him since mid-afternoon. Some Blades searched Jaensch's and Wildman's digs but again, nothing. Not a sign of them anywhere. The other odd thing is, one of Jaensch's pushers confirmed the pair were in a van in Johnston Street near Young Street. She says a few of 'em were doing a stake-out for Jaensch looking for a dark bloke. Neither she nor the other cockatoos saw the van leave but … it's gone. *M* is bloody furious. He thought he had Fox but now he's missing two of his clowns. You know your mate better than I do … could he disappear two people off the street like that?'

'I don't know, but, I have seen his army record … he's more than capable. I'll make some checks and get back to you.'

The first thing Johnson did was call Fox.

After several rings Fox answered.

'Ringing a bit late aren't you Spence? What's up.'

'Where are you?'

'On my way back to Perth. Right now I've just stepped out of a bloke's car in Skipton on the Glenelg Highway. Since I haven't been over this way before I thought I would hike back for at least some of the way. I want to have a look at Mount Gambier actually. If I like it, I might poke around there for a few days – don't know yet.' Fox was smiling as he spun his yarn to Johnson.

There was a long pause. 'So ... you're not in Fitzroy right now?'

'Nope. Checked out of the boarding house not long after I spoke to you earlier. I plan to be on the road at least a week, probably more.'

Another pause as Johnson considered the information. He was suspicious.

'Okay mate, take it easy on the road.'

Fox laughed. 'Anyway, why are you ringing me at this time of night?'

'Ahhh ... there's some odd things going on here with Milosevic and I wondered if you knew anything about it.'

'No. I changed my mind about all that. Like I said, Perth then the UK.'

'Okay. Keep in touch.'

'Sure, take care Spence.'

Fox was not happy lying to Johnson but steadfast resolve assuaged his conscience. He had received what he wanted at Keilor and intended to follow through.

After commandeering the van, Fox drove along Johnston Street then turned south into Napier Street. He knew of a street closure there with schools on either side of a barrier point. This meant no traffic and few people. He parked and, at leisure, sieved the van's interior. Apart from the things he had already seen, there were many varieties of tools and rope, but the paint tins were of particular interest – they contained decks of heroin, crystal meths and loose, fine-cut cannabis. Their street value suggested he was host to a fortune – at least $3 - 400,000. In a plastic tube roped to the shelving, he found three different sets of adhesive signs. One proclaimed: *Ronald's Deluxe Painting Services* and gave a phone number. Another said: *Plumbing by George!* Again, there was a phone number and address, both different to Ronald's while the third advised: *ABC Home Mechanic* with yet another phone number. He also discovered an axe and two razor sharp machetes. Finally, in a cunningly made, spring loaded drawer fitted over a wheel hub, he found three different sets of number plates. Good old Axe was capable of changing the van's identity at the drop of a hat. *How convenient*, thought Fox, *I might as well make use of it.*

He checked the opposite wheel hub and found a similar drawer. It seemed impossible to open and when finally he did spring it, found it jammed with packets of used $100 notes. He grinned broadly. *Ill gotten gains to fund the next phase of operations.*

In the quiet, semi-lit street, Fox swapped plates, fitted ABC signs to the van and headed towards Syme Street East Brunswick, headquarters of the Blades opponents, the Vikings. The two groups were poised on the edge of a massive turf war over tattoo parlours and blood, in substantial quantities, had already been spilled. Fox would leave them a gift. Meanwhile, in the back of the van, the object of his plan – feeling deathly after being mashed by Wildman's head – could be heard making frequent mewling noises.

Fox stopped near the Viking clubrooms, rolled his beanie/balaclava over his face, crawled into the rear of the van, cut some rope from a coil on a shelf and looped it around Jaensch's neck. With lights off, he drove quietly to a black painted brick building bearing an aggressive Viking sign across the top. Moving quickly, he cut Jaensch free of the shelving, dragged him over to the building's entrance and roped him to the security grill. With the gaffer tapes intact, Jaensch could not see, speak or move his legs or arms – he was a fitting bonus to the rival gang.

Fox left the club house and drove to a nearby side street. There he switched the van signs and plates again, lay back the seat of the now conscious, but uncomfortable Wildman, covered him with a painter's cloth and drove in search of a car wash. Although the van appeared battered, Fox discovered it was as smooth and tight as a Swiss watch with a responsive and powerful motor. Washing the van was yet another small change to its image.

Close to midnight, Fox pulled in to the long term car park at Tullamarine airport, a broad beach on which to hide his grain of sand. He drove up and down myriad rows of vehicles until he found an empty spot beside another van. Again, he removed and replaced the number plates and switched signs. *If* the van had been filmed at entry it would look confusingly different on the way out.

CHAPTER 59

Fox climbed into the van and removed the cloths from Wildman's body and the tape from his mouth. For the first time since responding to Milosevic's phone call, Fox spoke.

'Do you know who I am Wildman?'

'One of Sammy's fuckin' enemies. I can't fuckin' see so how would I know.' His belligerence was underscored by a trace of fear.

'Do you know why you are here … like this … right now?' Quietly.

'No.'

Wildman was frantically searching his memory. The voice had a ring of familiarity but, in truth, was unknown to him. One of the Vikings maybe. Deep shit goin' on with them. Something about the tone and stillness of the voice was chilling. He knew with certainty that life ahead was going to become very bad.

'Why did you leave Perth Wildman?'

'Personal reasons.' Before his words were finished, fear ratcheted up at the speed of light. *Fox! Fuckin' Fox! How did this happen?*

'To do with your health was it?'

No answer. Wildman's body began to tremble.

'Did you enjoy your view over the Swan River? From the eighth floor?'

Wildman's Adam's apple began to wobble. No response.

'Lots of different things to see from your balcony – runners, riders, houses, walkers, sailors. Do you remember them Wildman? You could even see when the mailman came, couldn't you?'

More tremors but no answer. *What does the prick want?*

'You could see people leave for work or school and when they came home again. Couldn't you Wildman? People like Caroline Connors and little Judy McNulty. You saw them often, didn't you Wildman?' Fox's quiet, insistent tone was relentless, unnerving.

Wildman's tremble became a violent shake.

'You didn't like their dog did you? It interfered with your being inside their home, interfered with your deliberate and sadistic stalking of a loving family. So you almost cut its head off didn't you? Don't you want to say something? Tell me it's all lies? Tell me I'm wrong Wildman?'

'F-f-f-fuck off.'

'Pathetic. You are a loathsome canker on life Wildman. Not so much the tough guy cop now eh? Just a weak, cowardly bastard who snuffed out two gentle and beautiful lives.'

'She ruined my life the fuckin' bitch.'

'Bullshit. As for Judy, words fail me. She was a child! She had nothing to do with you. Nothing! Yet you murdered her, crushed her as if she were a bloody cane toad.' Fox was searing, his tone a harsh, disembodied whisper.

Wildman made a massive effort to calm himself, to stop shaking, to assert control.

'You are goin' to get it big time Fox. You won't survive Sammy. He'll fix you right up and the only thing left for the cops to find will be pulp.'

Fox placed another piece of gaffer tape over Wildman's mouth ensuring an edge partially covered his nostrils. Wildman's breathing suddenly became difficult and he felt claustrophobic. His fear rose another three notches.

'Listen up you horrible piece of work. This van is your home tonight and tomorrow, we'll have another little talk. I have lots of questions and I want honest answers. Otherwise, tomorrow is going to be very unpleasant for you.'

There was no more conversation. Fox cut more rope from the coil in back, freed Wildman from his seat, dragged him into the back of the van and lashed him to the shelf frame. The knots were tight and excessive movement increased their tension. More tape was wound around his mouth. Wildman, as far as Fox was concerned, was a terrorist of the worst kind and his conditions were designed to encourage talk.

CHAPTER 60

Soon after sunrise Fox returned to the carpark from a short, but restful night at the airport's *Park Royal Hotel*. A quick look in the van showed, as expected, a prostrate Wildman. At that hour, the day was fresh, clear and crisp, the temperature a low five degrees. Fox took some fine leather gloves from his back-pack and slipped them on. Opening the driver's door he was assailed by the stench of urine. Fox said nothing, merely wound the window down and drove off. At the exit gate he paid the fee and headed along Airport Drive on his way towards Gisborne. At Sunbury he refuelled and bought two take-away coffees.

By 7:30 he was on Forbes Road just outside Gisborne. He followed the road west until it entered dense bush where he began searching for a fire track. After about twenty minutes he found a track with a drivable surface leading well off the road. Thus far Fox had neither spoken nor acknowledged Wildman's frequent noises from the back.

When eventually he stopped the van, there was an overwhelming sense of dense, almost suffocating silence. Slowly … whispering into the oppressive stillness came the ticking of the cooling motor, bird calls and a sighing breeze from above. Fox climbed from the van and opened the rear doors. Using a machete, he cut Wildman's ropes and pulled him from the van allowing him to fall with a thump to the ground. He yanked Wildman to his feet, spun him around and pushed his bum onto the floor of the van. Wildman tried to stand but, with legs partially numb from restriction and still bound by gaffer tape, he succeeded only in falling over.

Fox returned to the cabin and collected Wildman's almost cold coffee and took it around the back. He sat Wildman on the floor of the van again.

'A drink for you Wildman — be still.' He pulled the tape from Wildman's mouth and held the paper cup to his lips. Wildman drank greedily until it was gone.

'Don't move. I am going to take the tape off your eyes.' When Fox was done, Wildman blinked into the sharp sunlight, focussed and then shuddered when he saw Fox.

'Have you thought about what I said last night?'

Wildman nodded.

'You killed Caroline Connors and her daughter, Judy McNulty.'

Wildman slumped but nodded.

'I want to *hear* it.'

'I … I … killed them.' The voice was a monotone of abject defeat.

'Tell me how and *why.*'

In graphic detail, Wildman explained how he had pulled Judy from the ladder then pursued Caroline with her own kitchen knife and committed dreadful disfigurement.

Fox listened with growing, icy rage.

'You are one sick fuck Wildman and justice is coming.'

Wildman stared at Fox, loathing and contempt creeping into his eyes, his body beginning to shake uncontrollably.

'You contemptible black shit,' he screamed. 'Did you think I ever believed that you didn't kill your sister? You arranged with that fucking Connors bitch to unload me. She organised complaint after complaint and dropped me in it for bullying, harassment, intimidation and assaults. Did you think I didn't know it was all snake shit? That bitch got me drummed out of the force, made me an alcoholic wreck living in gutters. Can you imagine how disgusting that was? I was a good copper. I cleared plenty of crimes and that fuckin' bitch Connors dragged my name through the mud, no, not mud, the fuckin' cess pit! Yeah, she did that and it was my time to get even. Stick that up your arse …you … you … fuckin' bastard.' Wildman's face was livid, contorted with rage. Sweat beaded his forehead, spittle sprinkled his beard like frost.

Fox had to step away from the repulsive twisted creature to prevent himself committing a terrible mischief there and then. At the same time, he knew with certainty that Wildman was mad: stark, staring, crazy. No court would convict this lunatic. Fox wondered what forces, experiences or patterns had shaped Wildman's nature. Mullett fleetingly flashed to mind. In his own case, life had been sweet and sour. But Wildman's brutality to Caroline and Judy had changed Fox irrevocably. Wildman was unforgivable. Furthermore, Fox knew that many a lawyer would revel in constructing an amazing and impregnable defence for Wildman so that he would never properly atone for his bastardry.

'Untie me you weak bastard. I'll fight you to the death. We'll see just how good you are one on one.' Wildman was screaming, the veins on his neck standing out like ropes, his eyes glazed as he worked himself free of the van to hop around like an idiot on a pogo stick.

Fox saw that whatever was wrong with Wildman was taking him way beyond normalcy and he suspected the man had been in a similar mode when he attacked Judy and Caroline, beyond reason, beyond care and well beyond sanity. He returned to the van, grabbed a fresh roll of gaffer tape and went after Wildman who was hopping drunkenly down the fire track. When Fox caught him and spun him around, he unleashed a great gob of slag and fell to the ground. There he lay on his back kicking violently and bellowing foul and nonsensical language. Fox sat on him and noted that even though restrained, there was determined power in Wildman's bucking, ferocious kicks. Another length of tape over Wildman's mouth immediately reduced the noise but not the protest. Fox dragged the deranged man back to the van.

With rope from a coil in the van, Fox lashed Wildman to a tree. He drove back down the track out of Wildman's sight and earshot where he stopped, locked up and snuck back. Moving stealthily through the undergrowth, Fox selected a spot where he could see yet not be seen by Wildman. He settled comfortably against a gum and relaxed. The autumn sun rose steadily, warming the forest floor. High above the tree canopy a frail white tear appeared in the blue sky, the wake of a jet to some distant place. About a metre away, Fox watched a trail of red meat ants moving incessantly on their bush-litter highway. Some scurried purposefully, others jerkily danced backwards and forwards, seemingly checking their colleagues while still others lifted, carried and tugged booty many times larger than themselves. All around him insects hovered, zipped and dived amid a quiet symphony of humming and buzzing. The warming earth released a smell of dampness. Here and there, pale tendrils of mist rose slowly and everywhere, a concerto of birds – mynahs, magpies, wagtails, silver eyes, currawongs, rosellas, honey eaters, top-knots and the occasional blackbird. Fox recognised them all. The only blight on this heavenly place was lashed to a tree thirty metres away.

There, Wildman sat upon the ground, legs out straight, arms taped, wrists resting on bony thighs – as motionless as his previous outburst was frenzied.

Fox sat quietly and then, very softly, began chanting in his ancient *Gija* language.

CHAPTER 61

Milosevic's mood was incendiary. Nothing had been heard or seen of Jaensch or Wildman for two days. He'd pulled the strings of all his well paid snouts in the Police Force only to find that not one of them had even known the two men were missing. Heightening his rage was the fact that from the army of observers along Young and Johnston Streets and out to Kew Boulevard, not one had seen Jaensch's van move. It was a mystery that Milosevic neither understood nor liked.

That evening he summoned his six lieutenants to a remote factory at Rowville in Melbourne's east, one of the arenas for his dog fights.

'Listen you slack bastards, I need these two pricks found. Jaensch told me he had good information about this bastard who hospitalised our guys and disappeared George Lucas. Wildman confirmed it when he spoke to some crack-head, a girl. She's got to be found and grilled. I don't know how the fuck he's done it, but I think this bastard's got Wildman and Jaensch. We … I'll rephrase that, I want him found and we need Jaensch and Wildman. We've got more bloody dog fights in two weeks and if Wildman fucks up now, I lose big money – we all do. Any ideas?'

'What do we know about the fizz, the sheila?' asked Rocky Panzarella.

'Fuck all,' Milosevic responded harshly.

'Maybe the *Rochy* pub owner knows her,' said Kriptor Hourhily.

'Good thought. Check it out Krip. Also, see if any regulars were at the pub on Wednesday night. They could have seen something. Anything!'

Kranksy's mobile rang. 'What?' he barked. He listened and moved away.

'Where the hell could those two pricks be?' Milosevic was sounding genuinely perplexed. 'I know things are shitty with the Vikings, but not enough to result in a snatch.' He frowned and shrugged. 'Does anyone know the number of Axe's van?'

'Yeah,' said "Rhino" Alston, 'DGE 723.'

'Hang on,' said Hourhily, 'He's got several sets of plates for his wheels and swaps them. He showed me. His van could have any bloody number on it, including what you just said.'

Kransky rejoined the group. 'That was one of my fizzes in the cops,' he said grimly. 'A body wrapped in chains was found this afternoon underneath St Kilda Pier. Identity has been established from prints, tatts and scars – Jaensch. No clues about who or how at this stage, but ...we better leave the fuckin' door open on the Vikings.'

'Fuck, fuck fuck!' screamed Milosevic, 'Jesus fuckin' Christ! How the fuck did that happen? Doesn't anyone know anything? Come on you lazy pricks. Where is this black shit? One of you must know something.' Milosevic's eyes were dark with rage, his face was corded and his hands flexed as though he was going to belt one of them.

'Cut it out Sammy,' said Kransky mildly, 'we don't know it's the black guy, it could be the Eagles or even the Devils. Anyway, most of us haven't even seen this bloke you keep going on about. We definitely can't rule out the Vikings because we've given 'em big-time hassle over the tatts parlours. Right now we can't be sure of anything.'

'What? Have you become a fuckin' boong lover now? I don't

fuckin' care. Find him.' Milosevic's face twisted suddenly in spasm.

'Are you alright?' asked Toby Kent.

'Don't know,' gasped Milosevic, 'Feel … real strange … aaarghh.' He collapsed, a terrible rictus upon his face, right arm twitching uncontrollably, legs scrabbling on the floor, bladder emptying.

The six Blades looked at each other and then to Kransky.

'Get him to hospital' said Kransky. 'Toby, your car's here tonight?'

'Yeah, got me Humvee outside.'

'You know the Wantirna Hospital on Mountain Highway? I think that's the nearest. Let's get going, he's having trouble breathing.'

Three of them carried Milosevic outside to Kent's ex-US military vehicle and bundled him inside. Five powerful motor bikes barked to life then headed in pairs towards the hospital. Toby thundered behind.

Well after ten the emergency doctor approached Kransky in the waiting area. The others had left as soon as Milosevic was deposited.

The doctor, an Asian man, was diminutive beside Kransky.

'I'm Dr Lee. Your friend has had a massive brain haemorrhage and has to be transferred for specialised treatment. There will be residual paralysis but in time, when swelling is resolved, his face may return to normal. There may be some cognitive impairment, it's a bit early to tell but I believe there's been a lot of damage. It is likely he will need some long term hospitalisation. Really it's too early to say yet, but that's how it's shaping up. What was he doing when the event happened?'

'Talking. That's all, talking.'

'Was he under any pressure lately?'

'Well, he's a busy lawyer with a lot of big cases. So yeah, there's been pressure.'

'Hmmm. We'll know more after further examination,' said

Lee, 'but don't get too optimistic about the future.'

Kransky relayed the news to Johnson. Johnson, pissed that Milosevic might avoid prosecution was nevertheless buoyed by the thought of him becoming a vegetable. He thought of Fox … and wondered.

CHAPTER 62

Fox cruised along the Western Highway towards Bordertown, stopping occasionally at small towns to purchase discreet quantities of wine. He was fixed in purpose, Wildman was fixed to the spot – hands, legs and mouth still trussed with gaffer tape, body lashed to the shelving racks. The only concession to Wildman's comfort was some folded paint cloths on the floor beneath him and occasional toilet stops. Food intake had been minimal for both.

Wildman's journey was intended to be hard, Fox wanted him on edge, apprehensive about what was to come, wondering if he would live or die. Fox's warrior steel was gleaming. In the future and on his terms, Fox would deal with men whose status or position allowed them to abuse their power. People like Milosevic, Mullett and Wildman.

Two kilometres from Dimboola he pulled to the roadside, covered Wildman with a paint cloth and continued on. He refuelled at a BP servo on the edge of town and asked directions to the town's grocery store and pub. In town he bought food, pads, pens, plastic utensils and a swag of water containers at the supermarket. From the *Victoria Hotel* in Wimmera Street he purchased a flagon of cheap plonk and a bottle of sherry. Collectively, the grog purchases amounted to three flagons and nine bottles of sherry, more than enough for the intended outcome.

Shopping completed, he headed back to the highway towards Nhill, Kaniva and Bordertown. Since leaving Melbourne, Fox had driven more than 300 kilometres – the final destination was still 200 kilometres away.

He had not spoken to Wildman unless it was essential. The mere presence of the man generated feelings of intense revulsion in Fox.

Late Saturday afternoon they passed through Bordertown and were officially in South Australia. A further ten kilometres on, Fox turned north onto the B57 – the Bordertown-Pinaroo Road – a bitumen road of variable quality leading to the Ngarkat Conservation Park. He had researched the Park while in Melbourne. Comprising some 270,000 hectares, it was a curious landform which, from the air, appeared like enormous ripples left on a beach after a receding tide. Hardly surprising since aeons earlier, the park had been ocean floor. Essentially, it was a place of fine, ivory coloured sand dunes stretching ceaselessly in every direction. Large areas of the dunes were scantily covered with grasses or heath while other parts rolled interminably like rumpled olive coloured velvet, an effect caused by densely packed, low growing Mallee. It was country once walked by an ancient people.

Ngarkat was a popular destination for caravanners and four wheel drive enthusiasts who could choose from camp sites at Mount Rescue, Comet Bore, Pine Hut Soak or Pertendi Hut. With autumn as the favoured tourist period, Fox had to be vigilant. Moreover, as he wanted to be well away from defined tracks, his route had to be chosen carefully – the soft sands were harshly unforgiving of two-wheel drive vehicles.

As daylight began to fade, Fox wound the window down and drove slowly north. He was looking for terrain that would enable either an east or west entry into the mallee. It was tricky, as in parts, the scrub was so thick it was impenetrable for anything other than a hiker or perhaps, a trail bike. The warm air was laced with the heavy scent of eucalyptus and while the van ground onwards, the sense of space, peace and isolation became as tangible and welcoming to Fox as a mob campfire. Birdsong was gently audible over the motor and occasionally, he swerved to avoid a stumpy-tail lizard basking on the diminishing warmth of the road. Ahead, the road rose over a dune and on the left was an area where fire had thinned the bush – regrowth was juvenile. He stopped, got out, stretched, took a pee at the road edge and walked into the scrub. Picking his way between the lengthening shadows and leaning mallee scrub, he tested the ground for firmness and looked back to assess the difficulty of concealing tyre tracks. It was do-able. He calculated they were roughly midway between Comet Bore and Pertendi Hut.

Back at the van he deflated the tyres to about half pressure. When he climbed inside he found a fearful Wildman struggling against his ties and making pleading sounds. After their long journey Fox reckoned Wildman surmised the arrival of his worst nightmare.

'Won't be long now Wildman. Haven't seen your friend Sammy riding to the rescue. Police either. I will be, however, giving you an opportunity to survive, an opportunity you failed to give Caroline and Judy.'

Fox watched Wildman's eyes bug out, his imagination rampant.

In turgid slow motion, Fox managed to get the van a little over a kilometre off the main road before turning and stopping in a broad, gentle depression sheltered by a rich cluster of mallee. He parked well under the trees with the van pointed uphill.

'Welcome to Wildman's Purgatory.'

Fox was glowering as he alighted and opened the rear doors of the van. He cable-tied Wildman's wrists together before removing the gaffer tape, cut the ropes from the racks and dragged him outside. He removed the tape from Wildman's mouth.

'Wildman … we are going to do some serious business here and we won't be leaving until it's finished. How long that takes is entirely up to you but if it is done to my complete satisfaction, you will be entirely free to go. Do you understand me?'

Wildman nodded but said nothing.

'Work starts tomorrow. If you are cold tonight: tough. We can't be lighting fires because it's too risky. Not for us, the environment in case you're wondering.'

'You're a fucking black bastard and you'll get yours.'

Fox ignored him, reached into the van and withdrew some pieces of rope and tied them into a length of about six metres. He tied a loop around Wildman's neck, firm but not tight, dropped another loop down around his waist, free of his arms, and tied it behind his back. With Jaensch's bowie knife, he cut the tape from Wildman's ankles allowing the man to walk freely with only his hands and wrists pinioned. Fox then took the end of the rope and walked away from the van pulling Wildman with him.

'This will do. Consider it your private block of land.' Fox shinnied up the tallest and strongest mallee available and secured the rope almost three metres above the ground. The van was nearby on soft sandy soil.

'To the extent of this rope, you can walk around as much as you like until we are finished. After that, you may be free.' In the rapidly fading light, Fox could see apprehension writ large on Wildman's face. 'I'll bring you a drink shortly and again, you will have a choice.'

Fox was icy. This was crunch time, here was where justice began. He sent a silent prayer to Judy and Caroline, whom he knew would disavow his tactics, strode to the van and returned to Wildman with a bottle of sherry and a bottle of water.

'Your choice.'

'You fucking torturous bastard.' Wildman sobbed.

'Wildman – I will always give you choice. Think about the McNulty family, about Caroline and Judy. Think of all those other unfortunate individuals you beat up and fitted up as a copper. They had *no* choice!'

Fox made sandwiches and carried them with a couple of the large canvas painter's drop cloths to Wildman.

'This is your bunk. We'll talk in the morning.'

CHAPTER 63

The day dawned overcast, shrilling with cold. The dull light had settled a stony hue across what, the previous evening, appeared as a treed amphitheatre richly tinted with gold. Even the birds seemed muted. The breeze poked its icy fingers into every nook and cranny, scuffing debris across the ground and around the van. Wildman hated it. He rubbed at the grit in his eyes. His night had been sleepless through fear, cold and discomfort. A thousand times over he rued the day the Connors bitch entered his life yet not for an instant did he regret her death or that of her fucking daughter. *And that fucking Midnight! He's only a boong – weird and stupid. I can still win here. I just have to out-think him. Bastard. We'll see who has choice then!*

Wildman stomped about trying to get warm, ever mindful of his tether. He stared at the van wondering if Fox was still asleep. Wondering if there was any way at all he could climb the tree and untie the rope. There were plenty of weapons in the van. He would do the bastard in and no one would be any the wiser. He had no idea of his location. He would take the van and drive out. If Midnight could do it, so could he. He turned to study the tree and almost shit himself at the sound of Fox's quiet voice.

'Thinking like a monkey Wildman? Go on, have a go at it.'

Fox was just a metre behind him and Wildman had neither seen nor heard him arrive. *He's like a fucking ghost.*

It was 6:30 and Fox carried water, sherry and two jam sandwiches.

'I see you didn't touch either of your drinks last night. I'll keep these two. You might need them tomorrow. Here's the drill. I'm going to bring you a shovel and some toilet paper. You will not be moving from here until our work is finished. If you're wise, two days could be enough and you won't spoil your paradise. If not, it will take as long as it takes and paradise could become a little unsavoury. Work starts in half an hour. In that time I want you to think about all your criminal acts with Milosevic ... just Milosevic. You will record the nature of your activities, who is, or was involved, names, addresses, networks, companies and their roles – lawyers, accountants the whole box and dice. Everything you know in detail. I know a lot already so, no lies. Set it out like a police statement. Remember, you choose the consequences.'

Fox returned to the van. He knew these notes could not be evidence, only investigative pointers, but they would be useful to Johnson and others. He was using a lot of bluff.

Half an hour later, Fox again approached Wildman. He carried the bowie knife, a shovel, toilet paper and some cable ties.

'Put your hands to your left side Wildman and do exactly as I say, otherwise I am going to hurt you. Clear?'

'Arsehole!' Wildman spat but moved his hands as directed. Fox slipped a cable tie under the rope around Wildman's waist and then fastened his left wrist to it ... firmly. He then cut the cable tie binding both hands together freeing Wildman's right arm and hand.

'Now you can get on with your business and in twenty minutes you can start writing.'

Twenty minutes later Fox returned with a pad and pens. Carefully, he examined the rope tether, removed the shovel and said, 'Get on with it.'

Wildman had regained some composure and was mentally

drilling himself, *I still can win, I still can win.* So when Fox returned to the van and vanished, he threw the pens and pad into the bush.

'You're a fucking mongrel Fox and you can stick this up your arse,' he screamed. Sullenly, he dragged his makeshift bed of paint cloths over to a tree, sat in the sand and wrapped himself up. Above him, a wagtail chattered and jeered brazenly. He didn't see or hear Fox again.

There was no warming sun. The earlier breeze had become a cold, relentless wind and Wildman shuddered as the reality of his situation seeped into his bones. It was hopeless. For all he knew, Fox had gone. Anxiety blossomed. He thought at least an hour had passed and still, there was no sign of Fox. Suddenly, he felt himself being watched. The hairs on his neck rose, a metre long goanna emerged from the undergrowth a short distance away to his right. It studied him, hissed and waddled towards the van. It made him think of snakes. He was shit scared of snakes. Vulnerable, Wildman's fear climbed higher. Perhaps it was best if Fox was around. And then he thought about the night. Fox safe in the van while he was lying on the ground wrapped in cloth. There was no protection from snakes then. As his imagination exploded he began shaking, tears rimmed his eyes.

'Fox where the fuck are you?' he bellowed, a catch in his voice.

After leaving Wildman, Fox strode into the bush. He had a big job ahead of him. He had earlier gone back to the main track to inspect where the van left the road. Now, slowly, systematically and with great skill he began to remove all signs of their inland travel using a craft learned as a child at Turkey Creek. He was satisfied with his handiwork. No ordinary white person would ever see where they had left the road. Indeed, it would take a bloody good tracker to read the signs and, over time, Mother Nature would remove even these pale traces. Methodically, he worked his way back to the depression where they camped.

He was satisfied Wildman had little chance of driving out. Fox had nudged the van uphill and in the soft slippery sands, any movement would cause the depression to subside like an ant-lion pit. The greater the effort, the more the sands would collapse inexorably drawing victim to predator. The van would be trapped.

It was mid-afternoon, time to see what Wildman had produced. As intended, the man had become unnerved by Fox's silent arrivals a practice he would continue, although he didn't want Wildman incapable … yet.

'What have you got for me Wildman?'

Morosely, Wildman proffered the pad.

'I told you this has to be like a police statement, put your name and most recent address on it.'

Wildman scowled. Fox scanned the material, some eight pages. It was good. Wildman had commenced with his arrival in Melbourne and explained how he met Milosevic. The fact that he had been a copper caused Milosevic to recruit rather than kill him. It was clear from the notes that Wildman both feared and reviled Milosevic but was trapped. He had worked at turning Milosevic's control to advantage by making himself indispensable to the man. As a result, he had become privy to valuable information. The notes outlined Milosevic's bikie passion and his creation of the Blades gang. Wildman explained the gang's structure, named the six lieutenants, their responsibilities and described how the teams operated: drugs, burglaries, car thefts, guns, standover, debt collection, industry insurgency, night clubs, overseas interests, banking and asset management.

The final page, unfinished, began to outline Milosevic's legal protection. Milosevic appeared to use those lawyers and firms who, for substantial fees, were prepared to turn a blind eye to wrongdoing on the basis of protecting *individual* rights. The notes implied that Milosevic had, several times, talked of the great firm Wyvern and Sprite and their representation of mafia interests but decided they were too risky for him. According to Wildman's interpretation, Milosevic considered Wyvern and Sprite had grown too large, become too convoluted and too dispersed. He believed their volume of trade would ultimately undo them. Milosevic's approach was to use six small firms spread throughout Victoria. Wildman's understanding was that their use by a common party (Milosevic) was unknown to each other. The different firms, three of which were named, handled separate elements of Milosevic's interests. Wildman could not remember the names of the other firms.

'Well done Wildman, you've earned yourself lunch.' Fox could see Wildman's fear of his current reality had improved his co-operation nevertheless, he remained mindful of Wildman's erratic and volatile mood swings. This aspect of Wildman's personality could still sabotage his goal.

By the time the day had ended though, Wildman had produced twenty pages of notes and explanations. They charted money movement, listed the real estate he was aware of, some in Victoria some overseas, cars, boats and planes used for drug and gun importation, and three clandestine laboratories in outer Melbourne industrial parks. Milosevic's cooks were university chemists tied to him by gambling debts. He was able to name two. The notes portrayed a frightening overview of the Blade's drug activities. Entrenched, brutally enforced, state wide and targeting younger and younger users. Corruption and payoffs to numerous officials were rampant and included police who supplied intelligence from their official databases. Wildman was unclear about Milosevic's overseas banking interests but thought he had large sums of money in Indonesia and other parts of south-east Asia. He said that all Milosevic's money matters were handled by two prestigious Melbourne accounting firms, both of which he named.

Wildman also wrote of two matters that piqued Fox's interest. The first involved illegal dog fighting and the lucrative gambling surrounding it. Callous and ugly, its underpinning organisation implied a cunning sophistication that included Customs, police, Municipal Council workers, lost dog centres and commercial airlines. Wildman's pages revealed the activity to be Australia-wide and linked to international interests. A chilling aspect was the Flowerdale lime pit, final resting place for maimed and dead dogs and, to Wildman's certain knowledge, at least five humans.

The second item involved a man named Wally Keynes. Keynes owned a chain of warehouse storage facilities – *Keepsakes* – and on several occasions Wildman had overheard phone conversations between Milosevic and Keynes. Without exception, as soon as Milosevic twigged Wildman's presence the conversations ceased and twice had resulted in Wildman receiving a vicious bashing. Wildman reported similar action by Milosevic when a Blade arrived unannounced. Wildman's impression was that Milosevic was using one or more of the *Keepsakes* facilities to store drugs, guns, money or papers – he was unsure about what was concealed and could only infer that Milosevic wanted absolute secrecy.

The litany of crime, corruption and death was depressing. Fox wondered how it was that Wildman descended into such depravity and saw how ludicrous the claim Caroline had caused his fall from grace. That journey was initiated by his own hand long before Caroline appeared on the scene. Wildman, Fox believed, was not only deeply and seriously flawed, but a stark reminder of why he, Fox, must always exercise reserve and maintain balance when imposing his standard of justice on others.

CHAPTER 64

The following morning was colder but unlike the previous dawn, the rising sun had tinted the trees with gold and deepened myriad pockets of ground shadow with a purple hue. Some mallee stems were so luminescent it was as if sprites had, overnight, dashed about to daub every other stem with brilliance. High overhead the short sharp cry of a kite sent smaller birds into a tittering frenzy. Deep within the scrub, the resonant, low, slow *hooo, hooo* of a bronze-wing pigeon trembled softly on the air.

Fox was already up and about and hoped this was his last day with Wildman. He built a breakfast of tinned fruit, oats and mango juice and strolled over to Wildman who was fully concealed in his canvas cocoon. He nudged Wildman with his foot.

'Wake up! Important day today.'

A muffled curse came from the bundle on the ground.

'I'm leaving your breakfast here. At seven we start work. How long it continues depends on you.'

It won't be all that fuckin' long, thought Wildman. He had been awake for the last hour, plotting Fox's overthrow. Faint optimism had returned. He had, thus far, resisted the conveniently available plonk and drunk only water. But he knew, as certainly as rain fell, that if he didn't do something the grog would have him. The pressure was building. But … he had a plan. In Fox's absence while he crapped yesterday, he had found a short thick branch and with the shovel, fashioned a rough point to it. The weapon lay beneath his swag. Today, when Fox returned with the shovel and paper he would see just how good the bastard was. He had a few tricks of his own to play.

Soon Fox collected the shovel and paper roll and headed for Wildman. He saw that since receiving his breakfast, Wildman had moved closer to the tether tree and climbed back into his swag. He had eaten his breakfast and drunk from the water bottle. Yet, something was different. Fox sensed Wildman behaving like a king brown snake ready to strike – his head was raised, his eyes glittered, he was alert and he appeared to be mouthing silently through his matted beard.

Fox's brain whirred. He slowed his pace, smiled and kept walking but changed his grip on the shovel. About five paces from Wildman and well inside tether range, he stopped.

'Your ablution tools Wildman.' He tossed the roll to Wildman who made no attempt to catch it, and turned slowly to walk back to the van.

In that same instant, Wildman threw off the covers which merely lay over him and lunged at Fox with the short wooden spear clutched in his free hand. Too late he realised the object of his wrath was completing a full circle with the flat of the shovel scything through the air. It struck Wildman fearsomely on his left leg between ankle and knee, felling him instantly. He screamed – a mixture of rage, pain and bitter frustration.

Fox bent and picked up Wildman's spear, his face expressionless.

'Same as yesterday Wildman.' He plunged the shovel into the sand. 'When you've done what you need, toss the shovel towards the van.' He left Wildman sobbing, the air fissured by profanities.

Later, when Fox returned with fresh writing materials, Wildman was leaning against his tree, morose and sulking. He constantly rubbed his leg.

'Look at my leg you arse.' Wildman pulled up his trouser leg and revealed a rapidly swelling weal already beginning to bruise. 'I could get gangrene from this you black mongrel. I need help.'

'Do things properly today Wildman and tomorrow you're free. You can get all the help you want then. Earlier you told me why and how you set about murdering Caroline Connors and her daughter Judy. Without omitting a single comma, I want all that set out in another statement. I want it done clearly and comprehensively. I also want you to explain what motivated your actions, what you felt at the time and what you thought and felt after it was over. Leave nothing out!'

Hope sparked in Wildman's eyes at the mention of freedom. He turned mentally inwards. *I can hide afterwards,* he thought, *I've done it before. The coppers still haven't put me in the frame for this, only this fuckin' nignog Fox. I've got enough dosh stashed away, I can get out of the country using one of Milosevic's boats or planes. Piece of piss. I can do this. Choice – he said he'd give me choice.* Wildman looked up at Fox, a cunning expression on his face, madness in his eyes.

'I'll be free. Is that a promise?'

'Not a promise Wildman, but if you cover your actions fully, it will happen.'

Wildman scratched his head then absently twirled his putrid beard into rat-tails.

'And what happens when I tell the cops what you done to me? Assaulted me, kidnapped me, kept me prisoner, drove me miles from any-fucking-where. I'm the victim here Fox, you're just a heartless black bastard. What'll you do then when the cops are breathing down your neck? Eh, eh?'

'Do you think I care?' Fox's tone was even, his grey eyes hard and flinty. 'The police will only become problematic if you give evidence so … get on with it and I'll see what you give me before I decide.'

Fox spent the next hour carefully assembling items he required for the period after Wildman's release, most of which he would carry in his back pack. From time to time he glanced at Wildman who slowly rubbed his sore leg but was otherwise immobile.

When he had collected his gear, Fox stepped away from the van and slowly, with care, reviewed all of his actions since capturing Jaensch and Wildman. He had to be certain that no traces of himself remained on or in the van. He had worn either rubber or leather gloves for the entire time except for … yes, purchases – petrol and food. He wiped the petrol cap and all of the remaining tins, containers, packets of food and plastic utensils. Next, all liquid containers – water bottles empty and full, and the plonk. He scrutinised the van interior. Slowly he allowed his eyes to linger on every item: shelving, wheel hubs, tools, paint tins, flooring and windows. He reflected carefully. There was nothing touched without the protection of gloves and certainly, the steering wheel and glove box were clean and clear of prints. After collecting all pieces of gaffer tape, both discarded and on the roll, Fox turned to the driver's seat and floors. A meticulous search for body hair was demanded. Difficult with only the naked eye, but still useful. He found three of his own head hairs on the seat back but nothing else. The amount of rubbish was small and he stowed it in his pack. He was not worried about DNA samples – he knew the process was still in its infancy and not yet accepted by Australian courts. Notwithstanding that, he had made sure that his own dumps were widely spaced, well buried and more than a kilometre from the van. The likelihood of them being discovered was remote.

He was set for the next part of his plan.

In the late afternoon, Fox approached Wildman.

'What have you got for me?' His voice cold and steely.

'You asked for it, you got it you black fuck,' Wildman sneered. He handed Fox twelve pages of handwriting. 'Can't take the heat Fox? I bet you were rogering both of them. Reckon you're a bloody saint don't ya? Well let me tell ya, ya nothin' but a miserable, lying, cowardly, black … you hear that … *black* … fuckin' … sinner.

And, you will be caught and you will face justice.' A fiendish cackle rose from Wildman.

Fox stalked towards the van, a bleak, merciless fury battering the iron-like grip he had on his emotions. All the while, Wildman's mad, uncontrollable laughter soared.

CHAPTER 65

At 4:00 am Fox rose. He rolled his space blanket and drop cloth and looped them to the top of his pack. He was ready. From the van he took a machete, ghosted over to the snoring Wildman and slid it into the sand beside him. Back at the van he took the second machete and headed west. Everything he needed for the next phase was on his back. Wildman could go to hell.

Wildman woke, stuck his head out of the swag and saw the machete about fifteen centimetres from his face. *Shit, what the fuck's going on?* He was about to yell at Fox when it dawned on him: *He's pissed off. That's what he meant by free.* He struggled out of his swag, cut the rope from around his neck and the cable tie at his waist.

Machete in hand, trepidation in his heart, he sneaked across to the van. No Fox. He looked inside – plenty of food, tools, water and … plonk. Gallons of the bloody stuff. He checked the cabin and found keys in the ignition. Straight away he hopped in and turned the motor over. It went first pop and there was plenty of fuel. Still no sign of Fox.

Feelings of elation began to surge through him. What do you know, the prick kept his word! He left the van, took a long drink of water and opened a can of fruit. Still wary, he walked to the back of the van, opened its rear doors sat, and, after a nervous glance around, began eating from the can. He was beginning to feel chipper. The morning was mild, the birds were singing and Fox had gone. Gone! *Now all I have to do is get to the road and find civilisation – wherever it's at.* He slowly relaxed, drank more water and ate some biscuits. Feeling positive, he knew that very soon, he would be on his way. *Fox will be nothing but a horrible nightmare.* He sat and planned. *I'll check the top of the depression for tracks – that'll lead me to the road.* But, to his surprise, there were no tracks. He scowled and walked the rim — there was nothing resembling tyre tracks. *Had to be the wind blowing shit over them. I'll extend my circle. I'll pick 'em up, I know I will.*

Keeping the top of the van in sight, Wildman extended his distance from the depression by fifty metres and slowly walked another circle. Absolutely nothing. Jesus Christ! *What's the prick done? Where could the fuckin' tracks be?* Fear nagged, hyperventilation started and his heart raced as panic clawed at him. Having been blindfolded when they arrived, he had no idea where the road was and Fox had twisted and turned every which way when he drove in. *So where the fuck am I? What state am I in?* He paused … the scrub looked the same as Western Australia's … *but we didn't travel long enough to be there.* His fear morphed to stabbing pain. His gut knotted and felt lacerated.

Settle down, settle down, he told himself, *I've got the van. If I take it in a really big circle I have to pick up the tracks.* He returned to the vehicle, folded his swag, chucked it in the back, climbed into the front and started up. Pointed uphill, he realised he would need to take a run at the slope to reach the top. In neutral, foot lightly on the brake, he slowly rolled back until the van came to a natural stop. Then, in first gear, he gently commenced turning to take an angled approach to the top. *Shit, shit, shit!* No traction. He tried again. Releasing the clutch, and at ultra slow revs, hope shattered as the back of the van sank unresistingly. He leapt out and savagely kicked the door then punched the side of the van several times. The rear wheels were half buried in the fine sand. *This thing is fucking useless!*

'Fuck you, Fox!' he roared at the sky.

Pain and fear voraciously chomped at his insides now – he felt tired, his situation was hopeless. Pressure in his head began to thump relentlessly. He sat on the warm sand tempted to have a sherry. *No! Christ no! Not booze. Think, think,* he told himself. He rose and looked in the van again. *Jesus! I've got an axe and shovel! What's wrong with me?* He got the tools and carefully, began shovelling sand from behind and in front of the rear wheels to create a gradual incline for the tyres. He made similar broad channels at the front wheels for several metres ahead of the van and was thankful for the partially deflated tyres. *That ought to help the bloody grip.* He took the axe and began cutting mallee to create a hard surface to drive on. After two hours he had built his "highway" on both sides of the van from the rear to the front wheels and ahead of the van. *Time to test my handiwork.* With several boughs hammered into the sand behind the van in case it rolled back, he slowly let the clutch out. He could hear the tyres fizzing on the green bark and smelt burning rubber and eucalyptus. Then abruptly, the van lurched rapidly forwards and came to a grinding stop. He had moved so fast over the bough track that he'd shot off the end and buried the front wheels to their axles. The van was again trapped by super-fine particles of sand. His head almost exploded with frustration. *This is like trying to drive up a hill of ball bearings – fucking impossible!*

'Fox, you bloody bastard I will kill you.' His roar ended in a whimper. The desperation of his position was overwhelming. He was completely isolated. Free, yes, but with no help and lost, Christ knows where. Fox had fucking lied again. He was prisoner to the bush, his day had turned to crap and the birdsong was a perverse mockery. To make matters worse, the sensual warmth of the morning was now cloyingly hot and insufferably claustrophobic. He was parched and began shaking uncontrollably. As horrible images appeared in his brain, he sank into black despair. The day passed and he remembered little of it. Night descended, a deep velvety sky brilliantly pricked by millions of miniscule fairy lights. And still, he slumped against the van engulfed by a maelstrom of deep, dark confusion and swirling uncertainty – paralysed to the point of numbness.

Night moved on, washing the land with the crisp, clear, cold of the inland. Dew dripped from trees to fall onto the quenchless sand, plop-plopping, softly. Losing their grip on the chilled steel van, the drops rolled down the mudguard to seep into Wildman's clothes and onto his skin. *Shit I'm cold.* His foggy brain prodded until finally, his upper body sodden, he stood and stumbled into the back of the van where he dragged the paint cloths over himself. Frozen stiff, his head dull, he could scarcely think. *How did I get here? What have I done to deserve this? I've been a fucking good copper and this isn't right. I am not a bad person.* His addled brain recalled a hazy image of Caroline Connors. *That fuckin' bitch, she caused all this.* Wildman judged that life had been cruel to him. Eventually, hunger and glacial cold drove him to look for food. Crash! *What was that?* He turned the interior light on. A bottle of sherry had fallen from the seat to the floor. *Ahhhh. I'll just have a bit to get warm, just a little bit,* he thought. He hauled himself into the front where he hunched in the driver's seat, a dim, shadowy figure with a bottle to his lips.

A week later he lay on his back on the sandy incline, bottles strewn around him, a flagon, three parts full, beside his head. He had fouled himself and been on a bender for the week. Inert, he faded in and out of consciousness.

CHAPTER 66

By the middle of the third week, Wildman was staggering through the bush about half a kilometre south of the van. He was dishevelled, filthy, drunk and clutching a flagon. His progress through the trees was aimless, his gait jerky. Constant babble fell from his mouth – he was lost.

Back at the van food wrappers, tin cans and paper plates were strewn around the site along with empty water and sherry bottles and two dead flagons. The stench was enough to make anybody puke. In a little over two weeks he had converted the previously pristine site into a filthy, littered tip. The van interior was putrid. Yet, in a lucid moment he had attempted to chronicle his unwarranted victimisation and inevitable demise – a smudged, raggedy letter stuck in the glove box; a letter that heaped all blame on Fox.

On a Saturday morning in April of that year, Spencer Johnson went to the Epworth Hospital in Richmond. A little over a week had passed since Milosevic's transfer from Wantirna under police guard. Evidence resulting from the execution of search warrants on Milosevic's numerous premises had been more than sufficient to arrest him. The catalyst for the searches had been Tony Kransky's damning intelligence. One by one, individual Blades were arrested as watertight cases were built around them. Prosecution was still some way off but the Blade's presence and influence on the streets was already diminishing.

Johnson had attended the hospital in response to a message from Milosevic's police guard. Senior Constable Ian Thompson had overheard a conversation between doctors as they left Milosevic's room. "Sinking fast," one had said. Thompson wasted no time in passing the snippet on.

Johnson went to Milosevic's ward and asked to speak to the duty doctor. Fifteen minutes later, Doctor Peter Fitzpatrick called Johnson into his office.

'Your arrival pre-empted me Mr Johnson. I was planning to contact you this morning: Samuel Milosevic is not going to survive much longer. As you know, he had a massive brain haemorrhage resulting in significant paralysis to the right side of his body. Inexplicably, he then developed a skin disease we colloquially call TEN – toxic epidermal necrolysis. I've read his admission notes and there was no rash or other signs of infection recorded. We have no explanation for how he contracted TEN which has now progressed to Stevens-Johnson Syndrome. Unfortunately, Milosevic is headed for organ failure.'

Frowning, Johnson interrupted, 'This bloke is a serious drug pusher and does a lot of business in South East Asia. Could he have picked these problems up there?'

Fitzpatrick thought about it. 'Sure, that's a possibility but remember, I said there was no sign of this disease when he was admitted to hospital. That's only a week or so ago. For the disease to be as advanced as it now is there should have been visible signs and symptoms weeks ago. I can't think of any scientific explanation for Milosevic to be so gravely affected. All I can tell you is these two major health problems mean death is imminent.'

Fuck, thought Johnson, I was looking forward to prosecuting this bastard. Still, this is better than anything the courts would have considered.

'Okay Doc. Thanks for your time. Let us know when he goes.'

Johnson left the office and went down to the main cafeteria for coffee. *I'm buggered if I know how he's done it, or where he is, but I'm bloody sure Fox has pulled this stunt.*

CHAPTER 67

JUNE, 1989

Fourteen months later Johnson and Fox were zipping along the Hume Highway in Johnson's black Jaguar coupe. They were about forty clicks south of Gundagai and had been talking about the prosecutions launched against the Blades when an ABC news bulletin commenced.

'In a development emerging from fires raging through Ngarkat Conservation Park in South Australia's north east, police announced that the charred remains of a man's body were found today. The remains were approximately one kilometre west of a burn-out van discovered off-road midway between Pertendi and Comet bores.

Although the identity of the body has not been confirmed, police believe it is connected to the van. The van has been identified as belonging to a former member of the Blades, a bikie gang, whose body was found beneath St Kilda pier more than a year ago.

In a long running joint operation, Federal and Victoria Police closed down the Blades after an exhaustive investigation into their illegal drug manufacturing, dog fighting, gun running and ruthless stand-over tactics in the building industry.

In other news from South Australia …'

Johnson's conversation had trailed away and he drove in silence.

'So … What do you know about that? Anything?' he asked, throwing a glance at Fox.

'Nothing.'

'It always struck me as odd Fox that at the time you left Fitzroy, two of Milosevic's Blades vanished.'

'Spence, we've had this conversation before. How many times? I … can't … help … you.' Fox smiled to himself. 'Keep asking though if it makes you feel better.'

'And you don't know any Jaydn Fiske?'

'Never heard of him.'

'Only, we managed to track down young Bobby Dawson. His phone was mailed back to him via George Lucas at Bendalong on the New South Wales coast. Had a brand new SIM card in it – no history. If you had Dawson's phone, as I believe was the case, it would have shown that call to Milosevic by Fiske.' Johnson's tone, although bantering, held a flush of annoyance. He didn't like unfinished business.

'Can't help you mate.' Fox's silence was impenetrable.

'And what about those photo-copied notes that mysteriously turned up on my desk from Kingaroy in Queensland? Notes written by Wildman, notes confessing to a multitude of crimes including the deaths of your friends, notes telling us heaps about Milosevic. I s'pose you know nothing about that either?'

'Spence, I've told you before – I know nothing about any of it.'

'You keep saying that Mr Fox but now we have Jaensch's van and I bet the body turns out to be Wildman's. I know you're key to this.'

'Can I remind you Spence, there is no "we". You're not a copper anymore. And, since we've only heard this news now, I don't know any more about it than you do. Get over it.'

'Well, I don't believe you.'

They drove on in silence. Fox flitting over the events at which Johnson had probed.

The Ngarkat had provided Fox with an abundance of food and plentiful water. He made his way overland managing the roughly 250 kilometres easily, covering fifty-five kilometres over a consistent seven hour day – a simple trek for one used to the Brecon Becons. He reached Mount Gambier four and a half days later.

In Mount Gambier he booked into the Jubilee Motel on the Jubilee Highway. There he luxuriated in a shower, shaved, changed into his cleanest clothes, threw his grungy ones in the bin, took his back-pack and went out to explore Mount Gambier Marketplace, the town's major shopping area. After buying new, simple, work clothes – steel cap boots, twill trousers and shirts, a bluey jacket and underwear – he enquired at a local petrol station for the best motor bike distributor in town. He took a leisurely walk around the township, made a couple more enquiries then found Laurie Fox Motor Cycles in Wehl Street. He had to smile at the name.

Fox knew exactly what he wanted and was pleased to see it on the showroom floor – a brilliant red, four-stroke BMW K1 with flashing gold coloured wheels. The scintillating colour scheme was memorable. He strolled across to examine the machine and noted the price – $28,500.

'Can I help you?' a quiet voice asked.

Fox turned to the sales assistant, a man of about forty, grey crew cut, suntanned features and a look of strong physical fitness.

'You can,' smiled Fox. 'I'd like to buy this bike. Colin Fox.' He extended his hand.

'Dave Coates,' said the salesman cordially shaking hands. Pointedly, he looked at his watch. 'It's 4:30 now and we close at 5:00 pm. What about tomorrow?' Coates' voice was neutral but Fox detected reservation.

'How about we do the paperwork now, you organise the plates, registration and insurance, throw in a helmet and I'll pick the bike up around one tomorrow afternoon. Let's say an even $28,000 cash and I'll give you a $10,000 deposit now.'

Fox saw himself being appraised by Coates and observed his mental debate. Fox grinned good naturedly.

'Not used to us having money Dave?'

'No offence, but to be honest, no*t this* kind of money.'

'Fair enough.' Fox removed his pack and from a rear pocket took out five packs of Jaensch's used $100 dollar notes. 'There you go – $10,000. Count it.'

'No problem, let's get your details.'

At one o'clock the following day, Fox was mobile.

Over the previous night, he had read all of the motel's tourist information about Mount Gambier. Should anyone ask, he would be well informed about the town. For instance, he knew this was *Booandik* country, that white settlers had not seen the town's Blue Lake until 1839, that police arrived in 1846, that the first pub was built around 1847 and Dr Wehl, the Mount's first doctor, arrived in 1849. Like a sponge, Fox absorbed all of it and more. Easily accessible from Melbourne and Adelaide, the Mount was now a thriving town of some 30,000 people and numerous tourist interests.

As soon as he collected his bike, Fox hit all the prominent tourist spots in the shortest possible time. He was confident of withstanding any questioning about where he had been and what he had seen at the Mount.

He had then ridden straight through to Perth.

Jenny's and Kurt's wedding plans were confirmed for St Patrick's Day, March 1990 at St Georges Cathedral in St Georges Terrace and they wasted no time reminding Fox he was their Best Man and that he had better be available.

A week after his arrival, Fox and John McNulty met at Ecucina in Hay Street.

'So Fox, get everything squared away?'

'Yes Doc. I will be working with Spencer Johnson. He's

finished with Fedpol and is starting his own business. It's all still a bit flexible but I know he's got several irons in the fire, one of them being a body sculpting business. He's apparently won a lot of trophies in that game.'

'Anything else?'

'Yeah. He'll be taking on private investigations, jobs that very wealthy people want pursued without fuss. Looking for missing partners, industrial espionage, busting commercial blackmailers, stuff like that. For instance, think bikie, think standover, think extortion. We find out who, what, where and why and disconnect the circuit. Sometimes the outcome will not be pleasant but if our customers get peace of mind, that's a good thing. Spencer's also developing another angle to do with politics. I'm not sure what, but that's okay. I don't expect to be involved in everything he does and vice versa.'

'And …?' Fox noted the tremor in McNulty and saw pain in his eyes.

'Yes,' he said quietly, 'I found out who caused our grief. It has been justly dealt with and that is all I will say. We can all console ourselves that matters have been finalised. And John, that information is for your ears only.'

McNulty said nothing but nodded, his eyes filling with tears. Fox sensed a weight slide from his shoulders. 'I had hoped but was never sure. … Thank you Fox,' he whispered.

One month later, Fox was in Edinburgh with Callum. It was Sunday and they were travelling to Pittenweem in Callum's ancient Landrover.

'I see you haven't touched Lord Ravenscroft's trust account Fox. It's building at a good rate. What do you intend doing with it?'

'Callum, I'm comfortable and the way I feel about the Ravenscrofts, well … that money is tainted. How much is there by the way?'

'You've got just on £ 96,000. Some of the investments I've made have been very good. In Australian dollars I reckon you've got around $185,000.' He spoke with humour in his eyes.

Fox looked at him thoughtfully for a time before speaking.

'Okay, here's what I would like done with it. Jenny McNulty is marrying one of my former SAS colleagues on March 17 next. I'd like them to have $50,000. If that sum could reach me the week before their marriage, I would be most grateful.'

'Easy done.'

'Next, I have a favour to ask. It seems you are spending more time in the UK these days and less with United Nations. I know young Jason would love to come over here and get into some UN work or perhaps extend his education through Oxford or Cambridge. I would like to help. More particularly however, I would like you to mentor him, show him the ropes, settle him in and introduce him to the right people. What do you think?'

Callum laughed heartily. 'You're a mystery Fox. You've probably got every reason in the world to dislike these Isles yet you're willing to send this boy over here to learn. That's not a problem. You do realise though that if you pay for all this there won't be much left in your trust fund.'

'Well, if Jason would like to do this, I don't care. I'll also add any extra needed.'

They drove on in silence.

'I have a surprise for you laddie,' said Callum after a time. 'Following Lord Ravenscroft's death several family members, including your dear friend Heidi, savagely contested his will. She sought not only a sizeable chunk of his estate, but all the monies put into trust for you and the Early family. I didn't tell you because of the huge undercurrent and plethora of high powered lawyers. Contests involving wills are ugly. In short, the bigger the estate, the uglier it gets. As you might expect, Heidi really lit a fuse by alleging the Old Boy was crackers. It was all finalised only a month ago.

The matter involving yourself arose because, as time passed, Lord R reflected more and more upon Heidi's actions. Not long before he died, he telephoned me. He talked about the Early family and their needs, about Heidi's exploitation of a variety of people and then he talked about you – he had many well placed friends in the military. After you returned to Australia he made discreet enquiries about your background. As he learned more about you he became quite depressed and somewhat guilty over Heidi's actions. He decided to exclude her completely from his will and wrote me a very acerbic letter explaining his actions. He concluded by saying that he was adding another £100,000 to your fund. Well … you know Heidi, she called foul. The rub was that in this letter he bluntly stated she had the capacity to do well from her own natural abilities and she had to rely on them to make her way. Eventually, I was able to get that letter before the judge. With that, and argument from other family members, Heidi lost out. The Old Boy's will eventually stood unscathed. So Fox, I anticipate that when the dust settles, you'll have well over £200,000 to play around with.'

Fox regarded Callum with astonishment. It was an outcome he had never anticipated.

'That's the decision of a white man,' grinned Fox. 'Well mate, you can stay in charge of all this cash if it's not too much trouble. We'll see what happens with Jason because there is another thing I would like to do. Turkey Creek is well known for its art and I'm contemplating a way to stimulate that – a scholarship or an annual prize – something that recognises our local culture and a person's strong artistic spirit and ability. I'll talk to folk up there and let you know.'

On that Sunday Fox met many of his Scottish relations. He also enjoyed a long and heart-warming conversation with his now frail Great Aunt Louisa but was saddened by her failing health. Two weeks later he was back in Perth, revitalised, relaxed and ready to get on with the next phase of his life – working with Spencer Johnson.

A single phone call and it was done. Then, after a fortnight with the Mob in Turkey Creek, Fox flew to Melbourne to join Johnson.

Now, on their way to Gundagai, he reflected on the reason for their journey, a "love job" for one of Johnson's friends, a matter involving one of Sydney's most private and powerful firms – the Carstairs Group. According to the sparse details they had received it was a case involving cyber crime and it sounded challenging.

He wound the window down and let the cooling breeze buffet the interior of the car. He thought of this unseen force as a metaphor for his life: noisy, tumultuous, yet ultimately cleansing. With Caroline and Judy avenged, a new and unknown life with Spencer Johnson about to commence, effective arrangements in place to deal with the Ravenscroft money, Fox was at last beginning to feel good about life.

ACKNOWLEDGEMENT

My first novel, *No Witness, No Case*, featured a character named Fox. Only towards the end of that story do readers learn Fox is part Aboriginal, an aspect which numerous readers said surprised them. My initial "litmus critics" (fearless friends with aggressive red pens) for No Witness commented favourably upon Fox, said he intrigued them and wondered about his stark and deeply personal philosophy towards justice. They wanted to know more about him and the factors that shaped his life. The big question was: what could have happened that would allow the killing of others to become a component in his view of justice?

From these queries, my story of Fox was born.

Because he is Aboriginal, it was essential for me to ensure that nothing offensive, adverse or incorrect was published about members of our Indigenous community, especially the *Gija* people of north east Western Australia.

Writing about what is colloquially termed the stolen generation inspired considerable research. Many articles relating to the treatment of Aboriginal children from the Kimberly region of WA, other Australian states, the lifestyle and treatment practices at Sister Kate's, Forrest River and the Moore River Native Settlement (also known as the Mogumber Native Mission, source of the story, Rabbit Proof Fence) were combed for storyline, accuracy and historical context. Indeed, a host of sources were accessed to inform about the treatment of Aboriginal women, Aboriginals generally, their conditions during the period of this story, and especially the art and culture relative to *Gija* people at Turkey Creek. Reference was also made to the remarkable story of Geoff Guest, AOM, and his escape from Toowoomba, Queensland, Circa 1939.

Overall, more than fifty articles from reports, books, magazines, journals, the internet and newspapers were examined in my attempt to accurately portray a bleak period of Australia's history when federal and state government policies treated Indigenous communities as non-people, policies from which adverse consequences continue for many Aboriginal people today.

The horrific events experienced by the children, Colin and Lucy Fox, are real events that happened to real people. Colin and Lucy are, however, composites constructed from the lives of numerous young Aboriginal people of that time, not all of them from Western Australia. I have been at pains to ensure that no one Aboriginal person could actually say, "this is me, this is my life," in terms of Colin's or Lucy's experiences. Yet, unquestionably, there will be many Aboriginal adults of contemporary society who can truthfully claim to have experienced one or more of the events described. This is a regrettable truth and irrefutable part of our history.

Boxing tents were an iconic feature of Australian travelling sideshows often coinciding with some form of country agricultural show. Many a time, as a small boy, I stood with my dad outside Jimmy Sharman's tent at the Mildura Showgrounds listening to the unmistakeable drumbeat and call of "holdah … holdah … holdah." Regrettably, I was never taken inside to watch the action.

Fox's military experience is drawn from numerous sources and, to the best of my ability, depicts the various training regimes accurately. I do not know whether any Aboriginal soldiers have gravitated to the elite SAS Regiment but that, to me, seemed an honourable goal.

The Bramshill experience is my own, having attended the 27th Senior Command Course in the UK in 1990. During that course I was fortunate in being able to stay with my wife, Jennifer, at the home of Jim and Kathleen Main in Pittenweem, Scotland. Jim was then a member of the Royal Hong Kong Police and a course attendee with me at an inter-service terrorist exercise at Greenwich.

The letters given to Fox by his Great Aunt Louisa regarding the death of her brother, Fox's grandfather, are verbatim in every respect, except for the name Fox. These letters relate to my grandfather, Sergeant William Henry Gladstone Robertson, Regimental No. 2281, 60th. Battalion AIF, 1st Anzac Corps. Permission to use them in this story was granted by my family. The snippets Fox recalls as he runs the River Wye in Chapter 26 are cobbled together from various entries in my grandfather's work diaries of 1912 – 1915.

Much has been written about martial arts and its various forms. The "sombo" style of fighting seemed apposite for the battle between the two protagonists in Chapter 18. Following completion of this chapter, a practitioner of this world, Peter Muys, very kindly agreed to proof it for accuracy and authenticity.

The idea of Fox being the "victim" of a predatory female stalker was suggested by long time friend, Glenn Zimmer. Examination of this curiosity revealed a history of cases involving false allegations of rape and sexual assault, aborted trials and a world of psychological/psychiatric research into "bunny boilers." Knowledge of English law, prisons and the use of DNA profiling in that era became an essential corollary to the topic.

The bikie group of this story, The Blades, is a fabrication. There is, however, a wealth of material available from daily newspapers and television news about bikie groups, their activities, the law, police raids and proposed legislative change for dealing with them throughout Australia.

The ugly and brutal world of dog fighting is a silent and almost invisible criminal reality in our country. People should know it is there and that pets which disappear from the streets might well have become training pawns. The argument for allowing fighting breeds (such as American pit bulls) into Australia is vacuous ("Dog fight on bad breeds", Herald Sun, 29/8/13) given the existence of frauds, forgeries and criminal conspiracies around the world to nurture and promote dog fighting and smuggling. The fact is, these dogs do kill people and their easiest targets are children. Arguments about breed purity is mere obfuscation – if it looks like a pit bull, behaves like a pit bull and smells like a pit bull it is a pit bull and, in the author's opinion, should not be here.

A note is warranted about the villain, Dean Wildman. Some of my "litmus critics" found his personality somewhat unbelievable. One minute he is rational, logical and fully functional, the next he is a raging, violent, aggressive madman who vacillates between thoughts of invincibility and actions of cunning, cowering servility to sheer lunacy. What I have attempted to portray is a condition known as Intermittent Explosive Disorder, a condition embracing behaviours of explosive outbursts of anger, rage, aggression, screaming, mood swings, sweating, stuttering, twitching or palpitations. Physical injury to others, damage to property and assaults resulting in police intervention are not uncommon. It would seem the condition is not linked to any other medical or mental disorder and is manifest in people above the age of six years. Despite his condition, Wildman is just plain bad.

With the exception of the following, mentioned only briefly: Yitzhak Shamir, Yasser Arafat, Mohammad Mossedegh, Sir Robert Mark, Geoff Guest, Gary Foley, Anton Gallus, Major Les Hiddens, Elder Sam Woolagoodja, Sir Douglas Nicholls (Pastor) and the Aboriginal warriors Pemulwuy and Yagan, all people and characters in this story are entirely fictitious. Permission to use Elder Sam Woolagoodja's name was generously granted by his son, Donny, an artist from the Mowanjum Aboriginal Art and Cultural Centre in Derby, Western Australia.

My gratitude for assistance, ideas, improvement and support given so willingly and diligently by my "litmus critics", Glenn Zimmer, Donna Stoutjesdik, Kevin Gaitskell and Len Tosolini is boundless. It is not always easy to be analytically critical of someone you know. And mere words are inadequate for conveying my sincere thanks to Rachel Bin Salleh. Rachel, an Aboriginal woman from Broome employed by Magabala Books, helped me through the complexities of *Gija* culture and strove to prevent me from offending the Indigenous people of Turkey Creek through her instructive, fearless and at times, appropriately blunt comments. While her support and advice has been generous and educative, her overall contribution to this story from an Indigenous perspective has been profound. Rachel's assistance notwithstanding, I acknowledge the complexities of Indigenous culture and my own very shallow understanding of it. To my niece, Jessica Guinane, my deep appreciation for her help in understanding Milosevic's medical condition. Friends and family also patiently listened to my ideas, discussed storylines and put up with my obsession and helped my thoughts crystallise to this more concrete form. To them all, I am eternally grateful.

Again, I am indebted to Mark Zocchi, my publisher at Brolga Publishing for his belief in me as a story teller and his willingness to invest time, effort and support in a new writer. To his Chief Editor, Julie Capaldo, my praise is unstinting. It is both a pleasure and education to again work with Julie and observe her deft, light and ever so appropriate touch with a manuscript.

To my wife Jennifer, writer in isolation, my rock, my companion and constant sounding board who endures my "adventures with imaginary friends" with forbearance and understanding – my endless love and affection.

Finally, whilst I have made every attempt to be accurate with those events having a factual underpinning, errors, omissions or misinterpretations are mine alone.

BR
26/12/2014.

ABOUT THE AUTHOR

Bill Robertson is a retired Assistant Commissioner of Victoria Police. He served thirty-six years with the force at metropolitan and country stations and attended the noted UK Senior Command Course at Bramshill. After retirement he spent two years as a consultant with the Western Australian police and on returning to Melbourne was commissioned to review and make recommendations upon Victoria's Police Witness Protection Program for the former Office of Police Integrity. Subsequently, he assisted the Ombudsman's Office in researching and writing a history of corruption in Victoria Police between 1836 and 2005. He lives in Melbourne with his wife Jennifer and is the author of *No Witness, No Case.*

NO WITNESS, NO CASE

BILL ROBERTSON

Mafia member slain. Corrupt politician gaoled. Toxic waste scam exposed. Is this justice working?

This is a fast-paced crime thriller about greed, corruption and politics - dirty business, dirty politics and a callous disregard for the environment, the law and the community.

A black waste scam is concealed within a legitimate waste business; the business owner is in league with the Mafia; the owner's son is a corrupt and ruthless politician; and the Russians are trying to muscle their way in and oust the Mafia.

An exciting novel with memorable characters - some you will love, others you will love to hate.

NO WITNESS, NO CASE

BILL ROBERTSON

		Qty
ISBN: 9781922175243		
RRP	AU$24.99	.....
Postage within Australia	AU$5.00	.....
	TOTAL★ $_____	
	★ All prices include GST	

Name:...

Address: ....

....

Phone:...

Email: ....

Payment: ❏ Money Order ❏ Cheque ❏ MasterCard ❏ Visa

Cardholder's Name:..

Credit Card Number: ....

Signature:..

Expiry Date: ....

Allow 7 days for delivery.

Payment to: Marzocco Consultancy (ABN 14 067 257 390)
                PO Box 12544
                A'Beckett Street, Melbourne, 8006
                Victoria, Australia
                admin@brolgapublishing.com.au

BILL ROBERTSON

ISBN: 9781925367126   Qty

            RRP   AU$24.99   .....

Postage within Australia   AU$5.00   .....

                        TOTAL★ $_____

                        ★ All prices include GST

Name:..

Address: ....

....

Phone:...

Email: ....

Payment: ❑ Money Order ❑ Cheque ❑ MasterCard ❑Visa

Cardholder's Name:..

Credit Card Number: ....

Signature:..

Expiry Date: ....

Allow 7 days for delivery.

Payment to: Marzocco Consultancy (ABN 14 067 257 390)
                   PO Box 12544
                   A'Beckett Street, Melbourne, 8006
                   Victoria, Australia
                   admin@brolgapublishing.com.au

BE PUBLISHED

Publish through a successful publisher.
Brolga Publishing is represented through:
• **National** book trade distribution, including sales,
marketing & distribution through **Macmillan Australia.**
• **International** book trade distribution to
    • The United Kingdom
    • North America
    • Sales representation in South East Asia
• **Worldwide e-Book distribution**

For details and inquiries, contact:
Brolga Publishing Pty Ltd
PO Box 12544
A'Beckett St VIC 8006

Phone: 0414 608 494
markzocchi@brolgapublishing.com.au
ABN: 46 063 962 443
(Email for a catalogue request)

www.ingramcontent.com/pod-product-compliance
Lightning Source LLC
Chambersburg PA
CBHW072258020726
47501CB00002B/301